DREAM TRAVELLER

BY BETHANY DRIER

Published by:

Wherever Books LLC
A Division of Renegade Company LLC
Littleton, CO 80127
Dream Traveller book available at www.whereverbooks.com
Dream Traveller website at www.dreamtravellerbook.com

Wherever Books and Renegade Company are registered trademarks
of Renegade Company, LLC

Roku Channel:
Wherever Books
Fantasy Realized
Dream Traveller

Acknowledgements

I would like to start off by thanking Terry Ulick. I first met Terry at a writing group in Arvada, Colorado last October, and ended up at an ice cream shop afterwards. Time went by quickly, and we ended up chatting for three hours. Terry loved the name Dream Traveller, and the ideas I had for my book. We ended up working together, and he showed me how to put everything together, making the publishing of this book possible. Since I've known Terry, my life has been a never-ending workshop of inspiration and creativity.

Next, I would like to thank one of my best friends, Breanne. She has been one of my biggest supporters of this book over the past four years. As soon as I told her my idea, she became so excited and listened to every word. She continuously encouraged me, and wanted to read every new chapter as it came out.

Third, L. Briar. L. Briar is the leader of the Fantasy and Science Fictions Writers group in the Denver area, and has been a huge supporter of myself and the rest of the writers. She is always helpful and offers support whenever possible. Her enthusiasm for each idea I share with her lightens my world in ways I didn't think were possible. Thank you for welcoming me into your group and for becoming a wonderful friend.

Fourth, I'd like to thank my editor, Rachael McKay. She's been working on this project with me for the past two years. Working with her has made me a better writer.

Lastly, I would like to thank my ARC readers, and my friends and family for being the inspiration for a lot of my characters (the good characters, not the evil ones).

Trigger Warnings

Dream Traveller is considered a dark fantasy, with dark subject matter. Below I have a list of subjects that may be triggering to some individuals. Though I'm not descriptive in most instances, I understand some people are sensitive. Please read responsibly. Violence (Descriptive), Child Abuse, Child Sexual Abuse, Sexual Abuse, Rape, Murder, Kidnapping, Captivity, Human Trafficking, Suicide Attempt, and Mild Offensive Language.

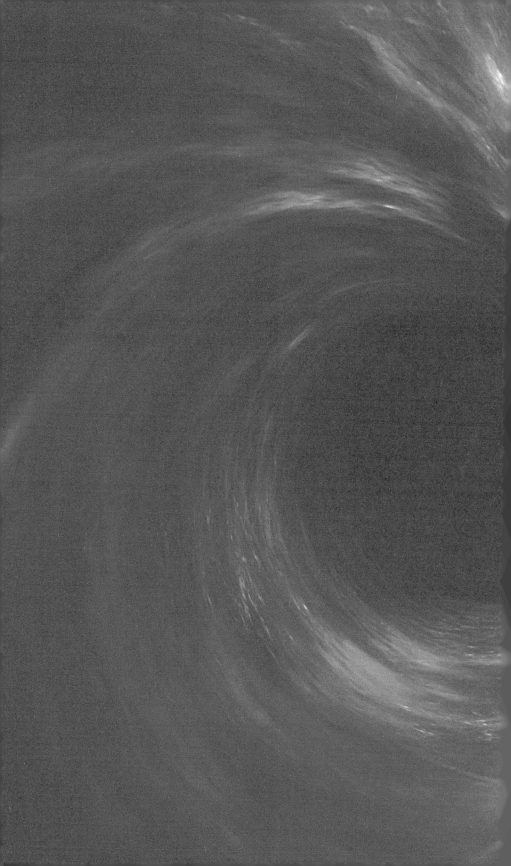

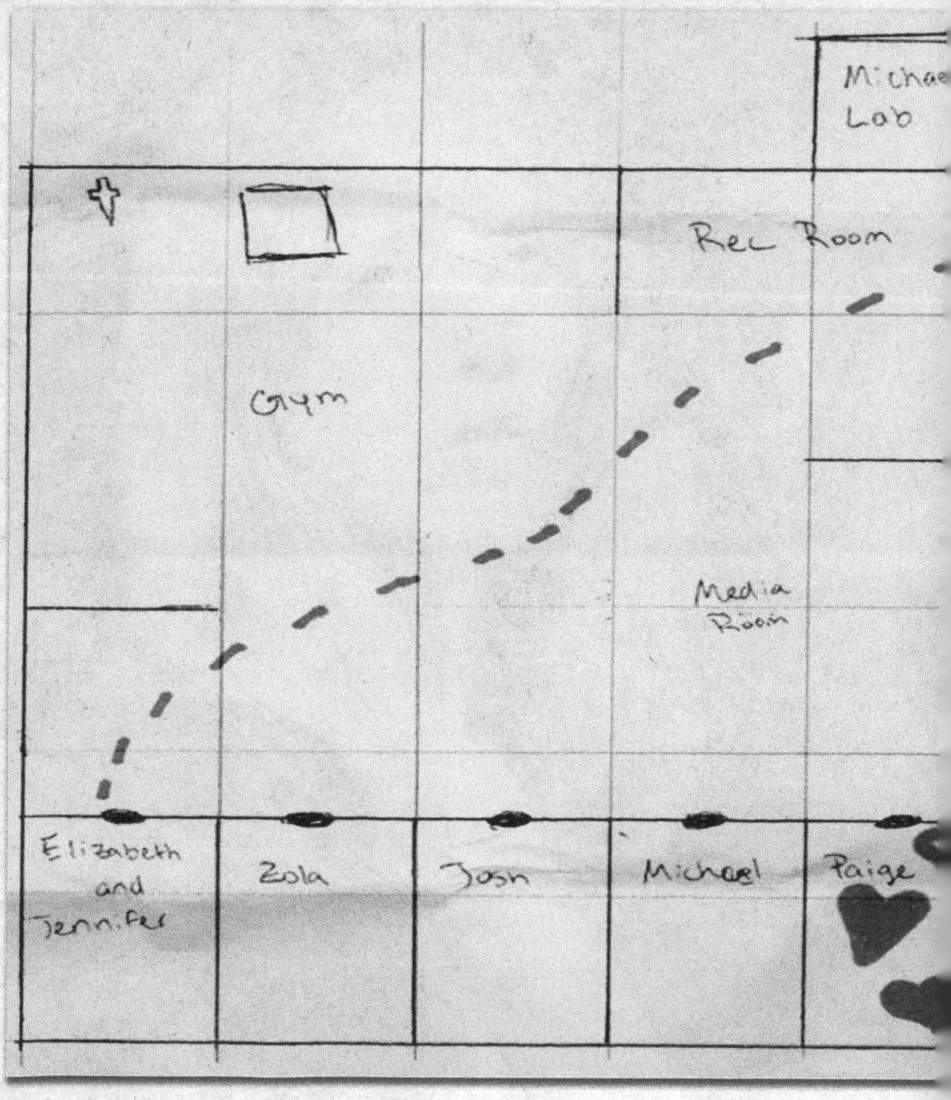

Michael
Lab

Rec Room

Gym

Media
Room

Elizabeth
and
Jennifer

Zola

Josh

Michael

Paige

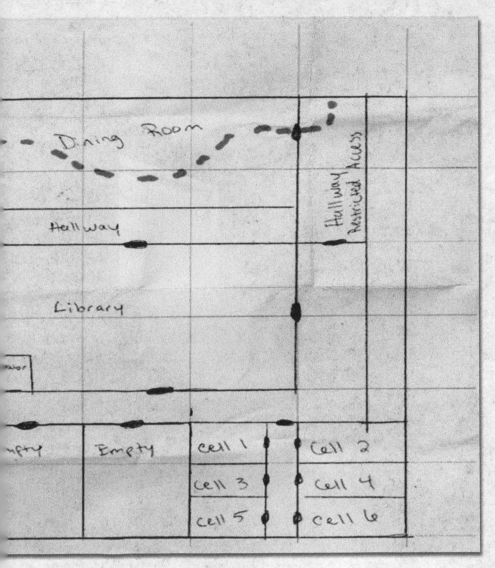

Map drawn by Elizabeth Voltz.
DUST Agency.
2nd Level Basement.

Chapter 1

"Lizzy..." A faint voice called out to Elizabeth.

"Liz... Elizabeth!"

Elizabeth peeked her eyes open to see her sister, Jennifer, sitting over her, her face pinched.

"Ugh! What's wrong? Did I sleep in?" she groaned.

"No, I have no clue where we are."

Confused and groggy, Elizabeth rolled away from Jennifer, hoping to get more sleep. Her bed felt harder than usual. Much harder. Muscles ached, and her spine was sore. Pushing her elbow out, Elizabeth used her arm strength to raise herself up until she sat almost level with Jennifer. She looked into Jennifer's eyes before looking around, then gasped at what she saw.

Elizabeth was not in her room. Not in her bed. Instead, she rested on a hard concrete floor, hence the soreness. Metal bars surrounded them. They were in a giant cage in the middle of a large room with only a small amount of light coming from a tiny window. It was silent except for the sound of their breath.

A musky smell crept up her nose. Shivering, Elizabeth wrapped her arms around her knees, bringing them up to her face. "This has to be a scary dream," she thought, but she hadn't dreamt in years. She stood, Jennifer watching her every move. Crossing to one side of the cage, she grabbed one of the bars and tried to shake it, testing its strength. It didn't budge.

"I've already tested everything." Jennifer said, softly.

Elizabeth felt her core go cold. Her head began to ache. Tears pooled in her eyes, and she hyperventilated.

Rushing to her, Jennifer forced her to her knees, holding on to her as her breathing became increasingly loud.

"Elizabeth, you need to breathe. In, and out."

Jennifer held onto the sides of Elizabeth's face, forcing them to look into each other's eyes. She made visible motions of breathing, encouraging her to follow.

"Breathe, Elizabeth."

Following Jennifer's prompts, Elizabeth felt her lungs stop burning, and her head stopped spinning as her breathing returned to normal. Her cheeks were wet from tears, and she occasionally sniffled.

"That's good. Just keep breathing. Stay calm. Passing out won't help anyone."

Jennifer continued comforting Elizabeth by rubbing soothing circles on her back.

"You good?" Jennifer asked, after a few minutes had passed.

Elizabeth nodded.

"Good."

"What are we going to do?"

"I... I don't know."

Jennifer's eyes followed the shape of the cage, the palm of her hand pressed to Elizabeth's back shaking.

"I checked every bar, looking for some sign of weakness. There's none But I have one last idea. It's why I woke you up. You're not going to like it, though."

Resting her head in her hands, Elizabeth already knew what Jennifer was going to suggest.

"I know you don't want to go dream travelling, but it's the best idea I can come up with. Maybe you'll find who put us here... or find something to help us escape."

"Yeah, I know. Jennifer, you're right. Dream travelling is probably our best bet at this point."

"So, you'll do it?"

With a resigned sigh, Elizabeth nodded.

"Yeah."

Wiping the tears from her eyes, Elizabeth laid down with her hands behind her head. Taking deep, relaxing breaths, she tried to lull herself to sleep.

She hadn't always been able to fall asleep so fast. Knowing what awaited her once she slept gave her too much anxiety for her to calm down. That had changed. After years of practice, accepting what sleeping brought, it took only a few minutes of coaxing to allow her body to rest.

Sleep, without a dream, yet like a dream—but not hers. Someone else's.

As if awake, Elizabeth slept, yet was standing in what looked like a boardroom filled with men and women dressed in suits. They were all yelling at each other.

Looking around the room she found herself in, she saw it had white walls and was filled with white chairs circled around a glass table. On the wall at the head of the table was a large, flat screen with Elizabeth's and Jennifer's pictures. Below each picture was text starting with their ages, twenty-five, followed by their physical descriptions. Before she could read more, the eyes she saw through moved to large windows with a view of the outside. She couldn't tell where they were, though. All she could see were large maple and pine trees, but she heard a voice.

"How in the world did that woman know about the hijacked plane? She knew before us, even!" said an elderly man.

"We should torture her. She must be one of the Society members," proclaimed a woman next to him.

The woman asked, "Jackie, what do you think?" to Elizabeth's occupied body, and she understood she must be in "Jackie's" mind.

"Shush, everyone!" Jackie shouted. It was silent for a short time while her eyes were closed. She smirked. "Well, I think I may have my answer," she thought.

"Answer to what?" Elizabeth thought to herself. Then, a shocking answer. To her.

"Hello, Elizabeth."

Then, something grabbed at her, pulling her from Jackie's mind. Elizabeth felt like she was being ripped apart. It was unlike anything she had ever experienced, like ripping off Band-Aids covering her entire body at once and flying through the air at the speed of light. Disorienting, painful.

Back in her own body, she jumped to her feet and woke up, feeling dizzy.

"What happened, Lizzy?!" Jennifer looked into her eyes.

"I don't know. I just saw a boardroom of people. I think... well, they think we're responsible for the plane being hijacked."

"That makes no sense. We warned them about that! Why would we have warned them if we were involved?"

"I don't understand it either. That's not all, though, the woman I travelled to... I think she may have talked to me through her subconscious. And I think she pushed me out."

Elizabeth felt a sense of dread.

"What! People can't do that! Can they?"

A door thudded, hitting the wall as it opened, and lights blinded them as they stepped away, gripping onto each other in fear.

"Hello, Elizabeth," said a strong, familiar voice. "I'm Jackie. I believe you invaded my mind."

Chapter 2

Jackie had long, wavy, dark brown hair, brown eyes, and olive-toned skin that looked smooth, like porcelain, but Elizabeth could tell she was middle-aged. Jackie watched her with an empty expression as her eyes adjusted to the piercing light. Elizabeth continued to look at her, unsure of what to say. No one had ever noticed her in their mind before.

"Oh, but I noticed you." She pushed her thoughts into Elizabeth's mind.

A chill ran down Elizabeth's spine, then throughout all the nerves in her body. She stared at the woman; her eyes grew wide. Nobody had ever pushed her out of their mind before. She had never felt pain like that. It was as if layers of consciousness were being torn apart. And now she had spoken directly into Elizabeth's head. Elizabeth opened her mouth to speak, but no words came out.

"Who are you?" Jennifer asked with authority.

"I've already told you, I'm Jackie."

"I know your name; I'm asking who you are."

"I'll answer what I can."

"Great, thanks." Then, speaking even more sarcastically, "I take it you're the one who put us here?"

"No. You put yourselves here. You made a 911 call about the plane before it disappeared, hijacked. Now the entire DUST thinks you may be part of the terrorist organization responsible, and a threat. To the United States."

"Are you going to kill us?" Elizabeth managed to utter the question.

Jackie stood silent, not answering, but Elizabeth thought she saw a flash of concern on Jackie's face. The silence was making her nervous, very nervous, and she looked to Jennifer, wondering if she'd know what to do. Nostrils flaring, eyes glaring, and fists clenched, Jennifer yelled, "You can't keep us here, we've done nothing wrong!"

"Oh, but I can."

Before her reply was even finished, two tall, large women, dressed in blue long-sleeved jumpers, walked through the door, straight to the cell. Jackie continued looking at the two captive women without expression.

"Don't fight them." Jackie thought to Elizabeth.

The two women in blue opened the cell and marched towards them. Elizabeth backed away, cowering, her back hitting the edge of the cell. She fell onto the floor, hoping it would swallow her. She closed her eyes, but opened them again immediately when she felt a sharp sting on the side of her neck.

"Watch out for the other one, she's a fighter," she heard Jackie warn the women.

Elizabeth's head started to feel woozy. Turning to Jennifer, Elizabeth saw her giving the two women a difficult time. Cornered, Jennifer undercut one woman, then kneed the other in quick succession. But while she was distracted, the first woman stuck a needle in her neck. Elizabeth cringed at the sound of Jen's yelp. Whatever drug had been injected into her sister quickly took over her body. Jennifer's attacks grew less powerful. Aside from the drug, she was fighting fatigue from waking up in a cell, with no food or water. Though Elizabeth tried to stay awake and watch Jennifer struggle to fend off the much larger women, she blacked out, missing her sister's defeat.

Once Elizabeth and Jennifer were placed on gurneys, Jackie watched as they were rolled away, saying, "Take them to the medical room for assessment."

Dream Traveller

"Yes ma'am."

Walking away from the cell, Jackie left, heading back to the boardroom. Before reaching her destination, she picked up her cell.

"William. Send me everything you have on Dream Travellers. Make sure that their apartment is clear of evidence. We don't want anything leading the police here."

She hung up.

Sitting in the boardroom, six officials were talking as Jackie walked in. All ignored her as she made her way to the front of the long table, except for Vance, cooly observing her every movement. He leaned back in his seat, looking her up and down with a judgmental stare.

She tried to reach into his mind, as she often did by habit, but something repelled her. She had never been able to reach him; it was as if he had a forcefield surrounding him. He gave her a knowing smile, making her shake inside. Jackie kept a straight face, not wanting to give him the satisfaction of making her uncomfortable.

"Oh, Jackie. Have them killed, please."

Jackie looked at him, hiding her disgust.

"I want them on my team, Vance."

Vance sat up straight, putting his forearms on the table. "And why is that?"

"Voltz is a Dream Traveller."

Vance got up from his chair, slowly walking around the table to her. "The last Dream Traveller we had went mad. Don't you remember him?"

Jackie flinched.

"Of course I remember him. Sir... But we have someone that can help her this time."

"Who? Michael?"

"Yes, and his sister, Paige."

All in the room were quiet as they watched the exchange. Vance moved behind her, his tall frame towering over her. She kept looking ahead as he leaned over her and said, "Tell you what, keep her as a trial run. If she steps out of line, does anything to jeopardize our operation, eliminate her. No questions asked."

Jackie nodded, agreeing to his demand, yet seeing an opportunity.

"I want Jennifer too. She could be a great asset to the team. She's a skilled fighter."

"We have plenty of fighters. Why waste resources on another?"

"She's more skilled than the others. It will be good to keep her and Elizabeth together. Don't you know they're sisters? Foster sisters? According to your 'researcher,' William, they've been inseparable since they were kids. That's the way I want them."

"As if you know anything about warriors. I was already on the fence about Elizabeth anyways. Why would I care if she stays with her sister?"

"There's more. Noels isn't who she says she is. She changed her last name."

"Care to elaborate?"

"Of course. Her parents were Alena and Jordan Hickory." Jackie turned to face Vance, stepping to the side for a bit of space. "If you remember, they were both Major Generals in the army until they were assassinated when she was thirteen. She was found unconscious, lying next to her dead parents. By the way, they found at least ten assassins dead, all killed by her, a child."

Jackie was sure she saw Vance smirk. "So... why is it that I'm just now finding out about her?"

"She was taken into protective custody. Last name changed to Noels. Elizabeth's family adopted her after fostering her for a year."

"Fine, fine, fine. I'll give them a chance. They're your responsibility now."

"Thank you, sir."

"Have them injected with trackers, and make sure they know that we'll kill everyone they love if they step out of line."

Jackie nodded, thinking how badly she wished to kill him, and started to leave.

"And Jackie? Do be careful. I would hate to have to take matters into my own hands."

Chapter 3

Elizabeth was in the body of a woman pushing a gurney. She could see her own body lying there, looking like death. She couldn't feel herself being bustled along, but could hear the squeaky wheels echoing off the walls. She'd never gotten used to seeing herself through the eyes of another.

To her right lay Jennifer. Elizabeth knew there must have been quite a fight because the woman pushing her had a black eye and a limp. She felt pain coursing through her host's body as well.

The women pushed them through a dimly lit, white hallway that reminded Elizabeth of a government owned building, like a prison or a school. When they wheeled her into a large elevator, she saw a red glowing LED panel indicating they were on the lowest level. The lady pushed a button, taking them to the next level. When the doors opened, they were brought into a pitch-black hall. Their keepers turned on flashlights and continued to their destination. Elizabeth couldn't see much of their surroundings; the flashlights were too weak.

They stopped in front of a door and opened it. The women carried their bodies in and placed them on beds. Elizabeth watched as the women tucked them in. It was a confusing gesture. Why care for their comfort? Once the women were satisfied, they left. Before the door shut, Elizabeth jumped back into her body. She never liked to be in another person's body for too long, afraid she wouldn't find her way back.

Wired and terrified, stuck inside her own darkness, she tried thinking of a way to escape. Instead, she thought of the reason she was there. She started to reminisce about the girl she stumbled into a couple nights ago. She had woken in the mind of a teenage girl sitting on a plane. Next to her was a little girl she assumed was her sister.

"Daisy," the girl whined, "I wanna play a game. I'm bored."

The child's innocent blue eyes pleaded with her, and her ash blonde hair fell gracefully over her shoulders.

"Fine, what do you want to play?" the older child asked.

"Go Fish!"

"All right, I'll get the cards."

She reached into her backpack, pulled out a stack of cards, and began dealing.

"No cheating, okay Sofie?"

"I never cheat, you're just a sore loser," the little girl stated.

Daisy glared at her, but continued dealing and shuffling the cards. Sofie happily took her cards and looked them over.

Just before they started playing, a loud banging came from the cockpit. The woman across the aisle spilled her fizzy drink on the man next to her, and the man cursed. The passengers in front of them stood and yelled to ask what was going on. Another loud noise blared, causing more distress. Daisy could see the man in front of them yelling, while the lady sitting beside him looked back at them, her raised brows creating wrinkles on her forehead. They were in first class, so it was easy to hear what was going on in the front.

"Daisy?" Her sister looked at her with fear in her eyes.

"I'm sure it's nothing." She patted the little girl's head, trying to soothe her.

Daisy spoke too soon. A woman with wild, curly red hair walked out of the cockpit and started strutting down the aisle. Reaching into her satchel, she pulled out a black handgun. Sofie hid her face in Daisy's side. Screams, cries of fear, and passengers' begging the woman not to hurt them blurred into background noise, but Daisy was focused on the gun.

"Hello, everyone, your destination plans have changed." The red-haired woman spoke with confidence.

The man in front of them stood. "Lady, please put the gun away; there are children here!"

He wore a light gray suit, and his brown hair was just starting to thin. She gave him a calculated look and tilted her head. She smirked, waving the gun around like it was a toy.

"You mean this little thing?" She pouted her lips.

"Why don't you just put the gun down? We can come to some kind of agreement." He tried to sound calm, but his voice shook.

She clicked her tongue. "Oh, congressman, you're so cute."

She pointed the gun at him, pulled the trigger, and he fell to the floor. Screaming, Daisy grabbed Sofie and pulled her to her chest. She wanted to shield her from the horrors before them. She looked to the aisle and saw the lifeless body with a hole between his eyes. Sofie was sobbing into her shirt. She could hear the woman screaming and crying in front of them. She looked up at the lady with a gun.

"Hmmm? I think not. Anyone else want to tell me what to do? No one? Okay, good. I only take orders from one person."

"Daddy!" Sofie cried. Daisy put her hand over Sofie's mouth. She didn't want any attention brought to them, but it was too late.

The lady walked over to them, knelt to the ground, and looked at them with what appeared to be sympathy.

"I'm sorry your daddy had to die, little ones, but where we're going, I'm the boss." She stood up to get everyone else's attention. "Let this be a lesson to all. If you don't want to die, address me with respect. I'm your new leader. We'll be landing soon, so be prepared."

Sofie was still soaking her shirt with tears as Daisy wrung her fingers through the little girl's hair. She was too shocked to feel anything. Their mother looked back at them with mascara-stained cheeks. Daisy could tell she was trying to stay strong, but the smeared makeup and watery blue eyes gave her away.

As soon as the red-haired woman turned her back, their mother closed in on them and protectively held the girls behind her. She looked back, then whispered, "Do whatever they say."

Relieved from the nightmarish flashback by her shoulders being shaken, Elizabeth opened her eyes to see Jennifer, with a panicked expression, looking down at her. She shot up, their foreheads colliding.

"Ow!" Jennifer cried.

They both rubbed their sore heads.

"We need to get out of here," Jennifer groaned. "Were you able to jump into any heads and figure out an escape?"

Jennifer's curly jet-black hair was in disarray. She had a split lip from the fight she'd put up, and her eyes darted behind Elizabeth, as if there could be an attack at any moment.

"No, I just was in one of those ladies' heads. They didn't say anything, though. Jackie probably warned them."

Jennifer pulled her hair back as she spoke. "Okay, well, do you think you could now?"

"I don't know, I have little control over my powers." Elizabeth dropped her head into her hands.

"Okay, okay. It's all right. Let's think about this logically. If they wanted us dead, they would have killed us. They obviously have the means and lack of morals to do so. And they've given us a comfortable room, so they seem to care for our wellbeing."

"So…"

"So, they want to gain our trust. They need something from us."

"Okay, well, we aren't giving them anything, right?"

"We need to play along. Let's scope out the perimeter."

"Good idea."

"Oh, and let me do all the talking. I know how to handle these situations."

Elizabeth looked around herself, seeing a lavender painted room, two queen beds with plain blue sheets and paisley comforters, three white doors: two in the front of the room and one on the left wall, and no windows. Elizabeth's bed was cozy, with four fluffy pillows surrounding her.

Elizabeth got up from her bed and stomped to the door. Getting sick of not knowing where she was, Elizabeth needed answers. Opening the door to the front right, she found it led to a bathroom. There was a large walk-in shower with a blue shower curtain, a shaggy black bathroom rug, an average toilet, two sinks with a mirror, white walls, and black tiles covering the floor. Elizabeth rolled her eyes and slammed the door.

She then tried the door next to it, but that only led her to a large walk-in closet. The closet was empty, but it could hold more than enough clothes for the two of them. After also slamming that door, she went to the final door, their last chance. Thinking it would probably be locked, she was surprised to find it wasn't.

She opened the door angrily, expecting to see Jackie with the guards, but they were nowhere to be seen. Instead, they saw a young man and woman, about their own age, playing ping-pong. Every time their paddles hit the ball, it echoed throughout the room.

The room was enormous, at least three times the size of their apartment. Despite the size of the room, the lack of windows made it feel claustrophobic. Next to the young adults were a foosball table, air hockey table, and some arcade games. In the far back left corner, Elizabeth saw what appeared to be a gym with treadmills, weights, punching bags, a rope tied to the top of the tall ceiling, and large mats. To the right was a living room area with a movie theater -like vibe. Although the functionality of the room looked fun, she could tell no interior designer put it together. It was total chaos.

"Oh, they're up!" the young woman playing ping-pong exclaimed. Cherry bombing the ball, she placed the paddle down, then ran over to them with a smile. The man stayed in his spot, watching them with curiosity. "I'm so glad you guys are up! I'm Zola, and that's Josh. What are your names?"

"Who are you?" Elizabeth demanded. She stood still, on high alert, ready to attack if needed.

She took in the woman's appearance. Zola appeared to be in her early twenties, her face round, skin tan, and eyes a light brown. Her shiny hair was dark brown and down to her waist. She wore an orange graphic T-shirt with a sunrise over an ocean printed on it, tucked into her high waist jeans. She didn't seem to be a threat, but her bubbliness in this prison was suspicious.

"I'm just excited you guys are here! I don't get to meet many young people. Most of the people we get to meet are old." Zola ignored Elizabeth's rudeness.

All Elizabeth did was hum. In any other situation, she would have been much friendlier, but their current predicament made her hostile. Jennifer raised her eyebrows at her. She would probably get a scolding after this, since Jennifer had just said to let her do the talking.

"Where are we?" Elizabeth asked.

Zola looked at them with an unfazed expression. "A government agency called the Department of the United States Threats Control. There's a part of the agency that is known to the public, but we're in a secret force of the branch. All I know is that all the people they bring here have something special about them."

"Wow, that's a mouthful," Jennifer commented.

"It is. I just call it DUST. That's what most other people do too."

"Do you know when we can leave?" interrupted Jennifer.

"Never." Zola looked to the floor sadly. "None of us can leave. We all have tracker chips, so even if we leave, they'll find us and bring us back."

"Tracker chips? Where?" Jennifer demanded.

"I believe it's on the back of your neck, at the base of your hairline."

Elizabeth felt the back of her neck. Right where Zola said it was, she could feel a tender bump. A sickening lump formed in her throat, and her face flushed.

"They've chipped us! Like animals." Elizabeth's voice shook.

"How do we get them out?" Jennifer asked.

"I don't know, I've tried. As soon as I dug into my skin, I felt a stabbing feeling around it and passed out. I woke up in a hospital bed a day later."

Jennifer grabbed Elizabeth's hand and she gave it a squeeze, knowing they both needed reassurance. At least they were here together.

"So you're being held captive as well?"

"Well, yes, but it's not so bad. They keep me safe."

"From what?" Elizabeth wasn't sure Zola was being held against her will. If she was, she should have been less appreciative. But Elizabeth decided to go along with it. One of the best ways to gather information was to act like you believed someone's deception; she learned that from her sister.

"Hurting people."

"You don't seem like you'd hurt someone."

"I've hurt lots of people."

Elizabeth squinted. It was worrisome that she would admit to hurting people. There was a loud noise across the room, alerting her to their surroundings again. Looking to where the noise came from, she saw the man who had been playing ping-pong with Zola, Josh, walking towards them.

"Hey, everything okay, Zola?" he asked.

"Yeah, I was just about to ask if they wanted a tour."

He nodded, gave them a skeptical glance, then walked away.

"Hold that thought, Zola. Let me talk to Elizabeth in private real quick," said Jennifer.

"Of course! Take your time."

Jennifer guided Elizabeth by the elbow until they were certain they couldn't be heard.

"We need to befriend Zola," Jennifer whispered.

"What? I'm not befriending any of these people! They're all crazy!"

"Maybe, but they might also just be victims like us. Either way, we need to gain their trust. It's the best way out of here."

Elizabeth glared at her. There was no way she could pretend to be okay with this. She was no actress.

"Come on, Elizabeth. They're obviously already brainwashed; how hard can it be?"

Elizabeth looked to the ground and shook her head. "Fine."

She followed Jennifer back to Zola. She understood how Daisy felt at that moment. Their lives had been hijacked.

Chapter 4

Jennifer saw Zola attempt to grab their hands, but she quickly retracted.

Cheeks flushing, Zola said, "Sorry! I get too excited sometimes. If you follow me this way, we can get started on the tour. First, I'd like to show where everyone's rooms are. Mine is right next to yours!"

Their room was the furthest left of the recreation center, then Zola's, Josh's, Michael's, and lastly Paige's room. All neatly labeled like they were a bunch of lab rats. Elizabeth cringed at the thought.

"Okay, on to the next thing!" She led them to the living room area. "This is the most important spot in this place... in my opinion." She laughed awkwardly. "We have frequent movie nights, and there's a gaming station."

The couch was huge, easily able to fit ten people. The television was almost as big as the wall. Jennifer took a seat on the couch next to Zola, making sure to leave space between them, and Elizabeth sat next to her.

"Tell us about yourself," Jennifer started. "Why are you here? How old are you? What about your family?"

Zola's face lit up. She seemed happy that someone was asking about her. "Okay! I'm twenty-two, and my family has no clue where I am. I was kidnapped... just like you guys! And I'm here because..." She hesitated for a second. "I'm here because I killed someone."

Jennifer looked at Elizabeth, shock etched both their faces. Jennifer felt panic rising within her, suddenly remembering the day she was almost killed, but she kept it at bay, remaining calm. Just how dangerous were these people?

"It was an accident! I swear! I was just really scared. I didn't know what I was capable of," Zola blurted out, probably noticing the uneasiness.

"It's okay." Jennifer played it off. She needed Zola to trust them, not think they were judging her. "We're just surprised."

"How'd you kill them?" Elizabeth asked. Jennifer nudged her knee. Elizabeth winced.

Zola smiled sadly. "You'll probably find out soon anyways. It's kind of a long story, but in short, I was in trouble. Some wolves attacked the men who were threatening me."

"Were they your pets?"

"No. I can control and understand animals."

Jennifer tensed up. Zola was the second person they had met with a special ability. She shouldn't have been surprised there were more people who were different like Liz, but she was.

"So, you told some wolves to kill some guys?" Jennifer wanted to hear more.

"No, I swear I didn't!" Zola was defending herself. Again. "I was just so scared… I must have wished for help, or something. I can't really remember everything."

Jennifer relaxed a little. Zola sounded a lot like the women that Elizabeth would tell Jennifer about when she dream travelled.

"We aren't judging you. If it was self-defense, it was self-defense," Jennifer said, knowing all too well what it was like to defend herself. The fear in the moment, then the guilt in succeeding. "This is all just new to us. Before being brought here, I didn't know there were people out there with abilities like you have."

"What did they do to you?" Elizabeth jumped in before Zola could respond.

"You don't have to tell us," said Jennifer, after shooting a quick glare Elizabeth's way.

"I'll tell you. I was at a bonfire with my friend while we were juniors in high school. Most of the people there were our age, but there were a few older boys there that bought alcohol for us.

"My friend and I thought they were really cute, so we were flirting away. Three boys eventually asked us to go for a walk with them to get away from the noise. Of course, we went with them," she said, and rolled her eyes, "and we got pretty far away from the party. We couldn't even see the light from the fire anymore. Everything was just lit from the full moon. That's when the boys started teasing us. They were asking us weird things like if we'd ever had sex, and if we'd ever done anything else with any guys.

"We didn't judge them for asking that, or anything. We just weren't doing that kind of stuff yet, so we said we weren't ready for that. That's when things started to get weird. They asked us when we would be ready, and being only seventeen, we had no clue what to say to those older guys. We started to get uncomfortable, and we wanted to go back.

"Those boys begged us to stay, but we said no, we're leaving. They didn't like that answer. They grabbed us and pinned us on the ground, telling us we owed them sex since they supplied us with beer. We started screaming for help, but nobody could hear us. It was disgusting."

Pausing, she shuddered at the memory, but managed to continue.

"They tried taking our clothes off, but didn't get very far. I heard howling from a distance, but it was weird because wolves usually didn't go anywhere near people. I was pleading for the boys to stop, but they didn't care.

"That's when I saw the first wolf, a huge, furry thing, leaping over me, taking one of the boys off me. I stood up and saw five wolves surrounding us. One of them ripped a boy off my friend. I still can hear their screams.

"By the time the wolves were done, all the boys' throats were torn open. Their limbs were scattered all around us. We were so terrified and confused, all my friend and I could do was hug each other. Then... one of the wolves came up to me, and I was sure I was going to die. That wolf looked me right in the eyes, then licked my face. Then it ran away, with its pack following behind."

"After that, we made our way back to the campfire and had someone call the police. We took the police to where everything happened, and they were absolutely shocked. Then, thinking we could do what the wolves did, they took us in for questioning. That's when I met Jackie. The police must have called the agency and told them about the incident. Next thing I knew, I had been drugged and woke up here."

"Did you try to escape?" Jennifer asked.

"I did, but was caught because of the tracker. When they knock you out, they insert a tracker with it. I was so scared they were going to kill me, but Jackie just gave me a warning. She said they'd kill my family if I tried to run away again."

Jennifer looked at the young woman beside her, noticing how sad her big, beautiful brown eyes were. Someone as sweet as her didn't deserve any of that, but Jennifer was impressed with Zola's strength. She was assaulted, witnessed a violent canine killing spree, then was kidnapped by the government and forced to stay here. All that, all that trauma, and she was still smiling.

Jennifer glanced at Elizabeth. She thought about how hard it would be to escape. Zola had been trapped there for five years. Even if they did manage to escape, they had trackers implanted in them, and there didn't seem to be any way to remove them. Leaving had started to seem impossible. She didn't want to let Elizabeth know she felt that way. She needed to give her some hope.

"I just want you to know," Zola said, "I realize you just met me, and you're scared, but I'm on your side. I hope, in time, we can trust each other."

"Maybe you could show us how your powers work sometime?" Jennifer requested.

"I'd like that."

Chapter 5

Thirteen-year-old Elizabeth sat in the waiting room with her parents. The chairs were old and uncomfortable, and the inner walls were made of glass, so she could see passersby walking along. She bounced her legs out of nervousness while her parents chatted about plans for the girl they were going to foster. Her name was Jennifer, and Elizabeth couldn't wait to meet her.

She had always wanted a sister, and then, a year ago, her parents had decided to become foster parents. They all went through training and had been waiting to find the perfect fit for their home. Finding a girl Elizabeth's age was merely a coincidence; but she hoped it would be beneficial for them both. After all, she had been having a hard time making friends her own age. Other children didn't quite know how to handle her.

Elizabeth had a darker mind than most people. She would be thinking of all the terrible things she saw when she closed her eyes, and her mind would drift off. Never able to pay attention, she always looked to be deep in thought. The other children liked to make fun of her quietness. Elizabeth hoped to be able to make friends with the girl about to become her foster sister.

It was perfect timing; the school year was about to begin, and thirteen-year-old Jennifer needed a safe family to help her.

The door opened, and in walked a girl with black afroed hair and beautiful dark skin. Beside her stood a social worker, an older woman. Elizabeth looked up at the girl and smiled. Instead of smiling back, the girl looked down at her feet.

"You must be Jennifer," Elizabeth's mom said sweetly.

Jennifer nodded.

"Well, it's a pleasure to meet you. We are so excited for you to come live with us."

Jennifer gave them a tight-lipped smile and stayed silent. They were aware that children in foster care were sometimes traumatized and unhappy in their situation, so they didn't take offense to her lack of enthusiasm.

"I'm Elizabeth." Elizabeth jumped from her chair.

"Nice to meet you," Jennifer whispered.

"And you can call us Mr. and Mrs. Voltz, Doug and Julie, or whatever you feel comfortable with."

"Okay." She had that same awkward smile.

"Let's go talk in my office for a second," the social worker said to the parents. "We will be right back, girls." The parents were led from the room, leaving Jennifer and Elizabeth alone.

Silence filled the room after the adults left. Elizabeth just stared at Jennifer, observing her.

Jennifer looked around the room, sadness in her eyes. "Okay, can you not stare at me? I don't know what your problem is," she snapped.

"Sorry." Elizabeth's face burned, and she looked at her feet.

"It's fine, just no staring, please. I feel like you're looking into my soul."

"Sorry, I'm just so excited to have a sister."

Jennifer glared at her. "I'm not your sister."

They sat in silence until the adults came back. After leaving for home, Elizabeth's parents tried making conversation by asking Jennifer questions about herself, but only received one-worded answers. Elizabeth stared out the window, disappointed by Jennifer's lack of warmth. This wasn't going to be the sisterhood she hoped for.

When they got home, Elizabeth showed Jennifer the bathroom and the room she would be staying in. Jennifer thanked her by slamming the door in her face, and Elizabeth went to the kitchen to help her parents with dinner.

Dream Traveller

"So, what do you think, Elizabeth?" her mother asked.

"Of Jennifer? I don't think she likes me."

"Just give her time. She's probably been through a lot. Apparently, her parents recently died."

"I know, I just had hoped we'd become friends more quickly."

"It'll happen, sweetie." Her mom smiled.

"We'll see."

After they finished making dinner, spaghetti with meatballs, Jennifer was called down, and the four of them ate an uncomfortable meal around the table.

"So, you're going to be in seventh grade this year?" Elizabeth's mom asked.

"Yup."

"That's exciting! Elizabeth is also going into seventh grade."

"Great."

"Are you interested in joining any clubs?"

"Nope."

Clicking her tongue, Elizabeth's mom took the hint that Jennifer wasn't in the mood for questions. They spent the rest of the time eating in silence.

Once dinner was over, Jennifer went straight to her room, while Elizabeth and her parents cleaned everything up. After, Elizabeth sat on the couch with her parents to watch a movie, but she couldn't pay attention. Her mind was occupied with her new housemate, and how much she'd botched her first impression.

She left mid-movie after telling her parents she was tired and walked upstairs to her room. Before she opened her door, though, she walked over to Jennifer's door. She leaned her ear to it to see if Jennifer was awake before she knocked. She could hear quiet sniffling on the other side and thought the other girl must be crying.

She didn't stand there long. Hearing the bed creak and feet coming closer, she jumped away from the door in time for Jennifer to throw it open.

"Are you spying on me?"

"No, I just wanted to see how you're doing." She looked into Jennifer's puffy eyes. "Have you been crying?"

"Why do you care?"

"I just want to be your friend."

"Well, I don't need friends." Jennifer shut the door. The second door Elizabeth got slammed in her face.

Elizabeth took a deep breath and left to go to bed.

The next couple weeks, before school started, things didn't improve between the girls. Elizabeth's parents told her to be patient with Jennifer, but time moves slowly for a thirteen-year-old girl.

Time came for them to start school again, and Elizabeth's parents dropped them off at the front of their school. After saying goodbye and good luck, the two girls walked up to the door.

"Let me know if you need help finding anything," Elizabeth offered.

"I'll figure it out."

Jennifer took off after they walked in, leaving Elizabeth to begin another lonely school year.

Elizabeth went through the motions, feeling like a zombie. She enjoyed her classes, enjoyed learning, but the other children outweighed all of that. Most of the time she was ignored. All of her classes allowed their students to choose their own seats, and she, being the first person to every class, got first pick. Unfortunately, the seats chosen last were the ones next to her. At lunch, she sat by herself while doing her homework. Between classes, she walked the hallways alone.

For the next couple weeks, Jennifer ignored her foster family the best she could. They kept trying to be inclusive and loving, but she didn't care to reciprocate. She wanted to be left alone, to wallow in her pain. Elizabeth was insufferable. She would knock on Jennifer's door every night to ask her if she wanted or needed anything. Jennifer hoped that if she wasn't the fit this family wanted, they would get rid of her, and she could move on to the next family. It was taking longer than expected, though.

Three weeks passed, and she was still adjusting to her new life, new family, and new school. She managed to make all the kids scared of her, which was exactly what she wanted. One of the boys in her class touched her hair several times, even after she warned him not to, and so she broke his finger. She was sent to the principal's office and was expelled, while the boy was given a two-day suspension. Her foster parents were furious, but after she told them why she did it, their fury turned toward the school.

The next day, she drove with her parents and Elizabeth to school, but instead of just dropping Elizabeth off, they marched inside, Jennifer following behind them. They walked into the principal's office and made a scene about how she shouldn't have been expelled since she was just defending herself. The fact that the boy had just been suspended after touching Jennifer without her consent, while she was expelled, was unjustifiable. After a couple hours of arguing, the principal caved, when her foster parents threatened to sue and go to the media with how "this school tolerates nonconsensual touching." He couldn't let her completely off the hook, so she was given the same punishment as the boy. Her foster parents seemed okay with that.

Nobody tried messing with her afterward, and they all avoided eye contact.

Jennifer noticed herself watching Elizabeth. As much as she tried not to care for her foster sister, the girl somehow got under her skin. On her third Friday of seventh grade, after school, she stood around the corner from Elizabeth's locker. There was a group of kids who were acting stalkerish toward Elizabeth, so Jennifer had been keeping a close eye on her. She heard some creepy snickering from one of the girls she recognized from her class.

"Hey, freak, why don't you talk?" one asked.

"Yeah, are you a mute?" asked a boy.

Jennifer heard a slam.

"Ah! Guys, you're scaring her!" a girl mocked.

"We aren't scaring you, we just want to be friends," the boy said. A chorus of laughter followed.

Getting a strange feeling, Jennifer couldn't stand by any longer.

"Hey, what's going on?"

They all turned to look at her.

"Nothing," a boy, who appeared to be their leader, replied. "I was just trying to make a new friend."

Elizabeth's eyes were bloodshot and zoned out.

"I don't think she wants to be friends with the likes of you."

The boy chuckled. "And who are you?" He walked up to her and puffed out his chest.

"Just leave her alone." Jennifer shoved him away.

"Did you just push me? I think she just pushed me!" He looked around at his friends.

"You were in my personal space."

"You know what?" He walked over to Elizabeth and wrapped a strand of her dark blond hair around his finger. He pulled on the piece, causing her to whimper. "I don't think I want to leave her alone."

Dream Traveller

The sight of him touching Elizabeth sent Jennifer over the edge. All of the sudden, she wasn't standing in the school hallway, but in her old home. She thought about how she was unable to save her parents, her tutor. She had vowed to never let someone she cared about get hurt again.

She ran up to the boy and wrapped her hands around his throat. The impact made him let go of Elizabeth's hair, and Jennifer slammed him against the lockers. Elizabeth dropped to the ground and wrapped her arms around her legs, looking up at Jennifer in awe.

Reaching for his throat, the boy tried to wrench Jennifer's hands away, but she was too strong.

"If you ever touch her again," she said, "I will make you wish you were never born."

The boy's eyes widened, and he nodded his head. To really solidify her threat, she waited a couple seconds before finally letting him free. He dropped to the ground and crawled away.

"Come on, let's get out of here," he choked out, then led his gang away from Elizabeth and Jennifer.

Jennifer knelt beside Elizabeth. "Are you okay?"

Elizabeth nodded, but tears started to stream from her eyes.

"Come on." Jennifer helped her up. "If anyone ever bothers you again, you come to me. I'll take care of them."

"Why? I thought you hated me."

Jennifer looked at her with sadness in her eyes, but said nothing as she put her arm around her shoulders and helped her to the front door.

Chapter 6

For the rest of the day after speaking to Zola, Jennifer and Elizabeth looked around to scope out an escape. Any rooms that looked like a possible way out were locked, so that was a bust. One thing they did find, which was as hopeful as it was concerning, was weapons by the workout station. Inspecting the edges of the swords, daggers, and arrows, Elizabeth was surprised to see they were sharp. They could easily be used to kill someone.

"Why do think they have these here?" Elizabeth asked, pointing to the weapons.

"Combat training would be my guess," Jennifer responded. "It's strange that the edges on the weapons aren't dull, though."

"Will they ask us to kill each other?"

Jennifer looked at her, drawing her eyebrows together. "I… I don't know."

"What if they ask us to fight each other? To kill each other?" Elizabeth's anxiety spiked.

"We will refuse. And if they find a way to make us, we'll figure it out. I would never hurt you."

"What if you don't have a choice?"

"There's always a choice."

Elizabeth gulped. She knew making fake scenarios in her head wasn't helpful, but couldn't help herself.

Jennifer walked over to her and put an arm around her shoulders. "Come on, let's see what else this place has to offer."

"Do they seriously just expect to keep us locked up for the rest of our lives?" Elizabeth groaned.

"Be patient, Elizabeth. Jackie will probably check on us at some point. Maybe we can get some information from Zola. She probably knows the schedules."

"You're right."

"We will figure this out. Don't give up."

When dinner came around, they followed Zola's chirping voice in hopes that they would find food. That brought them back to a dining area they had seen earlier. On the right side of the room was a long wooden dining table with twelve chairs surrounding it. The left side held a kitchen with all the essentials, such as a fridge, stove, oven, sink, and dishwasher. There was a long counter separating the dining and kitchen area, with pizza, a pitcher of water, drinking glasses, and plates laid out for them.

Elizabeth grabbed a plate along with a couple pieces of pepperoni pizza, got herself a glass of water, and took a seat at the table.

"Why is the table so big? Are there this many people being held against their will here?" Elizabeth asked.

"No," said Zola. "Usually it's just Josh, Michael, and I that sit here together. But now that you two are here, that makes five!"

"Then why not get a smaller table?"

"Not sure! It's just always been here. Rumor has it, there used to be a lot more people here."

"What happened to them?"

"I'm not sure! I've tried asking Jackie, but she just acted all grumpy and told me it's not my concern."

"Where's the big guy you were with earlier?" Jennifer chimed in.

"Josh? He might be with Jackie. I'm not sure though. He doesn't usually tell me."

Elizabeth wondered why he would be with Jackie, but didn't care enough to ask.

"What time does the staff come to bring breakfast?"

"Breakfast starts at six and ends at eight. They set everything up and clean afterwards."

"What doors do they come out of?"

Zola raised her brow, but didn't question her motives. "The one at the end of the room." she pointed to a large white door across the room.

"Perfect."

"Whatever you're planning, I hope you think it through."

"I don't know what you're talking about." Jennifer winked.

Stuffed with the pizza, Elizabeth felt drowsiness filling her head.

"Hey, guys, I'm exhausted. I think I'm going to head to bed."

"Okay, I'll come to bed in a bit," replied Jennifer.

"Good night, Elizabeth." Zola took her hand and gave it a little squeeze. "See you in the morning."

"Good night." Elizabeth forced a smile. She stood and placed her dishes in the dishwasher, then walked out. She had planned on heading straight to bed, but wanted to go back to the training area. She peeked around to make sure no one was watching and stepped closer to the weapon wall. Stroking the blade of one of the daggers, she decided to grab two: one for her and one for Jennifer. She shoved them up her sleeves, then quickly walked to her room.

After entering, she placed the daggers under her bed, then went to the bathroom to shower and brush her teeth. Before she stepped into the shower, she made the mistake of looking in the mirror.

Her face looked so pale, her hair brittle, and the bags under her eyes made it look like she hadn't slept in days. She wondered how she would look if she could sleep like a normal person. Unfortunately, that would never happen. She was cursed.

With a sigh, she removed her clothes, and didn't dare look at her body. She already knew she would be horrified at the sight. Despite having started training with Jennifer years ago, she was still too thin. Thanks to the constant dream travelling, her physical and mental health had been declining. It had taken a toll on her body. She entered the shower, letting the warm water wash away her anxiety.

After showering and brushing her teeth, she found a large T-shirt and cotton shorts in the dresser, which someone must have stocked for them. Curious, she decided to take another look in the closet. Before, it was empty, but now it was filled with clothes.

Elizabeth shuddered at the knowledge that DUST knew their clothing size, and that the closet held enough clothes to supply them for a long time. That meant their captors had no intention of letting them go. She closed the closet door, sighed, and climbed into bed. The sheets were soft and cozy. She took three deep breaths before being pulled into a dreamless sleep. She hoped she might land in the head of someone that had information about how she might escape. Her mind had a different idea.

As quick as a snap of the fingers, she awoke in another person's consciousness. The walls, floor, and ceiling around her were all brown, like the inside of a cave. The room was lit by several tall candles. Elizabeth saw a little girl resting her head on the occupied body's lap. They were both on a twin bed covered in white sheets and a white fleece blanket. Aside from the bed, the room held only a dresser and a bucket of water. The door was made of wood, but it didn't look very useful, as there were a few holes in it.

The little girl stirred in her lap, then sat up. Elizabeth recognized the girl as soon as she saw her face. It was Sofie from the hijacked plane, which meant she was in Daisy's head. She'd never been in the same mind twice.

"Where's momma?" Sofie asked.

"I wish I knew."

"Daisy, I'm hungry," Sofie whined.

She no longer looked like the happy, well put-together girl Elizabeth remembered from the plane. Now her hair was a frizzy mess, and there were dark circles surrounding her eyes.

"I'm sorry, we can't eat until morning."

"I know, I just wish I could eat something right now."

Daisy looked at Sofie's sad eyes until she gave in. "Okay, I'll see if I can get you some food."

Daisy stood up from the bed, and Sofie jumped up and down. Walking out of the room and down the cave halls, Daisy found her way to the kitchen and dining area. Finding it empty, she sighed with relief. This room was also lit by candles. The dining area consisted of ten long wooden dining tables, with wooden chairs that seemed to be handcrafted. The kitchen area had a line of counters and cabinets along the wall, a wood-fed oven, and a pit for a campfire with a large pot hanging over it.

She went to the cabinets and started looking through them. Most of the cabinets were filled with spices and boxed food like mashed potatoes and noodles, but eventually she found some apples and crackers.

"Ahem!" Daisy heard a cough, making her jump. "What do you think you're doing, young lady?"

Turning around, she saw the same lady from the plane. Her wild red curls framed her face like a halo, and she wore an elegant red robe made of silk.

"I'm sorry! I'm so sorry! I'm just so hungry and couldn't sleep!" She didn't want to blame her little sister. She was terrified of the woman. She'd killed Daisy's father, and Daisy was certain she would kill her too.

The woman chuckled. "Now, now, sweetheart." She walked to Daisy and stroked her cheek as if she was something precious. Daisy froze, unable to look into her intense stare. "There's no need to be afraid. You are most certainly welcome to take that food. But next time I would appreciate it if you asked."

Daisy let out a sigh. "Thank you."

The woman smiled. "You are Daisy, right?"

"Yes."

The woman tilted her head to the side, studying her as if she suspected something. "Well, it is lovely to formally meet you, Daisy. My name is Priscilla."

"Nice to meet you too," she lied.

"You'd better get off to bed, little miss. Don't leave the room again until morning." Priscilla warned.

"Yes ma'am!" She quickly left the room, with the crackers and apple in hand.

She ran through the halls, all the way to the bedroom, breathing heavily when she opened the door. To her disappointment, Sofie was already asleep. She guessed the food could be eaten another night. Climbing into bed with her sister, she closed her eyes and drifted to sleep as she thought about her strange encounter with Priscilla.

Elizabeth wondered where the rest of the people from the plane were, and if they were still alive. It was concerning that Daisy didn't know where her mother was. What was the purpose of keeping them separated? Elizabeth didn't know if she would ever find out.

Chapter 7

Back when Jennifer just started living with the Voltz family, Elizabeth confided that she would see things while she slept. Things that happened in the present time. She said it was like she was actually there, living in someone else's body. Jennifer, of course, didn't believe her; she just told Elizabeth that she had vivid dreams. At least, she did until one eventful night, ten years ago.

It was Jennifer's freshman year of high school, and two full years had passed since she came to live with Elizabeth's family. While she still felt sad over her reason for being there, she had to admit things were better than they could have been. She loved the Voltz family, especially Elizabeth, whom she now considered a sister.

Holiday break was in a couple weeks, and snow fell outside their warm house. Jennifer was sound asleep in her room when Elizabeth came rushing in. Jennifer jumped, awake as soon as she felt someone enter her room, and saw Elizabeth in sweat-drenched pajamas.

"Elizabeth! What's wrong?"

"We have to help her!" Elizabeth spoke as if she had just run a mile.

"Help who? Did you have a nightmare?"

"It's not a nightmare! It's real! The girl down the street. She's in trouble."

"What girl?" Jennifer got out of bed and put her hand over Elizabeth's forehead to see if she had a fever. "Are you not feeling well?"

"I'm fine!" Elizabeth swiped away her hand. "She's only eleven! She's in sixth grade. She shows up to school with bruises sometimes. She's being fostered by that huge family five houses away from us."

"She probably just plays rough sometimes. Children do that, you know."

"Please, Jennifer! I saw her being hurt by the dad and brothers. It's horrible. You're the strongest person I know. You have to help her!"

"If you're so sure she's being hurt, why don't you get a grown up?"

"Because nobody will believe me. Nobody ever does anything!" Elizabeth shouted.

"Okay! Quiet! You'll wake your parents." Jennifer looked at her with concern. Elizabeth looked terrified. It must have been a horrifying dream. "Okay. I'll tell you what. We can walk over there, maybe check in the windows, and see if she's okay. How does that sound?"

"Thank you!"

Elizabeth dashed from the room to grab her coat and boots, with Jennifer following close behind.

Jennifer wasn't looking forward to the harsh winter cold, but she had a feeling Elizabeth wouldn't go back to sleep until they made sure this girl was okay. Once wrapped up in winter coats, boots, and gloves, they quietly slipped out the front door.

They walked through the peaceful night as fluffy snowflakes danced around them. Once they made it to their destined house, they saw the lights were off, except in one room. The room was on the second floor, but there was a tree that could potentially be climbed.

Elizabeth looked at Jennifer. "I think that's the room," she whispered.

"Of course you do," Jennifer sighed. "All right, I'll climb up there and check it out."

"Okay, I'll wait down by the trunk."

The girls walked to the tree. Jennifer inspected the bark, pleased to see that it hadn't iced over. Giving Elizabeth a nod, she hoisted herself up. Branch by branch, she pulled herself higher, until she could see through the window.

What she saw would stick with her for the rest of her life. Tied to a four-post bed in the middle of the room was a girl. She was crying, while an older man, two young men, and a boy stood around her. Laughing. Unwilling to watch for another second, Jennifer used one arm to hold onto the tree, and positioned herself parallel to the window. Bending her knees to create more momentum, she pushed off the tree. She held her other arm in front of her face to protect herself as she hurled through the glass, shattering it. She was probably cut up, but her adrenaline was too high to feel any pain.

Going straight for the father, she punched him in the throat. He doubled over while holding his throat, coughing.

"What the heck!" she heard one of the young men yell. "What are you doing!"

"Stand back, and I won't hurt you," she warned.

"I'm not scared of a little girl."

"This little girl just jumped through a window. Piss me off if you want to see what else I can do."

The boy charged her. Without wasting a second, she kicked her leg up and hit his chin. He fell on his back and hit his head on the hard floor. When he sat up, blood dripped from his mouth, and he wiped it on his sleeve. The father recovered and decided to grab her from behind. It was difficult with a thick coat, but she managed to swing her legs up and pushed off the bed posts with enough force to slam him into the wall. She then flung her head back, hearing a crunch when it made contact with his nose.

He immediately dropped her, and Jennifer ran to the opposite side of the bed to get away from the men. She wasn't afraid of them; she just didn't want to traumatize the girl any more than she already had been.

"The police are on their way!" At least, she hoped that was what Elizabeth was doing. "So I wouldn't try anything."

The father held his nose and cursed. "Go wake your mother, boys", he said in a pinched voice.

Jennifer and the father waited in silence. She watched him closely in case he tried anything. Minutes passed, and Jennifer started to get nervous. What if no one showed? What would she do? She didn't want to have to kill these people to get this girl to safety. She would have to be moved to a new family.

Out of the corner of her eye, she saw the oldest brother appear through the doorway, with a gun pointed at her. The weapon she hated the most.

"Are you going to shoot me? Become a murderer?" she sneered.

"I'll call this breaking and entering. You assaulted my father and me. It'll be self-defense."

She couldn't tell if he was bluffing, but she had to keep talking to stall him from pulling that trigger.

"You're going to tell the police that you couldn't handle a fifteen-year-old girl? I thought you said you weren't scared of me."

"I'm not!"

"People know I'm here. My foster parents know I'm here," she lied. "If you pull that trigger, you'll be in prison for the rest of your life. Do you want that?"

He didn't take his finger off the trigger, but seemed hesitant. That's when she saw the blue and red lights flashing, then heard the sirens. She heard the door crash in.

"Police!"

"Help!" she yelled. "We are up here!"

Loud steps marched up the stairs, then Jennifer saw a man outside the door, staring at the gunman.

"Put down the gun, boy," he said. "Don't do anything you'll regret."

The boy grunted, but lowered the gun. The police officer rushed in and gasped at the sight of the bound child. Five other officers had similar reactions as they piled in behind him. While two officers untied the little girl, the father and son were cuffed and taken from the room.

A couple EMTs came in with a stretcher and lifted the girl, then carried her out of the room. A couple officers stayed behind and watched Jennifer while a EMT nurse cleaned some wounds on her face. The shattered window didn't hurt her too badly, since she wore gloves and a fluffy coat, but her face had some scratches. As soon as the nurse finished, Elizabeth ran in and wrapped her arms around her. Jennifer returned the gesture.

"We need to ask you two questions," one of the officers said.

"Okay," Jennifer replied.

"Why were you here?"

"Elizabeth thought something was wrong, so I came to check it out."

"Who all was involved with what you saw here?"

"The father, and the three boys who I assume are his children."

"No. They're all involved," Elizabeth interrupted. "The mom and sisters too. They've all been abusing the girl."

"You're sure?" the officer asked.

"Yes."

Then Jennifer could hear her parents shouting from the other side of the cop cars.

"Where are our babies?" her mother yelled.

"That's all the questions we have for now. You two should get home. Your parents are worried about you."

"Thank you, officer."

Elizabeth and Jennifer walked past the cars to see their mom and dad with worried looks. They ran to them and gave a group hug.

"Do you have any idea how scared we were when officers banged our door in the middle of the night! Never do that to us again!"

"Sorry, mom," Elizabeth replied.

"You two are in big trouble. But for now, let's get you home. I'm thinking you should stay home from school tomorrow."

"I'm okay with that," Elizabeth agreed.

The four of them got a ride home from a cop, and their parents saw the girls off back into bed. Before Jennifer fell asleep, she snuck into Elizabeth's room.

"Elizabeth," she whispered.

"Yes?"

"I'm sorry I didn't believe you."

"That's okay. It's pretty crazy."

"Yeah." She paused. "You saved a girl today."

"We saved a girl today. The way you crashed through that window was amazing. I wish I was as strong as you."

"I can teach you if you'd like."

"Really? I would love that. We could be a team."

"Yeah, we could."

"Starting tomorrow?"

"Tomorrow."

Chapter 8

When the clock hit five-thirty a.m., Jennifer leapt out of bed to shake Elizabeth awake. Even though she didn't sleep well, she was wired. This might be their only chance to escape; they couldn't screw it up.

"Come on, Elizabeth, we have to get going," she whispered.

Elizabeth groaned. "I'm up."

"Okay, come on! We don't have much time."

Sliding from her bed, Elizabeth rubbed her eyes and stretched. Then she reached under her bed for the two daggers she'd snagged. "Here." She handed one to Jennifer. "I grabbed these last night."

"You keep those. I actually thought of the same thing." Jennifer pulled two daggers out from under her pillow. "I just hope no one noticed four daggers missing."

"We'll just have to be extra cautious."

The two slipped from their room, walking stealthily until they reached the dining room. The light was on, and a group of workers, wearing all blue, were setting up breakfast. Realizing it would be too risky to try to sneak out with the way things were, Jennifer had to come up with a plan. She looked around and saw the door was closed, but on the right was a black rectangular box with a glowing red light. She thought it must be a spot for a key card or a fob, so the workers must have keys.

Jennifer looked around at their pockets, and noticed one woman had her key half hanging out of her pocket. If Jennifer could get the light switch, she could grab that key and dash to the door. But they would need to run fast, because once they were through the door, someone would see them. Alarms would most definitely go off. They would either have to use their weapons, or find a place to hide. Then maybe they would be able to find a vent or crawl space. Either way, they didn't have time to come up with a thorough plan. This needed to happen on the fly.

Unsure if the workers were innocent or not, Jennifer didn't want to get violent with them. It was never her desire to attack someone, she only ever fought on the defense. She might have been deadly, but that didn't mean she had no morals. Jennifer wanted to use her skills for good.

Looking back at Elizabeth, Jennifer signaled her to follow. All the workers were busy with their tasks and had yet to notice them. She saw four light switches, so she reached and turned all of them downward. Instantly, the room darkened, followed by a few surprised screams. It was light enough that she could see shadowed figures. She'd kept tabs on her targeted keys, and she grabbed Elizabeth's hand and ran to the woman to swipe them.

With swift motion, she gracefully dodged each body until she reached the red LED and placed the card over it. She let out a triumphant breath, then pushed open the door. She heard a voice call out to them, but didn't wait to see what they said. She dragged Elizabeth through the door and closed it, and started jogging down the hall so she could look around and see what the plan of action would be. To her surprise, the hallways were empty, and no one was running after them. She could hear no alarms.

"What now?" Elizabeth whispered.

"Not sure yet. Follow me and keep your eyes peeled. Let me know if you see anything helpful or suspicious."

Running through the halls, they tried to find an exit. Then they heard a door they'd already passed open. They whipped around to see Jackie standing in the middle of the hallway. She was already dressed for the day, with hair pristinely smooth and eyes wide awake. Jennifer and Elizabeth lifted their daggers.

"That won't be necessary. I won't fight you." Jackie spoke calmly.

"Well, we will fight you. If you try to stop us from leaving," said Jennifer.

"I told you. You can't leave. Why don't you come with me, and we can have a chat?"

"No. We aren't staying here another day."

"You really don't have a choice." Jackie sighed and shook her head. "Look, I'm trying really hard to keep you two alive right now. Either you can come with me peacefully, and I'll explain everything, or I'll activate the sedative inside your trackers. Then I would have to implant new ones, which would cause questions to arise from my superiors. So, what do you say? Can we keep this between us?"

"What if we get to you before you activate the sedative? Is it worth your life?"

"I won't be activating the agent; I don't have access to the trigger. Once my boss realizes you left, he won't hesitate to put you to sleep, then kill you. You won't make it outside anyways. This place is guarded to the teeth. The next agent you meet, though, will be less motivated to keep you alive."

Jennifer and Elizabeth looked at each other.

"How do we know you're not bluffing? Why do you care if we live or not?" asked Elizabeth.

"Because I need your help. Just hear what I have to say. I promise I'm not the enemy."

"Oh, you promise!" Jennifer laughed. "Well, that just clears everything up."

Jackie smiled. "Just follow me."

She turned down the hallway. Elizabeth looked to Jennifer to see what she would do, and to her seeming surprise, Jennifer did follow. Jennifer didn't think they had a choice. If Jackie was telling the truth about Vance killing them, she didn't want to risk it. She felt trapped.

They followed her to a large glass elevator, the ride silent. They kept a close watch on her every move as they clenched their weapons. Jackie stood there as if she wasn't standing next to possibly the world's deadliest warrior. Jennifer could still kill her and see if she was bluffing, but her request for help intrigued her enough to hold back for the time being.

The elevator doors opened, and Jackie let out a breath. She walked down marble halls, her heels echoing. Jennifer and Elizabeth followed closely behind until they came to a door that had Jackie's name plastered on the front in a business-like manner, Jackie Monley. Twisting the knob, Jackie walked inside. Her office was neat and organized, with a mahogany desk, a computer with triple monitors, and three chairs: one for Jackie and two on the opposite side of the desk for visitors. Around the walls were old and new pictures. The one closest to Jackie's chair was a group of fifteen children and young adults. Elizabeth squinted at the picture.

"I'm this one." Jackie pointed to a girl with dark hair in the center of the front row. "I was sixteen in this picture."

"Who are the rest?" Elizabeth asked.

"People like us. They had special skills or abilities."

"Had?"

Jackie coughed. "That's a conversation for a later time. Right now, let's focus on you two."

"Right."

"So, first things first. You probably want to know why I need your help."

"Yes," they said.

"I've been investigating strange disappearances of tourists and children for quite some time now. Until now, I've had absolutely no leads. I just know that it's been happening. Planes full of people go missing, cruises disappear, children vanish."

"And you think we have something to do with that?" Elizabeth questioned.

"No, I think you witnessed one of the attacks."

Elizabeth's eyes widened. "How do you know?"

"It sounds exactly like their MO. I don't one hundred percent know, but I'm positive enough that I think you could help."

"If I'm so helpful, why does your boss want me dead?"

"My boss is an idiot and has shown zero concern with these disappearances. Every time I bring it up, he just blows me off. He just thought you were involved in a random terrorist attack. I know better, though. I can see inside your head, and there's no way you orchestrated that."

"How can you see inside my head?"

"I'm a telepath. I can read people's thoughts."

Jennifer shivered. She didn't like that Jackie could see inside her head. What if she saw all the dark things Jennifer had done?

"How is this possible?"

"I don't know. I was born this way. Do you know how you became a Dream Traveller?"

Elizabeth shook her head.

"Well, then." Jackie shrugged. "Anyways, will you help me save these people or not?"

"I don't see how we can if your boss isn't on board."

"We don't need him on board. We just have to gather evidence, then present it to the agency leadership. Then they'll have no choice but to listen."

"And what about me?" Jennifer interrupted.

"Your voice was also on the voicemail recording, so I had no choice but to look into you as well. I was just going to take you home, but then I noticed something interesting."

Jennifer's face went cold; she knew where this was going. The one thing about her she'd kept hidden for the past thirteen years.

"You aren't Jennifer Noels," Jackie said, "you're Jennifer Hickory."

Elizabeth scrunched her brows and looked at Jennifer with shock.

"You've been protected by the Witness Protection Program since the murder of your parents when you were thirteen. I won't say anything else about that, since I know Elizabeth's hearing this for the first time. Anyways, I found out you were raised to be a great fighter. Your parents were both army Major Generals and hired the best teachers for you. At such a young age, you were defeating the best of the best. I think you would be a great addition to the team. We could use someone who is as skilled in combat as you."

As the memories from that day resurfaced, Jennifer looked down at her lap. "Okay," she said quietly. "I think I'm going to go back to bed, then." She stood from her chair without showing a lick of emotion.

"You know how to get back?"

"Yes, and I still have this key." She showed the key card.

Jennifer didn't say goodbye to either of them as she opened the door and walked out.

Elizabeth looked at Jackie. "What's wrong with you?"

"What do you mean?"

"Don't be daft. You just said you can read minds. You obviously just really hurt her."

Jackie sucked in her cheeks as she folded her hands and looked into Elizabeth's eyes. "You two wanted to know how you could help; I just explained. I'm sorry if my explanation was painful to hear, but I hope you know now how crucial you could be."

Elizabeth slid from her chair dramatically and walked to the door. "No, I don't". She exited.

Elizabeth walked back to the door she and Jennifer escaped through, and was surprised to find it unlocked. So, people could get in, but they couldn't get out unless they had a key card.

The other captives were sitting in the dining area eating breakfast as she stormed in.

"Elizabeth!" Zola shouted excitedly.

Elizabeth walked back toward the common area, ignoring her. She walked until she heard a familiar grunting. In the middle of the workout room, there was Jennifer covered in sweat, hitting a punching bag as if it were her worst enemy. Elizabeth stared at this woman who had been her sister for the past twelve years. How could Jennifer never have told her the truth? How alone she must have felt. She felt an overwhelming sadness come over her. No wonder she was always so reserved with her feelings.

Elizabeth walked over to Jennifer, then stood there quietly. She knew Jennifer sensed her presence, but she didn't want to force her to stop and talk.

"Look, I know you're probably pissed," Jennifer panted before she took another swing at the bag, "but I couldn't risk saying anything. If word ever got out about who I really am…"

"It's okay," Elizabeth interrupted.

Jennifer stopped before she hit again and looked over her shoulder.

"Is it?"

"I'm not angry. I'm just so sorry you were going through this alone."

Jennifer turned all the way around; she had tears in her eyes. "I've wanted to tell you who I am so many times."

Elizabeth threw her arms around her, and Jennifer sobbed into her shoulder. "I'm not going to force you to talk about it, but I'm here if you ever need to. I promise I won't ever tell anyone who you really are."

Lifting her head, Jennifer stepped away. "I was going to tell you, but then it just felt easier to pretend like it never happened. It hurts so much; you have no idea what I saw."

"I can handle whatever it is, or we can just keep moving forward for now. It's up to you."

Jennifer wiped her eyes, "I'm ready. Ask me anything."

"What were your parents like?" Elizabeth asked.

Jennifer stared off into silence, seemingly deep in thought. "I think about them every day."

Saying nothing, Elizabeth looked at her, waiting for her to make the decision.

"They were rarely home, but when they were, all their attention was on me. They loved me, as any parent should love their child. My mother was smart and funny; my dad was quiet and attentive. I would give anything to see them again, to tell them I love them."

Elizabeth watched as Jennifer smiled sadly, tears threatening to leave her eyes.

"Not that I'm not grateful to have you in my life. You and our parents are amazing. I'm lucky to have you."

"I know you're grateful, but that doesn't mean you can't miss your parents."

Jennifer's tears began to fall.

"Their death was horrible. I tried to save them, but I was too weak. I'll never be weak again."

Chapter 9

Twelve Years Ago…

Thirteen-year-old Jennifer was up late, reading in her cozy bed. She had a queen-size mahogany bed with silky red sheets and a dark red comforter. Her parents had it custom made while away on business. A wooden canopy was attached to the bed, and it had velvety, dark red curtains.

Her room was filled with toys for any child being raised as a warrior. She had a hand-carved weapon rack that held a long sword, a couple daggers, and a wooden bow with a bag full of arrows next to it. These weapons were for practicing on a straw-filled mannequin and a large foam target. She would usually destroy the mannequins and targets within a week, so they were often replaced. She wasn't sure why her parents were so adamant for her to be well versed in most forms of combat, but she did enjoy training. The adrenaline it gave her was addictive.

Her gray walls were decorated with hand-crafted swords, bows, and shields that her parents would acquire during their travels. The only weapons she didn't have were guns. She hated how loud they were. Her other weapons required a more personal and artistic approach.

Double glass doors led to the large balcony. The balcony had a couple benches where she often sat while reading. Her home was located on ten acres, and there wasn't another house in sight. The lawn was gorgeous, with a well-kept hedge maze and a garden filled with wild roses, tulips, peonies, and hydrangeas.

Since her parents were often gone for their work, she had one tutor living with her. Her parents arrived home that day, however, and Jennifer was excited. She missed her parents.

Jennifer's reading session was interrupted by an agonizing scream. Graceful like a panther, she jumped out of bed and listened for suspicious sounds. She heard the slicing of a sword and a loud thump from the room above her. After grabbing a sword and sticking a couple daggers in the pockets of her pajama pants, she crept out of her room and tiptoed up the stairs.

Knowing the sound came from the tutor's room, Jennifer walked to their room and opened the door. First thing she spotted was two adult figures dressed in all black, with black masks on. They hadn't noticed her presence as she snuck up behind them. She lifted her dagger and sliced the neck of one of the men from behind. This got the other guy's attention.

He quickly plunged toward her. His form was almost perfect; she could tell he was a professional. She dodged his sword and grabbed his hand. She pulled on his arm and when he pulled back and used the force to flip herself onto his shoulders. Without making a sound, she crossed her legs and squeezed her thighs on his neck, and dove her middle and pointer fingers into his eye sockets. Before he could scream, she used all her body weight to twist off him, breaking his neck in the process.

Looking to the side of the bed, Jennifer saw the dead body of the old woman that tutored her. She didn't have time to mourn, though, she needed to patrol the rest of the house and check on her parents. Jennifer dipped out of the bedroom and ran down the hall. She wasn't quiet this time. She wanted to get their attention.

Her distraction worked, three men dressed in the same dark clothing jumped out of rooms and surrounded her. She pulled out her sword, daring them to take her on. They obliged and lunged at her. Right before the blades could pierce her, she leapt onto the railing by their side and did a no-handed cartwheel, simultaneously slicing into the neck of the man closest to her. Once she landed, she crouched to the floor and cut through the achilles tendons of the man in the middle. He dropped to the ground and screamed as he instinctively grabbed his feet.

Jennifer was too quick for them to react. The last guy was face to face with her, but she could hear more running up the stairs. While the guy in front of her was distracted, she pulled one of the daggers from her pocket and threw it into his eye, killing him instantly.

Before Jennifer could turn around, she was grabbed from behind. She couldn't move her arms, so she threw her head back, breaking the man's nose. His grip loosened, giving her a chance to grab a dagger and stab him in the stomach. He let go of her, then stumbled backwards, holding the bleeding wound.

Jennifer kicked him in his right side, making him wobble on his feet. Men started shoving past him to get to her and accidentally pushed him over the railing. She effortlessly sliced and diced them. It was barely a challenge for her.

"Aren't you guys done yet? Y'all suck at fighting," she taunted.

The last guy hesitated, but tried to fight her anyway. She countered his sword and kicked him in the groin, and when he fell to his knees, she grabbed a dagger and pushed it into the middle of his chest.

"You weren't even wearing a cup? Come on."

Everything was quiet. Now it was time to find her parents. She had to make sure they were okay. She turned to make her way to their bedroom, then felt something heavy smack against her head. Everything went dark. She thought she only blinked, but when she awoke, her head throbbed, and she felt sweat running down her temples and the middle of her back. She squinted; it was so bright, and her eyes burned.

Jennifer groaned in pain. She tried to shift her weight, but something was holding her back. Senses started to come back to her, and she saw she was sitting at her own dining room table.

Across the maple wood, her parents sat, pinned to their seats with thick ropes.

"Mom," she choked, her voice raw and dry.

"They won't wake. I made sure of it," she heard a raspy male voice with a strange accent.

She looked around frantically, searching for the source. There, in the hallway to the kitchen, stood a tall figure, surrounded by smoke. He had a gas mask covering his mouth and nose, so she could see only the upper half of his face. There was a long, gnarly scar above his eyebrows. His hair was dark and pulled into a bun. The smoke was blocking it, but she thought she saw a tattoo of a spider eating a snake on his neck.

"Who are you?"

He smirked. "Master wanted you, but then he decided you're too old. It's too hard to train someone when they're older. Shame."

"What do you mean?"

"No need to worry, little one." He faked concern. "You'll pass out before you feel anything. I should have hit you harder."

"I don't understand." She started to tear up.

"I'd explain, but there's no point. It'll be over soon. And I have to get out of here. Before I leave, though, good job on my colleagues. I'm impressed."

He walked past her, in the direction of the entryway. Gracefully, steps silent.

"Wait!" She called out, but he didn't turn back.

Jennifer realized what was happening as she heard the front door open. The house was on fire. She could smell the smoke; it burned her lungs. She struggled against the bindings.

"Don't panic," she tried to reassure herself.

Panicking was never helpful.

Taking a deep breath, she drew her attention to the ropes, focusing on how they felt against her skin. Ignoring the sweat dripping down her skin and the toxic fumes, she tried to find a weak point in her restraints. Her parents had made sure she also learned how to escape situations like this. Since she was old enough to pick up a sword, she also took classes on how to escape capture. She had a specific trainer for escape tactics. The instructor would bind Jennifer with cuffs, ropes, or chains, and expect her to find a way out. Of course, the instructor would let her loose if Jennifer couldn't get out; her well-being was of first importance, but eventually she could escape without help.

"Found it," she whispered.

By her right shoulder, there was a little bit of slack. No binding was perfect, for perfection wasn't real. There was always a weakness. The smoke kept getting thicker, so she had to be quick. Wiggling her shoulders, inching the rope up, she worked one line over her shoulder, giving her slack to bend her neck and slide it over her head. Her neck bent unnaturally, causing a twinge of pain, but she kept going. After getting one piece to loosen, she was easily able to wiggle her way out of the rest of the rope, since it just spiraled around her. Her hands were still tied behind her back, but it was simple to tuck them under her and pull her legs through, like jumping rope.

The fire blazed, the doorframe from the kitchen now a ring of fire. She knew she didn't have time to cut herself free, so she'd have to make do with her bound hands. Finding a knife on the table, she used it to cut both her parents free. The parent closest to the front door was her mother, so she began to drag her out first. Sweat dripped from her brow as she used all her strength and concentration to make it in time. It took her about ten minutes, but she successfully got her mother out the door. She then ran back inside to get her father. Her situation had become worse, she could see smoke all along the ceiling, and the fire had entered the dining room.

"Dad!" she screamed.

She ran to him, and was relieved to see he wasn't burned, but knew he would be soon if she didn't get him out. Smoke circled around her, making it hard to see. Reaching for a cloth napkin, she tied it around her face to try and prevent herself from inhaling too much smoke. It wasn't a perfect solution, but it was all she had. She grabbed him and began to drag his body. He was quite a bit heavier, and she struggled. The fire followed them. If she didn't get him out soon, the kitchen could explode, and they would both be dead.

"Please! Wake up!" she cried.

She kept inching her way to the door, the muscles in her arms, shoulders, and back screaming. She coughed as she inhaled more and more smoke. She wasn't about to give up, though. She screamed through the pain, getting closer and closer. Just as she got her father through the front door, she heard an explosion. Her body went flying backwards, and her head hit the cement of their sidewalk.

The next thing she knew, Jennifer woke up to a bright light and a hard bed. She groaned and turned her head to look around. To her right was a monitor with translucent cords that led back to her arm. She was in the hospital.

"Hello," she called, her voice hoarse.

She heard the rustling of papers. "Oh! you're up," said a womanly voice.

Jennifer hummed. "What am I doing here?"

"You hit your head pretty hard, so it's probably going to take a second to remember what happened, but there was an explosion…"

And then everything came rushing back: the assassins, being tied up, the man that got away, the explosion.

"My parents — did I get them out in time?" she interrupted.

The woman had a sad look on her face, and she shook her head slightly. "I'm sorry, sweetie."

"But I pulled them out. I pulled them out!" Jennifer cried.

The woman stood and walked to the side of the bed. Tears streamed down Jennifer's face. The woman put a comforting hand on Jen's hand. "You did a wonderful job; you were so brave. Your parents died of an overdose, not the fire or explosion. By the time help arrived, it was too late. They had been dead for over an hour. I'm so sorry."

Jennifer sobbed so loud the entire floor could probably hear her.

"I'm a social worker. I'll be in charge of finding a placement for you. I know this is a lot to take in right now. When you're ready, there's also a marshal that would like to talk to you about the Witness Protection Program. I know you probably feel so alone right now, but just know that you are not. We are here for you," the woman said as she squeezed Jennifer's hand.

Chapter 10

Jennifer and Elizabeth had stayed in their room for the rest of the day and remained up most of the night talking about Jennifer's past. Jennifer fell asleep crying on Elizabeth's shoulder, making it impossible for her to close her eyes for longer than a minute. Not that it made much of a difference for her.

It was almost six a.m., and Elizabeth's stomach grumbled. Not a moment later, she heard a knock on the door. Jennifer groaned, and Elizabeth opened the door to see Zola standing on the other side.

"Hi, guys! Are you ready for breakfast? I thought I'd walk over there with you," she offered.

"Yeah, I think we are ready. Jen, are you good to go?"

"Yeah, I'm starving."

The three of them walked to the dining room and saw a buffet of eggs, sausages, bagels, and muffins.

"Is there always food prepared for us in the mornings?" Elizabeth asked.

"Yeah! It's different every morning though. On the weekends, there's oatmeal and cereal, though, since the kitchen staff is off."

"At least they aren't starving us."

Elizabeth watched as Zola filled her plate, surprised when Jennifer didn't hesitate to fill hers. She felt like they were being fed like pigs destined for the slaughter, but her hungry stomach and desire to maintain strength convinced her to grab some sustenance. Afterwards, she followed Jennifer and Zola to the dining table and took a seat to Jennifer's right, while Zola sat on the left. Zola dug in right away, seeming blissfully unaware of their situation. Elizabeth knew better, though. Zola gave up; she had become complacent.

While Elizabeth forced the food down her throat, Josh and another guy walked in together. The unknown male had messy, curly brown hair, blue eyes, a mustache, and a well-maintained beard that covered his defined jawline and complimented his high cheekbones.

Elizabeth took a break from her breakfast to look up at the stranger. Already staring at her, he gave a welcoming smile, then looked away and helped himself to the buffet. After he and Josh got a plate of food, they walked to the dinner table and joined the three women.

"Hi, I'm Michael!" the new guy greeted as he took a seat next to Elizabeth.

"I'm Elizabeth."

"And I'm Jen."

"Nice to meet you," he said, flashing a beautiful smile.

They were about to continue with the pleasantries, but were interrupted.

Standing in the doorway, Jackie waited for everyone to give her their attention. It didn't take long. Her presence seemed to suck the air from the room. At least, that's how Elizabeth felt.

"Good morning, everyone," greeted Jackie in a booming voice. "I hope you have been making Jennifer and Elizabeth feel welcome."

Elizabeth scowled at her while the rest nodded their heads.

"Elizabeth and Jennifer, when you're finished eating, come to my office on the second floor. Zola can escort you… in case you've forgotten where it is. Zola, I'll leave the second-floor access unlocked."

"Yes ma'am," Elizabeth sarcastically replied.

Noticing her tone, Jackie lifted her eyebrows. She ignored her, though, and walked out of the room.

"Sassy," Michael commented. "I like it."

While Michael seemed pleased with her behavior, Josh was the opposite. He was staring at her as if she had just insulted him.

"Thank you," Elizabeth said cautiously.

Jackie's surprise meeting took away the rest of Elizabeth's appetite, but Zola and Jennifer continued to shovel down food until their plates were clean. While Josh and Michael were still eating, the three of them took their plates to the dishwasher and left the room to meet Jackie in her office. Zola led them to the glass elevator and pressed the button for the second floor. It was the same elevator that they were brought up when they first arrived. Elizabeth took note that there were ten levels; however, all but the second and third floors seemed to have restricted access. They would need those key cards again if they wanted to go exploring upstairs.

"Why are the second and third floor accessible, but the rest not?" Elizabeth asked.

"The first and second floors are underground. The first floor is like a small prison, for people that DUST wants no one to know about. Including us. The second floor is where we live, obviously. And the third floor is where Jackie and William live and work. Jackie wanted us to be able to talk to her if needed, so she usually makes sure that there's no security restrictions for the second and third floor."

"But doesn't that mean anyone can get down here?"

"Well, yes. But the only people that know about this place would probably have access anyways."

The elevator came to a stop.

"Okay, guys. Make sure when you talk to Jackie you pay attention. She is extremely serious about everything she says." Zola seemed unaware that the girls had already had an unpleasant encounter with Jackie.

"I don't care."

"Elizabeth," Jennifer scolded.

"It's fine; I know she is harsh. But trust me, you don't want to get on her bad side."

The elevator dinged, and the door opened, and Zola led the way to Jackie's office, then knocked on the door.

"Come in!"

"Good luck, guys," she whispered, and walked back to the elevator.

"Take a seat, please." Jackie motioned to the two chairs opposite her. She was in her chair and had her elbows leaning on the desk, with a manila folder in front of her.

"So how is everything? The room okay? Clothes? Toiletries?"

"I'd like to pick out my own clothes," suggested Jennifer. Elizabeth gave her a skeptical look.

"Well, I've been thinking about what you said, and I've decided to decline. I will not be helping people that keep me here against my will. I want to go home," Elizabeth sneered.

"Stop asking to go home. You can never go home."

"Why?"

"Because the government doesn't trust you. If you try anything that will risk the secrecy of this agency, they will have your family killed. Do you understand?"

Elizabeth's body went cold. She couldn't imagine her family getting hurt. "How can they do that?"

"We know everything about you. And the powerful men and women upstairs? They don't care what happens to you. They don't care about your family. They care about power. They care to get what they want, and they'll do anything to get it. Do you understand?"

Elizabeth glared at her and leaned back in her chair. Jennifer placed her hand on her shoulder.

"We can get through this," Jennifer said.

"Good, then it's settled." Jackie didn't wait for Elizabeth to agree. She didn't have a choice anyways. "First things first: I need you to get into Daisy's head and talk to her. I believe she is one of the terrorist's captives." Jackie paused and concentrated on Elizabeth. "And from what I can see, you have already seen her."

"Excuse me? I can't just get into people's heads and talk to them! I have no control over this."

"You can talk to people when you're in their head; you'd be like their own consciousness speaking. The last Dream Traveller we had was able to do this, so I know you can too."

"The last Dream Traveller? Where are they? Maybe they can help me."

"He's dead."

"Dead!" Elizabeth shouted. "Did you kill him?"

"Absolutely not. He actually killed himself by accident. Which is the next thing we need to discuss. But first, I have something to give you." She opened a drawer in her desk and pulled out two small boxes. "These are your personal pagers. They have been programmed with the numbers of the other recruits, including myself and William."

Elizabeth rolled her eyes.

"These are strictly meant for communication with the team. Do you understand?"

"And what is this team?" Jennifer asked.

"Right, I should probably go into more detail. For the past few decades, the government has held this agency that counterattacks threats to the United

States, and they have a subgroup of the agency for people that scare them, essentially. Sometimes people come here for help and of their own free will, other times they are brought here as prisoners, for a lack of a better term. Every one of you has something special, whether that be a skill or a power. Myself, a telepath. William, a techno. Zola, who has made it her mission to befriend you, can understand animals. Then there is Josh; he's inhumanly strong. Lastly, we have the two siblings, Michael and Paige. Michael is a genius, and Paige is an empath. Your job as a team is to help each other gain control of your powers and grow. You will need to train and learn to move as a unit."

"We haven't met William or Paige yet. Why?"

"William has been here since we were kids. He hates people. And Paige fears her own powers, so she mostly hides in her room or the library."

"What's a techno?"

"That's the nickname we gave William's powers; he can speak to computers. I've never heard of another like him. He's useful for hacking into certain systems. It's how I get all my information. Any other questions?"

"Yes," Elizabeth groaned. "Will I ever be able to talk to my family again?"

"Maybe, but you have to earn it first. You have to prove that we can trust you."

"How can we do that?"

"By helping us. Elizabeth, you can start by telling me more about the hijacking incident that you witnessed. Jennifer, I want you to start using our gymnasium for training. Set up some exercises to help the rest of the team train. I'm counting on you for combat training and methodology."

Elizabeth crossed her arms and leaned back in her chair. "The last time I helped you, I got kidnapped."

"Well, now if you don't tell me you'll have to answer to my supervisor and other higher-ups. Trust me, you don't want that."

"Why, will they torture me?" Elizabeth tried to test Jackie's patience.

"Yes." Jackie leaned forward, looking serious.

Elizabeth gulped. "Why not just go into my head?"

"Because I'd rather you just tell me. I can't really create a trusting relationship with you if I'm always digging into your head, now, can I?"

"It's a little late for that."

Jackie sat back, waiting for Elizabeth's cooperation.

"Fine. But if I do this, no digging in my head without my permission."

"Deal."

Elizabeth didn't think she could trust Jackie, but if it prevented the woman from entering her head this one time, it was worth it. "Daisy and her sister were taken captive by the hijackers. I know that their mother and father were there. I think the father was a congressman, but I'm not exactly positive."

"Yes. The congressman on the flight is their father. Senator John Chatawick. We think they purposely took that plane, but we don't know why. Maybe to gather information about the United States government. Do you know where they were going?"

"Well, he's dead, so I'm not sure what information they'd be getting. And I don't know where they're going."

"Well, that's too bad. We still need to find them, though. Keep trying to contact Daisy."

"Fine. May we leave now?"

"One last thing. Behave, and don't draw attention to yourselves. You don't want the leaders of this organization to notice you. Okay? Now you can leave."

Elizabeth and Jennifer were about to walk out when Jackie said, "Oh, I almost forgot." They turned to face Jackie. "Elizabeth, I need you to speak with Michael. He can help you with your sleeping issues."

"I never told you I had sleeping issues."

"I'm a telepath. You don't need to tell me much."

"You just said you wouldn't do that." She glared.

"I've known for a while."

Elizabeth scoffed and they left the office. They made their way to the elevator.

Chapter 11

Once Elizabeth and Jennifer left the elevator, they began walking back, until Elizabeth halted abruptly.

"Hey! What's over there?"

Walking to the right of the elevators, she saw some beautifully carved, ceiling-high double doors. Elizabeth thought about how it contrasted from the plain, modern architecture she had seen so far. She grabbed a golden handle and twisted until the door budged.

Their jaws dropped as they stepped into one of the most beautiful libraries they'd ever seen. It seemed to be straight out of Beauty and the Beast. Wooden shelves lined the walls, and murals covered the ceiling. Comfortable looking chairs and couches were tastefully placed in the aisles and the center of the room.

Out of the corner of her eye, Elizabeth glimpsed another person. Sitting on a couch in the middle of the room was a young woman with silvery blond hair. She wore a plaid overall dress with a black turtleneck underneath. She flipped through the pages, seemingly in bliss. Elizabeth wondered who she was and why she was all alone. Unsure of how long she'd been staring, she caught the woman's attention. Snapping the book closed, she quickly stood. Elizabeth thought she would come over to say hello, but instead the woman put her head down and quickly walked off.

"Huh, that was weird," Elizabeth whispered.

"Yeah, I wonder who that was."

Elizabeth shrugged, and they continued to walk through the library. They walked past shelves labeled fantasy, nonfiction, romance, science fiction, anything one could think of. Eventually, they came to the other side of the room, where another set of double doors stood. Elizabeth opened them, and they were led to a hallway. The left was a dead end, so they turned right and kept going until they came across what appeared to be some cells.

These were different from the ones they had woken up in. They were in a row of four, and the walls were made from some sort of transparent material. Each cell had a twin bed, a small bathroom station, and a chair. Elizabeth gulped at the thought that these cells were meant for observing people like her. It was another thing that made her feel like a lab rat.

"This place gives me the creeps. Let's keep walking," Elizabeth said.

"I agree."

On their way back, they found another door that brought them back to the main common area.

"So, what now?" Jennifer asked while they walked back to their room. "Are you going to try and contact Daisy?"

"I don't know. I've never done anything like that before."

"Well, you have to try."

"Why should I?" Elizabeth looked at her. Was Jennifer being serious right now? Elizabeth felt bad for the girl, of course, but doing anything for the people holding them captive didn't sit right.

"Because that's what you're supposed to do."

"Wait, are you actually taking this seriously?"

"Well, yeah, they said they'll kill our parents and us if we don't."

"They can't do that; they're bluffing."

"I don't think so. I mean, they did straight up kidnap us."

Elizabeth sighed. "I don't know Jen."

"That's not the only reason why you should help the girl, though. She's innocent, and we should help those we can. I know it's hard, but if we can do something to save her, we should do it. You used to help people all the time! Remember? Then you stopped asking me to help you. It's almost like you've given up."

Thinking about what Jennifer had said, Elizabeth went silent. The two of them used to do more to help the people she travelled to. They investigated the people Elizabeth saw and left clues for the police to find. Sometimes they were able to save the victims, but often, they couldn't. As Elizabeth grew older, the events she saw grew more intense. More horrifying. The process of saving them, of knowing where to start, became impossible. It seemed easier to give up and pretend like the things she saw were bad dreams. She'd be lying if she said what she saw didn't affect her.

Now that Jennifer was asking her to help, she had to admit she felt more obligated. That, and the fact that she'd been in Daisy's mind twice. Maybe she'd have a better chance of saving her than the people from the past. If she couldn't, it would break her.

The other problem: she didn't trust DUST. Unsure of their true motivations behind rescuing Daisy, she had some reservations. They kidnapped people, but also wanted to rescue the people kidnapped by the terrorist organization. It was contradictory. However, if she rescued the two girls, maybe she could protect them from being hurt by the people that took her. Better than leaving them in the hands of the woman who killed their father.

"Yeah. Okay, I'll do it."

"Good. Trust me, Elizabeth. All I want is for us to be safe. So go and complete your mission. Contact Daisy. While you do that, I'll be sinking my hands into some of those delicious looking weapons." Jennifer was eyeing a set of daggers like they were a ripe, juicy apple.

Elizabeth laughed, albeit grimly, and shook her head. "All right, you have fun with that." They went their separate ways.

Walking to the bedroom, Elizabeth closed the door behind her, then lay down and closed her eyes. She'd never tried to see a particular person so far away before, so it would be challenging to even do that, let alone talk to Daisy. Still, she had to try. Her first thought was to simply imagine Daisy's face, and to her surprise, it worked right away. It didn't make sense, but that wasn't important at the moment. Elizabeth opened her eyes, and she was back in that same cave room.

The two girls were drawing pictures in the sand. Daisy was trying to put a strong front forward for her little sister, but Elizabeth could feel her fear.

"Daisy?" Elizabeth tried to speak out through her subconscious. Daisy didn't seem to hear her, so she called out again. "Daisy?"

Still nothing. This was ridiculous. How did Jackie expect her to do this with no training? She had to say she tried, though, so she thought of a different tactic. Elizabeth remembered Jackie saying something about how her voice would be like their own consciousness speaking to them. So, if she could become one with Daisy, maybe then the girl would be able to hear her.

From a psychology course Elizabeth had taken in college, she knew that a consciousness was made up from a person's awareness. Elizabeth was aware of Daisy's thoughts, feelings, sensations, and environment. While this wasn't everything that made up a consciousness, maybe it would be enough for her to speak through. She focused on making all of those pieces one with herself.

The first emotion came through, and Elizabeth felt all Daisy's anxiety wash over her. She heard her thoughts surrounding her anxiety; she wondered if her mother was still alive, what Priscilla wanted with her, if she would be able to protect her little sister, and if they were going to be killed. She felt the love Daisy had for Sofie as she watched her little sister draw in the sand. She wanted to shield her sister from the horror of their current situation. Hunger pained her stomach, her scalp itched from not being able to properly bathe, her body felt sore from sleeping on a thin mattress.

Daisy's feelings, thoughts, and sensations all became Elizabeth's.

"Daisy?" Elizabeth tried again.

Daisy froze. She stopped moving her stick in the sand. Confusion filled her head from hearing Elizabeth's voice. It must have been her imagination.

"Daisy?" Elizabeth tried again.

"I'm going crazy," Daisy thought.

"No, you're not."

In that moment, Daisy's entire body went cold. She dropped her artistic utensil and looked around frantically for the voice. There must have been someone in her room.

"Don't be afraid, Daisy. I'm not physically there with you."

"What's going on?" Daisy said out loud.

"Daisy?" Sofie said softly.

"My name is Elizabeth. I'm not going to hurt you. I want to help."

Daisy pulled at her hair and sat to curl into a ball. "This place is making me go crazy," she cried.

Sofie crawled over to her and put her arms around her.

"You're not going crazy, Daisy," Elizabeth said. "Please just listen to me. I want to help you and your sister. I'm able to go into people's minds. That's how I'm able to talk to you right now. I'm in the United States of America. I think I am, anyways, and there's a group of us that are trying to save you."

Daisy rocked her head side to side. "It's not real," she whispered over and over.

Of course the poor girl thought she was going crazy. Trying to talk to her was a stupid idea. There was no point in trying to get information from her like this. Elizabeth was about to leave, when another idea came to light. Daisy was maybe the wrong person to talk to; Sofie, on the other hand, was so young that maybe Elizabeth could convince her that she was an imaginary friend. Being so close, it shouldn't be difficult to travel to the next sister.

Stretching out her ability, she reached to the little girl hugging Daisy. She leaped from the current body and felt herself float into Sofie. It was strange, being in the child's head. She was afraid, but confused.

"Sofie?" Elizabeth called out in the sweetest voice she could conjure.

Sofie slowly let go of her sister and perked up. "Did you hear someone call my name, sissy?" she asked.

Daisy froze, the shaking of her head coming to a halt. "No, I didn't hear anything," she whispered.

"Sofie, I need to speak with you," Elizabeth said.

"Who's saying that?"

"I'm Elizabeth, I'm here to help you and your sister."

"Where are you?"

"I'm nowhere. I'm just someone who wants to help. I mean no harm."

"Who are you speaking to?" Daisy peeked up at Sofie through her matted hair.

"A lady named Elizabeth," Sofie said excitedly. "She says she wants to help us."

Daisy's face blanched at hearing Elizabeth's name. "How do you know that name?" There was absolute terror in her voice. "Did I tell you her name?"

"No, Elizabeth told me her name."

"Your sister is scared of me Sofie. I understand why," Elizabeth explained. "I didn't mean to frighten her."

"Why is she scared of you?"

"Because I'm a voice that can't be seen. People have a hard time believing what they can't see. But you're different, aren't you? You're not scared of me."

"Nope! I'm not scared of anything! Well, except for monsters."

"Well, I'm not a monster. I'm someone that wants to save you. Will you help me save you and your sister?"

Sofie bobbed her head excitedly, happy to do something to make her big sister feel better. Elizabeth mentally patted herself on the back. Now she was getting somewhere.

"I'm glad to hear that, Sofie. Now tell me, do you know where you are?"

"No, let me ask sissy," she said to Elizabeth, then poked her sister before asking, "Sissy, where are we?"

Daisy just shrugged her shoulders. Shoot, Elizabeth thought, how was she supposed to save them if she didn't know where they were?

"Okay, do you know who you're staying with?" She tried to avoid any words that might scare the young girl.

"I don't. Do you know who we are staying with, sissy?"

"No." Daisy sobbed a little.

"Okay, you're doing a good job answering questions for me, Sofie. I have one more question. Do you know where the rest of the passengers on the plane are?"

"I haven't seen mommy since we got off the plane. I haven't seen many other grown-ups either, just the kids."

"So, they must have separated the children from the parents," Elizabeth thought.

"Okay, thank you for helping me, Sofie. I'm going to tell my team and see if there's a way we can help you. Tell your sister that I'll be back to help. Be a good girl for her."

"Okay, bye, Elizabeth."

Elizabeth took one last look at Daisy's defeated form, wishing there was more she could do, and left Sofie's body.

Chapter 12

Reaching into her pocket, Elizabeth pulled out the pager that was given to her. She scrolled through her small group of contacts until she found Michael's name.

"Hey, Jackie told me to meet with you today," she messaged.

"Elizabeth, where are you? I'll come to you."

"I'm by my room."

A couple minutes had passed when Elizabeth spotted Michael walking in her direction from across the hall. He gave her a light smile and waved. She started to walk towards him, so he wouldn't have to walk the whole way.

"Hi, Elizabeth! Let's go to my lab."

Aloof, she stared at him, not wanting him to think she was going to be his friend. He continued to look at her with that warm smile anyways. When he realized she wasn't going to greet him in return, Michael turned in the opposite direction and motioned her to follow him. Without a word, she walked by his side as he led her to a room labeled "Michael's Lab."

"Impressive; you have a lab all to yourself?"

"Well, I'm the only one who uses it." He shrugged.

He opened the door, and Elizabeth's eyes widened. She saw beakers and funnels, neatly placed on the counter to the right, and a large refrigerator with a translucent door. Inside the fridge, she could see glass flasks and test tubes with different, colored liquids inside. In the middle of the room were a giant microscope and an MRI machine. White boards ran along the walls, covered with chemistry and calculus equations. To the left sat machinery to test results and mix solutions.

"Is this where you run tests on the other captives?" she questioned, with an accusatory tone.

"No, I don't run tests on captives. I only run tests and experiments on the things I want to."

Elizabeth raised a brow at him, making it clear she didn't believe him.

"Look, I know it's going to take some getting used to, being here and all, but I promise I'm on your side. I only want to help."

"What's in it for you?"

"First, I get to help people. People like you. And it feels good to help people, as selfish as that is. Secondly, I get to stay here, and be close to my sister in case she needs anything."

"Are you here willingly?"

Michael nodded.

Elizabeth tilted her head. She couldn't comprehend someone wanting to be here. "Why?"

"My sister had to come here." He turned to face her and leaned against the counter. "So I came along with her."

"Why did your sister have to come here?"

"Same reason you did. She's special. She wasn't doing well in society anyways. This place has been good for her."

Elizabeth crossed her arms and looked away from him. This guy must have been completely brainwashed if he thought being trapped here was good for anyone.

"Will you take a seat in that chair?" he asked.

He directed her to a small plastic table with chairs surrounding it in the corner. Cautiously, she walked over to the table and took a seat. Michael grabbed a notebook and pen from a cupboard, then took a seat across from her.

"Jackie told me a little bit about you. Your consciousness travels to others while your body is asleep. Can you elaborate?"

"As soon as I fall asleep, I involuntarily wake up in another person's body. But they can't… tell I'm there." Unsure if Michael was trustworthy, she didn't tell him she was able to communicate with Daisy and Sofie.

Michael started jotting down notes.

"How do you fall asleep? Do you need a sedative?"

"I used sedatives back when I was a teen and was testing out my powers, but they had a weird effect on my body. I would feel lethargic, and my head was spaced out all the time. So I started trying to fall asleep on my own. At first it was difficult; it would take me, like, half an hour to fall asleep."

Michael nodded, looking impressed. "Are you able to control who you jump into?"

"Usually only if they're in close proximity. Until recently, with Daisy. For some reason, I can travel to her pretty easily."

"Have you ever been able to control the subject you travel to?"

Elizabeth leaned back in her chair and eyed Michael suspiciously. "No, but I've never tried. Why would I want to do such a thing? And why are you even asking?"

"Could they possibly be wanting to use me for sinister things?" she thought.

"Just trying to understand what you're capable of. I promise I have no ulterior motives here." He smiled and changed the subject. "What does it feel like when you travel to another's mind?"

She rolled her eyes, not believing his intentions. "At first, it feels like I can't breathe and like I'm moving extremely quickly. But once

I land on a person, I can feel myself expanding. It's really a strange feeling, but not horrible."

"Hmm, interesting. Can you hear their thoughts or search through their memory?"

"I can hear their thoughts, but I've never tried to search through memories."

"How old were you when you started travelling?"

"The first time I remember it happening is when I was six." Elizabeth looked at her hands with concern. She remembered her first time dream travelling: she'd seen a room full of bodies wrapped in chains, a girl of about twelve years old with red hair running into the room, and a scary man.

"I think I have an idea." Michael brought her out of her thoughts. "May I measure your brain activity while you fall asleep?"

"Uh, why?"

"I have an idea, but you have to trust me."

Elizabeth looked him in the eyes, trying to figure him out. "How can I trust you? I don't even know you."

"Just hear me out," he pleaded. "If you don't like it, we won't do it."

"Fine, but I'm not promising anything."

Michael walked over to an examination table and pulled a machine over to it. He sanitized the table, then put a sheet and pillow on it.

"I would like you to fall asleep here and travel to my consciousness. I'm going to monitor your brainwaves on the EEG. This way, you can hear my thoughts in case I plan on doing anything you don't like. How does that sound?"

Elizabeth eyed him up and down. "I can do that. But if you try anything, I'll jump back to my body and make you regret the day you were born."

He nodded his head and smiled.

Elizabeth laid down on the table and tried to make herself comfortable. Her long, dark blond hair draped elegantly around her as she shifted. Closing her eyes, she took some deep, relaxing breaths.

"Do you mind not watching me for a second? You're making it difficult for me to concentrate."

"Oh, sure, sorry."

Michael turned away and walked to the other side of the room to give her space.

She took deep breaths until she drifted into sleep. She tried to concentrate on Michael, and she felt herself leave her body. She absorbed into him, and then she could feel his thoughts and feelings. His thoughts were sincere; he wanted to help her. He turned toward her to find her body looking like a corpse.

He walked over to the EEG machine and took out some suction cups. He carefully placed them around her forehead. It was strange for Elizabeth to watch herself sleep again, she'd only seen it once before, when she inhabited the body of Jackie's guard.

Michael walked to the back side of the EEG machine to look at a display screen. There were wave-like lines moving up and down. Michael clicked a record button.

Observing Elizabeth, Michael watched the slow rise and fall of her chest. Her ability to remain still was remarkable.

He thought about how much she reminded him of Paige. They both had abilities difficult to control, making it almost impossible to function in society. Just as he was determined to help his sister, he would help Elizabeth too. She may never live as a normal person would, but she should at least be able to sleep without having to experience other people's lives every night.

Paige had tried to kill herself over all the emotions she would feel on a day-to-day basis, unable to cope with the constant stress. He still wondered why she had never felt safe enough to tell him before she made the attempt. He had been able to tell something was wrong, but he was too young to understand. Now, at the age of twenty-seven, and after many years of studying human emotions from a psychological standpoint, he felt better equipped to help people like Paige and Elizabeth.

Elizabeth didn't feel safe telling him what was going on in her head, which he understood, but he hoped one day she would be comfortable enough with him to open up.

"All right, Elizabeth. Just a few minutes and you may wake up."

Michael watched the machine for the next few minutes.

"All right, you may wake up now."

She travelled back to her own mind and slowly opened her eyes.

"So, what are you thinking?"

"I'm thinking that maybe if I can create a device that gives off waves opposite to your brain's, then maybe I can neutralize it so that you won't leave your body."

"You want to flatline my brain?"

"No, I want to neutralize some of your brain activity. Let me show you something."

He walked her over to the table and grabbed a large book. He opened it in front of her and showed her some EEG diagrams of different brains.

"You see, this is what the brain activity usually looks like. According to the machine, yours is way different, as I suspected. You see how the crests on these waves stop about here?"

She nodded.

"Well, yours are at least an inch higher. And your troughs are a lot lower too. It's amazing you haven't gone completely crazy yet."

"Gee, thanks."

"I meant no offense, you're exceptional, actually." He smirked.

He seemed to be flirting with her, but Elizabeth wasn't interested in forming any romantic relationships.

"So, if your device works, I might be able to sleep? In my own head?"

"That's my goal. I can't make any promises, but I'm 92.34 percent sure that this will work."

Elizabeth laughed. "That's quite a specific number."

"Yes, I calculated it in my head."

"Sure, buddy, we'll just have to wait and see. If I could get some real sleep, though, I would really owe you one."

"No, you wouldn't. It's reward enough if it helps you."

"Right... so what now?"

"I'll come up with some sketches and give them to Jackie and have them implemented."

"Why Jackie?"

"She knows people. She will get you what you need, trust me."

"If you say so. Anyways, thank you for trying to help me."

"My pleasure. It's what I'm here for."

Elizabeth paused for a second, then had an idea. "Can I ask you something?"

"Sure."

"If you can create something to neutralize my powers, could you neutralize Jackie's?"

Michael eyebrows rose. "I could, but I don't think she'd like that."

"It wouldn't be for her; it would be for me. I don't like her being able to read my thoughts."

Michael sat down and rubbed his temples. "I could probably make something. Something you could wear to deflect her power. It would have to be a secret, though."

Elizabeth smiled; this guy was on her side, after all. "I won't tell anyone. And if she asks, I'll just say I learned how to deflect her powers using my dream traveling."

"That would be perfect. She might even be proud."

"Thanks, Michael." Elizabeth headed for the door. "Let me know when you have something, or if you need help."

She still didn't trust him completely, but she was willing to give him a chance.

Chapter 13

Just as Elizabeth was about to open the door, a knock interrupted her.

"Come in!" Michael called out.

Zola walked in, with a huge grin on her face. She wore a matched yellow set of shirt and pants, and her dark hair was in two Dutch braids.

"What can I do for you, Zola?" Michael asked.

She held her hands behind her back, and excitement lit up her features. "I've been thinking.... to celebrate the new arrivals, we should go out!"

"I can't, I have work to do," Michael declined.

"I don't really think our captivity is something to celebrate," Elizabeth muttered.

"Okay, maybe not celebrate, but we could still go out and have fun!"

"I don't know, I think I would rather mope in my room."

"Please?" Zola pouted.

"I thought we weren't allowed to leave."

"We aren't. But we will be back! I stole the key card and some car keys from Jackie's office. I even nabbed a little cash." She dangled the keys out in front of herself, and waved a hundred dollar bill past their eyes.

"I don't know."

"Come on, they'll never know we left! Josh and I have done it before, and we've never been in trouble."

"I'll cover for you in case anything happens," Michael said, drawing out designs and notes on a sketch pad.

"Jackie literally just threatened to have our parents killed if we tried to escape."

"Dude, if we didn't try to get out every now and then, we'd all go insane. When I first was brought here, I went a little stir crazy. Michael and Josh showed me where the cameras were and explained that there was no way we could leave without them knowing. However, every once in a while, some rats make their way into the building, and they just so happen to chew on some wires in the security room, disabling all the cameras until morning." Zola winked.

"Oh?" Elizabeth smirked. "And you wouldn't happen to be the cause of these rats knowing exactly where the security room is and what to be chewing on, right?"

"Oh, I would never!" Zola acted coy, pressing a hand to her chest in mock primness.

"I tamper with the audio in this room all the time, so I do it for the rest of this floor when Zola and Josh go out. Also, I can go into old footage and find videos of you sleeping and put it on repeat. I'll blend it when you come back, so no one will suspect a thing," Michael informed Elizabeth.

"They have cameras in our room?" Elizabeth scrunched her nose.

"I know, it's creepy."

"Are they in our bathrooms as well?"

"Oh, no. They do have the audio in there, though."

"Good call."

"Okay, if you all are sure about this, then I guess it would do Jen and I some good to get out."

"Perfect, bye, Michael." Zola grabbed Elizabeth's arm and pulled her out of the room. "This is going to be great! We have to find you an outfit and do your makeup. And trust me, we will be back before they even know we're gone."

Zola dragged Elizabeth to her room, where they found Jennifer sitting on the bed. Her hair was wet, and she was painting her nails black.

"She got to you too, huh?" Jennifer greeted.

"Yeah... are you painting your nails?" Elizabeth had never seen Jennifer wear nail polish before.

"Zola suggested it. You should see her collection; she has every color."

"I sure do!" Zola exclaimed. "We should do your nails too. We can have a girl's day until tonight comes along. Or until Josh comes to knock on my door. He gets bored sometimes."

"They'll be ruined by tomorrow, but sure. Why not?"

Now that Elizabeth had a minute to make herself comfortable, she looked around Zola's room. Her walls were covered in artwork that appeared to all be by the same person and were signed with "Z." The work was of abstract landscapes and animals.

"Who did the artwork on your wall?" Elizabeth asked, although she suspected she knew.

"I did," Zola replied.

"They're awesome; you're really talented."

"Thanks. I actually wanted to be an artist before, you know." A flash of sadness reached her eyes. "All of this happened."

Elizabeth and Jennifer looked at her with empathy. Before they could reply, however, Zola grabbed Elizabeth's hand and brought her to an elegantly carved dresser with a mirror attached and a chair to match. Zola opened a drawer, and inside was the nail polish. Elizabeth picked up a dark red.

"That one? Okay!" Zola got started on Elizabeth's nails.

"How was training this morning?" Elizabeth asked.

"Great! Josh and Zola joined me," replied Jennifer.

"Jennifer was teaching us some cool moves in… what's it called?" asked Zola.

"Krav Maga."

"Right!"

Having her sit first, Zola began doing Elizabeth's makeup. She picked a natural look: low coverage foundation, blush, brown eyeshadow, and mascara.

Zola was dabbing blush on Elizabeth's cheeks when Jennifer asked a question.

"How old were you when you discovered your powers, Zola?"

"I've been able to understand animals for as long as I can remember. I didn't realize I was different, though, until I got into kindergarten. Once, we were on a field trip at a ranch, and I snuck off. I went to look at all the calves and played with them. I got all the cows to follow me around. I don't remember everything, but I do remember the teacher being upset and apologizing to the ranch hands. They responded by saying something along the lines of, 'That was abnormal cow behavior.' That wasn't the only thing that happened, though. We had 'bring a pet to school day,' and I brought a raccoon I befriended a week before. The teachers were surprised by how well-behaved the raccoon was, especially after I told them how long I'd had it. Not only that, but everyone else's pets were more interested in me than anyone else."

"Did anyone suspect anything? Or did they just think you were really good with animals?"

"There was one lady that went to my church who seemed suspicious about it, but she mostly thought I was a demon. Everyone thought she was crazy, though."

"I see."

"When I was eight, my family and I went to the zoo in Florida, and my five-year-old brother fell into a lion's cage. He decided to climb up a ladder that a zookeeper left out. A lion was running to attack him, but I yelled, 'Stop!' and it listened."

"Did your parents figure out your powers?"

"I don't think they were able to comprehend what I was. They would just call me their 'Little Animal Whisperer.' But they always rationalized things with luck, chance, and coincidence."

Zola finished Elizabeth's makeup, then did Jennifer's. At around seven in the evening, they heard a knock at the door.

"It's unlocked!" yelled Zola.

The door slowly opened, and in walked Josh. His dark, sandy hair was slicked back, and he wore straight-leg black pants with a dark blue shirt.

"Is the operation a go?" whispered Josh.

"Yep! Our little friends just disabled the security cameras. You're right on time."

"When did you have the time to do that?" asked Elizabeth.

"I've had them on standby all day! I just told them to start, like, twenty minutes ago."

"Oh, so you don't even need to talk or see them?"

"Nope! It's all up here" Zola pointed to her head. "As I told you, I don't talk to animals in a verbal manner, I understand them, just as they understand me."

"Nifty," Elizabeth complimented.

"Sure is! Ready to go?" Zola turned to Josh.

"Yeah, I got the car keys."

"Sweet!"

Zola grabbed a tote bag and stuffed a couple clothing items and shoes into it. Then they walked out her room and down a hall until they were met with a door, at the very end. Zola took the key she stole and unlocked the door leading to a garage. Within, there were several different vehicles, including large SUVs and some sportier cars.

Josh clicked a button on the keys, and a light flashed in the dark garage. They followed the light and quickly found their ride. The car was a dark blue Porsche 911.

"I wanna drive," Jennifer shouted.

"No way, I'm driving," Josh rebutted.

"Come on, I'm a great driver."

"If we crash the car, I'm less likely to get in trouble since I've been here for so long, so I'm driving. End of discussion."

Jennifer crossed her arms and glared, but didn't argue further. Josh slid into the driver's seat, unfazed by her anger, while Zola took the passenger side and Jennifer and Elizabeth took the back. The seats were nice black leather, and the rest of the interior looked expensive.

Josh pressed a button on the car's ceiling, and the front wall of the garage opened. They all clicked on their seatbelts as he started the ignition.

As soon as they left the garage, they looked up into the dark sky. The lack of artificial lights allowed the stars to shine brightly. It was breathtaking. Then Zola pulled out her tote and passed Elizabeth and Jennifer each an article of clothing and a pair of shoes.

"What's this for?" asked Elizabeth.

"Your outfits for tonight. I grabbed a black jumpsuit for you since that seems to be your favorite color, judging by what I always see you wear, and a red, pleather mini dress for you, Jennifer."

"What's wrong with what we're wearing?"

"What's wrong with the pajamas you two are wearing?" Zola whipped her head around to look at them. "Nothing, except for the fact that we won't have many chances to dress up. Trust me, you want to take advantage. Plus, you two have your hair and makeup done. Why not go the extra step?"

"Fine. Josh, don't look."

"I would never do that," he reassured.

Jennifer and Elizabeth stripped off their pajamas and slipped on the borrowed clothes. To their surprise, the clothing fit them like gloves. Then Elizabeth put on some nude flats, and Jennifer put on black ankle boots.

"You two look awesome." Zola gleamed with satisfaction.

"Why do you have clothes that fit us? And where did you get something so nice?"

"They were in your closet already! I actually got to pick out your wardrobe. While you were in medical, they got your measurements, then William gave them to me so I could find you some clothes. Using the catalogs he provided, I was able to pick out whatever I wanted!"

"I see…"

Josh continued to drive down the barren road. They were sheltered by a vast forest on both sides.

"Are you sure there's anything out here?" Elizabeth asked.

"Yeah, there's a little town about fifteen minutes away. There's not much, but there is a bar. It's kind of a dive, but I like it," Zola replied.

They drove until a blinking yellow light came into view.

"There it is, guys," Zola exclaimed.

The town was indeed small. There was only a gas station, post office, police station, a bar, grocery store, ice cream shop, and some houses. It was dark, but the streetlights showed chipping paint and dirty siding. The stars and moon lit the sky, and in the horizon, the silhouette of mountains painted the landscape.

"Where are we?" Elizabeth asked.

"The Appalachian Mountains in Kentucky," Josh answered.

"No wonder we are so isolated," Elizabeth thought.

Josh parked the car close to the bar. Elizabeth slid out of the car after Jennifer, and they followed Zola and Josh. The town was almost silent, besides some music.

The bar was in need of some renovations, but it wasn't too bad. The floor was made from hardwood, and the walls were decorated with mounted deer heads. It wasn't busy, with only three men and the bartender occupying the facility. It wasn't the kind of place Elizabeth would normally visit, but being there gave her hope. If they could have freedom for a night, they could do so again. Clearly Zola didn't like being cooped up, so if the time came for an escape, maybe she'd help.

The four of them walked up to the bar to order their drinks. Jennifer and Elizabeth ordered hard ciders, while Josh and Zola ordered Moscow Mules.

"That one boy is kind of cute." Zola checked out a guy with blond hair and brown eyes. He was tall and wearing straight-leg jeans with a red plaid button-down.

"Maybe you should talk to him," Jennifer encouraged.

"I think I will," Zola winked and downed her drink.

"There she goes. Does this every time," Josh complained.

"Awh. Does she leave you alone at the bar?" Jennifer mocked.

"Yes," he pouted. "At least I have you two to keep me company, though."

Elizabeth gulped her drink. "So, what got you landed in this prison?"

"Well, it's not prison to me. They saved me."

"How so?"

"I was in the foster care system until I was four. Nobody was willing to house me because my strength terrified them. Jackie found me and brought me here. It's been my home ever since."

"Why were they afraid of your strength?"

"Well, I couldn't control it, so I would usually break things."

"Are you better at controlling yourself now?"

"A little," he said, shrugging. "What about you two? How did you end up in DUST?"

Elizabeth looked down at her drink, then lifted it to her lips, chugging the rest. Slamming the mug on the table, she saw Jennifer raise a brow.

"You don't already know?"

"I know what Jackie told me, but that's not why you're here. That's just how you were discovered. You wouldn't be here if you didn't belong."

"I don't."

"Yes, you do. You and Jennifer. You're special. Special people like you don't belong in the world, living mundane lives."

"So, we are supposed to be trapped?"

"No. We should have more freedom. But, more importantly, we need each other. No one normal will understand you the way people in DUST will. That's why you two are so close. Because you both know what it's like to be different."

"I guess I can see how that would be the case," Jennifer agreed.

Looking at her sister, Elizabeth saw how Jennifer stared, wide-eyed, at Josh. Jennifer never stared at a man unless it was to glare.

"I need another drink." Elizabeth went to the bar and ordered something stronger.

The bartender handed her the tumbler of bourbon, and she walked back to the table, finding Jennifer chatting away.

"Well, my biological parents did make it a requirement for me to learn how to fight, but I never really questioned them. I loved it. There's nothing quite like throwing a dagger and hitting the bullseye."

Elizabeth pulled her chair out, sat down, and took a sip. The bourbon slid down her throat, burning. She wanted the pain.

"That's awesome," Josh said. "How many fighting techniques can you do? What material can you use?"

"I've trained in Krav Maga, boxing, wrestling, and jujitsu. And as far as weapons go, I use bow and arrows, daggers, and swords. I prefer daggers over anything, though."

"No guns?"

"No. I've trained with most handguns, and it's pretty easy, but no. I don't like them. They're loud, first of all. Secondly, if I'm going to kill someone, it's going to be personal. What's personal about using a gun?"

"Good point. Okay, so you're a walking weapon. That's pretty cool. Now it's your turn, Elizabeth. Why are you here?"

"I'm cursed." Elizabeth took a swig of her drink.

"Cursed? From what Jackie's told me about dream travelling, it sounds pretty useful," Josh rebutted.

"When it's helpful, it's useful."

Pinching his brows together, he asked, "When is it not useful?"

Elizabeth didn't want to think about the times dream travelling had done nothing but show her something traumatizing, but as she took another drink of her bourbon, she found herself caring less. Josh stared intently, waiting for her reply as she chugged her drink once more.

"When I'm in the mind of a child being sold to some perverted man, and not seeing anything that could help me find them. When I'm a woman being murdered in the middle of the woods, and I can't see the man's face or recognize my surroundings. When I'm..." She needed another drink.

"I'll get you one," Josh offered, anticipating what she wanted.

"Thanks."

"You okay?" Jennifer asked.

"Yeah, fine," she lied.

Jennifer looking at her knowingly. "You've done more for those people than anyone else could've."

"It's not enough."

Returning to his spot, Josh pushed Elizabeth's bourbon across the table. Using two hands, she picked up the glass and took a large gulp. Some of the brown liquid escaped, running down her chin.

"I see a different victim every night. Some worse off than others. I can't save everyone."

"Of course not. That's impossible," Josh replied.

"It should be, though."

"You can't stop evil. No matter what you do. Take one down, another will pop up."

"Still upsetting, though."

"Yeah. I know."

Not realizing she was already finished with her third drink, Elizabeth tried to take another swig, but was disappointed by an empty glass. Starting to feel good as the alcohol dimmed her senses, Elizabeth was about to ask for another when she heard some obnoxious laughing. Turning towards the noise, she saw the three guys Zola went to flirt with laughing at something. Zola wasn't looking good; she seemed drowsy. One of the group pushed her into the guy she was checking out earlier.

"Well, that looks weird." Josh had a worried expression. "I'm going to check on her."

Jennifer and Elizabeth watched as Josh crossed the room and protectively asked what was going on. He seemed to be arguing with the men. When he went to reach for Zola's arm, the tallest man pushed him away and stood between them. He patted Josh's cheek, then laughed so loud it echoed over the loud music.

"Hey, what's going on?" Jennifer stormed over.

Elizabeth stayed back, ready to jump in if her new friends needed her, but unsure yet if she should interfere.

"We were just having a little fun," one of the guys said drunkenly.

"Okay, well, I think we are done." Jennifer grabbed Zola, who basically collapsed into her. "How much did you drink? We've been here for an hour!"

"Only two."

The cute guy started chuckling in a creepy manner.

"Come on, we aren't done chatting," he whined.

"She said we are leaving," Josh said angrily. "And I think she can think for herself." He snatched Zola away from Jennifer.

The tall friend came up behind Josh and started massaging his shoulders. "Relax, buddy, we are harmless."

Elizabeth saw Josh's expression change to one of complete rage. He grabbed the guy's hand and almost crushed his bones. Shrieking in pain, the man dropped to his knees, holding onto his broken hand. The other friend drunkenly stumbled towards Josh, ready to avenge his friend with a punch, but Jennifer blocked the hit and kicked him in the gut.

They were distracted enough to not notice the attractive man throwing Zola over his shoulders and trying to walk out with her. Elizabeth was paying attention, however, and stumbled after them.

"Hey, stop! What are you doing?" she screamed.

The man put Zola down. She was completely out of it at this point and slumped to the floor. Elizabeth was confused. Who would be this drunk after just a couple drinks? Then she realized: no one would be this drunk.

"What did you do to her drink?" she asked, trying not to sound drunk.

"Now, now, I don't want any trouble. Just looking for some fun."

"Okay, weirdo, you're ticking me off. Back off, or else. I know you did something to her drink!" Elizabeth walked up to him with her chest puffed out. When she got close enough, she tried to shove him away, but that backfired when he barely budged. He looked down at her with an evil grin.

"Josh! Jen!" she called out for help, but they were busy fighting the other two guys.

He lunged for her and wrapped his hands around her neck, choking her. He brought his mouth to her ear and whispered, "I own this town; there's nothing you can do to stop me." The smell of booze and smoke from his breath wafted up her nose.

Elizabeth tried to peel his hands off herself, but failed. Her lungs burned; her body begged for oxygen. She felt herself beginning to give up, the strength leaving her muscles, and she lost consciousness. As quickly as she left her own consciousness, she found herself in another's. The man who had just choked her. She saw her own body on the ground, with purple marks around her throat.

The guy went over to pick up Zola. "All right, sweetheart, let's go back to my place."

"No," Elizabeth shouted in his head.

She was furious. Disgusted. Then she felt something she'd never felt before. She began to feel herself expand and wrap around his nerves. His body felt like her own, and she was in complete control. She was connected with him in a way she had never been connected to another.

She forced him to put Zola back down.

"What's going on?" he cried as Elizabeth puppeteered him.

Elizabeth's only thought was to kill, blocking all judgment, all morality. Adrenaline filled her, making her feel invincible. She walked him over to the wall and started continuously banging his head against its surface. She could hear his screams, fueling her desire to hurt him. Blood was trickling down his temples, and he was crying for someone to help him. Elizabeth kept going until his body went out, then everything went dark.

Chapter 14

"Why can't I move?" Six-year-old Elizabeth thought to herself. She looked around and saw young people chained up along the walls. They all appeared to be between twelve and young adulthood, but she couldn't really tell. They wore clothes, but they were basically rags. She whimpered in fear. She had just fallen asleep after her parents read her a bedtime story; how did she get here? It felt so real, but it couldn't be. It had to be a nightmare.

Then a door opened, and light burned through the room. In ran a girl who looked to be about 12 years old with flaming red curly hair. Behind her, a pudgy, bald white man followed at a slower pace.

"You can't be in here." The man spoke sternly.

The girl looked around, unafraid and curious. "Why are they here?"

The man sighed. "They are to be sold or killed."

She looked back at him, "Why?"

"Because the boys aren't skilled enough to become warriors, and the girls were either not pretty or charismatic enough to be handy in the way you will soon be. We have no other use for them. They just take up space and resources."

"But…"

"Enough questions, get out of here." He grabbed her arm and dragged her to the door. Once he pushed her out, he turned back into the room, then began to inspect the people. He raised their arms and grabbed their faces, inspecting them like merchandise. Elizabeth's heart rate rose as he got closer and closer to her. Before she knew it, he was standing right in front of her, staring down into her eyes.

"Well, well, looks like one of you is awake." He knelt down to her level, since she was sitting on the floor. "Such a pretty thing you are. Too bad we can't keep you. You were just too mouthy. You'll make us a pretty penny, though." He used his thumb to stroke her lips, then started to lean closer to her face.

That's when Elizabeth jumped from her bed. She felt dizzy and crashed onto the floor, bruising her knees in the process. She scrambled to her feet and ran to her parents' room.

"Mom! Dad!" she cried.

"Baby?" Her mom spoke groggily.

"There was a man; he had people chained to walls. He's going to hurt me!"

"Come here, baby." Her mother lifted the blanket to invite her into the bed.

Elizabeth crawled between her parents while they tried to calm her.

"It was just a bad dream, sweetie," her father said. "No one is going to hurt you. Not ever."

Later, Elizabeth woke in her parents' bed, alone. The sun shone through the lace curtains, and birds sang from the apple tree on the front lawn. Despite the beautiful morning, Elizabeth felt nothing but despair and fear. She couldn't get the scary man's face out of her head. At that moment, all she wanted was her mom, dad, and the safety they provided. Afraid the man would find her if she stayed alone, Elizabeth leapt from the bed and dashed for the stairs.

Hurrying down the stairs and the hall towards the kitchen, Elizabeth came to a stop when she heard angry whispers. She flattened her back against the wall, frightened to interrupt.

"She doesn't need a doctor, Julie! She was just having a bad dream!"

"What six-year-old dreams about people being chained to walls? Those ideas don't come from nowhere," Elizabeth's mom replied.

"Maybe she heard something at school."

"Or maybe she snuck a peek at the scary movies you watch!"

"Oh! So, it's my fault!"

Elizabeth felt her body become stiffer as her parents' fight escalated. She didn't want them to fight because of her. After a tense pause, she heard her mother exhale.

"No. No. I'm sorry. I'm just worried about our daughter. I didn't mean to take it out on you. Can we please have her talk to someone?"

"I just think we should wait. This is the first time something like this has happened."

"So if it happens again, we can take her to see someone?"

"Yes. I think that would be a good idea."

Choosing that moment to walk around the corner, Elizabeth made sure her footsteps were loud enough for them to hear.

"Oh, good morning, sweetie!" Her mother greeted.

"How're you feeling this morning?" asked her father.

"Good morning. I'm good," she lied.

Looking graceful in her pink satin robe, Elizabeth's mother rushed to her, engulfed her in a hug, and kissed her forehead.

"My poor baby."

"Promise to come to us if you have another nightmare like last night?"

"Yes, dad," Elizabeth lied once more. She never wanted her parents to get upset over her again.

Chapter 15

Elizabeth's eyes fluttered open, her vision blurry, and she saw a dimly lit room around her. She didn't know how she'd gotten there. She remembered being choked until she passed out, taking over that man's body, and saving Zola.

She shot up and frantically looked for Zola, still out of it. A searing pain shot through her neck.

"Go slow. You're injured." Elizabeth heard Jackie's voice say.

"Zola," she coughed out.

"She's fine. She was poisoned with Rohypnol, but she's better now."

"And the guy that poisoned her?"

"He's in the ICU. He has a concussion. You almost killed him."

"I know."

Elizabeth remembered the blood running down his face and the excitement she felt as he became weak.

"I'm almost disappointed you didn't."

Elizabeth's eyes widened; she thought Jackie would be furious. Then, getting a better sense of her surroundings, Elizabeth saw Jackie standing on the other side of a glass wall, while Elizabeth lay on a twin bed. There was nothing else in the room except a chair, a toilet, and a sink. This was the creepy place she and Jennifer discovered while wandering.

"Where am I? Why am I here?"

"You are being held in this cell until things cool off."

Jackie walked away, and Elizabeth began to panic.

"Wait, don't leave me here." She ran to the glass, frantically banging on the wall.

Jackie clicked a button on the wall, and a white gas was released from the ceiling of the glass room. Breathing in and out, Elizabeth began to cough. A calmness came over her, and she dropped to her knees. She fell on her side and once again was overcome by darkness.

Walking to Michael's lab, Jackie thought about Elizabeth and her current predicament. Or, rather, their predicament. This affected the rest of the team just as much as Elizabeth. She hoped that she and William were successfully able to hide the excursion, but there was always the possibility Vance would find out.

Jackie had been hiding things from Vance for years. Zola and Michael were quite good at sneaking around as well. Zola because of her rebellious nature, and Michael because of his desire to protect his sister. It wasn't easy to hide things from William and Jackie, though. She could read their thoughts, of course, and William could tell when the security system was messed with. However, Jackie knew what it was like to be trapped. If they were being safe, she would give them a little bit of freedom.

They weren't safe this time. If Vance found out what happened, that Elizabeth almost killed a man, she wouldn't stand a chance. Jackie used her telepathy powers to erase the bar patrons' minds, but she was still worried. With sweaty palms and an aching jaw from clenching her teeth, she walked into Michael's lab, where he, Jennifer, and Josh were tending to Zola. Zola was unconscious, and the others were sitting around her. She had an IV in her arm, and Josh held her hand.

"How is she?" Jackie asked.

"Her vitals are stable; she hasn't woken up yet. She should soon, though." Michael replied.

"Where's Elizabeth?" Jennifer asked.

"She's being put under observation."

Jennifer's brows furrowed. "Why, what's going on?"

"How about we speak somewhere in private?"

Jackie stepped out of the lab, with Jennifer following behind her. They kept walking until they made it to the couch by the theater area and took a seat. Positioning herself so she sat diagonally to Jennifer, Jackie noticed the dismal look on the young woman's face.

"Tell me, Jennifer. Has Elizabeth ever expressed violent behavior?"

Jennifer involuntarily thought about how she came home from work one day to find their apartment trashed with broken plates. Elizabeth lay in a fetal position on the floor, crying, with scratches all over her body. When Jennifer tried asking her what happened, she muttered "sorry" over and over again.

Jackie saw the terrifying image in her head. "So, she has had manic episodes."

"She's never hurt anyone." Jennifer shook her head.

"Until now." Jackie sighed and stood.

"But he deserved it!"

"It doesn't matter what he deserved. Killing people is a last resort, and I know she was thirsty for his blood. I had to break my promise to her and look inside her head. Believe me, it's terrifying. There's something you should know."

Jennifer looked into Jackie's eyes, and for the first time since being there, she saw something other than the stoic expression. She saw fear.

"Okay."

"You remember how I told you we had a Dream Traveller who died?"

"Yeah."

"That's because he went crazy. He wasn't, at first. He was well put together, and rational. Then, out of nowhere, he started to act like someone else." She shuddered. "He killed a lot of people. He killed his own friends."

Jennifer's eyes were wide as she soaked in every word Jackie said. If Elizabeth didn't get the help she needed, would she turn out this way?

"What can I do?"

"Just keep an eye on her. I'm hoping the device Michael is working on will be completed soon. Now I have to double check everything to make sure this mess doesn't get back to the higher-ups." She felt annoyed, but also concerned.

"And what about Zola?"

"Zola will be okay. Physically." Jackie sighed. "I'm just glad nothing else happened to her."

"What will happen?"

"Hopefully nothing. I just have to convince the board that there's a rat infestation again."

Jennifer raised an eyebrow. It seemed Jackie knew of Zola's mischief.

"Did you know what we were planning?"

Jackie gave her a rueful smile. "Please, Zola does this every month. The only reason why I've let it go on is because she hides her tracks from the board."

And with that, Jackie stood from the couch and walked away, leaving Jennifer confused. Walking to her office to prepare for a meeting with the board, Jackie was surprised to see that her door was already open, and the lights were on. She stopped in the doorway, finding the last person she wanted to see sitting in her seat. His arms were crossed, and he leaned back as if in his own office. His wavy, dark brown hair was slicked back, and his white button-up shirt seemed a size too small, showing off his chiseled body. He had a manipulative smirk on his face as he looked Jackie in the eyes.

"Vance," she greeted, her tone showing her distaste.

"Well, if it isn't my favorite employee. How nice it is to see you here."

Jackie crossed her arms and raised a brow. "Well, you are in my office."

"Oh, I know, I just missed you."

"Cut the crap, Vance. What do you want?"

"Something happened tonight. I can tell."

"And that would be?"

"My guess, Elizabeth did something stupid."

"She didn't do anything to disturb operations or the agency."

"Then why is she in a cell?"

"That's for me to worry about. Don't you have better things to do than micromanage me?"

"It's my responsibility to keep DUST a secret from the rest of the world. So, keeping an eye on Elizabeth is on top of my priority list."

"And here I thought your top priority was seducing women too young for you."

"That too."

Rolling her eyes, Jackie said, "Elizabeth is fine. Everyone is safe. And, most importantly, your precious agency's secret is safe. The deal was to prevent Elizabeth from putting DUST in jeopardy, which she hasn't. Unless you have anything else to say, I would like for you to leave so I can get some sleep."

Vance raised a brow. "Fine." He stood and walked towards the door, brushing Jackie's arm as he passed.

"But just so you know," he added, pausing to lean down, his lips pushing against her ear, "I'll be watching. I know you're hiding something from me."

Then he left, shutting the door behind him.

Jackie let out a breath she didn't realize she was holding. They were so close to getting caught, but it seemed Vance had no proof of anything happening overnight.

Elizabeth had to learn to trust her, and soon. Or she at least had to understand that Jackie was all that stood between her life and Vance's deadly hands.

Chapter 16

Regaining consciousness, Elizabeth felt soft hands holding onto hers and thought maybe it was Jennifer. She slowly opened her eyes and was surprised to see a young woman, hair so blond it looked almost white, sitting on a chair and resting her head on the bed.

"Excuse me?" Elizabeth questioned.

The woman shot up. "What! I'm sorry." She spoke frantically.

"Ow, my hand."

She released her tight grip. "Oh, sorry."

"Who are you?"

"I'm Paige." Her pale gray eyes looked into Elizabeth's.

"And why were you holding my hand?"

"I was just trying to make you feel better. Michael told me you weren't doing well. You are holding onto a lot of anger and stress."

"Michael?"

"He's my brother."

"Oh, yeah, he mentioned you. Why haven't I met you yet?"

"Being around people isn't easy for me, I prefer to avoid it as much as possible."

Elizabeth laughed weakly. "At least you're honest. You said I'm angry and stressed. How could you know that?"

"I'm an empath. I can feel people's emotions and give them emotions."

"Is that why I feel weirdly at peace?"

"Yes. I took away the negative emotions. I gave you a calming one instead, so you wouldn't feel numb."

"How is that possible?"

Shrugging, Paige said, "Not sure. I've just always been able to do that."

There was a short pause as she stared at Elizabeth, then said with a timid smile. "Well, I should probably check up on Michael to see how his device for you is coming along." She started to walk out the door.

"Wait! Can you please let me out?" Elizabeth looked at her with hopeful eyes.

"I will see what I can do; in the meantime, why don't you relax?" She spoke in a soothing tone, and Elizabeth felt another wave of calmness wash over her.

Paige walked over to Michael's lab. He was concentrating while screwing together small gears; he didn't hear Paige come in. Paige sat at the table and let out a long, dramatic sigh.

"Oh. Paige." He noticed her presence and turned to her. "You look exhausted. I'm guessing you met Elizabeth?"

"Yeah," she sighed.

"Were her emotions too strong?"

"Well, yes, once I found them."

Michael looked perplexed. He'd never heard her say anything about finding emotions; she was always able to absorb the frequencies as she stepped into a room. "What do you mean?"

"I've never met anyone so guarded yet so emotionally intense. It was exhausting trying to get to her. I even had to hold her hand," she blushed.

"Oh? Did she know about the hand holding part?"

"Yeah," she had a dreamy look on her face.

"You seem to have enjoyed it. Did she?"

"She was indifferent."

"I see, anyway, back on topic. What is your analysis on her emotional state."

"Must you always talk like that! She's a human not a project."

"Sorry, how is she?"

"She's a time bomb. I tried to calm her but it only lasted 10 minutes. I've never dealt with this before. Nobody I've dealt with has been able to regain their emotions so quickly. And it's so difficult to reach her emotions it takes a while to regain control. When will your device be ready."

"It will take me at least two weeks to have it completed."

"We don't have that kind of time! When Jackie came to speak to me, she was worried. I know that they are putting her under pressure upstairs."

"I'm going as quickly as I can Paige, I haven't slept for 36 hours."

Michael kept his voice calm, but Paige could sense that he was worried for Elizabeth too, "I know, I'm sorry I just let my emotions get the best of me sometimes."

"I realize that, but you need to understand that I'm doing everything I possibly can at the moment. The minute this is complete, you and Elizabeth will be the first to know."

He was starting to get impatient with her and wanted to be left alone to finish his work. "All right, thank you. I will leave you to it." Paige walked out of the room.

Taking the elevator to the second floor, Paige went looking for Jackie in her office, so she could report her findings on Elizabeth's emotions. She quickly walked towards the room, but froze before she got there, when she sensed a sickening feeling in the air. She looked around, and her eyes came in contact with Vance. He was beautiful, but in a fallen-angel sort of way. His muscular arms bulged against his long-sleeved, button-up shirts, and his tan skin glowed under the harsh fluorescent lights. He had dark brown eyes, cheek bones that alone could have gotten him a modeling career, and a chiseled jaw with the perfect amount of stubble covering it. On the inside, though, well, that was a completely different story.

The hairs on Paige's neck stood up, and her chest went cold. Vance had an overbearing amount of evil and nasty emotions that he sometimes didn't bother to hide from her. That time was now.

"Miss Paige, did you finally decide to come out from your room?" He stepped closer.

She looked down and nodded. He walked until he towered over her, stroked her hair, and tucked a strand behind her ear.

"What are you doing on the second floor?"

"I'm looking for Jackie." She barely managed to speak.

"Ahh, she's on the top floor, in the boardroom. I'm heading up there right now. I'll tell her you want to speak. Why don't you wait in her office until then?"

Without getting out of her personal space, he reached over her and opened Jackie's door. Paige stayed as still as possible, hoping he wouldn't touch her again. He was close enough for her to smell the expensive cologne he must have sprayed in the crook of his neck.

Firmly grabbing the nape of her neck, Vance coerced Paige into the room. Her skin seemed to burn where he touched her. Forcing her feet to move, she stepped inside the office, while Vance stood in the doorway. He held onto her neck, no longer pushing her, so she knew to stay in place. Then he gave her a tighter squeeze. It wasn't hard enough to hurt, but enough to tell her he was the one in power. Then he let go of her neck and slid his hands through her hair, all the way to the bottom of her spine. almost touching her backside. She managed to hold in her sigh of relief when his hand left her body.

"You're such a good girl, Paige," he whispered.

Knowing what he wanted, she continued looking forward. A minute passed, and she heard the door click shut. The noise made her jump, so that she turned towards it. Paige grabbed her chest, feeling her heartbeat thump at what felt like a mile a minute. Seeing Vance had left her alone, she let out a shaky breath and tried to calm herself.

Paige remembered the first time she met Vance. She was twelve at the time, and she went up to Jackie's office with Michael. When they knocked on her door, it wasn't Jackie that opened it, but Vance. Paige was shy, so she hid behind her brother, peeking her head out to get a look at the strange man. He looked at her so intensely she couldn't look away. Vance didn't even look at Michael.

From then on, Paige saw Vance more and more frequently. At first, he would ask her questions in passing, then he started seeking her out. By the time she turned fourteen, he began to invite her to his office, escorting her to the top floor. His presence made her uncomfortable, but something about him made it hard to say no. A couple of weeks after her fifteenth birthday, he touched her for the first time. He gave her a present, a necklace. For the rest of the year, he would touch her here and there. Simple touches. He would stroke her hair, rub her shoulders, or give her a hug.

Everything changed when she turned sixteen. Zola had recently joined the team and decided to throw Paige a sweet sixteen. She enjoyed herself, hanging out with Michael, Jackie, Josh, and Zola. There was cake, games, and a dance party. She went to bed feeling truly happy and was glad she didn't see Vance. Then midnight came along.

Woken from a deep sleep, Paige's mouth was covered by Vance's large, rough hands. She whimpered, unable to move as his body covered hers. Vance stole her innocence that night and had her many times after that. She left her room less and less, under the guise that her empathy powers were too much to handle. In reality, she felt ashamed.

Not wanting to think about Vance any longer, Paige decided to meditate and regather herself. She sat down in the chair across from Jackie's desk and crossed her legs. Lengthening her back, she relaxed her face, and pushed out all emotions and thoughts until her body and mind were in peace.

A couple hours passed by, and Jackie left an extremely intense meeting. She needed to come up with a solution to save Elizabeth, soon. Elizabeth could blow up at any time, and she knew Vance was ruthless and wouldn't hesitate to discard her. She made her way to her office and was surprised that Paige was still there, since Vance had told her about Paige a while ago.

She was meditating, just like Jackie had taught her when they first met ten years ago. They had a lot in common, since they both specialized in mental powers. Jackie walked over to her computer and sat down across from her. Paige was completely unaware of Jackie's presence and continued to stay still in her seat, calmly breathing.

"Paige." Jackie telepathically spoke to her. "I'm back, sweetheart."

Paige's eyes fluttered open, and she came back to reality.

"Did he hurt you?" Jackie asked in her head, since she knew there were cameras in her office.

"How can I help you?" Jackie asked out loud.

"Who?" Paige replied telepathically.

"I'm here to update you on Elizabeth," Paige said out loud for the video feed. She and Jackie often communicated this way when they wanted to discuss things in private.

"Vance."

"And how is Elizabeth doing?"

"Oh, no, he just... he creeps me out."

Jackie tried to get more out of Paige by digging through her mind, but Paige had a knack for hiding things. During Paige's second year at DUST, Jackie found a memory of Paige going up to Vance's office. Nothing happened, they just talked, but Jackie knew she was uncomfortable by her thoughts in the memory. When she confronted Paige, asking her if Vance was hurting her in any way, Paige became defensive. Paige seemed upset by the question, and told her nothing was happening. Knowing she lied, Jackie kept pressing the issue until Paige actually yelled at her. Paige refused to speak to her for a week after that.

Since then, Paige's mind became more and more guarded. Now, Jackie could only see and hear whatever Paige wanted her to. Jackie also tried to dig around in Vance's mind, but every time she tried she hit a wall. He had a shield around his mind. She didn't know how it was possible for him to block her from reading him, she knew he had no powers.

"She is doing great. She's responding well to her therapy."

He had always been a weird guy, and seemed to prey on Paige every chance he got. "We need to do something about him."

"I'm glad to hear that."

"What do you mean?" Paige nodded and smiled.

"We need to get rid of him, Paige."

Paige looked up at her and thought Jackie was talking about assassinating him.

"No, not that," Jackie reassured her. "Although that's not completely off the table. We need to get dirt on him. I know he's a scummy person. He has all of us here against our will. He's been doing this since before I've been here. A person who does something like this isn't a good person."

"Can't you get in his head and dig around?"

"I wish it were that simple. He still has some sort of device that protects him from such a thing." Paige knew he did, but she still wished Jackie would try harder. At the same time, she was terrified that she would.

"Well, then, where do we even start?"

"I don't know yet. I think that Elizabeth could help us, though."

"How?"

"It doesn't matter yet because she wouldn't help us anyway. At least, not yet. First, we need to gain her trust."

Jackie wondered how they would get her to that point, and how long it would take to get her to trust them. "How was she when you saw her?"

Paige blinked. "She's strong. It was so difficult to feel her emotions, she suppressed them. And when I finally found them, I calmed them, but only for about ten minutes."

"Geez," Jackie shook her head. "She's a bomb. Do you know when Michael will be done with his headphone device?"

"He said at least two weeks."

"Then you're going to need to stay strong, because she needs you. We need to keep her calm until we can come up with something more permanent."

"Of course. May I say something?"

"Yeah, go for it."

"I don't think having her isolated in that cell is going to help, I think it's making her worse."

Jackie tapped a pen on the desk while she zoned out to think of a solution. After a few seconds, she perked up and excitedly looked into Paige's gray eyes.

"You're right. She will stay with you!"

"With me?" Paige stiffened in her seat.

"Yes, your room locks from the inside and outside. Only you, I, and some of the staff have a key. I will have the staff bring another bed in there, and you will watch her twenty-four seven."

Paige let out a loud sigh. She'd never been great with roommates.

"Paige, this will be good for the both of you. You will have practice controlling your powers, and she won't be so anxious."

"Okay, but just until the device is finished."

"Okay, well, if there isn't anything else, you may take your leave. Keep up the great work, Paige."

And with that, Paige exited the office.

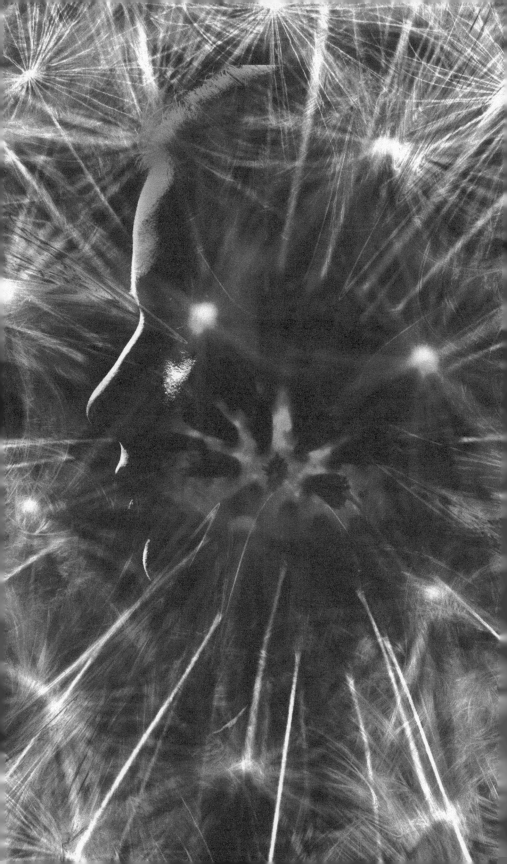

Chapter 17

Paige walked down the middle school hallways with her head hanging low. She could feel everything: the sadness, insecurities, and embarrassment of her fellow preteen classmates. Most of them just started puberty, and it was a whirlwind of emotions.

Paige stopped at her locker to grab her books. A powerful aura stopped by her side. She took a deep breath and turned her head to see a small girl with messy hair. The girl reached into her locker, exposing her forearm. Paige gasped when she saw bruises covering her wrist. The girl looked up, noticing her stare.

"What are you looking at, pig face?" she snarled, then slammed her locker.

Paige was too overwhelmed by the hurt the girl was feeling to be offended. Her stomach turned, and bile rose up her throat. Without bothering to close her locker, she ran to the closest bathroom and emptied her stomach. Sweat dripped down her face, and she shook.

She was startled by the school bell ringing, but still too nauseated to move. A few minutes passed, and she realized there was no way she could sit through class like this. She ran out of the bathroom and down the halls until she reached the doors leading outside.

She continued to run, trying to escape the hundreds of emotions she felt. However, every time she escaped one, she came in contact with another as she passed people's houses.

She finally made it to her house and slammed the door shut. No one was home, and she finally felt peace. The damage had already been done, though. Her head felt like it was going to explode into a thousand pieces. She couldn't take this for another second.

Paige's mother walked into the house. "Paige? Are you here? The school called and said you ran out." She waited, but there was no answer.

"Paige," she called out again. She walked up the stairs to Paige's room, but Paige was not there. Her mother then walked down the hall and saw the bathroom door was closed and that the lights were on.

"Paige." She knocked on the door. "Are you all right, sweetheart?"

She still didn't answer.

"Paige, I'm coming in."

Her mom twisted the knob, but it was locked.

"Paige, don't make me walk downstairs and get a key."

She sighed and went downstairs for the key. She searched through a drawer in the entryway and found the little key which they'd labeled "upstairs bathroom."

She walked back up the stairs and placed the key in the lock below the doorknob. She twisted the key and pushed the door open. Everything felt like it was in slow motion. Red water covered the tiled floor.

Paige's mother shrieked in horror as she saw her daughter's seemingly lifeless body lying in the bathtub's bloody water.

After being rushed to the hospital, Paige was in a coma for several days, but the doctors were able to save her. Her parents decided to have her admitted into a psychiatric hospital, in hopes they could help her with the intense depression. Doctors would not be able to help her, though. This was beyond their knowledge.

The hospital was worse than school. Paige felt everyone's depression, anxiety, and fear. She refused to leave her room, no matter how many times the staff asked her to.

Michael visited her every day, after school and on the weekends. He spent as much time as allowed in her little room. He desperately wanted to know what was going on with her.

One Saturday morning, he brought her bagels and orange juice. A couple weeks had passed since she attempted suicide, and the psychiatrist was still at a loss at the cause of her pain. At first, they thought she had schizophrenia, but she didn't hear voices or see things that weren't there. Then it was a bipolar disorder, but they ruled that one out as well.

Michael walked to his sister's room and noticed her doctor standing outside the door, fiddling with her notes. He walked closer, and the doctor finally noticed him.

"Oh! Good morning, Michael."

"Good morning. Why are you here so early on a Saturday?"

"Your sister has a visitor, and I'm just here to make sure everything is okay."

"A visitor? Who?"

"One of my nurses informed me of a psychoanalyst specializing in emotional management. I thought it could be helpful... nothing else has been helping," she muttered.

"Why wasn't I informed of this? I would have liked to do a background search on them."

"We asked your parents. You're only fifteen..."

Michael cut her off and rushed to open the door. The doctor tried to stop him, but he was too determined. Nobody was as protective of Paige as him.

He was surprised to see Paige and a woman with dark brown hair sitting on her bed. They weren't speaking, and their eyes were closed. It seemed like they were meditating. The woman turned her head and looked at him through kind brown eyes.

"Open your eyes sweetheart," she said to Paige, her voice soothing. "There's someone here to see you."

Paige opened her eyes. Excited, she jumped over to Michael, leaping into his arms.

"Good morning, Paige," he said as he wrapped his arms around her.

"I smell something good." She smirked up at him.

"Do you? Could it possibly be the bagels I brought?"

Squealing, she snatched the bag from his hand. She opened it and pulled out her favorite, an everything bagel.

"There's also orange juice in there. Enjoy your breakfast while I have a word with your guest outside." He looked at the stranger.

The lady nodded and walked gracefully towards the door. She opened it and held it while Michael followed. The doctor was still standing there, looking embarrassed.

"Hello, Dr. Fray."

"Hi. I'm sorry, I tried..."

"No worries," the woman cut her off. "I'm glad Paige has such a wonderful brother."

"How'd you know I'm her brother?"

"Let's take a walk," she commanded.

Michael followed her. The clicking of her heels filled the silent hallway. Nothing was said until they were far enough away for nobody to hear them. Stopping, the woman turned to him.

"My name is Jackie, and I already know your name. Michael."

"Hi, Jackie, what are your credentials?"

She no longer had a kind smile, but now looked serious. Michael liked this much more; the look before seemed forced.

"I am the only one who can help your sister. I am the only one who knows what she's going through."

"Oh, yeah? And what is it that she's going through?"

She looked as if she was trying to reach his soul as she intently stared into his eyes. There was silence for an uncomfortable amount of time.

"I don't think you'd understand."

"I understand everything."

"You don't understand emotions. You may be an academic genius, but you aren't an interpersonal one."

"You just met me."

"I've known people like you my whole life."

How did this woman know anything about him? He never had been great at expression, but when it came to his sister, he would do anything for her.

"I can see that you want the best for your sister. So, trust me, Michael. I can help her."

"I don't trust you. You think I don't understand people, but I have a weird feeling about you."

Turning back the way they came; he left her there and headed to his sister's room.

Chapter 18

Paige and Michael were sitting outside in the psychiatric hospital's garden, appreciating the Christmas lights streaming in the trees. They were enjoying the tranquil sounds of chick-a-dees and the refreshing, crisp air.

Paige had been seeing Jackie a few times a week for a month and was doing much better. Finally, she was leaving her room, giving everyone hope. Michael was excited to see her returning to her happier self, although she never was truly happy. He knew she wasn't a cheery person, but he just thought it was a personality trait.

"So, Christmas is tomorrow. Are you excited? Mom, Dad, and I are coming here for the day."

"I don't get to spend Christmas at home?" She looked up at him with furrowed brows.

"Unfortunately not, but we will have so much fun with you here." He smiled, trying to make it seem not so bad. Truthfully, however, he did ask his parents to let her come home for the day, but they didn't think it would be safe. He wholeheartedly disagreed; he would have kept an eye on her, but it wasn't up to him in the end.

"Hmm," Paige hummed, with an indistinguishable tone. She seemed deep in thought.

"So, Jackie seems to be helping you."

"Yeah! She's awesome! I really like her. I feel at peace around her, kind of like I do with you! Except she's teaching me how to feel that way around other people."

"I guess I misjudged her."

"You have a bad habit of not trusting people."

"And you have a bad habit of being too mature for a twelve-year-old." He roughed up her hair.

"Hey." She swatted him.

"All right, all right! We should probably get you inside before they force us back in. It's almost time for your bedtime!"

Paige grumbled, but went inside anyway.

The next day, Michael and his parents showed up during mid-morning, and were surprised to see Jackie already there, doing Paige's hair with festive red ribbons. Paige was wearing an adorable, long-sleeved red dress and ankle booties with black tights. The dark colors wonderfully contrasted with her fair skin and silvery blonde hair. Jackie did her hair with two half-up space buns, symmetrically placed on both sides of her middle part, with ribbons wrapped around them and tied in cute bows.

"Mom, Dad." Paige gleamed, running towards them for a hug.

"Merry Christmas, sweetheart." They kissed her forehead.

"What do you think of my hair?"

"It looks adorable. You look lovely," their mother complimented. "You did a wonderful job, Jackie."

"Thank you. I'm glad you like it." Jackie smiled. "I just came by to drop off this Christmas present and keep her company until you all arrived." She handed Paige a red gift bag.

"May I open it now?" Paige asked.

"I would love that. I also got presents for the rest of your family." She passed Michael and their parents small boxes wrapped in green paper.

Paige excitedly took the tissue paper out of the bag and pulled out a book and a small box similar to her family's gifts. They all unwrapped their presents, finding boxes of festively decorated chocolates.

"Oh, Jackie, they look delicious! Thank you!"

Jackie put on a smile, but Michael thought it looked forced. "I'm glad you like them. I will be on my way, then; I don't want to intrude on family time." She bowed her head and gracefully showed herself out.

"Jackie is concerned," Paige blurted.

"Nonsense, honey, she seemed perfectly fine," her mother replied.

Paige was still suspicious, and Michael trusted her instincts.

They filled the day with singing and dancing along to Christmas music, and later they decorated cookies. They finished by watching a couple Christmas movies on a television the hospital lent to them. Paige fell asleep, curled between her father and mother.

"I guess we'd better let her sleep," her father whispered. Both parents kissed her on the top of her head and tucked her in.

"May I stay with her?" Michael pleaded.

Their parents looked at each other as if each were trying to read the other's mind. "I don't see why not," they replied.

"Yay!" he quietly exclaimed.

"Sure, sweetheart." His mother kissed him on the forehead. "I'll be here in the morning to pick you up."

Michael asked a nurse for a spare blanket and pillow, then curled up on the couch by the wall next to his sister's bed. Even though the couch was comfortable, he couldn't sleep. Ever since his sister attempted to end her life, he had a difficult time sleeping. He'd stay up thinking of ways to help her and researching. He'd read multiple books on depression and suicide and written down several ideas. He gave them to Paige's doctor to try, but nothing worked.

Jackie was the only person who made progress with his sister, but the woman was unwilling to give away her secret. That made Michael not trust her; the doctors had been open with him about everything.

Hours passed, and Michael was still unable to relax, as his mind kept working for an answer to cure his sister. He looked at the alarm clock next to Paige's bed and confirmed it was midnight. Sighing, he felt frustrated with his overly active mind.

He snapped his eyes to the door when he heard the lock click open. Someone twisted the handle, trying to not wake them. Michael closed his eyes when a dim light beamed through. He heard the stomping of three pairs of heavy shoes, and the clicking of one pair of familiar heels.

They crept closer to Paige's bed, making her stir. Before she could wake, Jackie took out a syringe with pink liquid and pierced it into her neck. Michael heard Paige squeak, and, not a moment later, he sat up. He was about to shout for help, but the gun pointed at his face made him think that was unwise. He gulped, and his throat felt like sandpaper.

"You're not supposed to be here."

Michael looked up to see her positioned next to the gunmen. Her arms were crossed; she looked annoyed and a little concerned.

"I knew you were acting suspicious," he snarled.

"What should we do, boss?" the gunmen asked.

One of the men picked up Paige and was holding her as if she was delicate as a baby. A woman kept guard outside the door. Jackie just looked at Michael.

"You'd do anything to save your sister, wouldn't you, Michael?" she asked sweetly.

"I would."

"I can save her, but not here."

"Where, then? What about our parents?"

"You need to trust me. There's so much about this world that no one knows about."

"How can I trust you if you don't answer any of my questions?"

She walked closer to him, then sat gracefully on the couch. "Give me your hand."

He hesitated when he reached for her palm, but once he placed his hand into hers, it felt like electricity shot through his veins. He saw things, memories that weren't his own. A boy running so fast that he looked like a flash of light, a girl that could float, and more supposedly impossible things.

Jackie let go of Michael's hand. "What just happened?" He was in shock.

"I showed you some of my memories. I have the power of telepathy; it's how I've been able to help Paige. My time here is running out. In order for me to continue helping her, she has to come home with me, to the headquarters of where I work."

Michael just stared forward, unable to speak or move.

"Joe, put the gun away. He's coming with us."

"But, ma'am, Vance said only the girl."

"I don't care what that sad excuse of a human has to say. He's an idiot." She glared at him.

"Yes ma'am."

He backed away and slid the gun into a satchel.

"Come on, sweetheart."

Michael followed her and the three guards out the door and into a new life. He wasn't sure why, but he suddenly trusted Jackie with his life. Maybe it was because she let him in her head and shared her deepest secrets. The future would tell.

Chapter 19

Paige nervously walked to Elizabeth's cell. She looked through the transparent wall and saw Elizabeth sitting at the edge of the twin bed with her head in her hands. Anxiety and a feeling of defeat rolled off her, sending chills down Paige's spine.

"Don't even think about it," Elizabeth spoke up, then looked up at her. "These emotions are mine, and I want to feel them."

Paige gulped. "Are you sure? I can make you feel better."

"I don't want to feel better."

Paige nodded, then walked over to the door. Taking a deep breath, she pulled out the key card and swiped the lock. The door automatically opened, and Elizabeth curiously looked at her.

"Follow me," Paige ordered.

Elizabeth scrunched her eyebrows and stood. Her hair was slightly greasy from not showering for a few days, but her green eyes beautifully contrasted against her pale skin. She followed Paige through the white hallways and up a quiet stairway, then through the heavy metal door to the common living area. Instead of leading Elizabeth to her old room, Paige stopped in front of a different door. After taking a deep breath, she opened it and motioned for Elizabeth to walk inside.

Elizabeth did so, emanating curiosity. In the room were two queen beds; one with a flowery comforter and one that matched the bedding in Elizabeth's room. The walls were covered in art, and there were no windows. While Elizabeth was distracted, Paige closed and locked the door.

"So, you are going to be staying with me until Michael finishes his contraption."

"Am I allowed to leave and walk around?"

"Only if I'm with you."

Elizabeth scoffed, "So, you're my babysitter?"

Paige sensed her annoyance. "Well, I'm not too happy about it either." She rolled her eyes, "Go take a shower. You look like you need it."

Elizabeth didn't argue with her. She walked towards the bathroom and left the door open a crack to let the steam out.

While she was in the shower, Paige lay on her bed, thinking about how she was going to survive this undetermined amount of time with another person. She felt bad for not being more welcoming towards Elizabeth, but this whole thing was just sprung on her, giving her no time to emotionally prepare. She wrung her hands frustratedly through her hair and scrunched her eyes. Then her thoughts travelled to how easy it was to get lost in Elizabeth's tired, beautiful green eyes, and how her expressions danced on her smooth skin. Her soft hair made Paige want to twist it around her fingers, and—

A cough interrupted Paige's thoughts, and she sprung up to see Elizabeth in a towel. Her hair was sopping wet and dripping onto the floor. Paige admired her damp skin, glistening under the lights.

"I kind of need clothes."

"Oh, right, they brought your clothes here. Your dresser is next to your bed, and your side of the closet is on the right," Paige replied.

"Sweet." She walked to her dresser and pulled out a sweatshirt and some black sweatpants. She let her towel fall to the ground, and Paige gasped, flipping her head the other way. She felt heat rushing to her cheeks.

"You're not shy at all, huh," she nervously remarked.

Elizabeth turned her head to see Paige's profile and her obviously flushed cheeks. "Oh sorry, next time I'll change in the closet." Paige knew she was sincere.

"Or just a warning next time would be nice."

"You got it." Elizabeth winked. She seemed to be in a better mood as she pulled on her clothes. "So, what do we do now? Can I go see Jen?"

"I was hoping we could meditate. I haven't been able to today."

"How about you do that, and I'll go hang with Jen."

"That's not possible. Until you have better control of yourself, you can't leave my side."

Suddenly, the aura surrounding Elizabeth darkened. "Oh? Are you the only one strong enough to control me?" Elizabeth slowly stalked towards Paige, but there was a playful glint in her eye. Paige's face turned bright red. She felt both shocked and intrigued by the change in mannerisms.

"Are you scared of me? You could let me out of this room, and I'll no longer be a problem." Elizabeth sauntered closer, until she was standing over Paige's sitting form. She grabbed a handful of Paige's hair and pulled it until she looked straight up at her. Using her other hand, Elizabeth grabbed her cheeks and squished them together, so her pink lips pouted out.

Paige started breathing quickly; she wasn't scared, but heat slid down her body that she'd never felt before. If Vance did this to her, she'd have a different reaction, but Elizabeth was just being playful. She didn't anticipate the boldness Elizabeth was capable of. She could make Elizabeth feel anything she wanted, including extreme exhaustion, making her completely defenseless. With little resistance, Paige reached up to the hand holding her mouth hostage and gently pulled it away.

"You may not leave without me by your side, and no, I'm not scared of you." Elizabeth scoffed and walked away. "Fine, but I won't meditate."

"Suit yourself. I think it could be helpful, though."

Elizabeth rolled her eyes and lay down in her bed. She rolled on her side, facing away from Paige's observant stare. Paige crossed her legs and straightened her spine, preparing herself for meditation. She focused on her breathing for a while, until her thoughts drifted to Elizabeth. She could sense that Elizabeth was anxious and afraid, but she was trying to mask those feelings with anger. Paige didn't blame her; it was less painful to be angry than it was to feel afraid. How was she supposed to keep Elizabeth from getting into trouble for the next two weeks? Paige was barely able to control her own demons. It seemed impossible for her to help someone as out of control as the woman now sharing her room. It didn't help that Elizabeth thought of her as the enemy. Maybe she wouldn't if she knew her life was at stake and that their goal was to keep her alive. Would she believe it, though?

Paige remembered when she first arrived at DUST. She could still recall the betrayal she felt from Jackie, a woman she trusted. She didn't leave her room for weeks. Michael brought her meals, which she barely ate. She lost weight to the point where Michael begged her to eat, with tears in his eyes and a desperation she'd never felt before. Paige ate for the sake of her brother, but the unending emptiness bore through her soul.

Jackie didn't visit her for the first month, which only made things worse for her. Jackie said she had an important mission, which, unfortunately, took way longer than she thought it would.

Jackie also revealed all the horrific details of Paige's departure from the outside world. Her parents thought she had tried to run away, along with Michael. When no one could find them, they were presumed dead. Paige screamed at Jackie, not understanding how she could do this to people who put their trust in her. Jackie bowed her head, but gave no indication of emotions. She explained that it would take time for Paige to understand her actions. She said she understood that what she did was evil, but it was the best plan she could come up with. If Jackie hadn't taken her Paige would have died.

Now that many years had passed, Paige understood Jackie. She had come to the conclusion that Jackie did not waste anything or anyone. She didn't kill or abduct without reason. And most importantly, Jackie had little control over her actions, for her life belonged to an unknown branch of the government. In actuality, she was only able to save the people forced to be there by manipulating the higher-ups. She would do whatever it took to save them, even if that meant she had to hurt the ones she saved.

Chapter 20

Still meditating, Paige tried to ignore Elizabeth's stubbornness. She knew meditating would be helpful, but Elizabeth wouldn't listen. Elizabeth wanted to hold onto some control, Paige understood that. However, lying around getting lost in one's thoughts wasn't healthy. With meditation, she could learn to center herself, to silence her mind.

"I know how you feel." Paige interrupted the silence.

"Well, that was a short meditation session," Elizabeth grumbled, even though Paige knew she hadn't really been trying.

"I gave up. It's impossible to concentrate right now."

Elizabeth turned to her other side to face Paige, her hair falling like a waterfall over her shoulders. She looked into Paige's eyes with curiosity. "How could you possibly know how I feel? You seem to be right at home here." Elizabeth flushed. "Aside from being an empath, obviously." She rolled her eyes. "You know what? Never mind."

"It didn't start that way. I was kidnapped from a psychiatric institution."

Elizabeth used her left arm to raise herself. She raised her eyebrows. "May I ask why you were there?"

"I tried to kill myself."

Elizabeth gasped.

"I had no control over my power. It was too much. My mom found me, and then I was committed." Paige looked down at her hands. She felt guilty for putting her family through that.

"How did Jackie find you?"

"She had a contact in the hospital. After weeks of nobody being able to help me, Jackie showed up. Since she has similar abilities, she knew how to help me. During the middle of the night on Christmas, she had me drugged and kidnapped. My brother came with her willingly."

"Were you mad at your brother?"

"No, I was too upset with Jackie to be mad at him. The only reason he came was because he didn't want me to be alone. Plus, they would have had to kill him."

Elizabeth's eyebrows raised. "Wow." She searched Paige's face. "I don't understand… why are you doing what she wants? How could you forgive her?" Paige could feel Elizabeth's judgment.

"I had no choice. I later found out Jackie had no choice either. She belongs to the government. She's the only reason why we are still alive."

"I don't understand."

"Of course you don't. You will, though. It takes time."

Elizabeth scoffed at that.

"I know it sucks that we don't have the freedom to come and go as we please, but it could be so much worse for us. The government is afraid of people like us, so if it weren't for Jackie, we'd be killed on the spot. Here we are fed, clothed, and given resources to help us control our powers. Jackie's goal is for us to have freedom someday, but we have to prove ourselves first. We can't do that, though, if you spiral out of control."

Elizabeth bit the insides of her cheeks. "Maybe you're not my enemy, but Jackie sure is. She may have some of the people here brainwashed, but I'm not falling for it. If Jackie really is our savior like you seem to think, why did she have us kidnapped instead of approaching us peacefully? And what's with all the secrets?"

"I know it's hard to believe,' Paige interrupted her, "but one day you will understand."

"I'm in control. I'm ready to understand now."

"Oh, are you? What would you have done if you killed that man? Do you know what murder does to a person?"

The chemistry surrounding them changed. Elizabeth's face blazed with fury as she slid from her bed and approached until her face was inches away from Paige's. "He would have deserved it," she huffed. Her minty breath wafted up Paige's nostrils.

"That just proves you're not in control."

At that point, Elizabeth lost it. She grabbed a lamp on a nightstand and threw it at a wall, while making animalistic noises. It seemed like one second she was fine, and the next she would turn into a different person. Paige took note of this observation.

"I'm in control, who are you to tell me I'm not!" She continued throwing random objects until Paige pulled her anger from her and pushed exhaustion in.

Elizabeth stopped in an instant and fell to her knees, looking like the life was just pulled from her. "What did you do to me?" she said, in a raspy voice.

"I need you to calm down. If Vance catches you in a break down... He might hurt you."

Elizabeth's breathing slowed, and she slowly slumped to her side on the carpet. Her eyes slowly closed. "I'm sorry, Elizabeth." Paige placed a soft pillow under her head, and then encased her body under a warm blanket.

Chapter 21

Elizabeth tried to fight off the sleep, but her efforts were futile. Sleep was no escape. Within her rest, she witnessed the darkest parts of society. Even safely enclosed in the comforter tucked around her body and with her head placed on the lush pillow, she would never be comfortable. Not while she had to watch innocent people being tortured.

Elizabeth felt herself shift out of her own mind. She opened her eyes to find Daisy staring back at her through an old mirror. Now her eyes held intense hopelessness and despair. She looked like she hadn't eaten in days, and her face and neck were covered in bruises.

"Daisy?" Elizabeth thought. "What happened to you?"

Although she kept an eerily straight face, tears dripped down Daisy's pale cheeks.

"Can you hear me, Daisy?" she thought again.

There was a knock at the door, and then she heard a creaking sound as it opened.

"You have been summoned, child," said a male voice.

Daisy turned towards the voice, but the man's face couldn't be seen, because he had a black hood covering his face. He slowly turned in the opposite direction and walked, Daisy following behind him.

"Don't go, Daisy." Elizabeth had a bad feeling.

Daisy kept following him, though, until they came to two tall double doors. The man pushed open the doors, which creaked loudly and echoed off the walls, then stepped aside to let Daisy pass.

She looked around the candlelit room and saw Priscilla, surrounded by five young men with black hoods. Priscilla had a wicked smirk on her face, contradicting the more motherly tone she set the last time Elizabeth had seen her. Her hair curled around her head, looking like wildfire.

Daisy stopped in her tracks, frozen in terror. Elizabeth sensed something wasn't right. She hoped to will Daisy into running out of the room, but she stayed in place. The five men lifted their heads, revealing their sickening faces. They all had scruffy beards and piercing eyes. They looked at Daisy like she was a sacrificial lamb.

"Step forward, child," Priscilla creepily whispered. "It's time for you to become initiated."

Daisy nodded her head and looked to her feet, which refused to move her from her spot. Priscilla tsked and motioned for two of the men to grab her. The two closest to her briskly walked towards her and grabbed both arms. They dragged her until she was right in front of Priscilla, then threw her to her knees. Daisy shook in fear, and tears threatened to escape her eyes. She continued to look down, too afraid to look anyone in the eyes.

She heard noises behind her; it sounded like chains and chairs being moved around. Her anxiety increased until her heart felt like it was going to jump from her chest. Sweat trickled down her temples and her spine. This was the moment she would die, she thought; they were preparing to sacrifice her.

"Look up child," she heard Priscilla order.

She slowly lifted her head, then, reluctantly, her eyes. Priscilla stood and walked to her. She lifted Daisy's chin with two of her fingers and gave her a sickening smile.

"How old are you?"

"Sixteen," Daisy managed to choke out.

"What a wonderful age to be."

Daisy obediently nodded. Priscilla circled her, inspecting her like she was a prize. She stroked Daisy's hair, then inspected her face.

"You poor thing. Your father was a naughty man. It's too bad you'll have to pay for his sins."

Daisy began to tremble. "What do you mean? I don't know how to do that."

Priscilla chuckled lightly and stroked her cheek, in an almost loving manner. "Don't worry, my dear. You will." She then left, and her steps became increasingly quiet until it was silent. Daisy stayed kneeling on the ground, hearing only the sound of her own breath.

It felt like forever had passed, but then she heard someone walking up behind her. Large hands grabbed her hair, pulling it back until her entire neck was exposed. She expected a knife to slit her throat, but was surprised when hot, wet lips pressed below her ear. She flinched away from the strange intrusion, earning herself a sharp tug on her scalp.

Two sets of hands then grabbed her wrists and dragged her backwards, ignoring her pleas for mercy. They carried her over to a small table in the middle of the room and encased her wrists in cuffs connected to chains bolted to the ground.

"Please." Tears streamed down her face. "Please let me go."

Elizabeth knew what was about to happen. She couldn't let Daisy go through this.

Elizabeth had done so once before, so she knew she could take over Daisy's body. She had to encase her psyche in the far back of her mind, so she wouldn't feel or experience any of the horror that was about to happen.

"It's okay, Daisy," Elizabeth whispered in her head. "I will protect you. You won't feel a thing. I promise."

Her emotions were so intense that it was easy to complete her task. She was then Daisy, and Daisy was asleep. Tears flowed from her eyes as she focused on keeping Daisy tucked away. She felt all the pain for her, and took all the emotional trauma. She laid there for what felt like forever.

Until the men undid her chains, and they walked away.

Elizabeth shot up from the makeshift bed that Paige had made for her on the floor. Her loud pants awoke Paige.

"Elizabeth! What's wrong?"

"We have to stop them. We have to save her," Elizabeth muttered.

Chapter 22

"Help who? What did you see?" Paige asked.

"Her name is Daisy. She needs our help," Elizabeth said, still panting.

"Okay, you are making no sense. Slow down. Tell me what happened."

Elizabeth opened her mouth to speak, but her throat was dry and painful. "Water," she choked.

"Okay, I'll be right back."

When Paige walked out, Elizabeth stood on shaky legs. Black spots clouded her vision, but she continued to make her way to the door. She shook the handle but found it locked. Sliding to the floor, she curled her legs up to her chest and sobbed out all the emotions she had been holding in. What she had experienced was horrid; she knew humans were evil, but this was a whole new level of disgusting.

Paige came back after a couple minutes, with a glass of water, to find Elizabeth in her pitiful state. Paige rushed to her and urged her to sit up and drink some water.

"There," she cooed. "It's going to be okay."

Paige stroked her hair and brought the glass to her lips. Elizabeth gulped down water to quench her thirst. When she had enough, she told Paige everything. She told her about the plane being taken over, witnessing a murder, and the kidnapping of the passengers. She told her about Daisy, and Priscilla, and how Priscilla ordered five men to rape the girl.

"I felt everything she felt. Saw everything she saw. She looks so broken. Her face was covered in bruises. We have to save her before it happens again."

Paige looked into Elizabeth's sad eyes. She felt everything as well, Elizabeth knew. It was overbearing. She knew then Paige was about to take it away.

"Don't take it away," Elizabeth pleaded. "I don't deserve it. I need to feel what she feels."

"Why would you deserve to feel pain?" Paige asked.

How could Elizabeth explain it to her? She felt guilty for not being there. Feeling scared and traumatized from the abuse Daisy endured made her feel less guilty. "I feel more connected to Daisy. You have to let me keep the emotions. It should be up to me, after all."

"Okay. I'll let you keep the emotions. But we need to tell Jackie."

"Will she care?"

Nodding, Paige reached for her pager. She messaged Jackie, asking her to come to their room. While they waited, Paige stroked soothing circles around Elizabeth's back. At this point, Elizabeth was staring into space, with tears streaming down her heated face. They sat in silence until there was an urgent knock on the door.

"Come in!"

Jackie walked in, without an ounce of emotion on her face. She approached them cautiously, and Elizabeth watched her every move.

"What happened? What have you seen?" Jackie asked as she knelt before her.

"It was Daisy." Elizabeth's voice shook. "We need to get her out now."

Jackie reached her hands towards Elizabeth, but she flinched backwards. "I just want to get into your head. It's easier if I touch you. Is that okay?"

She took a deep breath and nodded, allowing Jackie to take hold of her hands. Paige watched as Jackie searched through Elizabeth's memories. Elizabeth knew Paige had kept her word and let the feelings stay, because Elizabeth was afraid, hurt, and angry. She held onto the anger the most; it was her driving emotion.

"Pay for her father's sins? What did Chatawick do?" Jackie seemed to ask herself, then to Elizabeth, "Is this the first time you've seen something like this?"

"I've witnessed rape and abuse before, but nothing that violent." Elizabeth's lips quivered, and her tears flowed more harshly.

Paige looked at her with wide eyes and put her arms around her. "I'm so sorry. No wonder you got so upset at the bar."

Elizabeth looked at her. "I'm always so helpless. I can't help them. When I had a chance to help Zola and get revenge for her, I took the opportunity."

"We can help you increase your abilities. We can make you stronger," Jackie interrupted.

"That's not important right now. What we need to do is help Daisy."

"We can do that too. Did you find out where she is?"

"No. She has no clue where they are. Just that they are in a cave."

"We can't help her if we don't know where she is." Jackie spoke calmly.

"You don't think I know that! You don't think I know I'm useless!"

"Okay, it's okay." Paige rubbed Elizabeth's arms. "You are not useless. You can figure out where she is. I have faith in you."

"How? How can I figure it out? I've only been able to control this power once in my entire life."

Elizabeth bowed her head. She looked defeated.

"You can start by not moping," said Jackie.

"Jackie!"

"I'm serious, Paige. Coddling her isn't going to be helpful." She looked at Elizabeth. "You want to be strong and change things? Then work hard. Focus. Sitting around will change nothing. You can either sit on the floor and cry, or you can stand up and fight."

Elizabeth gulped. Her cheeks were wet. She took her hand from Jackie's and wiped her face off. "You're right." She stood and held out her hand to help Paige from the floor, and Jackie also stood. "I just don't know where to start."

"All of us have had to work on ourselves. While we don't have the exact answers, we have the tools to find those answers. Paige can help you, along with the rest of the team. When I leave here, brief them on the situation. I'll trust you to handle it."

Paige and Elizabeth nodded.

"Great. I will work on getting the supplies we need. I'll also need approval from the board, but first, you all need to prove that you can work together. They don't trust you yet, so show them they can." She turned from them and walked to the door. Before she left the room, she turned back to the two young women. "Good luck. I believe in you." She gave them a soft smile and left.

After Elizabeth was sure Jackie was far enough away, she turned to Paige. "Does this mean I can leave this room?"

"Yes, but behave yourself." Paige wiggled her eyebrows.

Elizabeth sniffled. Her eyes still burned. She then wrapped her arms around Paige. "Thank you for believing in me."

Paige returned the hug and placed her nose in the crook of her neck. "You're welcome," she whispered.

Chapter 23

Jennifer wrapped her arms tightly around Elizabeth, and she returned the hug. It had been too long.

"Don't leave me like that again."

"I'm sorry, I mean, you bash a guy's head in once, and people are suddenly afraid of you."

Jennifer laughed. "I'm glad you're so casual about it."

Feeling a tap on her shoulder, Elizabeth turned her head to see a glowing Zola staring happily into her eyes. Elizabeth let go of Jennifer and jumped to Zola. Zola froze at first, but then returned the hug even harder.

"Are you okay?" Elizabeth asked Zola.

"I guess; I have no choice. I have to be okay, or he wins."

Elizabeth squeezed her tighter. "I won't let anyone hurt you again. None of us will," she whispered.

"Thank you for what you did. I know Jackie was angry, or upset, or whatever, but after I heard what you did, I.... I have never felt so loved." Her eyes glistened.

"Of course. I know we haven't known each other for long, but I will always protect you."

Jennifer grabbed Elizabeth's shoulder. "So, what have you been doing? Why did Jackie let you out?"

Elizabeth released Zola and turned to the group. Josh, Michael, and Paige were also there. Josh stood like a soldier ready for battle, while Michael and Paige seemed worried. Paige had been hounding Michael to get a dream-traveller-proof device working, as they weren't sure having her roam free was the best idea.

"I've mostly been in isolation, but, for the past few days, I've been staying with Paige. I'll be staying with her until my power is under control."

"What? Why? You have always done just fine," Jennifer complained.

"I know, but I don't have much of a choice." Elizabeth's voice quieted. She didn't want to admit it, but she was close to losing control. She didn't want to accidentally hurt Jennifer or the others. "I will regain my freedom completely once I have a better grasp on things. Until then, Paige will make sure I don't do anything crazy."

Paige's cheeks burned in embarrassment as all eyes went to her.

"We haven't met," Jennifer said suspiciously.

"I'm Paige. Sorry I never greeted you. I rarely leave my room." She looked down at her feet.

Before Jennifer could harass Paige more, Elizabeth interrupted her. "The reason why I'm here speaking to you all today is that I need your help. There is a girl named Daisy who has been kidnapped by a terrorist group, and we need to save her. The terrorist's leader is a woman named Priscilla, and she is a psychopath, I assume. She also has Daisy's little sister, Sofie, trapped with her."

"What do you want us to do?" Josh asked.

"The first step is that I need to gain better control over my abilities. I need to infiltrate Priscilla's mind so I can find where they are. I would like to use you guys as my guinea pigs. If I can practice reading your memories, maybe I can latch onto others. Once I have their location, I'll tell Jackie. I've been in contact with Daisy a few times, so she can help us a little bit."

"You can start with my mind."

"Great, thank you, Josh. Michael, you can work on the device designed to help me sleep. Everyone else should work on training with Jen."

Everyone nodded in agreement and went their separate ways.

"You really took charge there," Josh said, when only the two of them were left.

"I know firsthand what happens in that terrorist cult, so I kind of have to be the one to give instructions. But feel free to give ideas. This isn't a dictatorship."

"Will do. Anyways, how shall we go about you digging into my head?"

"Okay, so I'm going to go into Paige's room while you hide. I don't want to know where you are, because it'll be more of a challenge for my consciousness to find you."

He nodded.

"Just so you are aware, I might see things you don't want me to see, are you okay with that?"

"If it helps you save Daisy, I'll do anything." He seemed determined to help.

"Great. Okay, go hide."

Elizabeth left him and returned to Paige's room. She closed the door behind herself and lay on her bed. She wiggled into a comfortable position, then relaxed her breathing. She didn't know how she'd get into Josh's head, but focusing on him would be a start.

She thought about his curly brown hair, freckled nose, and hazel eyes. She quickly fell asleep and forced her mind to stay close. She opened her eyes to see strong hands tinkering with fancy equipment. She saw Paige helping, so she assumed she was in Michael's mind.

After realizing she was in the wrong head, she forced herself awake. "Ughh," she groaned. "How was I able to do this last time?"

She thought about how she was able to control herself after Zola was assaulted. She remembered feeling angry and focused. All she wanted to do at that moment was destroy the predator. However, creating artificial emotions wouldn't be easy.

Maybe Paige would be able to help? Elizabeth paged her, asking to meet in her room.

"Hey, what's up?" Paige asked as she walked into the room.

"Can you put emotions into people?"

"Yeah, why?"

"I need you to make me angry."

Paige raised her brows. "I'm supposed to be keeping you calm. Not the other way around."

"Please? You can take it away if things get out of control. I remember being able to control my powers when I was angry."

Paige clenched her jaw. "I don't know..."

"I promise, if I lose control, I'll never ask again," Elizabeth begged.

"Ugh." She rolled her eyes. "Fine. You're really trying to exhaust me, aren't you?"

"Yay! Okay, make me really mad."

Elizabeth laid down and stared at her until Paige sighed and pushed anger into her consciousness. It felt strange. It wasn't like when she naturally felt enraged; this time it felt much more toxic. She was angry, but it felt more controlled. She focused more on completing her task, rather than feeling the chaos, like during her last temper spell.

She forced her body to sleep, and her mind took off. It seemed like she was flowing through a colorful tunnel. This was her first time experiencing this void. Usually, she just woke up in a different body, and there was no physical travel involved.

She focused on Josh once again, eager to find him. It was necessary to practice on him in order to save Daisy. She let that further the drive to succeed.

Suddenly, she saw a door, the type of door she couldn't describe. However, she still somehow knew what it was. Maybe she had been here, but never remembered it. She pushed the door open and fell into an abyss of darkness.

Chapter 24

Elizabeth opened her eyes and knew she had found him. The awareness was astounding, she felt so connected; her and Josh were one.

"Okay, Josh'," she thought. "let's see what I can find out about you. Considering I know nothing except that you are inhumanly strong, this should be interesting."

She heard yelling, from a man and a woman. They were arguing over the little boy huddled in the corner. His little hands were pulling on his hair, and tears wet his face. He covered his eyes.

"He can't stay here. He breaks everything! He broke the girls' dolls this morning. I'm done!"

The little boy opened his fingers to see a red-faced man charging towards him. The man grabbed his hands and pulled him to his feet.

"Why do you do these things?" The man yelled while shaking Josh violently.

"I'm sorry, I didn't mean to! I just wanted to play!" he cried; he meant it too. He would usually play dolls with his foster sisters. They loved him. He accidentally broke their favorite doll, making them both cry. He'd already broken so many things in the house, and the parents were masking their fear with anger.

"You're a freak," the woman yelled. "You are leaving in the morning!"

The man threw the little boy into the wall, and the collision made him black out.

When his eyes opened, he was alone on the carpet next to the wall. Sitting up, he looked around, confused. Behind him, Josh saw the wall. The plaster was smashed in, with a hole where his skull hit. That's when he remembered his foster father throwing him into the wall. He didn't feel any pain, but he was thirsty.

Creaking from the floor caught his attention, and he looked up to see a woman, her silhouette outlined in the sunlight coming from the window behind her. Josh stared at her in awe, wondering if he was seeing an angel. Then she walked closer until she knelt in front of him, concern covering her face.

"Hi, Josh, my name is Jackie."

She had the kindest voice he'd heard from an adult.

Reaching for him, she grabbed his head, turning it as if to inspect him. Her hands were soft, gentle.

"You poor thing," she whispered, "you have cuts and bruises all over your face. Are you hurt?"

Josh shook his head.

"I'll have a doctor check on you later. You're going to stay with me now." She smiled sweetly and stood, holding out her hand. Knowing he had no choice, Josh took it. This was his life; being called a freak, then being passed on to the next person. A part of him also wanted to follow her, however. She seemed nice, at least, nicer than anyone he'd ever met.

"Right this way, little guy."

He walked beside her until they made it outside and to a black sedan. She opened the back door and helped him into a booster seat.

"How old are you?" she asked while buckling him.

"I just turned five," he said in his sad little voice.

"Your birthday was a week ago, right?"

He nodded.

"Oh, that's exciting. If it's okay with you, I'd like to have a little party to celebrate!"

He looked up at her with hopeful eyes. "With me?"

"Well, of course, silly, it is your birthday party, after all."

Jackie closed his door and moved to the passenger seat. There was a big man in the driver's seat. She instructed him to drive home, then turned back to Josh.

"You are going to love your new home. There will be lots of toys, your own playground, and whatever else you want. You are going to live like a prince."

Instead of giving her the reaction she seemed to expect, he looked down sadly at his lap.

"Why the long face, bud?"

"You'll find out," he mumbled.

Jackie already knew what he was thinking, of course. She would let him find out for himself, though.

Eventually, Josh fell asleep. He must have been carried to his room, because the next time he opened his eyes, he was lying on a comfortable mattress, tucked underneath a soft, fluffy comforter.

The ceiling was covered in glow-in-the-dark stars, which felt relaxing in the pitch-black room. He sat up and rubbed his eyes. They quickly adjusted to the darkness, allowing him to take in the outlines of the furniture and doorways.

Josh pushed the blankets off himself, shivering as the cold air bit his skin. He noticed a lamp next to him on a bedside table and switched it on. He looked around the room in awe; there were shelves lined along the walls filled with books and toys.

He climbed from the bed, his toes hitting the soft, gray carpet, then opened a door. The room on the other side looked like a giant warehouse. He did see the playground Jackie was talking about, but hadn't expected it to be inside. There were also no windows.

"You're up!" He heard Jackie's voice, then saw her stand from a couch. "How'd you sleep?"

"Good, thank you."

"That's good to hear! You slept all day. It's dinner time now. Come with me, and I'll show you the dining hall."

He followed her through the mostly empty room until they came upon double wooden doors. She pushed them open and motioned for him to sit at a long wooden table. At the center was a large chocolate cake and a box of pizza.

"Happy birthday, Josh! Eat up, then I'll give you your present."

He sat and scarfed down two slices of pizza. He hadn't realized how hungry he was. Jackie came back holding a large box wrapped in red paper. She set it down next to the cake, then cut a slice for Josh.

"Eat your cake, then you may open your present!"

After eating the rich chocolate cake, he eagerly opened the mysterious box. Inside, he found a set of small boxing gloves. He looked up at Jackie with curiosity.

"I heard you are super strong, I thought you might make use of those. I also set up a punching bag and some mannequins for you to practice on."

"You heard I was strong?" His forehead crinkled.

"Yeah! I think it's awesome. You know, I'm special like you, too."

"You break things?"

"In a way. I break relationships and figure out secrets. I can read minds."

"Really? You know what I am thinking right now?"

"You are thinking that I'll get rid of you in a couple months. But let me tell you something, mister: I will never get rid of you. I'm so sorry that other people haven't been able to handle you, but here, you can be yourself. Anything you break can be replaced. You were made for great things."

She smiled at him, and for the first time in a long time, Josh felt like he belonged. He was home.

The memory faded, and now Elizabeth saw Jennifer from his male gaze. He was studying her smile, her strong curves, the way she easily threw knives into a target. He felt butterflies forming in his stomach; she was the most beautiful and terrifying woman he'd ever seen.

Then she was running away from Jennifer, a door was thrown open, and she saw her body lying on a bed. Josh shook her body, trying to wake her.

Elizabeth was thrown back into her own mind. She shot up, bonking her head on something hard.

"Ouch!" she heard Josh shout. She looked up to see him holding his head.

"Josh! It was just starting to get good! Why'd you wake me?" She pouted.

"I think you've done enough practicing on me. I don't want you to know all my secrets. You've been out for three hours. So, tell me, what did you learn?"

She noticed Paige had left the room, so it was just her and Josh.

"You were in foster care. Jackie brought you in when you were five. I can see why you are loyal to her."

He nodded.

"Your other foster parents were scared of you. That must have been awful."

"Yeah, I thought something was wrong with me. Jackie brought me to a place I could fit in."

"I also saw you checking out Jen."

His face burned red, and his eyebrows rose.

"Don't worry, I won't tell her. I'll let you do that." She winked.

"Okay, I think that's enough sharing for today," he said awkwardly as he jumped from her bed, walking out the door as quickly as possible. When he stepped out of the room, Paige entered.

"What did you do to him? I could sense his embarrassment!"

Elizabeth laughed and shook her head. "Nothing! I swear!"

"Uh huh…" She raised her brows, but left it at that. "So, what's next?"

"I want to try Jackie's head and see if I get caught."

"No, that's a bad idea."

"Really? Because I think it's a great idea."

Elizabeth smiled and closed her eyes.

"You'll get us both in trouble, stop!" Paige cried.

Chapter 25

Jackie sat behind her desk, her hands wringing through her dark hair. She looked down at the photo of herself and her old team. She was seventeen in that photo. There were twelve people, aged five to eighteen. Most had powers, and the rest were skilled in combat or defense, or were insanely intelligent.

The only people still alive were her and William. She often had nightmares about that deadly day. She failed them, but she wouldn't make that mistake again. Elizabeth reminded her so much of one of her teammates. He, too, was a Dream Traveller. Unlike Elizabeth, he was able to control his gift. He could plant thoughts and memories, control minds, find every secret withheld.

His mind slowly warped over time, and no one noticed. Jackie should have, with her ability to read minds, but she didn't. She blamed herself every day. Because of her inability to pay attention, the majority of her team died. She wouldn't let Elizabeth assume the same fate.

She looked at the monitor she'd placed inside of Paige's room. She had cameras placed all over the lower level. There was no corner she couldn't see. She didn't usually watch them; it was just in case something happened. However, she had been closely watching Elizabeth. She didn't find out much; that woman wasn't one to share. She was hoping that sharing a room with Paige would help Elizabeth open up. So far, the only thing she'd witnessed was the subtle flirting between the two.

She was pleased to hear that Elizabeth had success with Josh's memories. However, she heard that they were going to try her next and dashed out of the office. She walked briskly down the hall and stairs until she swung open Paige's door.

"I don't think so."

Paige placed a guilty smile on her lips, while Elizabeth rolled her eyes. "My mind is off limits. I have too many confidential secrets that would get everyone killed if revealed."

"You're so dramatic," Elizabeth deadpanned. She got off her bed and stormed out the door.

Paige started to walk after her, but Jackie grabbed her elbow. "Paige, you're doing well. Thank you."

Paige smiled and nodded, then Jackie let her go. She ran to catch up to Elizabeth, who was heading towards Josh, Zola, Michael, and Jennifer. Josh and Zola were practicing with wooden swords, Jennifer was instructing them on different techniques, and Michael was observing.

"Sword fighting is a dangerous dance. It's a deadly improvisation. You must learn the opponent's strengths and weaknesses before they find out yours, else you die," said Jennifer.

Jackie could see Josh and Zola were circling the mat, staring daggers into their eyes. "For example, Josh is large, therefore slower."

"Hey! Not cool." He looked at her with mock offense.

While he was distracted, Zola slid on the ground and used her sword to whack his shins. Josh instinctually fell on his butt and winced in pain. Jackie tried to hide a smirk of pride for Zola; she knew Zola was stronger than she thought.

"Ow, Zola!"

Zola laughed while she sprung back to the other side of the mat to avoid retribution.

"A point for Zola. Don't get distracted, Josh. And don't fall just because you get hurt. Fight until you die. Because otherwise, death is inevitable. And Zola, in the real world there is no honor when fighting bad people. You strike when they're down."

"If this was the real world, he would have lost his feet."

"You couldn't cut through my bones!"

Josh charged her, but she dodged to the other side. "Ha, too slow!"

Josh charged for her again, but this time he anticipated her move and stuck his foot out. She tripped and landed on her side, the sound of her body slamming on the ground echoing in the room. Josh's eyes widened and crouched down beside her. "Oh my gosh, are you okay? I didn't expect you to land so loudly." He spoke with concern.

"Yes, I'm fine. I'm not fragile."

"Good job, Josh, way to think ahead," said Jen. "That's exactly the kind of thing I'm talking about. A great warrior uses their head as well as their strength."

Josh held out his hand for Zola and helped her up. She brushed off her knees and turned to give Paige and Elizabeth a perfect smile. They were surprised to see Jackie standing there as well.

"Miss Jackie," Josh greeted. "We weren't expecting you." His face remained stoic, but Jackie could read his thoughts, and hear that he hoped she was impressed by their sparring match.

"Josh, I see you and Zola are having a great start to your training."

"Yes ma'am." Josh bowed his head slightly in respect.

"What's the plan for today?" Jackie turned her attention to Jennifer.

"I was just waiting for Paige and Elizabeth to come out. Josh said he and Elizabeth just finished testing her powers on him. I thought I would start with some strength training, then go on from there."

"Great idea." Jackie smiled. "I'll let you get to it, then."

"Why was Jackie here, and why do you seem more irritated than usual, Elizabeth?" Jennifer asked.

"I got caught trying to infiltrate Jackie's mind." Elizabeth sighed.

"I told you it was a bad idea. Just count yourself lucky we didn't get in trouble." Paige gave her a knowing look.

"Oh, and what's she gonna do? Ground us? We are already in a worse situation."

"Elizabeth, you need to listen to Paige," Jennifer scolded.

"Oh, so you're on her side?"

"I'm on our side. Have I ever steered us wrong?"

"Well, there was that one time in high school...."

"Elizabeth, I'm not messing around," Jennifer interrupted. She was worried because of what Jackie had told her while Elizabeth was in confinement.

"Fine, I will behave myself. Happy?"

"Yes."

"What do you have planned?"

"Oh, just the basics. I want to keep things light and fun the first couple times. We need to become closer as a group if we are to become more like a team."

Located in one half of the gym was a climbing rope that was three stories long. Targets lined the walls for knife throwing and crossbow shooting. There were also punching bags, foam mannequins, and a wrestling mat. On the other half of the gym were more standard equipment. There were six treadmills and four stationary bikes. In the middle were a few squat racks and cable machines. On the side were free weights and bench press machines.

"I'm surprised you're here," said Michael to his sister. He stood and walked over to her, then engulfed her in a bear hug.

"Yeah, I have to keep my eye on Elizabeth at all times, remember?"

Elizabeth rolled her eyes, but smirked to show she didn't mind too much.

"Enough chitchat! Let's get started on a warmup. To the treadmills," Jennifer ordered.

Jennifer had each of them run a mile, and it was obvious a lot of them would need to up their cardio. Most of them were panting heavily, not even halfway through. Paige only made it a quarter of the way before she had to stop and take a rest. Next, Jennifer had them all go to a squat rack and separated them into pairs. Jennifer was with Elizabeth, Paige and Michael partnered, and Josh went with Zola. Jennifer was squatting 150 pounds, and she encouraged everyone to push themselves. Josh tried putting 900 pounds on his bar, but it ended up bending it.

"You know that's not how physics works," Michael playfully scolded as he inspected the bent piece of metal.

"I didn't know this would happen," Josh groaned. Zola lay on the ground, laughing hysterically.

"Maybe we should just bring a car in here for you to lift!" Jennifer suggested.

"Actually, that may not be a bad idea," Josh replied.

"No, we are not getting a car brought down here," Michael shot the idea down. "I can see if we can get a barrel full of lead or something."

"For now, lift the couch with everyone sitting on it or something," Jennifer said.

"You got it, boss."

Once everyone got through their squats, they went to the free weights for some sets of lateral raises, bicep curls, and shoulder presses. Everyone was working hard, pleasantly surprising Jennifer. As hard as they were working, though, their technique could use some serious work. Only her and Elizabeth had proper form. They knew how to breathe in a way that wouldn't leave them exhausted. Josh was able to lift heavy, but if he learned how to properly lift and move, Jennifer wondered if he could do even more.

Jennifer had a long way to go, as far as training the team and making them an unstoppable unit went, but this session had shown her where everyone was. She decided that this was a good stopping point.

"Okay, everyone, I think we are done for today. You are going to be sore tomorrow, so make sure you stretch and drink lots of water."

She heard sighs of relief and smirked. She was happy to know that even though they were exhausted, they continued going with no argument. If they kept up with this attitude, they would be ready sooner than she'd thought.

Jennifer, on the other hand, was far from tired. She walked over to a weapon rack and picked up a knife. She admired the sharp edges and the smooth metal. She began to reminisce about her childhood spent training in the fields near her home.

She quickly snapped out of her trance when she sensed someone watching her.

"You look as if you're in love with that knife," Josh said.

"You shouldn't sneak up on someone holding a sharp object." She spoke confidently, before turning to face him. She then turned to the target and threw the knife right into the center. The man gulped.

"You're terrifying and amazing," said Josh.

Jennifer laughed at his nervousness.

"Thank you."

"Got any other tricks?"

"They aren't tricks." Jennifer raised an eyebrow.

"I meant no offense." He looked down to his feet.

"It's okay, I'm not easily offended. I was just messing with you."

"Oh." He let out a sigh of relief. "What else can you do?"

"I'm a great fighter. Care to go for a round?" she challenged.

"I don't think so. I'm pretty strong. I'd hate to cause any serious damage," he warned.

"I might surprise you. Trust me, I won't get hurt."

"Fine, I'll try to go easy on you." He grinned.

Josh and Jennifer went to the wrestling mat and positioned themselves on opposite sides. Jennifer noticed Zola and Elizabeth standing on the sidelines to spectate the fight.

"Go, Jen!" cheered Elizabeth.

Jennifer stayed focused on her opponent, studying his movements. His stance looked strong, making him seem confident. She nodded, indicating that she was ready to begin. He rushed over to her with his fists raised. At the last second, Jennifer jumped into the air, and her feet landed on his back. Josh sprung upward, giving Jennifer the momentum to do a backflip and land perfectly on her feet, facing him.

He spun around to face her again and lifted his fists. They were two feet away from each other. Josh swung at her again, but she effortlessly dodged it and grabbed his hand. She used it to fling herself onto his back and planted her feet into the backs of his knees. Josh fell to his knees and whined in pain. Jennifer took this opportunity to slam the side of her hand on the artery on his neck.

Josh grabbed his neck. "I yield, I yield!" He was barely able to speak.

"All right, good job." Jennifer patted his back. "Next time, don't charge head-on. Try to observe your opponent first."

Josh nodded, still rubbing his neck. "You're great. Can you teach me how to do that? Once I recover, of course."

"Yeah, I'd love that."

"That was so fun to watch!" Zola interrupted from the sidelines.

"I bet it was." Josh shook his head.

Chapter 26

One month later...

It was taking longer than expected for Michael to create the device to help Elizabeth stop dream travelling. They had been testing, but every time she made it through. She was also becoming stronger, so if Michael wanted to create a contraption to hold her, he would need to do the opposite of underestimating her. Unfortunately, that meant Elizabeth had to continue staying with Paige.

Paige and Elizabeth sat on yoga mats on the floor of their bedroom. Their eyes were closed, and all they could hear were the sounds of each other's breathing. Elizabeth felt eyes on her, so she peeked hers open slightly. As it had been for the past month, she caught Paige staring at her. Elizabeth usually let her get away with it, but today she felt like making the woman squirm. She smirked, then opened her eyes all the way. Paige quickly shut her eyes and pretended like she had been meditating the whole time.

"Oh, Paige..." Elizabeth said teasingly. "Don't think I haven't noticed you staring at me during our daily meditation sessions."

Paige's neck and cheeks bloomed a glorious red shade. "Huh?" she squeaked.

Elizabeth laughed. "You're so cute when your face turns red."

That comment only made Paige's face turn a deeper shade, but she remained silent and tried to keep her face straight. Elizabeth enjoyed teasing Paige, so she decided to take it up a notch. She crawled over to Paige and got close, until her face was inches away from Paige's. Elizabeth noticed Paige's breath becoming faster. She raised her hand and delicately tucked a strand of Paige's silvery blond hair behind her ear.

"What are you doing?" Paige whispered.

Elizabeth brought her lips right up to Paige's ear, so they were barely grazing it. At this point, Elizabeth's arms were on both sides of Paige's hips, caging her in. "You just had some hair on your face. Thought I'd help you out," she whispered seductively.

Then Elizabeth stood, leaving Paige wide eyed and panting. She clearly enjoyed the attention Elizabeth was giving her, but didn't know what to do. Elizabeth admired her for a second, and then held out her hand. "Come on, Paige, morning meditation is over. Let's go see what Jennifer has in store for us today."

Paige nodded and grabbed her hand, allowing Elizabeth to pull her up. Elizabeth didn't let go of her hand as she led her out the door and to the gym, until they found everyone sitting and chatting. The first person to turn around was Jennifer.

"Well, hello, you two," she greeted. She noticed Paige and raised an eyebrow. "Why do you look like you just ran a mile?" Then she looked at Elizabeth. "What did you do to her?"

"What do you mean?" Elizabeth acted coy.

Jennifer rolled her eyes. "Don't give me that innocent act, I know how you are."

Elizabeth responded with a grin.

"Whatever," Jennifer said. "Let's get started." All chatter became silent as they gathered in front of her. "You all have been doing great work for the past month. In a few minutes, Jackie is going to come downstairs to talk about how things are going with the board. Until then, I'm going to give you some reviews on your performance.

"Josh, you have improved your ability to work as part of a team, but you have a long way to go. Just remember, alone, you are strong, but together, we are stronger.

"Zola, you do a great job of looking out for your teammates. You and Josh work well together, probably because you are great at having his back.

All you have to work on is increasing your techniques using weapons and throwing a punch. As we continue training, you'll get more confident.

"Michael, you get more confident every time we train together, but your timidness will be seen as a weakness by our enemies. Try to continue growing in that area. Remember you have a team that has your back.

"Paige, you are doing great. I've seen how you use your abilities to try and increase the confidence of our team. Just make sure you don't tire yourself out. They can't rely on you too heavily.

"And lastly, Elizabeth. You need to learn to trust the team. Remember, they are in the same boat as us. The better we become, the more likely we will be able to get out of this mess. How does everyone feel about how things are going?"

"Great," Josh replied. "But it would be nice to have training in a different environment. Also, if we could train against someone other than each other, that would be beneficial."

Everyone nodded in agreement.

"I agree. I've actually set something up for after we meet with Jackie. We will meet outside after this. Michael and I have already been briefed, so we are going to get things ready. Michael, if you will follow me? Jackie will be here soon."

Jennifer and Michael left to set up, and as soon as they were sight, the elevator doors opened and out walked Jackie.

"Good morning, everyone," she greeted.

"Good morning, Miss Jackie." Josh bowed his head politely.

Jackie smiled at him. "As you all know, I have been talking to the board about us going on a rescue mission for Daisy, her sister, and everyone else being held captive by the terrorist group that calls themselves the Society. DUST will extract the hostages once we know where they are located. Elizabeth, I'm going to leave that quest to you."

"I can do that," Elizabeth said confidently.

"Good. My supervisors have decided to lengthen your leash by letting you go outdoors. You'll be able to go pretty far, but there is a fence a couple miles out which you are not allowed to cross. If you do, the trackers will be alarmed, so don't even try it. Are we clear?"

The team nodded.

"All right. May I speak with you privately, Elizabeth?"

"I guess, but it won't really be private." She gestured to the cameras.

"Anything I say to you they can hear too. It's necessary."

Elizabeth rolled her eyes, then followed Jackie to the dining room. They sat on opposite sides from each other.

"I'm going to speak to you telepathically, because there's some delicate things I'd like to talk to you about. Respond to the things I say aloud, though."

Elizabeth was perplexed, but smiled to show her she understood.

"How are things going with Paige?" Jackie asked.

"I need your help."

Elizabeth wrinkled her forehead. "Good, she's been helpful."

"With what?"

"I'm glad to hear that. Have you had any violent thoughts lately?"

"I want to take down this organization."

Elizabeth was shocked. She thought Jackie was just one of their puppets. She was supposed to be the bad guy.

"I haven't."

"How do I know this isn't some trick? How do I know you won't go to your leaders and tell them I'm trying to take them down?"

Jackie smiled. "I'm glad to hear that. Have you been in contact with Daisy again?"

"It's no trick. I'm sick of being their lap dog. I don't trust any of them."

"No."

"I feel the same way about you."

Elizabeth recognized a hint of sadness in her eyes. "Well, let me know when you do."

"I hope, in time, I can gain your trust."

"Bye, Jackie." Elizabeth stood and quickly walked from the room, eager to get away from her.

Chapter 27

Paige was waiting outside the dining room. "How'd it go?"

"I need to blow off some steam," Elizabeth rumbled.

"That bad?"

"Yeah, where is everyone?"

"Outside, follow me."

Once outside, Elizabeth felt refreshed by the scents of pine trees and of honey from goldenrods. The sun kissed her pale skin, immediately relaxing her. The two of them walked until they found Josh waiting for them on the trail.

"You're so white, the sun reflects off you," Josh said to Elizabeth.

"Shut up."

"Hey, where did Zola go?" Paige asked.

The three of them followed a trail until they came upon an open space surrounded by trees. They saw Zola standing to the side, petting a fawn and a doe.

"What are you, a Disney princess?" Josh spoke sarcastically.

"They're so cute! Hunting isn't allowed here, so the wildlife is abundant."

The trees were filled with birds, and rodents scampered along the field. As Elizabeth looked deeper into the trees, she noticed many different kinds of animals.

"They're just standing there. Why aren't they afraid?" Elizabeth asked.

"I told them we mean no harm. Would you like to say 'hi' to my friends here?"

Elizabeth cautiously approached the young deer and its mother. She placed her palm under the fawn's nose, waiting for permission to pet it. Its wet nose sniffed, then pushed upward, encouraging her to pet the top of its head. She smiled as she stroked the soft fur.

Elizabeth could suddenly sense someone staring at her.

"Beautiful," she heard Paige whisper.

Elizabeth looked up at her. Time seemed to stop as they stared into each other's eyes, and heat blossomed from Paige's cheeks.

"The fawn, it's beautiful," Paige amended, as though she hoped nobody had noticed.

Elizabeth smirked and nodded in agreement. Then they heard Jennifer's commanding voice.

"Okay, guys! Everything is ready!"

Jennifer entered the clearing. Following behind her were Michael and eight guards, five men and three women. The guards wore all black and had shaved heads. It was creepy how they all moved fluidly in sync. It was like they were one machine.

"What's up with the creepy octuplets?" Elizabeth asked.

"They're here to help us with a training exercise, and I wouldn't insult them if I were you. They have been training for many years. They're DUST employees."

"Sorry." Elizabeth shrugged. "They don't seem offended, though." The robotic strangers looked forward, with no hint of emotion.

Jennifer playfully rolled her eyes. "Whatever. Let's get started. We are going to play a game. It's like capture the flag, but more violent. It will be us against them." She motioned to the eight warriors.

"Six against eight? That hardly seems fair!" Zola complained.

"In the real world, nothing is fair. Besides, your powers will level the playing field."

The warriors went to their side of the field, while Elizabeth and the others followed Jennifer to their side. Once they were far enough away, Jennifer turned to them.

"I already explained things to the other team, so now it's your turn. Each of us has a flag. Ours is yellow, theirs is orange. We have to get theirs before they take ours."

"Sounds simple enough," said Elizabeth.

"We will see." Jennifer smirked. She pulled a whistle from her pocket and blew into it. "Let the game begin!"

Josh charged to the front lines; Zola chased behind. Jennifer groaned in frustration. "Josh! Zola! Come back!" she yelled. Josh was too focused on the target ahead to listen to her, and Zola fixated on having his back.

The other team guarded their flag, carefully watching the two gaining the area. Josh went straight for the orange flag, determined to knock through the wall of bodies. He dove through the people in the middle, sending them to the ground. One of them dove for him, but was sent flying back with a brush of his arm. Then, four of the remaining teammates tackled him at all angles, overpowering his strength. While this happened, another grabbed Zola, binding her hands behind her back.

Josh struggled to shake them off, but too many bodies held him down. The warriors that were thrown to the ground recovered and grabbed ropes to contain him. They tied them around his body and arms, making sure he couldn't escape.

Josh tugged at his bindings when the opposing team members turned their backs, but they wouldn't budge. Usually, he would be able to break through them, and they looked like a normal rope, but he couldn't even move them an inch. "What's up with these ropes?" he yelled.

"They're not normal ropes. They have Tungsten woven into the fibers," Michael shouted back.

"What! How is this fair?" Josh yelled, as they pushed him and carried Zola to a far corner of their territory.

"Nothing in battle is fair when fighting bad people. Remember that for the next time you charge in head on without consulting your team!" Jennifer yelled. "Now you've left us with just four people to protect our flag. Thanks a lot."

"Jen, I think we are screwed," Elizabeth whispered.

"That doesn't matter. We keep trying."

Three of the enemy warriors stalked to the opposite side of the field, determined to capture the yellow flag. Paige, Jennifer, and Elizabeth stood their ground, nervously waiting for a fight. The enemy moved fluidly, not showing any emotion.

Elizabeth watched Jennifer and Paige out of her peripheral, in case they made a move. Then Paige took a light step forward and grabbed all her attention; she couldn't help herself. Most of the time, Paige seemed meek, but, at that moment, she had a fierce expression. Paige focused on one man as she outstretched her hand. Stopping in his tracks, her opponent dropped to his knees, his mouth open as he let out a low cry.

"Paige?" Elizabeth called out to her. "What's going on? Why is he acting like that?"

"Stay back, Paige grunted. "I don't want to accidentally hit you with my powers."

Elizabeth froze. Seeing Paige control that man with whatever feeling she was giving him made her realize just how powerful Paige could be. It frightened and amazed her.

Then Jennifer shouted, warning her the enemies were close. Elizabeth looked away from Paige just in time to miss an attack from one of the men.

Jennifer grappled with one of their opponents and masterfully choked her out while Elizabeth fought with the man. Using the techniques Jennifer taught her, Elizabeth dodged, punched, kicked, and wrestled with him. He was larger than her, so she tried to use his weight against him. Unfortunately, Elizabeth's skills were not up to par, but she was able to keep him distracted till Jennifer jumped onto his back and put him in a choke hold. Paige stood over the man she'd used her powers on. He was curled in fetal position, sobbing uncontrollably. They dragged all their defeated captives to the makeshift jail.

"Geez, Paige," Jennifer said, "what did you do to him?" Paige's victim now stared off into space, the tears dried on his cheeks.

"I exhausted his emotions. He'll be fine in a couple hours."

"That's awesome, and terrifying."

Paige smiled at the compliment.

Now that the enemy team was left with five members, the balance was restored. Four more warriors came for the yellow flag, giving Michael, Jennifer, Elizabeth, and Paige each an opponent. While everyone was distracted, Zola lured a raccoon and a few rats to chew through her and Josh's bindings. It took a few minutes, but the ropes broke, and Josh tackled the fifth guard to the ground.

With all the enemy warriors distracted, Zola dashed for the orange flag and lifted it from its holding place. She ran until she reached her team's side of the field.

"I got it!" she shouted breathlessly.

All fighting ceased. Her team rushed to her and gave her a huge group hug.

"Gross, you all are sweaty!"

"Well, while you got to enjoy jail, we had to protect our flag," Jennifer joked.

Jennifer turned to the other team, "Thank you for helping us train, everyone. Hopefully you will be willing to help us again tomorrow."

They nodded, carrying off their unconscious teammates.

"I think we did well," Elizabeth commented.

"They took it easy on us," Jennifer retorted. "We have a lot of work to do."

They started to walk inside while Jennifer gave notes.

"Josh and Zola, doing what you did would get you killed in the real world. Do not do that again. As for the rest of us, I think we just need to work on our fighting techniques. I'm sure there are other things to work on, but I focus on the fighting aspect of things. You're on your own when it comes to strengthening your powers. Practice using them and help each other."

Jennifer was stern as she spoke. She told them they would practice every day with either the same eight warriors or different ones.

Once they reached their own rooms, they all showered off the day's sweat and dirt, then got ready for bed.

"You were awesome today," Elizabeth complimented Paige.

Paige turned her body to face Elizabeth. There was a soft glow around her face from the dim light of the lamp between their beds.

"Thanks, so were you."

"I was all right, but you? I had no idea you held that kind of power. The way you stopped a man twice your size simply by warping his feelings... it was amazing."

"It's not enough, though. I need to be able to do that to more than one person."

"If that's your goal, I believe you can do it."

"Why are you being nice to me?"

Elizabeth just smiled at her, then reached for the lamp to switch it off. "Good night, Paige," she whispered.

Chapter 28

The next couple weeks, the six members worked on improving their skill: whether it be powers or fighting techniques. They practiced archery and swordsmanship. They practiced different martial arts techniques. They even practiced with snipers and handguns, but since Jackie wanted them to focus on using their powers, and Jennifer hated guns, they focused on close range combat and silent attacks.

Elizabeth became exponentially better at digging through memories from her volunteers, and Paige could alter the emotions of three people at a time. Zola made friends with some wolves that were willing to protect her, and Josh started getting used to thinking as a teammate rather than an individual.

Everything was coming together. They were becoming the unstoppable force Jennifer had envisioned. There was still the matter of Elizabeth's being able to control people, finding where the terrorist cult was located, and Michael's finishing a device to help her sleep, but the results were still impressive.

"Hey, Elizabeth," Jennifer said one afternoon, "have you been in touch with Daisy at all?"

Elizabeth looked guiltily towards the ground. "I've been going to her almost every day, using her mind to jump to other people, trying to find a location."

"Why do you feel guilty?" Paige asked.

"Because I've found nothing."

"I know what it's like to feel like you're not doing enough." Jennifer placed her hand on Elizabeth's shoulder. "You can only do your best. Nobody is blaming you for anything. I can't imagine how difficult dream travelling must be."

"I'm blaming myself."

"Maybe the terrorists you've travelled to don't know where the island is. Maybe only specific people know the location. Have you tried traveling to Priscilla?"

"Yeah, I tried that first. And several more times after. I always end up in one of her guards' heads instead, though."

"That's strange."

"Yeah. I guess all I can do is keep trying."

"That's all anyone can do. Have you tried finding her right-hand man? There must be at least one other person who knows the location."

"Maybe. I haven't tried finding a right-hand man. I have no idea who it would be."

"Ask Daisy or Sofie. They may have noticed something."

Elizabeth hated to ask those girls for anything. They became more withdrawn every day.

"Once we get them off the island, we will get them the help they need. We won't give up on them," Paige reassured her.

Elizabeth wouldn't stop until she saved Daisy and Sofie, but how would they be after getting rescued? She'd seen the aftermath of abuse many times. It affected every person on a different scale. No matter how much therapy a victim went to, they couldn't erase the trauma. With the level of abuse Daisy had endured, Elizabeth worried she wouldn't be able to function in society again without living in constant fear. Paige was right, though; they would do everything they could for her. Elizabeth would do anything.

"When we find those pedophiles, we are going to make them beg for death," Elizabeth growled.

"Absolutely," Paige and Jennifer agreed.

Elizabeth walked to her room for some privacy to speak with Daisy. It was time to get them out of there.

Chapter 29

Elizabeth lay on her bed, and Jennifer and Paige sat on the other bed to provide support.

"You got this, Elizabeth. We are here for you," Paige encouraged.

Elizabeth nodded and closed her eyes. It was much easier to connect to Daisy with all the practicing she'd been doing. As soon as she fell asleep, she woke in Daisy's mind. She was sitting on her bed, looking down at her feet. Blue, purple, and brown bruises covered her legs.

"Daisy? It's me, Elizabeth."

There was no answer. It was like she wasn't even there; she was hollow.

"What have they done to you?" asked Elizabeth rhetorically. "Daisy, listen to me. I know it feels easier to disassociate, but you can't give up yet. We are ready to come get you. I need your help to do that."

Nothing. Elizabeth could force her to come back, but she'd been through enough already. She wanted the girl to do so on her own.

"Daisy, where's Sofie? Where's your little sister?"

"Sofie," she choked.

"Yes, where is she?"

Daisy turned her head until the little girl came into view. She was curled in a ball behind her sister, breathing softly with her eyes closed.

"Please, Daisy. I know this is hard for you, but you can't let them win. Help me help you. I will get you and Sofie out."

Daisy scrunched her eyes closed; tears cascaded down her face. Elizabeth gave her as long as she needed.

"I'm so scared," she sniffled.

"I know. It's almost over. I just need you to do something for me. Can you do that?"

Daisy nodded.

"Do you have any idea who Priscilla's closest guard would be? Or her right-hand man?"

"No."

"Shoot," Elizabeth thought. She would need to make her best guess, then.

"Okay, I need you to get close to Priscilla. Avoid being seen."

Daisy stood from the bed on wobbly legs. Elizabeth could feel all her pain. Everything hurt. She tried to keep her fury at bay; she needed to keep her focus. The time for revenge would come, but for now, she needed to find the island they were being kept.

Daisy slowly walked down the hall. Shocks of pain shot through her nerves with every step. She kept going until she made it to the throne room, then ducked behind a plant.

Peering through the leaves, Elizabeth spotted Priscilla, sitting on her throne, surrounded by men in black robes. Most of the men sat before her, worshipping, but one stood out. He kneeled by her feet, looking into her eyes with devotion. Priscilla said something, and the man stood, walking to her side. Tilting her head as the man bent to her level, Priscilla whispered in his ear.

"I hope he's the one," Elizabeth thought.

"Perfect. Thank you, Daisy. I'm going to leave now. As soon as I'm gone, head back to your room."

Elizabeth focused on the guard standing next to Priscilla, then made herself travel to him. The next second, Elizabeth opened her eyes, and she was staring right into Priscilla's green orbs. Priscilla smiled at Elizabeth's new body, then looked down at the other kneeling guards lovingly.

Satisfied that she was safe to dig through the guard's mind, Elizabeth began. There was an abundance of information on Priscilla. This man was truly obsessed with her. All the guards were probably obsessed. That was what being a cult leader brought, mindless devotion.

It didn't take long for Elizabeth to find exactly what she was looking for: the location of the Island. There were even memorized coordinates. The island was small, located 400 miles from Madagascar.

The island had everything they needed to survive, a small lake in the middle, tropical fruits and some animal species, and a large cave for shelter. There was also a landing strip on the western side of the island, and a port for ships. Priscilla must know some powerful people for her to be able to hide such a place.

Thankfully, the guard was like an encyclopedia on all things Priscilla. Apparently, she grew up in a lodge in the mountains of China. The lodge appeared to house a cult. The man she was invading grew up there as well. He and Priscilla had been friends since childhood.

Elizabeth watched the memories. The men trained in techniques similar to Jennifer's. Except they were given these skills to be used sinisterly. The boys were covered head to toe in black cloth. She noticed a symbol on the right side of their necks, a spider eating a snake. The girls wore white dresses, and had no tattoos on their skin, but an occasional bruise or scrape.

A tall and muscular woman was barking instructions at the children. A boy was mercilessly beating another boy until he laid on the ground, not moving.

"Wonderful job, number ten," the woman praised with a rich Russian accent. "I like your ruthlessness. You!" she shouted at a nearby adult. "Check to see if that child is alive. If he is, take him to medical. Otherwise, throw him off the cliff. The snow will bury his body."

The woman's ruthlessness was shocking. These were just children. Elizabeth wondered if they were kidnapped, abandoned, or sold. Unfortunately, that wasn't her focus for now.

Satisfied with the gathered information, Elizabeth retreated back to her own mind. She awoke to see Paige curled up next to her, while Jennifer slept on Paige's bed. Elizabeth shook the small woman's shoulder.

Paige shot up; redness spread on her cheeks.

"I'm so sorry! I didn't mean to fall asleep like that..." she continued to blabber nervously until Elizabeth cut her off.

"I don't mind. You can cuddle with me anytime," she teased.

Paige's eyes widened. Her hair had turned into an adorable mess, and a blush crept down her neck. The moment was over when they heard a groan from Jennifer.

"Sorry to interrupt, but did you find anything, Elizabeth?" she asked groggily.

"Sure did. We need to orchestrate a team meeting now."

"I'll go wake everyone up. Meet in the dining room?"

"Perfect."

Chapter 30

Elizabeth, Jennifer, Paige, Michael, Josh, and Zola sat at the dining table, drinking coffee. They all looked exhausted, but sleep would have to wait. They had to create a plan to infiltrate the Society cult.

Jackie burst through the door and quickly took a seat. "You have some useful information?" she asked Elizabeth, who sat next to Jennifer.

"Yes. I know exactly where they are located. It's an island 400 miles east of Madagascar. I have the exact coordinates I can give you too. There is a landing pad on the western side of the island, so we should arrive on the east."

"Great."

"So, when do we leave?"

Jackie's forehead crinkled as she looked down at the table.

"Jackie?"

Elizabeth could see Jackie's jaw flex as she clenched her teeth. "DUST will be sending out their own agents. The team won't be going on this mission."

"What?!"

"What have we been training for, then?" Jennifer yelled.

"I'm sorry." Jackie looked at Elizabeth. "I tried to advocate for the team, to make it possible to rescue Daisy and Sofie ourselves, but the board wouldn't budge. They're afraid of you and Jennifer escaping. To them, the threat of exposure isn't worth it."

"I will do anything to save Daisy and Sofie! I won't escape; I wouldn't even try. I wouldn't risk their safety!" Elizabeth argued.

"I know. I'm sorry. DUST will do their all to make sure the girls and other hostages are safe."

Grinding her teeth, Elizabeth said, "I suppose I have no choice. When are they planning on executing their mission?"

"I'm not sure. They'll have to come up with a strategic plan, figure out who to assign to what roles, gather supplies… it could take up to a week."

"A week?! We can't leave them there for another week!" Elizabeth stood from her seat, slamming her hands on the table. "They need to go rescue her now! They haven't seen her like I have! She's wasting away! She's basically a shell of herself!"

"I'm sorry, Elizabeth. I'm sorry, everyone. I wish I could do more." Jackie withdrew from the table.

As she was walking out the room, Elizabeth yelled after her, "You better hope those girls survive, Jackie! The whole agency better hope they survive! If they don't…" Elizabeth started to feel faint. "If they don't…" She collapsed on her chair as the stress from her body washed away. "I'll…" Panting, she said, "Paige, what did you do…"

"Sorry, Elizabeth, I don't want to see what will happen if you threaten the agency." Paige's eyes lowered; her brows drew together.

"I don't care."

"Come on, Elizabeth." Jennifer helped her from her chair. "Let's get you to bed."

"I don't want to sleep. I'll just see her." Her voice slurred.

Paige bent to Elizabeth's ear. "We won't make you sleep. I'll stay awake with you."

"Okaaayyy."

Wrapping an arm around Elizabeth's waist, Paige helped her to their room. She pushed the door open, then she and Elizabeth walked over to Paige's bed. Elizabeth sluggishly crawled on the bed, while Paige sat at the headboard.

Staring at Paige, she said, "I want to be mad, Paige."

"I know."

Elizabeth moved to Paige's side and rested her head on Paige's shoulder.

"Paige? I'm worried about Daisy and Sofie."

"I know," Paige sighed, "it doesn't take long for you to get your emotions back."

"Let me keep these. I don't like it when you take them away."

"I won't, as long as you don't start threatening the agency again."

"They're so sensitive," Elizabeth scoffed.

Chuckling, Paige stroked Elizabeth's arm as they sat in silence. Elizabeth tried to stay awake, but Paige's soothing touch had her drift to sleep. She didn't know how long she was out, but the next time she opened her eyes, she was no longer resting on Paige. Instead, she lay on her side, alone.

As she stretched her body, her arms overhead, her shoulders and spine cracked. Elizabeth could hear rustling around her, and when she turned her head towards the noise, she saw Paige dressed in gray cargo pants and a long-sleeved black shirt. with her hair in a low bun. She was packing a backpack with various items from the dresser.

"Paige?" Elizabeth whispered. "What's going on?"

"We are going to rescue the hostages."

Hearing those words, Elizabeth leapt from her bed. She had no questions to ask; she just wanted to get ready as soon as possible. She pulled on some black tactical pants from her closet, a black t shirt, and a black hoodie over it. After washing her face and brushing her teeth, she heard the door to their room open. Peeking her head from the bathroom, she saw Jennifer standing there, smiling at her.

"You ready?" Jennifer asked.

"Yes. I'm so ready."

"Awesome. You ready, Paige?"

"Yeah." She flung the backpack over her shoulders. "I packed some clothes for Elizabeth and I, just in case."

"Good idea. I packed some for me, too." She showed them her backpack.

Elizabeth left the bathroom and slipped on some combat boots from the closet. While she laced the boots, Jennifer continued talking to Paige.

"Jackie said you know where to go?"

"Yeah, I've been there before. Once Elizabeth is ready, we'll head over there."

"Great, everyone else is waiting in the living room. How'd Jackie convince DUST to let us go?"

"I'm not sure... She'll probably explain when we see her."

"Okay, done," Elizabeth stood. "Let's go."

Elizabeth and Jennifer followed Paige. Just as Jennifer said, Josh, Michael, and Zola were waiting in the living room. Paige led them to the same place they'd gone to when they went out to the bar. Jackie was waiting in the garage, standing in front of a black van.

Without saying a word, Jackie opened the doors on the passenger side, then opened the door for the driver and hopped in. Paige got in afterward, slipping into the back, and everyone followed after her. Josh sat in the front, next to Jackie. Once Josh sat, the last person to do so, Jackie whipped out the garage.

Elizabeth knocked into Paige from Jackie's jerky driving.

"Everything okay, Jackie?" Josh asked.

"One second."

She drove on, silence filling the car. Once she passed the gate, Jackie took a deep breath.

Dream Traveller

"Okay," she exhaled.

"So…" Elizabeth started, "are you gonna tell us what's going on? Why are you driving like a bat out of hell?"

"I'm just in a hurry, is all."

"How'd you convince the agency to change their minds? It seemed they were pretty against it." Jennifer asked.

"I didn't. I didn't ask for permission."

"What? But what about the chips? The cameras? Didn't you say they'd kill us if we tried to leave?"

Elizabeth froze, afraid, excited. She wanted to save Daisy and Sofie, but what if the agency killed her before they got there?

"I know. William and I took care of everything. He tampered with the cameras and audio. At this moment, you are still sleeping, according to the video feed. He also redirected the signal from our trackers. He was able to make it, so it still looks like we are in the agency. We should be back before they notice we're gone."

"What if they find us out?" Elizabeth asked.

Jackie paused. "Let's just hope they don't."

Throughout the drive, Elizabeth sat in nervous silence. Paige grabbed her hand, smiling up at her.

"Everything will be okay."

After driving for a couple hours, they arrived at a small airport in a little mountain town. Parking the car, Jackie jumped out, and everyone followed her. She came to a garage and put in a code. The door opened, revealing a small plane.

"Do you know how to fly a plane?" Jennifer asked.

"I can drive anything," Jackie responded. "You all wait out here while I get the plane out of the garage. Josh, will you spot me?"

"Yes ma'am."

Jackie handed him two neon signs and left to enter the plane. The rest of them stood on the side, watching as Jackie drove the plane out and Josh guided her. Elizabeth felt anxious watching her, but Jackie made it look effortless.

Once the plane parked, a set of stairs appeared from the side, mechanically rolling down to the ground. Jackie opened the door and waved them to come in. Josh stood on the side, guiding them, and watching to make sure they were safe. He followed the last person, Michael, up the stairs.

Inside, the plane looked luxurious. Unlike a normal commercial plane, this one had comfortable couch-like seats, tables in front of the seats, and a mini fridge in each row.

"Wow…" Elizabeth gaped.

"Everyone, take your seats! I don't have anyone to guide me, but I think it'll be okay. I've flown out of here plenty of times," Jackie announced.

"Wait, don't you have to, like, tell someone you're flying?"

"Umm, I left them a message."

She went back to the cockpit, closing the door before they could respond.

"Well, this will be terrifying."

"Buckle up," Josh shouted.

"Like that'll save us if she crashes."

Elizabeth took a seat by the window, and Paige sat next to her. Facing them, Jennifer and Josh sat on the other side. Buckling, they heard the plane starting to make a whirring noise. Then it began to move. Elizabeth looked out the window at the sun rising over the mountains, turning the sky a beautiful pink and orange.

The plane followed the runway, speeding up until it lifted from the ground. The ground shook, and Elizabeth braced herself. She'd never been on a small plane, but from her experience, planes didn't usually shake so roughly. Everything smoothed out, though, and the ground grew smaller.

"Wooo," Elizabeth let out.

"I'm surprised I didn't pee myself," Zola joked.

"How long do you think we'll fly for?"

"I'll go up there and ask." Josh unbuckled his seatbelt and went to the cockpit.

"This is a stressful situation," Elizabeth admitted once Josh closed the door.

"It's worth it, though, right?" Jennifer asked.

"Oh, absolutely. As long as we save Daisy and Sofie before they catch us."

"I don't think they'll catch us," said Paige. "Jackie and William are really good at what they do."

"Well, I don't have the same trust in them you do."

"Well, you can trust me. Right?" Paige looked hopeful.

Smiling, Elizabeth said, "I suppose."

The cockpit door opened, and out walked Josh.

"Okay, I got the whole plan." Josh got everyone's attention. "We are flying to the ocean first, stopping for gas, then flying to Madagascar. We might need to stop for gas a couple times, but Madagascar is the final destination. From there, we will take a submarine to the island Elizabeth told us about."

"Ughh, this is going to take forever," Elizabeth groaned.

"Well, we'll get there before DUST, at least."

"Still, Michael, can't you invent a teleportation machine?"

Staring at her, with a serious expression, he said, "Maybe tomorrow."

For the rest of the plane ride, they talked among themselves, napped, and tried other ways to entertain themselves. Michael sat in silence, tinkering with his invention to help Elizabeth sleep. They made one stop in Mexico for gas, then another in Brazil, before flying over the ocean. Stopping on the west coast of Africa for the last refuel, they made it to Madagascar.

After Jackie parked, they shuffled off the plane. Jackie led them to a marina's office, and they walked in to find people working the front desk. Speaking in French, Jackie and the front desk employee chatted. He must have understood what she wanted, because he picked up a phone and spoke a few words, and another worker came from downstairs.

She walked over to Jackie, a friendly smile on her face, and said a few words that Elizabeth couldn't understand.

Jackie turned to the group. "The submarine is ready for us. We'll follow this woman and then get situated."

The group followed silently behind as they were led downstairs. The marina opened up to the ocean, and a long cement dock went into the water. They walked on the path, the waves crashing around them. Then they saw the submarine floating on the water, its metal exterior becoming larger until they came to the end on the dock.

The woman and Jackie spoke, nodded at the rest of them, then motioned for them to enter the vessel. The submarine was gigantic, way larger than she thought it would be. It looked like an underground safe house the size of a two-story home.

"Come on, everyone." Jackie went to a door that opened at the top, then climbed down a ladder.

One by one, they climbed down the ladder. Elizabeth looked around in wonder. The inside was immaculate. There were fine leather seats lining the sides, rooms for them to sleep, a kitchen, and an armory.

"You could live on this thing," Elizabeth commented.

Jennifer went straight for the armory, checking out the weapons. "Can I take these with me?" She held out two daggers.

"Yes, take whatever you think you will need," said Jackie.

"Is this DUST's sub?" Josh asked.

"Technically, it's property of the US government, but DUST can use it. William was able to hack a board member's account and request access."

"Risky."

"Yeah, but it was necessary. We'll cover our tracks."

"So, what now?" Elizabeth asked.

"Now, we get the sub on auto pilot, then we come up with a plan."

Chapter 31

Walking into the console center, Jackie stood in front of a large touch screen, pressing buttons that looked random. Elizabeth watched her, confused, as she found a seat at a long metal table. Once everyone else filed in, Jackie opened a map of the world on the screen, then searched for the coordinates.

The map zoomed in to the coordinates, but it only looked like there was a body of water there. Jackie double tapped on the screen anyways, then pressed another button, and the screen went away, showing the water in front of them. The ocean was dark, and various sea animals floated on by, dodging the large vessel invading their home.

"Okay, everyone," Jackie said, interrupting Elizabeth's fish watching, "the submarine has the coordinates, so let's talk about the plan."

"Yeah, what can we expect, Elizabeth?" Jennifer asked.

"They have next to no technology, so unless they have lookouts on the far side of the island, we shouldn't be detected. When we arrive, I can lead us to the cave. Before we confront Priscilla, we need to find Daisy and Sofie. Then we will get the other hostages. We can borrow five robes from some guards. Jackie will wait by the sub, and Paige will lead the two girls out while we create a distraction."

"How many guards are there?"

"Thirty-two guards, all men. The only female terrorist there is Priscilla."

"And how will we find these guards?"

"I think I know where they'll be. It shouldn't be hard to find them."

"Anything else?"

"There is one more thing. While I was in the mind of a guard, I found out some interesting information. Priscilla grew up in some lodge in the mountains of China. The men all had these spider tattoos on the side of their neck. You should be able to tell the terrorists apart from any victims by looking for that tattoo." She rubbed her neck where she'd seen the tattoos.

Jennifer perked up, a flash of anger and sadness filling her eyes. "A spider eating a snake?"

"Yeah, does that mean something to you?"

She clenched her jaw, then said, "Yeah, they are the people who…." She seemed to be having a hard time saying it as memories bubbled to the surface. "They killed my parents. And my tutor. They almost killed me."

"What?!" Zola jumped from her seat on the opposite side of the table.

"We will make them wish they were never born," Josh growled next to Zola.

Jennifer gripped the sides of the table, her nails scratching the metal. "I have been dreaming of revenge for years." She determinedly looked into Elizabeth's eyes. "Who knew my sister would be the one to deliver that to me."

Elizabeth lifted her left hand to squeeze Jennifer's shoulder. "Let's make them pay."

"I will see if William can find any information on them," Jackie offered matter-of-factly.

"Well, great. We can save Daisy, Sofie, and the other hostages, and we can avenge Jennifer. Now all we need to do is reach the island, find the cave, and get past the guards."

"You make it sound easy," said Michael, across from Paige.

"It won't be. But it will be fun." Elizabeth smirked.

"Is there anything else we need?" asked Jennifer.

"I finished another prototype of Elizabeth's sleeping device," Michael said excitedly. He pulled a small box from the pocket of his pajama pants and flipped it open. Everyone leaned in to see small white earbuds. "We might have to tinker with it a little bit to make it more comfortable, but I wanted to see if it works first."

"Can I try it right now?"

"Yes, of course." He quickly passed her the box. "Please do."

"Okay, everyone, try to get some more sleep. I will take care of the preparations," announced Jackie, before she quickly stood and walked out the door.

The rest of the team followed suit and retired to their rooms. Elizabeth cuddled under her warm comforter and placed the earbuds in her ear. Week after week, Michael had kept her trying out his devices, but nothing worked so far. She appreciated his effort and that he was determined to get her anti-dream-travelling device working, but it seemed impossible. However, as long as he kept trying, then so would she.

Tossing until she found a comfortable spot on the foreign bed, Elizabeth fell asleep. Her mind felt relaxed, at one with her body.

Her conscious didn't want to leave; it felt content. She felt content. Minutes, hours, days, and years of spending her nights dealing with other people's issues when her brain should have been dealing with its own, had built up massive tension.

She had real dreams for the first time that she could remember. Impossible, goofy dreams, that made no sense. Knots in her brain were being massaged by her subconscious, relieving her anxiety and fears. There was still a ways to go, but it was a step in the right direction.

She didn't wake again until she felt gentle hands shake her shoulders. She slowly opened her eyes to see Paige kneeling next to her.

"Good morning! How'd you sleep?"

"Wonderfully. I slept. Actually slept. I want to sleep more. That was heavenly." Elizabeth turned away from Paige and cuddled into her pillow.

"Yay!" She jumped on the bed. "Michael will be so happy to hear that."

"Paige," Elizabeth groaned.

Paige jumped to Elizabeth's other side and lay down next to her. She snuggled to her side, then blew on Elizabeth's nose. "Wake up," she whispered.

"You brat." Elizabeth wrapped her arms and legs around Paige, trapping her small body.

"This is not getting up," Paige grumbled.

"I'm so comfy, and even more so, now." Elizabeth spoke flirtatiously, causing Paige to blush.

"Come on, Elizabeth, we have to go get Daisy. Remember?"

That immediately stirred her. She released Paige and jumped out of bed. "I'm so selfish. I shouldn't have slept at all! I should have been planning."

Sensing her stress, Paige placed a hand on her shoulder. "There's nothing more you could have done."

Swiftly, Elizabeth changed into black leggings and a black tank top, then tied a gray sweater around her waist. After brushing her teeth, washing her face, and putting her hair into a low braid, she walked with Paige to the dining room.

"How do you feel?" Paige asked as they walked.

"Focused."

"You do seem to be a bit more centered. Your skin looks brighter too. I wonder how much you'll change in a month."

"Me too."

When they entered, everyone was already there, enjoying their breakfast and coffee. They'd all had the same idea and wore athletic, non-flashy clothes, with pulled-back hairstyles for the girls. Paige and Elizabeth took their seats and fueled themselves for the journey, finding sausages, eggs, and oatmeal. Everyone else was already eating.

"Did Jackie cook?" Elizabeth asked.

"No, Josh and I did," Jennifer replied.

"Oh, thanks!"

"Yeah, I went to check on you, but you seemed to be at peace. Less corpse-like while you slept. So, I thought maybe the device was working. We all decided to let you sleep longer."

"Yeah, the device worked!"

Michael rose at once, excitement written on his face. "Really?"

"Yes! Thank you so much, Michael. You have no idea how much this means to me." Elizabeth's cheeks started to hurt from how much she was smiling.

"That's amazing, Elizabeth. I'm glad the earbuds worked. When we get back, I'm going to try to make something more comfortable. Maybe something that can just surround your bed instead. Then the earbuds can just be your portable device."

"Okay, thank you. Again."

"You're welcome. That's what friends are for."

Chapter 32

Taking a spoonful of oatmeal, Elizabeth noticed a mug sliding in front of her. Steam rose from the cup as the scent of coffee welcomed her.

"I made you coffee," Paige said sweetly.

Elizabeth took a sip and hummed in satisfaction. "This is delicious! You made it just how I like. Thank you."

"You're welcome."

"Can you two not flirt in front of me?" Michael cut in. Everyone at the table giggled in response.

While everyone went back to talking amongst themselves, Elizabeth turned to Paige.

"Are you scared?"

"More worried than scared." Paige shrugged. "You are scared, though. I can feel it."

"Of course you do."

"Don't worry. I won't let anything bad happen to you. No one will. We are a strong team. Jennifer has been training us for weeks. We got this." She placed her hand on Elizabeth's thigh.

"I know I just can't stop thinking of everything that might go wrong."

"Nothing will go wrong."

Before Elizabeth could reply, Jackie stormed into the room. "We are arriving in 15 minutes. Please take this time to go over plans and make sure you have everything."

"What, no pep talk?" said Elizabeth sarcastically.

Paige snorted. "Can you imagine Jackie giving a pep talk?"

"That would be terrifying."

"Any updates, Elizabeth? Did the anti-traveling device work?" Jackie asked.

"It did."

"Good. That's good. How does it feel?"

"After sleeping for the first time since I first dream travelled? Like a weight has been lifted off my chest."

"Great. This is great news. We can talk more about this later. Everyone, get ready to go! Strap yourselves with weapons from the armory." And Jackie left the room.

Jennifer led the way to the armory, instructing the teammates which weapons they should carry. Tactical belts hung from a wall, and each person grabbed one, then sized it to fit around their hips. Jennifer equipped herself with five daggers, her favorite weapon. She then told Elizabeth to carry a couple daggers and a whip; while Josh was told to carry a mace and an axe; Zola, a bow and set of arrows; Michael, darts dipped in poison and stun grenades; and Paige, a baton with an adjustable electrical current.

Jennifer also stuffed a backpack with ropes, extra daggers and knives, and some water, just in case. As Jennifer put on the backpack, Jackie walked into the room, carrying a duffel bag. Placing it on the ground, she knelt and unzipped it. Inside was a small case, which she handed to Elizabeth.

"Inside that case, you will find earbuds. I want you all to wear one." Jackie informed them.

Elizabeth opened the case, pulled out an earpiece, and studied the small, tan item. It looked like a mini hearing aid.

"Pass the case around, and everyone stick it in your ear. They automatically turn on when they leave their case."

Elizabeth passed the case to Jennifer, and she plopped the bud in her ear.

"Use these to talk to each other if you separate. To activate, simply tap the earpiece, then tap again to turn off. You don't need to do anything to hear someone. Call me if anything unexpected happens. I will stay here, keeping an eye on the vessel and your movements.

"We have reached our destination and are coming to the surface. Let's go wait by the door."

Following her, they stopped in front of the same door they entered.

"You're not coming?" Elizabeth questioned.

Turning to face the team, Jackie clasped her hands in front of her, fiddling with her fingers.

"I don't do field work anymore. I haven't for years."

"Why?"

"I'm just better in the background. I always end up becoming a liability."

Elizabeth narrowed her eyes. She knew there was more to the story, but didn't want to pry. Maybe she'd ask her later.

"Okay, stand on the platform in the center of the room. You will notice a rowboat; use it to reach the shore. I will be close by. Paige, let me know when you have Daisy and Sofie, and when you exit the cave. I will be waiting for you. Then we will go back in to rescue the rest of the hostages."

After everyone was in a safe position, Jackie pulled a lever, which caused the platform to steadily lift from the floor. The rowboat laid on the platform next to them, rising with the floor.

Once they reached the surface, they were surrounded by salt water, and their nostrils were assaulted by the intense smell. Spotting the island, Zola and Josh each grabbed an end of the boat and walked it to the side of the submarine. They were close enough so that the water just barely touched them.

One by one, they climbed into the boat while Josh held onto it. After they were all evenly spread out, he jumped in and took over the oars. His strength allowed him to effortlessly push the oars through the water. After thirty minutes of silence and the salty breeze blowing through their hair, they arrived on shore.

As expected, there were no guards. The terrorists were too cocky to assume someone would find their little oasis. The team hid the boat in a bush and put branches over it until they were satisfied that no one would discover it.

"All right, everyone," Elizabeth said as she wiped the sweat from her brow, "follow behind me. Stay low."

They trekked quickly behind her, running quietly through the tropical forest. The sounds of squeaking and chirping from the local animals hummed soothingly through the air. This island would actually be a beautiful place if it didn't house such evil.

After 30 minutes of running, they were all panting and drenched in sweat. They reached into their backpacks and chugged some water.

"Are you there yet?" Elizabeth heard Jackie through her earpiece.

"Almost, Jackie," she replied. "All right, team, the cave is just over this hill. Jennifer, you go first. Let me know what you see."

Jennifer sprinted up the hill as if the last couple miles were easy. She must have spotted the cave immediately, because she ducked to the ground. She crept closer to the edge of the hill. Once she was confident no one was around, she talked into the earpiece, telling them it was safe.

When the team peeked up from behind the hill, Jennifer waved her arms for them to come to her. They cautiously ran to her and flattened their backs against the cave wall. They inched along the side until they found the entrance. Jennifer looked around the corner, then used her hands to signal it was safe to enter.

"This feels too easy," Elizabeth whispered.

"I agree," responded Jennifer. "Keep your eyes peeled for anything suspicious."

They sneaked around the cave halls, making sure to be aware of all their surroundings. It was eerily quiet, and the path was lit by dim candlelight. They eventually came to a split path, and Elizabeth took the lead, heading towards the right.

"Almost to Daisy's room, guys. Just follow me."

They passed by a few closed-off rooms and some rooms that were without doors, lit by candles. The halls were empty, and the rooms were silent. Their own breathing and the light clicking of feet echoed around them. The air felt cool and damp and smelled of mold.

Finally, Elizabeth came to a halt and turned to a wooden door. There were cracks in the door, so a soft light could be seen. Elizabeth tapped her knuckles on the door.

"Daisy, you there?"

She could hear the scuffling of feet, then the door opened a crack. Sunken eyes stared up at her, then widened.

"Elizabeth?"

Elizabeth nodded and smiled softly. Daisy opened the door all the way and ushered them to enter. When they were all inside, she frantically looked up and down the halls to make sure no one had witnessed their entry. Sofie was sitting on the bed. She looked at them curiously.

Tapping her earpiece, Elizabeth spoke, "We found the girls, Jackie. Daisy and Sofie are safe."

"Great job. And the other hostages?" Jackie replied.

"Haven't found them yet. We'll get them, though."

"Keep up the good work."

Elizabeth tapped the earpiece to cut the communication.

"You're actually real," Daisy said in awe.

"Told you." Elizabeth winked, then looked at the little sister. "Hi, Sofie," Elizabeth greeted sweetly.

"Elizabeth! You came! I knew you would come for us!"

Sofie beamed with happiness. She jumped over to her sister and hugged her around the waist. Daisy looked worse than Elizabeth could have imagined. She looked far too thin, her dress like a tent, and her skin was so pale she was almost transparent. Her skin was bruised around her neck, wrists, and ankles.

Daisy looked down at her feet in shame from Elizabeth's worried stare.

"We will make them pay," Elizabeth growled. "Are you ready?"

Daisy blinked dreamily and looked around at everyone. "I'm ready."

"Good. Paige is going to guide you and Sofie out of here and back to our boss. Then we will take you back to the United States. Are you okay with that?"

"Yes."

"Did you by chance figure out where the other hostages are?"

"No. I couldn't find them."

"Okay. It's okay. We'll find them."

Paige walked up to Daisy and grabbed her hand. "I'll take care of you two." She smiled. She pushed a state of calmness outward, instantly relaxing them.

"You girls be careful. We have five guards to play with." Elizabeth smirked.

"You should be careful too." Paige walked out the door, hand in hand with Daisy and Sofie. Elizabeth walked to Daisy and Sofie's bed, preparing to travel and search for the five men responsible for assaulting Daisy.

Chapter 33

Elizabeth laid on the bed, relaxing her mind, to find where the guards were hiding. Coincidentally, they were all hanging out in the chambers where she first witnessed them assault Daisy.

"I know where they are. Follow me."

The five of them crept down the halls until they came upon tall double doors. Elizabeth swung them open, catching the guards by surprise. They turned with widened eyes on their ugly faces.

"Hey! You can't be in here!" the oldest one shouted.

Elizabeth ignored them and casually walked closer. The others spread out around them, like a group of hyenas stalking their prey.

"Careful, she doesn't like being told what to do," said Jennifer in a creepily sweet voice.

"Can I have the big one?" Josh asked.

"You can have whichever one you want." Elizabeth smirked.

"You all need to leave, now! The lady won't be happy."

"Oh, no!" Zola shouted, with mock fear.

They crept closer, backing the men into a corner of the room. They pulled their chosen weapons from their belts. Elizabeth had the whip, Michael had a dart in each hand, Josh had his giant axe, and Jennifer had a handful of daggers. The most terrifying of all was Zola. She held no weapon, but as they got closer to the men, a stream of rats ran into the room. Too many to count gathered behind her, while some climbed up the door to seal off the exit. Chitters and squeaking filled the air, until everything went silent. All that could be heard was the frightened panting of the guards.

"What's wrong?" Jennifer pouted. "Not used to picking on someone that can fight back?"

"What do you want?" One of them tried to sound brave.

"Oh, it's simple. We just want you to apologize to Daisy."

"Daisy?"

"The girl you raped."

The man just snickered. Elizabeth swung her whip, the tail landing right by his feet. He jumped and yelped.

"I wouldn't piss off my friend. She has anger issues." Jennifer warned.

"I'm sorry! I'm sorry!" he blubbered nervously.

"What do you think, Elizabeth? Is he sorry?"

Elizabeth let her arm relax, drawing the whip away from him, making the man sigh in relief.

"They aren't sorry. All of you take off your robes."

They hesitated for a second, but Elizabeth flinched, causing them to quickly strip off their clothes. She walked past each of them, gathering their robes and placing them away for later use.

"You all are just a bunch of cowards," she sneered.

"Please let us go! We won't tell the lady anything!"

She cocked her head to the side and pretended to contemplate. She walked closer and placed a hand on the speaker's shoulder. She smiled softly, making him think she was going to have pity, but her smile quickly turned malicious. Pulling a dagger from her belt, she jammed it into his upper thigh, just inches away from his second brain. He screamed, causing the other men to dash towards the door.

Unfortunately for them, there was no escape. The other four team members casually turned towards the door, watching the men trying to dig their way through the rats.

"What's going on? Everything okay?" Elizabeth heard Jackie through the earpiece.

Not wanting to be distracted by Jackie, Elizabeth took out her earpiece and stuck it in her pocket. She saw Josh press a finger to his earpiece as he muttered something she couldn't hear.

"Leaving so soon? The party is just starting," said Jennifer.

Zola commanded the rats to surround the men. Climbing up their legs, the rodents shoved them to the ground. The men screamed and tried to scramble away, but the combined strength of the rats overwhelmed them. They were dragged over to five chairs. As the rats sat the four men in the chairs, Jennifer pulled rope out from the backpack, then tied them with it. Josh dragged the man Elizabeth wounded to sit next to the others. Once they were secured, the rats scattered and made their way back to Zola's side.

"Do you feel helpless like she did?" Elizabeth asked.

"Are you scared like she was?" Jennifer chimed in.

"Please! We are sorry!" the oldest one cried. Like a coward.

"No, you aren't," Zola grunted.

Josh grabbed his victim's shoulder and slowly squeezed it. A pained whine emerged from the man's throat.

"Not so tough, now. What happened to the big, strong men who tied down a child?" Elizabeth mocked them.

Elizabeth pulled out her dagger and began walking toward the oldest guy, ready to stab him in the stomach. Before she could plunge her knife into his bulging belly, she felt a hand on her shoulder, and then was pulled away from the man. She furrowed her brows and turned to see Jennifer looking at her, her brows drawn together.

"Don't do this; it's not worth it."

"I have to, for Daisy and any other woman they've hurt."

"They'll get what's coming to them. If you kill them, then their punishment will be over. Don't give them that mercy."

Elizabeth contemplated Jennifer's words, then breathed aggressively through her nose. Looking into her sister's eyes, she saw the determination to prevent her from killing these men. She also saw sadness. This woman killed her first person at the age of thirteen. She killed several men. Did this scenario remind her of her parents? Did seeing them tied in chairs bring back those traumatic memories? These men were killers, too. Who knew how many innocents they'd hurt? They were also connected to the people that killed Jennifer's parents.

If Jennifer could hold herself back, show mercy, then she would too.

"Fine." She put her dagger back on her belt.

The man's face showed a brief look of uncertainty. Then Elizabeth curled her fingers into a fist and smashed it as hard as she could into his nose. Blood gushed from his nostrils as he screamed in pain.

"Doesn't mean I can't leave him with a broken nose," she taunted, and gave an evil smile. "That's for Daisy, you fucker." She pulled the earpiece from her pocket and stuck it back in her ear. Activating it, she said, "Jackie, we have apprehended the men I saw hurt Daisy."

"Great job. Keep me in the loop."

"Let's go get Priscilla," Jennifer said. "We've wasted enough time on these worms of men."

Elizabeth nodded in agreement. They put on the black robes, then opened the exit doors and left the men. It was time for the next part of their mission.

Chapter 34

Elizabeth led the others down the eerily quiet stone hallways. She was navigating her way to the throne room, hoping that was where Priscilla would be.

"Elizabeth..." she heard a sweet, taunting voice call out.

"Did you guys hear that?"

"I didn't hear anything," replied Jennifer.

She scrunched her eyebrows and felt a chill crawl down her spine. Something didn't feel right.

"Come find me, Elizabeth..." The voice spoke again.

She stopped in her tracks; her face grew hot as the realization came to her.

"What is it?"

"She knows we're here. Priscilla knows."

Instincts kicking in, Elizabeth took off. The rest dashed behind her. She came to a double door and swung it open.

Twenty-seven men in robes snapped their focus to her and the team. They had apathetic looks on their faces, as if they were not surprised their home had just been invaded.

The throne where Priscilla usually sat was empty. Elizabeth panicked as her eyes darted around the room.

"Up here, Elizabeth."

She looked up to see a stone bridge about twenty-five feet from the ground. There was Priscilla, along with two of her right-hand men. She looked regal in a velvet robe the color of blood. The men had Sofie and Daisy, blindfolded, gagged, and tied up, while Priscilla had — Paige. She had Paige up there, with a blade pressed against her throat.

"Hello, Elizabeth."

Elizabeth gulped and stared into Paige's terrified eyes. From her peripheral, she saw Josh tap on his ear, and she assumed he was updating Jackie. Elizabeth returned her focus to Paige.

"What's going on?" She heard Jackie through the earpiece, her voice panicked. "Where's Paige?"

Elizabeth couldn't respond, afraid that if she let her attention leave Paige for one second, something bad would happen.

"I'm calling for backup," Jackie said.

Michael walked forward.

"I wouldn't come any closer, Michael," Priscilla warned.

"How do you know who we are?" Elizabeth struggled to keep her voice even.

"The same way you know about me. Except I got it straight from the source."

"I don't understand…"

Priscilla sighed. "My, my. They've done a poor job in training you, my dear. From one Dream Traveller to another, let me give you some advice. Guard your mind."

Elizabeth's insides froze. Priscilla, a Dream Traveller? How could nobody have known? "You got inside my head?"

"I did more than get inside your head. I've been manipulating you for a while now. Did you think it was an accident when you stumbled upon my little operation? I've known about you for years. I've been watching you."

Elizabeth shook her head in disbelief. "How? How did you find me?"

"I can teach you. I can teach you so many things, Elizabeth. Together we can take over the world. You have no idea the power you hold. That's why Jackie has been keeping such a close eye on you. That's why she had her pet, here, spy on you." She shook Paige.

"I wasn't! I swear!" Paige cried out.

"Don't hurt her."

"She's been controlling you. I've felt it."

"You're wrong. She wouldn't do that."

Priscilla chuckled. "She's an empath, that's what they do." She stroked Paige's cheek with the knife, making Elizabeth growl possessively. "You're young and naive. You're just a puppet to them. With me, you'd be an equal. We could make the world a better place together."

"I'm nobody's puppet! And I don't think instructing men to rape a child is going to make the world a better place!"

"She grew up around privilege, thanks to her father who built his reputation and wealth off the backs of those he viewed as lesser. I know it wasn't her fault, but in war there are always casualties. She's just a means to an end."

"You're crazy to think I'd ever join you!"

"Maybe not now, but you will join me."

Then it felt like everything went into slow motion. Priscilla lowered her knife and pushed Paige forward. Paige's body fell from the ledge, and Elizabeth sprang into action. She ran forward in hopes of breaking some of Paige's fall, but the guards grabbed her and held her back. Adrenaline pumped through her veins; she could neither hear nor think of anything else but getting to Paige.

"Let me go!" She struggled to escape their grasps, but it was hopeless. Paige's body hit the ground with a loud thud. "Paige!" she screamed. Paige's body was unmoving.

Rage took over. All she could see was red. "Take them all down. Make them hurt. Save Priscilla for me," she directed her team.

They wasted no time. Zola called to every living creature in the area, and they came crawling from the walls. Insects and rodents surrounded the men. Their screams maniacally bounced from the walls as the bugs swiped them away. Zola looked ethereal as she stood there, focused on commanding her small army of creatures. Her eyebrows pinched together, and her eyes were focused straight ahead.

Jennifer threw a dagger into the shoulder of a man charging her. As he fell to his knees, holding onto his wound, Josh ran behind him, wrapping his arm around the man's neck until he passed out. Jennifer sprinted forward, pulling out another dagger in time to throw it into the foot of a man trying to catch them off guard. When another enemy closed in, she lifted her leg and smashed her heel into his chin. The force caused his teeth to clash together, biting through his lip in the process.

Elizabeth saw five guards surrounding Jennifer and Josh, and almost shouted to warn them. Josh let go of the man he'd choked, however, and noticed just in time. Pulling out his axe, he swung it around him, making the mass of men back up.

While Jennifer and Josh kept their opponents at bay, Zola menaced guards with her creatures. Bees swarmed around two men, not stinging, but disorienting them with their loud buzzing. Beetles and ants climbed up legs, spreading along bodies. Men swatted at their bodies, trying to kill the insects crawling on them. Rats overpowered limbs, trapping their enemies, concealing them on the ground. Bats circled around heads, screeching into ears.

The path cleared for Michael to go straight to Paige, guarding her body from anyone that wanted to do harm. He held his ear to her heart and checked her pulse.

The more skilled warriors guarded Priscilla and held onto Elizabeth. Fury filled every bone in Elizabeth's body, until she passed out. She concentrated on the guards holding her captive, traveling to them, then made their bodies walk over to Josh and Elizabeth. They knelt on the ground and spread their arms like they were sacrificing themselves. Josh head butted one, while Jennifer elbowed the other in the nose. Their bodies slammed onto the ground, and Elizabeth travelled to the guards protecting Priscilla.

The men protecting their queen changed course by grabbing her. Priscilla laughed.

"You are so powerful, Elizabeth! Imagine how much you could do if trained by the right person!" Priscilla shouted.

The men dragged her down some handmade stone stairs until they came to Jennifer and Josh. Elizabeth made the two guards grab some leftover rope and tie Priscilla, until she felt confident the woman couldn't leave, not that she was putting up much resistance. She just kept laughing, like it all amused her.

"Can you retrieve Daisy and Sofie while Josh and I hold off the rest?" Jennifer asked.

The two men nodded in sync, then turned for the guards holding onto the girls. Daisy and Sofie were being held by their hair, and their mouths and eyes covered. Elizabeth's anger grew at the sight.

"Brothers?" one of the free guards asked Elizabeth's puppets, "What are you doing? Where is our lady?"

"She's safe." Their voices spoke together. The men restraining the two girls scrunched their brows.

Elizabeth made her puppets, the men she controlled, move to the guards holding the girls. Each puppet wrapped their hands around the other guards' heads, palms at their temples with their thumbs pressed to their eyes. Their victims screamed, instinctively letting go of the girls to try to pry away their hands. Daisy and Sofie dropped to the ground, shaking in fear, wrapping their arms around themselves.

The puppet guards squeezed until their thumbs gouged their victims' eyes in. Blood squirted from eye sockets as they fell to the ground, crying, grasping at their eyes. Letting the men go, her puppets grabbed the girls and held them.

"It's Elizabeth," they whispered to them, "Don't be afraid."

The guards brought them to Elizabeth's sleeping form.

"My body is right in front of you. Keep the blindfolds on for now. I don't want you to see this," they said.

While Jennifer and Josh had gotten through about a quarter of the men, Elizabeth knew she had to speed things up, for Paige's sake. The anger burned through her veins, through every inch of her body. Letting go of control, she let her dream travelling take over. Elizabeth expanded her reach to all the guards still conscious. All the screaming and fighting stopped. All that could be heard was the squeaking and buzzing of the animals.

Jennifer, Josh, and Zola looked around, confused.

"Elizabeth?" Jennifer called out to her, "What's going on?"

She didn't answer. Elizabeth wasn't there anymore. She'd let her power take over, and it was out for blood.

The guards moved towards each other, so each man was facing another. Lifting their arms, they pointed their weapons at each other's throats.

Jennifer's face blanched, and her eyes widened.

"Lizzy? Liz... Don't do it!" she cried.

Elizabeth wasn't in control. She commanded the men to stab each other, feeling every sharp pain. She didn't care and welcomed the sensation.

Blood soaked into the sandy floor; splattered the walls. Some splattered on Jennifer, but she didn't flinch. Zola stood frozen, her mouth gaped open, the color leaving her face. Josh stepped in front of the two women, as if protecting them from Elizabeth's body. His bravado faltered slightly as he watched the bodies fall.

"Elizabeth…" Jennifer's voice was barely a whisper.

The last body fell, and Elizabeth jumped back into her body. Looking around, she saw the death she caused.

Nausea washed over her. Her eyes stung, like she wanted to cry, but she was too shocked to express emotions.

"What have I done?"

Hysterical laughter and clapping could be heard from Priscilla in the background.

Jennifer stepped around Josh, cautiously walking towards Elizabeth, like she was a rabid animal. Kneeling in front of her, she bent to Elizabeth's eye level. Elizabeth stared off into nothingness, and Jennifer reached forward, trying to bring her sister back to reality.

"It's going to be okay, Elizabeth," Jennifer said, with a soft tone.

Raising her hand, Jenifer stroked Elizabeth's cheek.

"Elizabeth…"

At that moment, Jackie came bursting into the room, with DUST soldiers following behind her. They all paused at the sight in the room. The masks on the warriors' faces hid their emotions, but Jackie's could be seen. She seemed equally horrified and worried.

Jennifer stared at her, then in her head said, "I'll take care of Elizabeth. Get Daisy and Sofie out, and have DUST find the rest of the hostages. They have to be around here somewhere. Paige needs immediate medical attention. She's with Michael under the bridge."

Josh must have told Jackie about Paige's fall, because she instructed two soldiers carrying a stretcher to go to the wall, where Paige and Michael were. Jennifer glanced their way and saw Michael sobbing over his sister's unconscious body. The stretcher was lowered, and Paige was carefully placed on the stretcher. Michael followed them as they carried her out of the room.

Zola and Jackie guided Daisy and Sofie from the room. Holding their hands, the women encouraged the girls to stay blindfolded, so they wouldn't see the dead bodies. Josh grabbed Priscilla and passed her off to a couple soldiers to take care of.

Five soldiers remained, watching Elizabeth, Jennifer, and Josh.

Jennifer and Josh helped Elizabeth to her feet, her eyes still seeming unfocused. Knowing Elizabeth needed time to process, Jennifer didn't try to say anything. They helped her walk back to the sub, with the soldiers following behind. The soldiers weren't reassuring; if they came, that meant the agency knew they disobeyed.

Chapter 35

Elizabeth, Jennifer, Josh, Jackie, Michael, Paige, and Zola rode back to the base in the plane the agency had used to arrive so quickly on the island. There were DUST agents located in Madagascar, which was how they got to Jackie's team in just an hour. Some DUST soldiers took charge of returning the submarine and the plane Jackie borrowed.

The new plane was large enough to carry the hostages and some of the soldiers, although it was a tight squeeze. They were able to recover twenty kidnapping victims, plus Daisy, Sofie, and their mother. They were kept in the back, where soldiers and a medic attended to them. It was chaos all around as tortured victims screamed and cried and soldiers barked orders. The soldiers that didn't fit on the plane stayed back, working on cleaning up some of the mess. Another plane would arrive to take them back.

Priscilla was being kept tied up in the front, where Jackie's team and some more soldiers could keep an eye on her.

Jackie checked on Daisy and Sofie and found them sitting on the ground being hugged by their mother. Mrs. Chatawick's dyed blond hair was greasy, with her darker roots starting to show. Like the rest of the victims, she looked far too thin, collar bones jutting out.

Kneeling to their level, Jackie said, "Hello. I just wanted to come check on you. Your daughters are the reason we were able to find you."

Wetness formed in Mrs. Chatawick's eyes. "Thank you."

"Where's Elizabeth?" Sofie asked.

"She was injured during the fight," Jackie lied, not wanting them to know the truth. "She'll be okay, but right now she's having trouble speaking."

"When she's feeling better, can we thank her?" Daisy asked.

"Of course. I'll reach out when she's better. Is there anything I can get you?"

"No. I just want to go home and return to normal."

"Of course. We will get you home as soon as we can."

"Elizabeth... she... I know things happened to me, bad things... somehow, she made it so I can't remember them. Will you make sure she knows how thankful I am?"

Tears ran down their mother's face at Daisy's words, but Daisy just looked exhausted. Reading her thoughts, Jackie knew she felt too tired to cry.

"I'll make sure she knows, but I assure you, she protected you out of her own volition. Knowing you're safe will be thanks enough for her."

Daisy nodded.

"I'm going to check on my team now, but let me know if you need anything," Jackie said before turning back to the front of the plane.

Then Jackie tried to check on Paige. The young woman she swore to protect, and whom she'd failed. She never should have let her go into that cave. Jackie knew Paige was a powerful empath, but like her, Paige wasn't a fighter. They weren't agile or fierce in that way. Their minds were their weapons. Paige wasn't confident enough yet. She had so much potential, but she didn't understand how to unlock the full use of her powers. That would take time. Time they might no longer have.

"Get away from her!" Michael yelled at Jackie as she inched closer. "You promised you'd protect her!"

Nodding, Jackie kept her distance. His words stung, but she knew he was deflecting. In truth, he blamed himself; she could hear his thoughts. She would take the blame if it made him feel better. After all, it was more her fault than his.

"You're right. I did. I'm sorry, Michael. The agency will do everything they can for her."

Michael didn't respond. Instead, he turned back to his sister, watching as medics did what they could to keep her stable until they arrived ashore. Knowing there was nothing more she could do in that moment, Jackie left Michael and Paige to go back to the rest of the team.

Jennifer sat next to Elizabeth, her thoughts loud with worry.

"Why did she do that? How did she do it? It's like she wasn't even there. How can I help her through this? Oh, god, what if DUST kills her?"

"Jennifer." Jackie interrupted her thoughts. "How is she?"

Jackie sat across from them, next to Josh and Zola. Elizabeth stared forward, looking at nothing, in shock.

"She hasn't said anything. She won't even look at me."

"She just needs some time to process."

Jennifer's brows pinched together. "Are we in trouble? I assume DUST knows that we disobeyed."

"Yes, I unfortunately had to call them. We needed help. As for in trouble, no. None of you are in trouble. Everything will be okay."

Jennifer didn't believe her, but Jackie was determined to make sure her team didn't get in trouble. She was in charge, she gave the order, now she would deal with the repercussions.

The rest of the ride back, Jackie kept silent. The sounds of the hostages haunted her, and she knew they also haunted her team. Elizabeth seemed to be digesting the day's events, as she began to look more like herself and less like a hollowed-out person.

"We will be arriving at the airport soon, where a vehicle will await to escort you back to the agency," a soldier alerted them.

"Thank you," Jackie replied.

"What's gonna happen?" Elizabeth whispered.

"We are going to get back to the base, shower, get some food, and sleep."

"There's no way they'll let us off the hook."

"I'm not going to let anything happen to you." Jackie stared into Elizabeth's eyes, giving her a serious look to show her how much she meant it.

"We are descending," an announcement issued through the speakers. "Please buckle up, and prepare for landing."

Jackie and the team put on their buckles. As she surveyed her team, the nervous looks were obvious.

The plane landed, and the team members were brought to the van. Noticing how intimidatingly the soldiers were acting, Jackie knew she was in trouble. Another vehicle pulled up behind them, and Jackie saw Priscilla comply as soldiers pushed her into the van. Paige was hauled into an ambulance, and Michael followed in after her. Tears filled Jackie's eyes as she hoped Paige would be okay. Jackie lost so much already; she didn't know how she'd survive if she lost Paige too.

Blinking back her tears, Jackie masked her emotions. She couldn't let the team know she was upset. Jennifer and Elizabeth squeezed each other's hands, both thinking they were going to be killed, regardless of Jackie's reassurance. Josh and Zola occasionally whispered to one another, too low for Jackie to hear over the murmuring of the vehicle, but she could hear their thoughts.

Josh was worried about what would happen for different reasons. He didn't think they'd kill him, not after all the times he'd lashed out with his powers, but he was worried about punishment and for his new friends. He thought they'd lose privileges or be watched more closely. Zola was also afraid for her new friends, and she didn't want security to ramp up. She didn't think she could handle any more restrictions.

Morning was approaching, and with no sleep, Jackie struggled to maintain her composure. As much as she knew this whole ordeal was her fault, she had no control over Vance's actions. Fairness wasn't in his repertoire. He could see this as an opportunity to get rid of Elizabeth.

They arrived at DUST's base, the soldiers stepped out from the front seats, then opened the doors for Jackie and the rest of them. The chilly morning mountain air hit Jackie's face, reminding her of Vance's demeanor, his icy stare.

The other van pulled up behind them, and Priscilla climbed out of the van. Jackie eyed her as she allowed the soldiers to manhandle her. As soon as Josh told her Priscilla was a Dream Traveller through the earpiece, Jackie went on full alert. She remembered the panic, the adrenaline running through her body. Priscilla being a Dream Traveller was a curveball none of them anticipated. Calling the agency, asking for help, was supposed to be a last resort.

Priscilla must have used her dream travelling powers to figure out they were on the island. Jackie didn't know how she captured Paige, and she couldn't read Priscilla's mind to find out. She found Priscilla's compliance suspicious. She didn't fight the soldiers once. The whole thing seemed humorous to her.

Gently nudged forward, Jackie and the rest of her team walked towards their fate. They went through the garage, then down the stairs to the lowest level, where they were brought into the large room before the cells. Vance sat on a cheap plastic chair. Ten men she'd never seen before stood behind him. Jackie internally gulped, but she wouldn't show Vance her fear.

"Thank you, soldiers," he said to the people that escorted them, "We can take it from here. You can go home."

They left Jackie, Elizabeth, Jennifer, Josh, and Zola alone with Vance and his cabal. The whole thing felt ominous. No person should be treated this way, but it seemed DUST didn't view them as human.

"Vance, what's…"

"That's enough, Jackie," he interrupted her. "I'll be the one speaking."

Jackie could feel the nervous stares of her team.

"You deliberately disobeyed my orders. You put the whole team at risk. You almost lost one. You might still. You knew we were going to be sending out our own agents to save the hostages from the terrorist group, yet you decided to go on your own. You stole government property to do so."

Vance walked closer to the group, and Jackie stepped in front of them protectively.

"It was my best judgement to go as soon as possible. I didn't think the hostages could survive much longer, I…"

Vance stopped right in front of her, lifted his hand, and struck her across the face. The impact was hard enough to make her fall to the ground. Jackie heard a gasp from behind her, but was too disoriented to tell whose. Josh went towards her, but she put up her hand, hoping he would listen and stay.

Clenching his jaw, Josh nodded and stayed back. The last thing Jackie wanted was for Josh to get himself in trouble.

"Your insubordination makes us all look bad." Vance went back to his cool demeanor. "What if we got in trouble for taking government property without authorization? We still might. What if your team got discovered? How can I trust you if you go off and do your own thing when you disagree? Now I have to come up with a punishment for you all. Your actions have consequences. I could have you all killed."

"NO!" Jackie showed her panic for the first time since walking into the room. "It was my fault! My team had no clue they were doing anything wrong! Please don't punish them for something they had no part in!"

Vance cast his eyes down at her, head raised high, while Jackie stayed down on her knees. Playing on his ego was in Jackie's best interest. He cocked his head.

"And how should I punish you?"

Vance glanced back at her team, no doubt gauging their reaction at his degrading question. Jackie realized he didn't just want to hurt her; he also wanted her team to lose their respect in her.

Unsure of what to say, she managed, "However you see fit... sir," she added on the end, to solidify her defeat.

"Very well."

Reaching forward, Vance grabbed her hair, then dragged her across the room. She winced, struggling not to scream out in pain. She grabbed at his hand, trying to relieve some of the pressure. Looking back at her team, she saw the horror on their faces. Josh was holding Zola back from running after her. Elizabeth and Jennifer both had a look of absolute rage. Vance threw her down in the middle of the room, Jackie groaned as her body slammed on the concrete.

"Now, I want all of you to watch. Watch what happens when you disobey me," he growled at Jackie's team.

Without warning, he kicked his booted foot into Jackie's stomach. She made an effort to not make a sound. Now Josh began to charge for her. Jackie couldn't have him interfere. It would only make things worse.

"Stay back, Josh!" she said telepathically, "He'll only make the punishment worse. He might even kill you if you try to stop him."

Josh froze in his place. Jackie could see his red face and teary eyes before Vance struck again, kicking her in the same place. He kicked her thighs, and her back. Everything but her face throbbed. Losing track of time, she didn't know how long he hurt her for. It felt like an eternity, but being abused by Vance wasn't new to her. She took joy in Vance's annoyance at not being able to break her. This time would be no different.

After what felt like forever, he finally paused, panting from the exertion of beating her.

Hoping he was done, she looked up at him. She didn't know when she started crying, but her cheeks were wet from the tears.

"Now, you know the drill, Jackie. This stays between us, and I won't kill your precious team members."

Jackie could only grunt in response, her body unmoving on the ground. It hurt to breathe.

He turned to her team. "I expect you to take care of her. I'm too busy to bother."

Vance walked away, brushing between Jennifer and Josh, and his men followed behind. Once the door closed, Josh ran to her. He dropped to his knees, holding her face in his hands.

"Oh, Miss Jackie." His voice filled with distress and worry. "I wish you would have let me do something."

"He would have killed you." She coughed.

"Let's get her to Michael's lab," said Jennifer. "We can probably find something to help her in there."

"Michael might be mad, but he'll take care of you, Jackie," Josh reassured her.

Jackie could hear them talking, but the pain started to get to her. She couldn't make out what they were saying as the darkness began to sink in.

"Get William," Jackie whispered, before she passed out.

Chapter 36

Back at the base, Priscilla was taken to a cell much like the one Elizabeth had been trapped in, strapped to a chair with Michael's special headphones in her ears so she couldn't dream travel. They had to extract information from her, but it was difficult since she had built walls so strong in her mind. By leaving her strapped to an uncomfortable chair, they were hoping to make her so exhausted that her mind would become weak. She had been holding her composure, sitting and grinning confidently.

Meanwhile, Elizabeth lay curled up next to Paige's comatose body. It had been two weeks since Paige fell from that ledge, and she still hadn't given any sign that she would wake. The memory of the terror in Paige's eyes while Priscilla held the knife to her throat was embedded into Elizabeth's head. Paige looked so sad when that wench said she was trying to control Elizabeth, to spy on her. If only Elizabeth could tell her she never believed that to be true. She knew Paige would never hurt her; she was too pure and kind to be that manipulative.

Now all she could do was be there for her, just in case she awoke. She watched Paige's chest rise and fall. Slowly rising to prop herself on her elbow, Elizabeth made sure to not mess with the IVs stuck in Paige's arm. She stared at the unconscious woman's emotionless face, something she wasn't used to seeing. Paige's lips were chapped, and her beautiful silvery hair had been shaved so the doctors could perform surgery on her split skull.

Elizabeth's train of thought was interrupted when she heard the door open. In walked Jackie. Her emotions were difficult to read, as always. She acted aloof, but now Elizabeth knew she cared. She took a beating for them. They knew they were going on the mission to that island behind the agency's back, and they knew there could be consequences, but Jackie took the blame anyways. So why did she still act like she didn't care?

"Elizabeth, how's Paige today?"

Elizabeth shrugged. "Same as yesterday."

Jackie went to the bedside and leaned close to her face. "Hmm, still can't get a read on her thoughts. That's not a good sign."

"I'm not giving up on her."

"Good. Thank you for being here for her."

"She would do the same for me."

Jackie nodded. "You're right."

"How are you?"

Biting her lip, Jackie looked at the ground. When Josh carried Jackie up to Michael's lab and laid her on the examination table, he lifted her shirt to inspect the damage. She was black and blue everywhere. They had to page Michael and take him away from his sister to come down there. He had to run an MRI on her to make sure there was no internal bleeding. Her kidney was bruised, and she had a concussion, but she had no serious injuries. They put some ointment on her bruises, and had her rest. Once Jackie felt up to it, they got her a hot bath, then an ice bath. Zola and Elizabeth carried a bed into his lab, and Jackie stayed in there while they took turns watching her, in case something happened.

A week later, she was able to walk, but Elizabeth knew she still hurt. Even now, Elizabeth couldn't ignore Jackie's slight winces as she stepped on her foot wrong. Watching what Vance did to her, being forced to stand there and do nothing, was horrifying. Elizabeth was afraid they'd kill Jackie. She didn't know how Jackie was walking, or why she was walking. She should be sleeping, healing.

"I'll be fine. It's just a little ache today," Jackie replied.

"That's good."

"Anyways, I need you to keep trying with Priscilla."

Elizabeth sneered at the thought of her. The last thing she wanted to do right now was leave Paige to attend to the women responsible for her injury.

"I know you don't want to leave Paige right now, but I'll be here with her. And I'll text Michael to have him see her too."

"Fine. At least I can torture the woman a bit."

"I hope you mean figuratively," Jackie said, not seeming to agree with the idea of torturing Priscilla.

"Yes, Jackie."

Elizabeth rolled off the bed and marched to Priscilla's cell. Just as it was every day, Priscilla sat in her wooden chair, smirking egotistically.

"Hello Elizabeth," she greeted.

Elizabeth's response was to glare, making Priscilla fake pout.

"Aww, still mad about your little girlfriend?"

Ignoring her, Elizabeth sat on the ground. Every day she came to the cell and practiced dream travelling on Priscilla. She still couldn't get any secrets from her, but eventually, she'd learned how to enter her mind and see through Priscilla's eyes. Elizabeth didn't even need to sleep anymore, now she could meditate and dream travel, like Paige taught her.

Almost instantly, she entered Priscilla's mind.

"Getting tired, I see," she thought, "I got in here faster than yesterday."

Elizabeth thought it odd that she got into Priscilla's mind so quickly. Every day, entering Priscilla's mind got a smidge easier. Almost like she purposely let Elizabeth in. Shaking away the thought, Elizabeth continued on. It didn't matter if Priscilla orchestrated Elizabeth's ability to get into her head, it only helped Elizabeth anyways.

"You did, great job love."

Elizabeth mentally rolled her eyes. "You're cocky now, but just wait until I'm done with you."

"Oooh, kinky."

She ignored the bait and instead looked for the darkest memory she could find. She saw children getting whipped and beaten. This was no place a child should have grown up. There was no love, only fear. Their version of toys seemed to be arrows and daggers. Then she came upon something so sickening that she felt her stomach coil.

"They beat a child to death right in front of you."

There was no response from Priscilla, indicating that this was a traumatic experience for her.

"She was your friend, wasn't she? She stole food. Not for herself, but all of the children. They were starving you."

"They were teaching us how to survive."

"They were abusing you. No child should be starved like that."

"Children must be disciplined."

Curious as to why she was defending her old masters, Elizabeth asked, "Why are you standing up for them?"

"I'm not."

Elizabeth could feel herself being nudged out, so she grabbed on tighter. She wanted to see this memory of Priscilla's. It wasn't difficult to stay in her head. As soon as Elizabeth willed herself to stay, Priscilla stopped trying to push her out.

The image was vivid, like a movie. It became more and more clear.

"Hmmm. Anyways, they whipped her bloody. Her skin was sliced and hanging. They flayed her. She bled out. I'm guessing she was only eight. How old were you?"

"Six. She was like a big sister to me. Taught me how to hold a knife."

"Hmmm, you were scared. I can feel it. Then, while she was bleeding out, they forced their hands down your throats and made you vomit out the food she stole for you. The whole time she stared out at you, with sorrow in her eyes, her last words were..."

"I'm sorry," Priscilla whispered.

Elizabeth left her mind and came back to her own. A single tear streamed down Priscilla's cheek. She looked into Elizabeth's eyes, the tear the only indication she felt sad.

"Don't you want revenge on the people who hurt you?" Elizabeth asked.

Priscilla said nothing, but the cockiness was gone. Elizabeth sighed and stood up to leave, but before she turned the corner, she heard Priscilla croak.

"Yes."

Chapter 37

She screwed up. Jackie promised Michael she would keep Paige safe. She shouldn't have let her go into that cave. Now she was staring down at Paige's unconscious body, which hurt more than the bruises littering her own limbs and torso. The doctors were unsure if the young woman would wake. She loved Paige, like a daughter. It was a weakness she tried to hide; if Vance knew, he would use it against her.

She couldn't lose any more people; she'd lost too much already. Twenty years ago, she lost everyone. She was seventeen years old and stuck in the same place she'd been born in, or so they told her. She lived with fourteen other people in the basement of the huge government building in the middle of nowhere. They were the government's underground superheroes, the ones who saved people behind the scenes, the ones who never got credit.

Seventeen-year-old Jackie sat on the couch, reading her favorite romance novel, when she felt large, calloused hands cover her eyes.

"Guess who?" a manly voice asked.

"Santa?" she asked, with a mockingly innocent voice.

He removed his hands, and she turned to face him. Standing there with a huge smile on his face was the leader of their troop, which he liked to jokingly call, "The Forgotten Children." His green eyes were surrounded by long, thick eyelashes, and his facial hair was cut short around his lower face. He had sandy-colored hair that never looked brushed. He was tall, with a strong build from all the time he spent training and weightlifting.

"I'm better than Santa!" he said.

"Good morning, Andrew," Jackie greeted.

Her cheeks flushed at the sight of his beautiful smile. Andrew was their Dream Traveller, and a couple years older than her. Jackie had a huge crush on him, and he knew it. It was more than a crush, really; she was in love with him. It was inevitable, though, since they had known each other for so long, and had to constantly spend time together.

She knew he noticed her blush by the way his thoughts presented themselves to her. She wasn't able to read much on him, though; his mental capabilities allowed him to hide a lot from her.

Andrew leaned his elbows on the back of the couch, getting closer to her face. Jackie noticed him becoming more and more tired lately; a slight purple shade decorated his under-eyes, but he still looked lovely.

"I spoke to Vance today." He grimaced.

Vance, their liaison for the agency, and the one her team reported to. He gave them all the creeps. As a power-hungry young man at the agency, Vance tried to act alpha-like around the men, and he always looked at the ladies with hunger as he spoke down to them. Jackie could hear his thoughts, his commenting on their bodies as he checked them out. It was predatory. He knew that Jackie was telepathic and didn't even try to hide what he thought of her, and what he'd do to her if he could. She knew he did it on purpose to embarrass her.

"What for?" Jackie asked.

"Everyone is tired, so I asked him if we could take a break for a while. All of us. Maybe go on a vacation."

"Let me guess, he said no."

"Actually, he said yes." He shrugged, "After our next mission."

"Another one already? What about their paid employees? Can't they do it? We just finished rescuing survivors from the hurricane in Florida."

"I know. I tried to suggest that, but I didn't want to tick him off and risk him taking back the vacation idea."

Jackie sighed. "Maybe it could just be us older ones? The children are so tired. They need time to be kids…" She paused, noticing the disappointment in Andrew's thoughts. "But you asked about that too, didn't you?"

"It's a big one, Jackie. He said we need Vanessa's strength and Jack's speed. Then there's Julie, we apparently need her to tell us what's going to happen, and—"

"I get it. He has an excuse for everyone."

"I'm sorry. One day, I'll be so high up the chain I'll be able to tell him off. But until then, this is the best I can do."

"I know, and I don't blame you. I just can't wait until we answer to you and not him."

"I can't either, things will be so much better then."

"So, what is this so-called important mission?"

"A group of terrorists have taken over the White House."

Jackie jumped from her seat. "What?! And you're just telling me this now? Why aren't we already on our way?"

"Because I don't think we should go."

Jackie scrunched her eyebrows. "Why?"

"I tried to dream travel there, but I couldn't." Andrew looked worried. "Which means we are dealing with someone like us. Someone with powerful mental capabilities."

Jackie stood from the couch and walked around to face him. "Did you tell Vance?"

"Yeah, he just said it was a great way for us to challenge ourselves. He seemed completely unconcerned."

"But you're worried?"

Andrew looked around as if someone could be watching. He nodded for her to follow him, and he turned in the opposite direction. She walked quickly beside him as they made their way to the library, grabbed a book after she saw him take one, then found a seat opposite him at one of the study tables in the middle of the room. He then tapped on his head nonchalantly, indicating he wanted to speak telepathically, and opened his book to make it look like he was reading.

"What's wrong?" She opened her book to make it look like they were both reading.

"There's something not right about this mission. Vance is acting suspicious. I know he's not stupid, and going into a hostile situation blind would be foolish."

"I agree. What should we do about it?"

"Leave," he said, turning a page.

She turned a page of her book, too. "Yeah, that sounds great, except how would we? And where would we go?"

"Plan A would be to have William turn off all the cameras and lights. Then I would travel to everyone's mind and have them go to sleep. Lastly, you would lead the rest of our team to the woods, run as far as you can, and not stop. William and I will catch up when we have the chance."

"It's a solid idea, but what if we get caught?"

"Then we will do the mission. The worst that could happen is we get caught, then surrender."

"Okay, if you think this is the best option, I trust you."

"Spread the word to everyone else. Tell them to be prepared at eleven tonight and to wait for the lights to shut off. And make sure they all have snacks and water packed. Wait five minutes after I leave so nothing seems suspicious. I'll see you tonight."

Jackie's eyes watered at one of the last memories she had with Andrew, but she quickly wiped them away. She grabbed a chair and pulled it up next to Paige's bedside. She sat carefully, then leaned close to Paige's ear at an angle, so that if anyone was watching the security cameras, it would appear she was just lying there.

"I made a mistake once, long ago. Out of pure naïveté." she whispered, too low for any listening devices to pick up. "It cost me everything. All but one of my team members, including the man I loved.

"He came up with a plan to escape one night, one I thought was genius at the time, but we were fools. We thought we were being so sneaky. Vance isn't stupid, though, he was watching us carefully that day, and could tell we were up to something. He could see Andrew and I were communicating telepathically and saw us sneak supplies into backpacks.

"As soon as he figured out what we were up to, he had the guards usher us by gun point to the cellars. Andrew was there before all of us, knocked out, with a metal collar around his neck. They put collars on the rest of us, until all fifteen of us were collared. Vance announced that if any of us used our powers while the collars were activated, it would shock the entire group. Then he insinuated that the older members would be in severe pain from the shock, but the younger members, their small bodies, wouldn't be able to survive.

"We were forced onto a jet. Andrew was slung over a guard's shoulder and placed on the floor, and then we were taken to the White House."

Jackie looked around the jet at everyone's faces. The younger ones had red eyes from crying, Andrew was still knocked out, and William was looking into the distance with no evident emotions. There were six guards with them, standing evenly spaced along the sides, holding rifles that were likely to kill anyone. It was unnecessary and inhumane, the way they were being treated. Jackie looked at Andrew, lying on the ground, and began to crawl towards him. She would have spoken to him telepathically, but she didn't want to test out the consequences of the collar.

One of the guards flinched as soon as she moved towards Andrew, making her freeze on the spot.

"I'm just going to try and wake him."

The guard narrowed his eyes at her as if to warn her, but nodded, then looked straight forward again. Jackie resumed crawling towards Andrew. Once she was close enough, she shook his shoulders.

"Andrew," she whispered in his ear.

He responded with a groan.

"Andrew, wake up."

He groaned again.

Jackie sighed, then began to shake him more violently.

"Ow, please, my head!" he groaned.

"Are you up?" she whispered.

"Yes, unfortunately." He squinted his eyes open and winced as he sat up. He brought his hand up to the back of his head.

"Are you hurt?"

"I got smacked in the back of the head, hard enough to knock me out."

"How? What happened?"

"It was shortly after I left the library. I went to my room and was ambushed. I didn't even have time to see who hit me, but my guess is Vance sent someone to do his dirty work."

"You've been out this whole time? They must have hit you hard."

"They really did. I think I have a concussion."

"Can you still travel?"

"Yeah, don't worry. I won't let anything happen to you or the team."

She watched as he smiled through his pain, and he leaned towards her and placed his hands over hers.

The jet ride was quick, taking just a little over an hour. They landed in an abandoned parking lot, then were ushered onto the back of a large military vehicle. Jackie looked around at her team; they looked solemn, defeated. She caught Andrew's eye several times, and he would give her sad smiles. She wished she could speak to all of them and try to get their spirits back up. What could she say, though? Time and time again, they were treated as subhumans. They were just machines, tools for their government.

After a long, solemn drive, the vehicle finally came to a stop. The back door was opened, and a guard motioned for them to exit. As soon as Jackie got out of the car, she heard a beep from her collar.

"The collars have been shut off. You can now use your powers," a guard announced, handing Jackie a small backpack probably filled with weapons and other supplies. "There is a tunnel entrance that will lead you into the basement of the White House." Other soldiers passed out backpacks to the other children as well.

"Yes, I know," a little boy that went by the name of Henry answered, "I can see it now." He had the gift of seeing paths based on where he wanted to go. He was a walking GPS.

Jackie ran up to his side and grabbed his hand. Andrew followed her and stood in front of them protectively.

"You can leave," Jackie snapped at the guard.

"Our orders are to follow you inside the tunnel, boss's orders," the guard said, with no expression.

Jackie huffed, "Fine," then knelt to be on Henry's level. "Okay, Henry, you tell us where to go, but Andrew is going to lead, as always."

"But he always leads." Henry pouted.

Andrew turned in front of him. "One day you will lead, little dude," he said as he ruffled Henry's hair. "When you're older and can beat me in hand-to-hand combat. Deal?"

"Okay," Henry grumbled.

Then they got into formation. The oldest kids stood around the sides of the group, flanking the younger ones between them. Jackie knew the younger kids were helpful, but it was still ridiculous that they were made to come. They should have been back at the base, where they were safe. However, Vance didn't care about their safety; he didn't care about them at all. The guards took up the end of the formation, and then they began to move as one unit, one machine.

Jackie linked her team's minds so they knew each other's moves and thoughts. She told them to walk fast. Without the guards, it would have looked like they were on a school field trip, but with the armed soldiers behind them, they stood out. Henry led them across the parking lot and to some abandoned-looking brick buildings on a low-trafficked street. There wasn't a person in sight as they walked through an alley and came to a stop in front of a door with chains bolted on it.

Vanessa, a twelve-year-old with wavy black hair, walked up to the door, grabbed the chains, and ripped them off with little effort. Andrew and Jackie nodded to her in appreciation before she stepped back into formation. Andrew cautiously opened the door and looked around, then nodded to Jackie. Jackie's mind link told the rest of the group that the coast was clear and that they were good to enter the building.

The inside of the building was dusty and filled with cobwebs. Broken pieces of furniture and empty paint cans were scattered randomly, making it obvious nobody had been in the building for a while. Henry guided them to the corner of the room, where Andrew found a wooden trap door under a table. Jackie assisted him with moving the table out of the way, then he opened the door. A loud creaking noise echoed throughout the eerily silent warehouse.

Since the soldiers had the decency to remain silent while they worked, Jackie could run commands and hear any important thoughts from her team. Andrew sent a thought of a metal ladder through the link, then sat down next to the open door. He shifted his body so he could shuffle his way down the ladder, then told Jackie to wait up there until he made sure the coast was clear.

After a few minutes, she heard his command to follow him down the hole. Jackie went first, then Henry, and one by one the rest followed. Jackie saw the dark tunnel before them. The ground was wet, probably from sewage or rain. Andrew had a flashlight out, so she took out hers and asked the rest of the older kids to use theirs as well. She could hear squeaks and see shadows of rats scampering around, angry that their territory was being invaded.

Henry told them they had a few miles to walk through the tunnel, so they trudged forward, the sound of water sloshing under their feet.

"Is everyone okay?" Jackie asked.

"I can't see anything," Julie replied with fear, and she didn't mean visual surroundings.

"You can't?" Jackie asked, with concern. Julie could always see what was going to happen.

"It's like there's a heavy fog in my head. I can't see through it."

She and Andrew gave each other worried looks. First Andrew, now Julie was unable to use her powers to see what was happening at the White House. Going forward with this mission seemed too risky. Jackie wanted to turn back.

"Andrew?" Jackie telepathically called to him.

"Yes, Jackie?"

"I have a bad feeling. I think we should turn back."

"I agree, the only problem is the guards behind us. And who's to say Vance won't have more guards sent? He probably has trackers in these collars. And he will probably turn them on again, and maybe leave us defenseless until the last minute. I don't want to risk anything."

"I know, but if we...."

"This is our best chance, Jackie. I've thought through every scenario, and trust me, they could all go wrong. The best thing to do is find out what's blocking my powers and take it or them out."

"Them? You think it could be a person doing this?"

"It could be. I'm not sure we are the only ones like us out there. But it could also be some device. Either way, it's a threat."

"Okay, I'll trust you know what to do."

The group continued forward in silence.

"Half a mile to go, everyone," Henry thought to the group after a half hour.

After Henry's comment, Andrew suddenly came to a halt.

"Andrew, do you see something?" Jackie asked.

Dream Traveller

But there was no answer. She couldn't hear his thoughts anymore. She couldn't hear anyone; the mind link was broken. Andrew slowly turned around to face her. His eyes were vacant, and Jackie felt a twinge of fear churn in her gut.

"Andrew?" she whispered aloud.

She watched as his pupils dilated, and a sickening smile came about his lips. Taking a casual step forward, Andrew lifted his hand. The backs of his knuckles softly grazed the side of Jackie's cheek, before he harshly grabbed her jaw and brought her face so close to his that she could have easily kissed him. Instead, he forcefully turned her head and playfully bit her earlobe, before whispering seductively, "Jackie…"

"Hey, what's going on up there?" one of the soldiers snapped.

He let go of her face and towered over her as she watched him glare at the guards behind them. She turned her head to see what was happening. One second, the guards looked confused and irritated, the next they shifted to a casual stance, with no emotions on their faces.

"Good boys." Andrew grinned.

"Andrew, what's going on? You're acting strange!" She gulped.

He looked down at her, then tucked a strand of hair behind her ear. She tried to read his mind, but it was like penetrating a thick wall.

"Don't worry, love, we will see each other again."

Before Jackie could react, Andrew lifted his flashlight and smacked Jackie so hard on the top of her head, everything went dark in an instant.

When she became conscious again, she felt a throbbing pain pulsing through her head. Why was she wet? And why did it smell like mold? Her eyes opened slowly, and then everything came back to her. They were on their way to the White House, until Andrew started acting strange. She shot up at the memory and gasped at the horror surrounding her.

Flashlights flickered under the shallow water. She picked one up and shone it around her. The water was red, and the bodies in it were unmoving. She looked to her right and saw Henry, his lifeless eyes staring right at her.

"Oh, my god," she sobbed.

She stood up and flashed it on everyone else. They were all dead. The soldiers. Her friends. She flashed her light in front of her, and there lay Andrew, with a bullet hole between his eyes. She crashed to her knees and pulled his dead body to her chest, rocking him as she wailed.

"I don't understand! I don't understand!" she cried.

She sat there, crying and holding him close, for what felt like forever. All that could be heard was the sound of her whimpers. Then she heard a cough and turned towards the sound.

"Who was that?" she wheezed, her throat sore from crying. She shone her light around until she came upon a body moving slightly.

She gently let down Andrew and walked towards the body.

"Oh, William!" she cried, "Are you okay?"

"Jackie," he coughed again.

"Where are you hurt?"

"My leg, they shot my leg. I must have passed out from the pain." He looked ghostly pale, and his eyes were half open, like he was struggling to stay conscious.

"We need to get you out of here." Tears streamed down her face. "We are so far into the tunnel. I can't carry you for that long." She pressed her face to his chest. "Everyone is dead, William."

He rubbed her back weakly. "I'm sorry, I tried to shield the kids, but they shot my leg. I was helpless to save them."

"I don't blame you. I just wish I was dead with them."

"Don't say that."

"I mean it. Why aren't I dead? Why only knock me out?"

"I don't know. But we need to get out of here if we want to find out."

"How? We can't go to the White House injured, with no backup, and the entrance is so far back."

"I mapped all the tunnels before we came here. I have them memorized. There should be a way out just a few feet behind us. Help me up." He held out his hand for Jackie.

He stumbled, but Jackie caught him before he could fall. She swung his arm around her shoulders, and he leaned his weight against her. They stumbled through the water, trying to avoid the bodies beneath. She felt tears stinging her eyes again as she looked down at the small children. They had so much more to give the world, and now they never would.

Slowly they got past all the bodies and through the water, until William stopped them at a ladder.

"Here. There should be a manhole at the top."

Jackie looked up and saw a small bit of light shining through some holes.

"Can you climb that?"

"I'll have to," he said.

She nodded and began ascending. At the top, she pushed at the heavy metal opening, and was able to budge it until her fingers could slip through the crack. She pushed and pushed until her body could fit through, then waited for William so she could help pull him up.

Chapter 38

"I just love our little visits…" Priscilla purred.

Elizabeth sat in silence on an uncomfortable plastic chair, with her elbows on her knees, and glared at her.

"Ughh," Priscilla groaned, "You are being so boring! Look, I could apologize for pushing your little girlfriend and almost killing her, but you and I both know I wouldn't mean it."

Elizabeth tilted her head. "She's in a coma, you psycho. If she dies, I will personally make sure you regret ever touching her, and Daisy."

"Oh, Daisy! I forgot about that lovely girl. How is she?"

Elizabeth growled, "You forgot about the girl you tortured? You don't get to know how she is."

Elizabeth made sure to check on Daisy every day. She travelled to her and asked for updates on her life. Daisy was currently living with her mom and sister at their vacation home on a peaceful island, to get away from the media attention and focus on healing. While Daisy's wounds had healed, she had been struggling with PTSD. Elizabeth made sure to remind her that there was no timeline in healing. She was a strong girl, and she had survived a horrific event.

"Are you always this grumpy?" Priscilla teased.

"Only when I am talking to you."

"Oh, boo!" She pouted. "I'm trying to make it up to you! I said I'd help you find my master."

"Like I trust you! You made it way too easy."

"Well, I'll just have to prove it to you then," Priscilla said flirtatiously.

"What if I help you become a better Dream Traveller?"

Elizabeth crossed her arms and leaned back in her chair. "How would you do that?"

"I've been watching you for a long time." Priscilla smirked. "And you are a very powerful traveller, but there's much for you to learn."

Elizabeth tensed. "So, you've actually been watching me? What do you mean?" Priscilla somehow knew about her team's rescue of the hostages, but maybe she knew more.

"You didn't think it was a coincidence you found me, did you? It's not like there's an abundance of Dream Travellers walking around."

"How long have you been watching me?"

"Since I first met you."

"Which was when?"

"I'll tell you when you're older." She winked.

"Stop playing games with me!" Elizabeth yelled.

"Such anger." Priscilla tsked. "Lesson number one, don't wear your emotions on your sleeve."

Elizabeth rolled her eyes, aware that Priscilla was watching her every move. Even with Priscilla locked away in this room, with Michael's headset preventing her ability to travel, Elizabeth felt powerless around her.

"Answer. My. Question." She seethed.

Priscilla sighed, "Fine. But only if you can find it."

Rolling her eyes, Elizabeth began her meditation. She easily entered Priscilla's head, since Priscilla allowed her to, and appeared to land in a room surrounded by doors. The doors were all different, some metal, some wooden, some in pristine shape, others that looked like they belonged in a junkyard, and some in between. She had never seen any mind like it. Organized. The only problem? The rooms weren't labeled, so how would she know which door to open?

"Use your instincts, love." She heard Priscilla's voice.

She walked to a metal door and pulled it open. She held it wide, and a red light assaulted her vision. She blinked a couple times to allow her eyes to adjust and was surprised to see a younger Priscilla in the center of the room. Her arms were held above her, bound by a chain hanging from the ceiling.

Her curly red hair was a mess, with some strands sticking to her sweaty forehead. There were tears in her dress, with blood seeping through shallow cuts beneath. Behind her was a man holding a whip, but Elizabeth couldn't see his face; it was encased in darkness. She saw him raise the whip and quickly slammed the door before she could witness any more. She didn't even realize her muscles had tensed, and that she was panting.

She rolled out her neck and took a deep breath before looking back at the room. She had a strong urge to go in there and save her, but she knew it would do no good.

Then Elizabeth noticed—she was experiencing Priscilla's memory from the perspective of a different person in the room.

"This is what happens when you dream travel. When you leave your body, you're no longer experiencing what happens in your body. Dream travelling becomes useful when you're going through something painful, or scary. You can simply leave. So here I am, not experiencing the pain inflicted on me. I sure felt the soreness after, though."

In the memory, Elizabeth lifted her arm, then landed a lash of a whip on Priscilla's leg. Elizabeth closed her eyes. She was unsure of why they were hurting her.

"Because they knew I was a Dream Traveller. They would hurt me while I was out so I would feel it when I went back into my body. I couldn't decide what hurt worse. Experiencing the torture in the moment, or feeling it all at once when I had to go back into my body."

Elizabeth winced as she struck the young Priscilla on the arm.

Then she heard a seductive chuckle surrounding her. "What's the matter, Elizabeth? You're not starting to feel bad for me, are you?"

Elizabeth felt a tinge of sympathy. She couldn't feel bad for Priscilla, though, because if she did, it would feel like betraying Daisy and Paige. Priscilla could have been messing with her, too, orchestrating her finding this memory. After all, it would be in Priscilla's best interest for Elizabeth to feel bad for her.

Elizabeth decided she had enough, so she carried on. Not wanting to stumble upon another horrific memory, she decided to heed Priscilla's advice and follow her instincts. She walked along each door, feeling no draw to any of them. Eventually, she came across a dark hallway. It was as if a magnetic force was pulling her in, so she decided to go with it. She kept walking until she came across an odd space in the wall. It was as if her body was screaming to stop there.

Oddly enough, all the doors were evenly spaced except in this spot, which was missing a door. There was nothing but a brick wall.

"You're getting warmer…" Priscilla hinted.

Placing her hand on the wall, she began feeling around. She noticed one of the bricks jutted from the wall slightly, so she put some pressure on it. The wall started shaking, making her jump back in fear it would collapse on her. Instead, the wall started to separate down the middle, where that odd brick was placed.

Once there was enough room, she slipped through and found another hallway. She immediately halted and gasped when she saw multiple doors, each the same one from her bedroom at her parents' house. It was a plain white door, surrounded by that intricately designed wallpaper of different flowers.

"Stalker, much?" Elizabeth whispered, with more fear in her voice than she intended.

One door looked different from the rest, however, with parts of the white paint yellowing and peeling. She gulped, her instincts telling her this was the one that would answer her question.

Cautiously, she walked over to the door and opened it. Her stomach dropped at the horrors inside. Chained to the walls were male and female teenagers, unconscious. Elizabeth took a few steps inside, and the door automatically slammed shut, causing her to twist towards it in a panic.

"No!" she screamed.

She began to run towards the door, but then it opened. A young teenager ran in, and Elizabeth instantly recognized it as Priscilla. Her eyes widened as she began to remember this moment. As if Priscilla could tell Elizabeth remembered, she felt herself being violently yanked from the room. It was like her body was being dragged through hallways, until she flinched back into her own head.

Her eyes opened to see Priscilla grinning at her. "You were there when I first travelled?"

"It's as if we're connected. Isn't it?" Priscilla replied.

"I don't understand. How can that be?"

"I think it's the universe's way of telling us we are destined for one another. You and I were made for great things."

Chapter 39

Elizabeth left Priscilla to go find Jackie and report their progress. The only problem was she couldn't find Jackie anywhere. She wasn't in her office, and she wasn't with Paige, so Elizabeth went to the only other person she could think of who would know her whereabouts.

She found Josh getting his butt handed to him by Jennifer on their designated sparring mat. It was amazing, watching a guy as large as Josh losing to Jennifer. Not that she was small; she was actually quite tall, but compared to him she was short. Josh was a good sport about it, though. Instead of pouting over her beating him, he would ask her for pointers and about what he did wrong.

Elizabeth gasped as she watched Josh throw a hook into Jennifer's side, worried that he would break a rib. Instead, Jennifer used his momentum against him, by grabbing his arm and swinging around him. Josh's ankle turned at an awkward angle, causing him to lose his footing and land on his side as Jennifer landed on top of him.

"How many times do I have to tell you this? Learn how to fight your opponent. If you're going to throw punches at someone like me, wait until I'm tired. You totally let me see exactly what you were going to do."

"But I just love being beneath you," he teased.

She punched his arm and got off him. "Shut up." Elizabeth saw her smirk, though, when Jennifer turned away.

That's when they noticed her watching.

"Enjoying the show?" Josh asked as he sat up.

Elizabeth laughed, "I'm enjoying watching you get your ass kicked by my sister."

He made a mock pouty face.

"Actually, I was looking for you, Josh. Have you seen Jackie? She seems to have disappeared."

"Yeah, she's outside at the cemetery." His joking facade suddenly faded.

"Cemetery? I didn't know there was one."

"Yeah, I'll take you," he said as he stood. "Be back in a bit, Jennifer. I know you probably need a break."

"Oh, sure." She rolled her eyes.

Josh walked over to Elizabeth and nodded, signaling her to follow. His strides were longer than hers, so she had to pick up her pace to keep up.

"You look like you've been improving since Jennifer first started training you."

"Yeah, she's a great teacher."

"She sure is."

They walked outside to the same place where they played capture the flag. She looked at him, hesitating, but continued to follow him. There was no cemetery to be seen, only dense trees. He walked all the way to the end of the field and stepped through the trees.

"Are you leading me to a cemetery, or to my death?"

"Please, if I killed you, Jennifer would kill me. Plus, we still need you. Paige needs you."

"If she wakes up."

"She'll wake up. She has to," he muttered softly.

Ever since Paige had been hurt by Priscilla, Elizabeth couldn't stop blaming herself. If she hadn't been so hell bent on revenge, she would have paid closer attention. She would have noticed that Paige and the two girls were taken, and she would have been able to stop it. And if she hadn't been so preoccupied with escaping and hating everyone, she would have spent more time strengthening her abilities, and she would have been able to take control of the men in hoods before Paige had been pushed. What-ifs weren't going to help Paige now, though, so if she ever did awaken, Elizabeth would spend every day of the rest of her life proving herself to her.

Elizabeth continued walking next to Josh through the trees in silence. It was peaceful, they were sheltered from the wind and sunlight, and all that could be heard was the sound of chirping birds. About a half mile into the forest, Elizabeth spotted a clearing. She walked closer until she could see a small graveyard, and Jackie, kneeling in front of a headstone.

"Miss Jackie?" Josh said, softly, so he wouldn't startle her.

She turned around to face them, and Elizabeth could tell that she'd been crying. She looked at Josh and saw a hint of worry in his eyes.

"Can I get you anything, ma'am?" he asked.

"No, I'm fine. Thank you, though. Did you need something?"

"Not me, but Elizabeth was looking for you. Hope it's okay I brought her here."

"Oh, yes, that's fine."

"Okay, I'll leave you to it," he said to Elizabeth, before he turned to disappear into the forest.

Elizabeth walked next to Jackie and sat down in silence.

"He's so polite and professional towards you. It's weird. Seems like he sees you as a mother figure."

"Is it not to your standards?" Jackie said sarcastically.

Elizabeth flinched at her tone, not used to any show of emotion from Jackie. "It's just not how my mom and I are."

"Well, neither of us had a mother, or a father, or any parental figure for that matter."

Elizabeth looked at the side of Jackie's face to see her perfectly trimmed eyebrows scrunched together. She looked angry and sad at the same time. Elizabeth worried she'd offended her with the attempt at humor.

"I'm not offended, Elizabeth. I'm very much aware of the unconventional ways I have parented Josh."

"I wasn't trying to be judgmental."

"I know you weren't. Don't worry, though, you have to have thick skin when you're a telepath."

"Makes sense." Elizabeth looked at the headstone. "Who's Andrew? And why does the headstone only have his first name?"

Jackie was silent for a minute. "He was the Dream Traveller I told you about."

Elizabeth looked around at all the headstones. "They all only have first names," she said, in a confused voice.

"That's all they would allow me to give them."

Elizabeth gave her a pitying look. "Who were they?"

"They were my family. My team. It's been twenty years since I saw them."

"What happened?"

"Vance sent us on a mission to the White House, and everything felt off. Andrew couldn't use his powers to see what was happening there. He told Vance that it was a bad idea, but he didn't care. Something was in the house; it drove Andrew to madness. He knocked me out, and I woke to find everyone dead, except William." She spoke with a numbness that seemed to come from years of sorrow wearing her down.

"I'm sorry, that must have been horrible."

"I was horrified, confused, angry, and heartbroken. To make matters worse, nobody cared. William and I were left to mourn alone. We even had to beg to have them bury the bodies here. Vance was considerate enough to give me two months of peace before sending me to fetch Josh.

"When I saw that scared little boy, a sense of purpose filled me. His poor heart had been broken time and time again, and he thought so lowly of himself. He thought he was a monster. I was determined to prove him wrong.

"He broke every single one of his toys, almost every plate, controllers, pencils, almost everything he touched. I remember the first time he broke a toy. It was mid-morning, and I was trying to find him for his tutoring session. It didn't take me long. I could hear his thoughts, his sad, agonizing thoughts. He was in his closet, curled in the corner, with a smashed toy car in his hands. He thought I was going to hit him, but instead I praised him for his strength and told him I'd buy him another one.

"He still felt guilty every time he broke something, but eventually he started to feel like less of a monster. That's when I realized what I was capable of. I could find people like me and make them feel more human. Help them to realize that they aren't evil.

"Andrew had a dream: to take down Vance and take over our group of powerful misfits. We'd be free to be better, to live normal lives or to save normal people. With him gone, I thought everything was over. I'd be a slave to our government for the rest of my life. But Josh gave me hope. He gave me someone to protect.

"William and I started gathering intel, him with his hacking abilities, and me with my telepathy. I used my abilities to play politics and gain favors from powerful people. I learned how to push people's buttons and manipulate them, all for the sake of keeping my kids safe and taking down Vance."

Elizabeth stared at her with wide eyes. Jackie had never opened up to her like this.

"But I made a mistake," Jackie choked out. "I never should have let you go to that island. Now Paige is…" That's when she broke down. Her hands covered her eyes, and she bowed her head to the ground as she wept.

Elizabeth was shocked by the loss of Jackie's usual bravado. "It's easy to blame yourself," Elizabeth whispered. "I blame myself too. If I hadn't been so focused on hurting those horrible men, I would have been paying attention, and she wouldn't have been captured."

Jackie shook her head, disagreeing, while she continued to lay her head in the soil.

"Before we left, Paige told me she was tired of hiding," Elizabeth said. "She was sick of feeling weak. She's anything but weak, though. You know that too. Josh is right. Paige is still in there, and we have to have hope that she can wake up.

"You are not to blame, Priscilla is. We had no way of knowing that this would be the outcome, but I know that mission was one we had to take. Daisy and Sofie would still be in that hell if we didn't go save them."

Jackie sat up, her eyes bloodshot, hair falling out of her bun, and dirt smudged her forehead. Elizabeth gave her a small smile.

"Priscilla has been watching me since I was six, Jackie." She saw Jackie's eyebrows crinkle. "She planned the entire thing. She wanted us to find her. I think she wanted us to capture her, too."

"Geez. That's nineteen years of watching you."

"I know. She says we were planned for greatness. I'm not sure what she's talking about, but she's probably being evasive on purpose."

"Be careful with her. She's dangerous."

"I know she's dangerous. But if I keep getting close to her, she can lead us to who her boss is. She also said she would help hone my dream-traveling skills."

"No." Jackie said sternly. "Gain her trust. Get as much information out of her as possible. But do not allow her to teach you how to dream travel. You have no clue what her end game is. She could be trying to get inside your head."

"But if I can be as strong as her, no one could hurt us ever again. We could take down Vance easily."

"Absolutely not. We will take down Vance in a different way. Priscilla is not to be trusted in any way. Find out who she's working for, and nothing more."

Elizabeth sighed. "Fine. But I think we are passing up a great opportunity."

"We don't know all that she's capable of. What if she takes over your mind and starts puppeteering you? I won't take any chances."

"Okay, okay, I get it." Elizabeth stood and wiped the dirt from her knees. "I'll be careful, I promise."

"You better be. I can't lose you, Elizabeth."

Elizabeth smiled at her. "You won't. I promise." She walked away.

Chapter 40

Elizabeth had been avoiding Paige for the past few days. She would sit outside Paige's door, but couldn't get herself to go in. After seeing her every day for two weeks, seeing her body looking paler and smaller, all Elizabeth could think about was the loud thump of her body as it hit the ground.

Sitting outside the room, Elizabeth hugged her knees to her chest when she heard the door open. She jumped to her feet to meet the doctor that checked on Paige every day.

"How is she?"

"Same as yesterday. Stable."

"Do you think she'll wake up soon?"

Frowning. "I don't know… If she does wake up, she'll probably have severe brain damage. It's amazing our system is still showing activity." The doctor looked concerned.

"Is there nothing you can do?"

"I've done all I can. All we can do is hope. She doesn't have a normal brain, so I don't know what's going to happen."

Grinding her teeth, Elizabeth looked at the floor angrily. She stormed off to the person responsible for Paige's sorry predicament. She flung open the door, its heavy frame banging on the cement wall. In the center of the room, still tied to her chair, was the powerful redhead, the source of her current anger.

"Careful, love," Priscilla said calmly. "You might hurt yourself."

"Shut up."

"Now, now," she cooed, "what seems to be the problem?"

"You! You're the problem!"

Priscilla gave her a teasing smile. "If I had a dime for every time I heard that. Maybe you could be more specific?"

"You know what you did! Paige is still in that stupid coma you caused!" Elizabeth yelled.

"Still?" she mocked.

Elizabeth walked straight to her and leaned so close their noses touched. "Yes," she hissed.

Priscilla didn't cower, allowing Elizabeth to stare into her green eyes. "Why not?" She whispered.

"How should I know?"

"Well, have you asked her?"

Elizabeth backed off and began to pace. "I'm not in the mood for your games, Priscilla." She said her name like it was the most disgusting thing she'd ever said.

"I wouldn't dream of playing games when you're so stressed. You're a Dream Traveller, darling, why don't you just go into her head and try to find her?"

Elizabeth paused. "I can do that?"

"Well, of course. I'm surprised you haven't tried. Isn't she the woman you love?"

"Love? Who said anything about love? Is that why you hurt her?"

Priscilla's brows rose. "No, I'm an opportunist. It did cross my mind, though."

Elizabeth glared at her. "What would you know of love, anyways? I doubt you're even capable of the emotion."

"If you say so." She shrugged.

Elizabeth began to pace again. If she could find Paige, maybe she could talk to her. Talk to the real her, not just a memory. "How do I find her?"

"Who?"

"Stop playing! Paige! How do I find Paige in her own head?"

"Are you asking me for help?"

"Unfortunately."

"If I help you, what would I get in return?"

"How about this." Elizabeth walked behind her and wrapped Priscilla's ginger locks around her hand. "If you help me, I won't kill you," she said, pulling until Priscilla's head was bent at an awkward angle.

"If you kill me, how will you find my master?" Priscilla asked cockily.

"There's always another way." Elizabeth searched her eyes. She knew she couldn't kill her, but she was hoping Priscilla wouldn't call her bluff.

"Relax, love, I'll help you."

Elizabeth slowly let go of Priscilla's hair. "Good. My friends wouldn't be happy if I killed you."

"Oh, we wouldn't want that," she teased.

"Tell me." Elizabeth circled to the front of her.

"It'll be similar to how you entered my mind; you'll have to be somewhere quiet, maybe even in her hospital room. Her head is way different than mine, though. It's not so organized."

"How do you know that?"

"Well, I've been in her head before, of course."

"Of course." Elizabeth rolled her eyes.

"Every person is different. Sometimes you find them easily. They might be wandering aimlessly through a world they created. Sometimes they're lost in a memory, sometimes they're hiding... there are so many possibilities.

So, first things first, you need to find her. Then, depending on the state her subconscious is in, you'll need to get her attention or convince her that you're real. Then you'll need to convince her to wake up."

"Sounds simple enough."

"The mind is a difficult place, but you'll get through it. Just make sure you don't get lost."

"What do you mean, lost?"

"One time I got lost in someone's head for a few days and didn't know it. Don't worry, though, I'll get you out if I need to."

"Oh, no, you are not going back into her head."

"Suit yourself. Just be careful. It would be so boring without our daily visits."

"Yeah, whatever." Elizabeth turned and left the room.

Elizabeth walked to the door of Paige's room and took a deep breath. Cautiously walking to Paige's bed, Elizabeth grabbed her hand, almost expecting her to hold her hand back; but instead, it was lifeless and cold. Her lip trembled, and she held Paige's hand tighter.

"Hi, Paige." Her voice cracked. "I'm sorry I haven't been visiting the past few days."

There was no answer, of course. Just the rise and fall of her chest under the boring hospital sheets. Elizabeth wanted nothing more than to curl up by her side, but now was not the time to cuddle. She let go of her hand and found a chair to pull up closer. Once she got comfortable, Elizabeth closed her eyes and went into that familiar, deep meditative state.

Priscilla was right; Paige's subconscious was different. There weren't doors, but tunnels, surrounded by different colors of smoke. The tunnels, walls, and floor were made of cobblestone, with creases filled with moss. It even smelled different, like lilacs and vanilla. Priscilla didn't tell her how to tell which tunnel to go through, but she did warn her not to get lost, so that meant she'd better go through the correct one. She knew that she'd had a strong sense as to which of Priscilla's doors to go through, depending on what Priscilla wanted her to see and what she was trying to find. She'd gone through the wrong door at first, but that was only because Priscilla wanted her to go through that door. Elizabeth didn't think Paige would steer her wrong; at least, she hoped she wouldn't.

As she walked past different tunnels, she felt different emotions. It seemed that Paige organized her brain by colors. Any tunnels surrounded by blue smoke oozed sadness, versus yellow smoke, which made Elizabeth feel happiness. She kept walking down the path, crossing several different tunnels.

After a few minutes, Elizabeth realized that none of the tunnels called to her. It was taking too long.

"Can you give me a hint, Paige?" she asked, hoping Paige could hear her. She felt a shift in the air, but nothing else. "Come on, Paige, I know you can hear me." She felt wind coming from behind her this time. "Paige, please," she whispered sweetly. "I need you."

That seemed to get to her, because the next thing Elizabeth knew, she was being pushed forward. It was as if there was a magnet in her chest, pulling her so quickly that the colors around her blended into one another. Within a couple blinks, the force stopped, propelling her to the ground. She closed her eyes and was prepared to hit the stone, but instead she felt softness.

She gasped and looked up. Grass surrounded her, the softest grass she'd ever felt. It led into another tunnel, but this one didn't have any smoke around it. Elizabeth could feel her; she was definitely in there. Cautiously, as if the tunnel could be spooked away, she rose to her feet and walked to the tunnel. The other side was completely dark, hiding whatever lay there, but if Paige wanted her to go through this tunnel, then Elizabeth trusted her.

When she got through, she immediately had to shield her eyes from the sunshine. Once adjusted, she took a look around. If heaven was real, this was what it would look like. The grass was green and soft, the trees were large and whimsical, and the sky was a bright blue with fluffy clouds. There was an enormous waterfall that could be seen in the distance, which led into a river, cutting into the middle of this small world that Paige had created. Elizabeth could also see animals majestically feeding off the grass and the fruits living on bushes and trees. They seemed unafraid of her, even as she walked past them in such close proximity.

Elizabeth kept walking, absolutely in awe of how beautiful it was, until, underneath a willow tree, she saw the woman she had been searching for. Paige looked magical, her hair long and silvery, her skin tan, and her body covered with a flowy pink sundress. She looked just as Elizabeth had remembered her. Happy and healthy. Paige knew she was there, judging by the way she stared, with that lovely smile on her face.

Unwilling to waste another second, Elizabeth took off running towards her. They collided, arms encasing each other, body to body.

"Oh, I've missed you, Elizabeth," Paige whispered in her ear.

"I've missed you too."

Paige stepped back and grabbed Elizabeth's hand. Elizabeth let her lead until they came to a quiet spot by the river. She could hear the tranquil stream, and saw fish swimming.

"Is this where you've been this whole time?" Elizabeth asked.

"All this time?" Paige questioned. "Hasn't it only been a day?"

"No, it's been a couple weeks."

"A couple weeks! I've been here that long?"

"Unfortunately."

Paige wrinkled her brows, and her eyes became sad. "That's much longer than I thought! Am I dying?" she asked softly.

The question stunned Elizabeth. "Not exactly, but the doctor said that if you don't wake up soon, you won't ever wake up."

"Oh." She seemed disappointed.

"So can you wake up now?"

"Can't I stay here a little while longer? Like, how soon is soon?"

Elizabeth pinched her brows together. "No, you can't. I need you to wake up right now. You didn't even know that you'd been in a coma for this long! Who knows how time processes here?"

"Well, I'm not ready."

"What do you mean you're not ready? What's there to get ready for? Your brother is worried sick! Don't you want to see him? Everyone misses you… I miss you."

"Well, they've missed me for two weeks. They can miss me a little while longer."

Paige began to walk along the river. Elizabeth followed her.

"Did you not hear me?" Elizabeth began to get a little frustrated. "The doctor said you need to wake up soon."

"I don't care."

"How can you not care? Don't you want to wake up?"

"Not really."

Elizabeth grabbed her shoulder, making Paige stop and face her. "You just want to stay here for the rest of your life?"

"It's peaceful here. I can be whoever I want and go wherever I want.

There's no worries. I can't even feel your emotions."

Was she that exhausted? Had Paige truly been giving so much of herself that she was done, wanting to live in her own head for the remainder of her days? Elizabeth wondered about how hard it must be to have to feel others' emotions all the time. She'd actually never thought about it before. Sure, she had been exhausted from dream travelling, but she only travelled when she was asleep. Paige had to deal with her powers all the time, while everyone else could choose when to use theirs.

Elizabeth couldn't imagine her life without Paige in it, though.

"No, you're waking up!"

Elizabeth reached for her, but then Paige vanished.

"Paige!" Elizabeth yelled.

Paige was nowhere to be found, and Elizabeth could no longer sense her. She ran back to where she came from and out the tunnel. Aimlessly, she ran down the cobblestone path, searching for a way back to her. Then she saw her, standing calmly in the path.

"Paige." Elizabeth was startled. "You scared me."

"I don't want to leave yet."

"I don't want to leave without you."

"Why? I'm worthless, useless, a coward."

"How can you say that?" Elizabeth inched closer. "How can you think that?"

"I barely contribute to the team. I can't even leave my room without feeling like an anxious mess. I saw you when you first came here, but instead of saying hi... I ran away."

"You saved me. Even when I pushed you away, you stood by my side. I haven't been here for long, so I'm not sure how you've been with everyone else, but wake up and you can show them. It's not too late to come out of your shell. I can help you. It'll take some practice, but you'll get there. You're stronger than you think."

"I don't know…"

"Please!" Elizabeth begged. "I really need you."

Paige bit her bottom lip as she looked into Elizabeth's eyes. Elizabeth could tell she was having an internal battle. On one hand, Paige was exhausted and loved the peacefulness she had been experiencing while comatose, but on the other, she was too selfless of a person to turn down someone asking for help. Elizabeth didn't necessarily need her, which made her feel a little manipulative, but she did want her. The past weeks had been lonely without Paige. It was odd, considering how at first Elizabeth wanted nothing more than to get away from her. But their conversation before leaving to rescue Daisy helped her to understand Paige better. She had shown her vulnerable side, making Elizabeth feel something she had never felt for another person. Watching Paige fall from that ledge solidified her thoughts; she loved Paige and couldn't imagine life without her. She wasn't about to tell her that, though.

"Okay," Paige sighed. "I'll wake up."

Not even a second later, Elizabeth was pushed from Paige's mind, and she flinched back into her own body. Her eyes snapped open, and she looked at the petite blond in front of her. Paige's eyes still weren't open.

"Come on, Paige," she whispered.

She heard a soft groan. Shifting to the edge of her seat, she held her breath as Paige's eyelids fluttered. Slowly, her eyes opened into slits, and she winced at the bright lights in the room. Elizabeth got up to dim the lights, then ran back to Paige's side. Paige looked up at her and smiled lazily.

"Hi," she croaked.

"Hi, Paige." She smiled back.

Chapter 41

Elizabeth called for a nurse to check on Paige, then paged Michael, telling him Paige awoke. She paged everyone else, too.

Michael's eyes were bloodshot as threw the door open to the hospital room and charged straight for Paige. She sat up on her bed and smiled at him, then looked shocked when he wrapped his arms around her.

"I was so worried" Elizabeth heard him mumble.

Jackie walked around to the other side of the bed, while Josh, Jennifer, and Zola crowded at the foot. Elizabeth stood next to Michael, feeling a rush of happiness as she saw Paige beam. With everyone so happy that she was awake, how could she feel useless after this?

"How is she, nurse?" Jackie asked the nurse that was fiddling with a machine connected to Paige. Jackie's ice-cold persona was back in place after the last time Elizabeth had seen her. Elizabeth saw Michael's body tense at the question.

"She's doing well. Vitals are stable; she's coherent, speaking well. We should expect a full recovery. I don't know how she woke, though. It's a mystery."

"It was Elizabeth. She woke me up," Paige replied.

Jackie looked at Elizabeth inquisitively.

"I was able to travel into her subconscious and wake her up from there. If only I'd have known that was possible sooner."

"How'd you figure out you could?" Jackie asked.

"Priscilla told me."

"Priscilla?" Paige questioned. She dropped her arms from around Michael and sat up a little straighter.

"I've been interrogating her," Elizabeth said. Paige was unreadable as Elizabeth searched her eyes. "Why?"

"I just wish you would've waited until I woke up."

"You wouldn't have woken at all if I hadn't spoken to her in the first place." Elizabeth was beginning to feel frustrated again. "And it would have been a bad idea for you to be near her anyway. She's the one who hurt you in the first place."

"I can help! I can shift her emotions or something."

"I know you can help, but I also know that she hurt you to get to me. I don't trust she won't do it again."

"Okay, can you two table this conversation?" Michael interrupted. "Paige, you just woke from a coma, and I've been worried. Can we talk alone for a bit?"

Paige turned her attention to him and forced a smile. "Sure, Michael. But we will talk later, okay, Elizabeth?"

"Fine, later," Elizabeth grumbled, feeling annoyed that Michael asked Paige to boot her. Even though she knew Michael had been consumed with worry and that he should get some alone time with his sister, Elizabeth selfishly didn't want to leave. But she led the rest of the group out the door.

Once everyone was out of the room, Paige turned to Michael. "I'm sorry for worrying you," she said softly.

"Don't worry about me." He grabbed her hands and held them firmly. "Not when you're the one who's been hurt. I'm so glad you're awake now."

Paige could see beads of moisture collecting on his lower eyelid.

Dream Traveller

"I'm okay now. There's no need to worry anymore."

"I came here to protect you, and I failed. It's my job to keep you safe."

Little did Michael know, he'd never truly protected her. He couldn't, not when he had so little power. Paige would never tell him that, though. The only person that could protect her was herself.

"You couldn't have possibly protected me from what Priscilla did. Don't blame yourself."

"I'll try." But even as he said it, Paige could still feel his guilt.

"Now, tell me everything you know about Elizabeth and Priscilla. Is it going okay?"

Paige couldn't help but be a little worried for Elizabeth, and she couldn't believe Jackie was letting her go through with this on her own.

"I have a headset basically chained to Priscilla's head, making her unable to dream travel, and she's also tied-up to a chair at all times, except for when she has to do her humanly things like eat, drink, and use the bathroom. But when she does that there's an armed guard to watch her and make sure she stays in line. She's agreed to help Elizabeth, but she isn't making it easy, of course. It's like she's playing a game. We don't trust her at all, but other than that, I think it's going okay."

"Hmmm," Paige mumbled. She still didn't like that Elizabeth was doing the interrogating, but it did seem like they had everything handled.

Then she heard the door creak open. Michael was blocking her view, so she couldn't see who it was, but she knew as soon as an icy chill ran down her spine.

"Paige." She heard his confident voice boom in the room. Michael turned around, and that's when Paige saw him. Usually, Vance wore business clothes, but today he was dressed in a tuxedo, and his brown hair was gelled back. He carried a white cloth over his shoulder.

"What are you doing here?" Michael said, his tone unfriendly.

Paige could feel his worry, and she agreed with his emotions. She was also fearful. Anytime Vance showed up, nothing good happened.

"I have a surprise for you."

Paige froze as his blue eyes stared at her. Vance walked closer to her and placed the white cloth at the end of her bed, laying it flat. It was a beautiful white dress, with intricate lace designs, spaghetti strap sleeves, and a modest neckline.

"What's this?" She pointed to the dress.

"I'm throwing a small party to celebrate you all. I wanted to throw it as soon as you got back, but I didn't want you to miss all the fun," he smiled.

"I just woke up," she said pathetically, as she tried to ignore the dress. She definitely wasn't feeling up to a party. She felt weak, and she hated being around lots of people.

"It's not for a few hours. You'll have plenty of time to make yourself look less like…" he looked her up and down, but didn't continue the thought. "Anyways, I've taken the liberty of choosing this dress for you, and there is a room filled with makeup, and some wigs." He made it obvious by the look on his face that he didn't care for her short hair.

"She hasn't even walked for two and a half weeks, how do you expect her to go to a party, sir?" Michael asked.

"The nurse said she's doing better than she would have expected. She said her reflexes and speech seem fine. I'm just asking for her to show up. If she gets too tired, she's welcome to leave at any time." Vance held up his wrist to check his watch. "Anyways, I have to go and get things ready. Remember, the party starts at seven." He walked out without a second look.

Once she heard the door close, Paige groaned and landed on her pillow.

"It'll be okay, Paige; I'll be by your side the whole time. I promise."

Paige smiled at Michael, all the while thinking, "Don't make promises you can't keep."

Chapter 42

Josh, Zola, Jennifer, and Elizabeth were waiting in the hall outside Paige's hospital room when Vance showed up. He ignored them completely as he held his head high and walked towards the room. Elizabeth watched him with suspicion, glad that Michael was in there with Paige. Everyone stayed quiet, and Elizabeth watched the door like a hawk, ready to burst in there in case there were any screams.

Vance only stayed in there for a short period of time, and then he came waltzing out with a cruel smile on his face. For the first time since getting there, he acknowledged them.

"I would just like to say congratulations to you all. I am very grateful for how quickly you were able to rescue our late congressman's two daughters and wife," he said, coming closer. "To show my appreciation, I have organized a small get-together that will begin at seven tonight. My staff should have already set up a station in one of the empty rooms by your rooms."

Elizabeth could see Zola's eyes zero in on the ground, her body appeared to go completely still. Josh's face shifted to a look of hate, then he stepped forward, as if he wanted to protect them all.

Elizabeth rolled her eyes and looked back at Jennifer. She could tell Jennifer felt just as uneasy around him. She had her jaw clenched and her eyes intensely focused on him, as if he would strike at any moment. Elizabeth turned back towards Vance. "You didn't seem grateful when you beat Jackie to a pulp. Plus, we'd rather not celebrate with the very people forcing us to be here."

His facade didn't even falter. "Elizabeth, is it?" He spoke with a sickly-sweet tone. "Jackie speaks quite highly of you." He walked closer to her and looked her up and down, as if sizing her up. "She's even begged us not to terminate you, and Jackie never begs."

Elizabeth felt like her heart was going to leap from her chest, and she was speechless. Vince shifted past her, and, without another word, he left them behind. Her heart continued to pound, and all her bones felt cold. She hadn't felt unease like that from a person in a while. Jennifer came to her side, put an arm around her, and looked into her eyes.

Jennifer opened her mouth to say something, but then they heard the hospital room door open again. Out walked Paige, holding Michael's arm to steady herself. Immediately, Paige froze in the doorway, with a look of fear on her face.

"What happened? Why are you so scared?" Paige asked Elizabeth.

"Vance. He just told Elizabeth something... disturbing," Jennifer growled.

"Oh, Vance... Yeah, stay away from him. Don't get in his way, stay out of his sight, and he'll leave you alone. At least, he will most likely stay away. Just make sure you listen to Jackie when she says not to do something. She's probably protecting you from him."

"Oh, we know. After what he did to Jackie, we'll be staying as far away from him as possible," said Jennifer.

"What do you mean? What did he do to Jackie?"

Jennifer and Elizabeth looked at each other. Elizabeth didn't know if she should tell Paige about what happened. She didn't want to add to her stress.

"Tell me!" Paige commanded.

"He hurt her," said Elizabeth, not wanting to say more.

"Physically?"

Nodding, Elizabeth said, "Yeah, pretty badly."

Paige's nostrils flared. "Is she okay?"

"Yeah, we took care of her."

Paige's face was still pinched, but she nodded.

The team walked back through the common room to the area Vance mentioned, where staff in business attire hustled all around, carrying boxes and pushing clothing racks into a room. A man dressed in a tailored suit saw them coming and rushed towards them.

"Hello, ladies and gentlemen," he greeted politely. "I have taken the liberty of setting up two rooms for you to get ready in. If the men will follow me? Ladies, your room is right over there." He pointed to a woman wearing a blue pantsuit and a tight bun. She stood by the racks of clothes with perfect posture, hands clasped behind her back, and her chest puffed out. She didn't move a muscle, and her eyes looked straight forward. Elizabeth grabbed Paige's hand, and Michael and Josh left them to get ready.

"Giselle!" The man snapped.

Giselle flinched at the command, then came rushing over to them. "Hello, young ladies," she said sweetly. "It will be my pleasure to assist you tonight. We have provided you ladies with several dresses each in your sizes. However, if you like one and it doesn't fit you, let me know, and I'll be happy to alter it before the party. Inside there are mirrors for each of you, each stocked with makeup and hair supplies."

"Thank you!" Zola said, looking amazed.

"You're welcome. Is there anything else I can get you? Do you need help with hair and makeup?"

"No, we prefer to do it ourselves," said Elizabeth, her tone bitter.

If Giselle noticed Elizabeth's tone, she didn't show it. "Very well. I'll be in the dining area if you need anything."

Once they were alone, Elizabeth sighed. "Well, this will be fun."

"I know, I love dressing up!" Zola shouted excitedly.

"That was sarcasm, Zola. They are showing us off like we're prizes."

"Oh." Her face dropped.

"Let her be excited, Elizabeth," Jennifer scolded. "We all need something to hold onto."

"Sorry, Zola, I'm just grumpy. It wasn't directed at you."

"It's okay. I'm not stupid. I know how they see us. But I'm still excited to dress up."

"You're right. We might as well take advantage of all this makeup and beautiful clothes."

Noticing Paige's confused look, Elizabeth said, "What's wrong?"

"Giselle... she seemed off. Her emotions were so mild that she seemed hollow."

"She did seem pretty robotic. She's probably a DUST agent trying to impress her superiors."

"I don't know about that. None of the other agents I've come across have felt like that."

Tilting her head, Elizabeth contemplated Paige's worry. If Paige sensed something was wrong, they would investigate it. "Let's ask Jackie about her later. Maybe she would know."

"Okay."

Next, they started to get ready. The girls chose their outfits first, just in case alterations were needed, but of course there weren't. The dresses fit them like they were made specifically for them. It creeped Elizabeth out. She turned to look at what the other girls chose, and was surprised to see Paige in a white dress. There were no white dresses on the rack.

"Where'd you get that?" Elizabeth asked.

"Vance brought it to me; he wants me to wear it."

"That's a little odd. It kind of reminds me of a wedding dress."

"Yeah, me too," Paige agreed.

"Do you want to wear it?"

"No, it makes my skin crawl, knowing he picked this out."

It made Elizabeth's skin crawl, too. "Then don't wear it."

"I don't want to make him mad."

Looking at her curiously, Elizabeth wondered why Paige was scared of him. Elizabeth feared him because he basically said he wanted her dead, but that was probably because she was a threat to the organization. She knew she could be reckless. Paige, however, had a hold on her emotions. She was sweet and kept to herself. Vance even brought her a dress, so it didn't seem like he wanted her dead. Then a sickening thought came to Elizabeth.

She walked over to Paige and pulled her to the corner of the room. Zola and Jennifer began to put on their makeup, seeing that they wanted some privacy to talk.

"Why are you afraid of him?" Elizabeth asked.

"Because he's a powerful, scary man," Paige said matter-of-factly.

"I think it's more than that, Paige. Why does he want you to wear a white dress?"

Paige shrugged and looked to the ground.

"Has he hurt you? Has he..."

"Stop," Paige whispered, her voice breaking.

Elizabeth saw her eyes turn watery. She knew Vance had done something awful to her to make her fear him.

"Does Jackie know?"

"Nobody knows. I don't want anyone to know. They couldn't do anything anyway."

"What if they could?"

"Can we just stop talking about this?"

Elizabeth sighed. She wanted to make it better. Frustrated, she was internally screaming at Paige to let her help, to let her in. She'd do anything to help her; didn't Paige know that? But if Paige didn't want her help, she wasn't going to force the issue. Elizabeth knew from lots of experience that making a sexual assault victim do something about their abuser was not the way to go about things. No, she had to be respectful of Paige's wishes, be there for her, and to give her control of the situation.

"Okay, we can talk about it later. I do think you should pick your own dress, though. Don't let him hold power over you."

Paige looked at her thoughtfully for a moment, before she finally agreed with a nod. Satisfied, Elizabeth led her back to Zola and Jennifer, where they began to apply their makeup.

"What's Priscilla like?" Paige asked after a while of silence.

Elizabeth was powdering her cheeks with blush when she responded. "It's hard to tell, honestly. She said she wants to help us find the headquarters of the Society, but so far all she's done is play with me. I don't know what she's trying to do, exactly, and her head is like a fortress. I can only get something out of her and dive into her memories if she allows me to."

"Maybe she's stalling," Jennifer commented. "Letting her cronies get ready for an attack, or she's trying to get to know us. I bet she has something up her sleeve."

"She probably does. Or she could just be crazy. She is a Dream Traveller, after all, and she's been one for a while. I've been inside her head, and the things she's been through are the kinds of things that would make anyone go insane."

Before they could continue, there was a knock at the door.

"Come in!" Jennifer shouted.

The door opened, and in walked Josh, with Michael behind him. They both wore fancy tuxedos. Josh wore a blue tie, while Michael wore a red one.

"Well, look at you two in your monkey suits," Jennifer teased.

Elizabeth could have sworn Josh blushed.

"I do feel like we're their trained circus animals. Ready to be showcased," Michael joked.

Elizabeth snorted at his comment.

"Jackie wants to know if you'll be out soon." Josh looked behind himself before whispering, "She seems anxious."

"Yeah, I think we are almost done, right, ladies?" Jennifer asked.

They all chimed in with their agreement, so the two men left to let them finish. After a short period of time, they walked out, makeup and hair done, dresses and heels on. Jackie rose from the couch and walked over to them. Josh was right, she did seem nervous. She walked over to Jennifer first, scanning her head to toe.

"Green is a great color choice, Jennifer, I'm glad to see that Vance, or whoever he chose to choose the wardrobe, picked this out." Jennifer's dress ran all the way to her heels, with a slit that went up her thigh. Jackie gave her a smile before she went to inspect Zola.

"Yellow has always been my favorite color on you. I'm not surprised you chose it. I love the flowers embroidered around the waist."

Moving on to Paige: "Bold choice, Paige, I love it." She winked.

Elizabeth checked Paige out. She wore a deep red dress that wrapped tightly around her curves and classic black heels. Paige had lost a little bit of weight, but she still looked perfect. She'd chosen a red lip, matching the dress, and black eyeshadow, making her gray eyes pop. The foundation and blush brought her face back to life, so no one would be able to tell she had just woken from a coma.

Elizabeth's favorite part was the hair, or rather, no hair on her head at all. Vance must have instructed them to bring wigs for her, because there were five different ones, all silvery blonds. Elizabeth was glad Paige dressed how she wanted.

Then Jackie went over to Elizabeth. Elizabeth had decided on a long black dress with a black corset-like top, and a skirt that flared out slightly at the hips. "This look is perfect for you," Jackie complimented.

"I'm happy with everything you all chose, so that will be fine." She let out a loud breath. "Now, as far as the party goes, you all have to be very careful with how you act. The people that you are about to be in a room with are dangerous, powerful people. Try your best to stay away and not draw any attention, and everything will be fine. Understood?"

Elizabeth swallowed what felt like a large lump in her throat. They all nodded.

"Great! Let's get this over with."

Chapter 43

Paige followed behind Elizabeth as they walked through the double doors to the gathering. She looked around the room in awe, and nervousness cramped her stomach. This was no small gathering, but a huge party. There were people everywhere, dressed up in fancy dresses and suits. Lantern lights strung from the ceiling, a small orchestra played at the front of the room, aerial dancers hung from large ribbons in the ceiling, and people dressed in black uniforms walked around with trays of food and drinks. Some people stood close to the orchestra and danced, while others flocked on the outskirts, talking amongst themselves. A chaotic mess of emotions filled the room, and Paige was having a hard time shutting them out, but she held on for now.

Paige was startled when she felt someone grab her hand, but relaxed when she saw Elizabeth.

"Let's go get some food; that's probably the best thing here."

Paige agreed and let her lead them to a table filled with a buffet. They got in line to fill their plates, letting go of each other's hands. While they were distracted, Paige felt large hands clamp on her shoulders, and she was dragged away so quickly she didn't have time to call out to Elizabeth. Whoever it was, they held her in front of them, so she couldn't see their face without turning around, and she was too afraid to do so. She had a pretty good idea of who it was, though.

They turned her around, and Paige found herself face to face with Vance, the last person she wanted to see. He grabbed her hand and pulled her closer so he could rest his hand on her waist. He started swaying her side to side in beat to the music. He was silent, but he also stared into her eyes with such intensity that her skin felt on fire.

"That doesn't look like the dress I chose for you."

"The one you chose didn't fit me right," she lied.

He scoffed, obviously not buying it. Then she squealed when he suddenly spun her around and brought her into a dip.

"Don't forget who you belong to," he said, as he brought his lips to her ear.

His hands clung painfully to her arms; she was sure it would bruise.

"MMMHMMMM," Paige heard a familiar feminine voice say.

Vance brought Paige back upright, and she saw it was Elizabeth, eyeing him warily.

"Elizabeth…" he hissed.

"Vance."

"Come to chat? I thought our previous conversation would have scared you away from me forever."

"I've met scarier," she said, even though Paige could feel her fear.

"Oh? Like who?" He smiled, showing his perfect white teeth.

"You can't be worse than Priscilla."

"Oh, that little minx? How have your conversations with her been? Has she given you some tips on how to be a better Dream Traveller?"

Elizabeth's jaw clenched, and her fear became more potent. Then she looked at Paige and held out her hand.

"May I have this dance?"

Paige smiled awkwardly, eager to get Elizabeth and herself away from Vance. She knew he wouldn't make a scene in front of all these people. She grabbed onto Elizabeth's hand like it was her lifeline, but made the mistake of looking back at Vance. He was seething, she could tell, but Elizabeth dragged her away before he could do anything.

Once they lost themselves in the crowd, Elizabeth grabbed one of Paige's hands and put her own palm on the small of Paige's back, where there was no clothing hiding her skin. Paige felt a gushy feeling in her heart, something she had never felt before.

"Are you okay?" Elizabeth asked her as they gently rocked.

"Yeah, I think he's mad about the dress."

"I'll protect you."

Paige chuckled and shook her head. "Michael says the same thing."

"I won't leave your side."

"You can't always be watching me."

What she really needed was to be able to protect herself.

"What can I do?" Elizabeth looked at her pleadingly.

"You're doing all that you can," Paige assured her. "I think I need to learn how to protect myself."

"Jennifer can teach you how to fight. Why don't you use your powers on him?"

"He has some sort of block on him most of the time. I can't feel his emotions, and I can't make him feel emotions. I've tried before."

"Why don't you tell Jackie? She would help you."

"I don't know how to tell her." Paige didn't want anyone to know; she was embarrassed. She felt weak, hopeless. If she told Jackie or Michael, they would judge her or get mad. She wouldn't be able to handle it. Then there was Vance. He could kill anyone. She wouldn't have told Elizabeth anything if she hadn't figured it out on her own.

"What if I told her for you?"

"Drop it, Elizabeth!" Paige shouted, in an unanticipated surge of anger. Elizabeth's persistence made her anxious.

"I'm sorry, I'm just trying to help."

Paige could feel her guilt, frustration, and confusion. "No, I'm sorry. I didn't mean to raise my voice. You know what? I'm tired, so I think I'm going to lie down."

"Let me come with you, I…"

"No, I want to be alone."

Paige pulled from Elizabeth's embrace and hurried out of the room.

Elizabeth watched as Paige left. She didn't understand what she'd done to upset her. All she wanted was for Paige to be safe. Knowing that Vance was taking advantage of her made her sick. The moment Paige was out of sight, she decided to follow her. Swiftly, she walked to their room, guessing Paige wouldn't go back to the medical wing. She made it to their door and was about to open it, until she heard sobs on the other side.

Her heart broke at the sound of it. Should she go in there and comfort her? Or should she leave her alone, as she wished? She was at war over what to do, and suddenly, she felt her feet moving, toward a certain room holding a crazy redhead. She came to the holding cell, and, behind the translucent walls, there sat Priscilla, looking straight at her.

Elizabeth opened the door and walked in. She dragged a chair so that she could sit right in front of Priscilla. She plopped down, rested her elbows on her thighs, and put her head in her hands. She let out a sigh.

"What's the matter, my sweet?" Priscilla spoke in a motherly tone.

Elizabeth groaned, then looked around, looking for a camera. "Vance, that creepy guy that seems to be in charge, has been watching us."

"Ma…. Vance?"

"Yeah. It makes me uneasy."

"I see. Why are you so dressed up? This isn't all for me, is it?" She gave a coy smile.

"Ha. No. Vance had a party for us. For taking you down."

If that jab hurt Priscilla, she gave no show of it. "So, this Vance is busy?"

"Yeah, I suppose."

"So, we can talk freely?"

"I don't know. I don't know where the cameras are. I don't know how he's able to watch us."

"Why don't you want him to know what we talk about? It's not like we talk about anything too scandalous. Or did you want to tell me something spicy?" Priscilla shimmied her shoulders a little.

"What? No. He's just… he's off."

"How so?"

"Why would I tell you?"

"Why else would you be here? I'm great at keeping secrets. I've built my entire career on it."

"Career? If that's what you want to call it," Elizabeth grumbled.

"Tell me what's bothering you, love."

"It's Paige. She's in trouble, and she won't let me help her."

"Oh, your little girlfriend."

"She's not my girlfriend." Elizabeth felt her cheeks burn. She wasn't ready to admit her feelings.

"Whatever you say. What kind of trouble is she in?"

"Like I'd tell you," she scoffed.

"Fine. Don't tell. It doesn't matter to me. I will say this, though. If someone I loved was in trouble, I would do anything to help them. I would even kill for them."

Leaning back, Elizabeth looked at her hands. Priscilla might be willing to do anything for someone she loved, but was she? Could she? The fact that she questioned it made her feel guilty.

"What if that someone was being hurt by a powerful person? Someone untouchable."

"Oh, dear, no one is untouchable."

Chapter 44

The sound of fists pounding into a punching bag echoed through the empty main room. Elizabeth woke early, and since she no longer needed Paige to watch over her every move, she left her sleeping. Unsurprisingly, Jennifer was up too, practicing her moves with a couple daggers. It had been a while since the two of them had time alone to have one-on-one training.

Jennifer smiled, sweat dripping down her temples, and asked Elizabeth if she wanted to do some boxing. Eager to relieve some stress, she quickly agreed. They would take turns on the same bag, Jennifer coming up with the routine and Elizabeth executing it afterward. As she started to get into it, all thoughts about Vance exited her mind.

"Great job, Elizabeth! Way to use force. Your enemies will never expect it," Jennifer encouraged her.

Elizabeth hit harder, her breathing becoming louder, sweat drenching her hair and drizzling down the nape of her neck. The sweet pain in her knuckles distracted her from the pain in her heart. Jennifer circled her and the bag, shouting encouraging words, until Elizabeth couldn't hear her anymore. Her adrenaline spiked, and the background faded. It became silent, except for the blood pounding in her ears. She hit harder and harder, imagining herself caving in Vance's face. She couldn't feel anything, and her vision began to tunnel, until all of a sudden, she felt arms wrap around her, Vance's face no longer there, and she was thrown to the ground.

She screamed viciously as her arms were pinned down. She thrashed, trying to escape, but her captor was too strong.

"Elizabeth." She heard muffled words, like she was under water.

"Elizabeth. Calm down." She stopped thrashing. "Take a deep breath." The calming voice was soothing her, and she started to breathe in through her nose and out her mouth, until her vision became clearer, and she could see Jennifer pinning her down. "Good, Elizabeth. Are you back? Or is the demon still possessing you?" she joked, but there was a slight look of fear in her eyes.

"I'm good," Elizabeth groaned.

"Thank goodness." Jennifer climbed off her, but Elizabeth stayed down. The exertion finally getting to her, Elizabeth felt exhausted, and she struggled to breathe. She brought her hands up to smooth her hair back, and Jennifer grabbed one of them.

"Geez, lady," she breathed, "your poor knuckles are raw."

Elizabeth turned her hands so she could see the backs of them. They weren't just skinned; each knuckle was oozing blood. "I guess I got a little carried away."

"I'd say. Is something bothering you?"

"No, I'm good."

Jennifer sighed. "Right, because hitting the bag until your knuckles are bleeding is completely normal," she said sarcastically. "Does this have to do with Priscilla?"

"No, it's not about that."

"Then what? Talk to me." Jennifer grabbed a first aid kit that was hanging on the wall and sat down in front of her.

"It's Vance."

"Vance? About what he said to you yesterday?" she asked as she began to clean Elizabeth's wounds.

Elizabeth hissed in pain when the alcohol wipe met her torn flesh.

"No, not that, something else. Have you noticed him being weird towards Paige?"

"I have not, but I've only seen the guy three times."

"I'm 99 percent sure he did something bad to her, or is doing something bad to her, but she won't let me help her."

Jennifer finished cleaning Elizabeth's wounds and began to wrap them with gauze.

"What do you think he's done to her?"

"I can't tell you. She won't let me tell anyone."

"Do you know why?"

"No, I tried to ask her more about it, but she just yelled at me and stormed off. I don't know what to do."

"Yeah, that's hard. It's hard when someone you care about won't open up to you and let you help them." She paused her wrapping and looked sadly into Elizabeth's eyes. "I would give her space and time. Let her come to you when she's comfortable. Unless you truly think she's in danger. Then, definitely tell Jackie."

"That's the thing, I think she's in danger. I think Vance is going to hurt her."

Jennifer finished wrapping Elizabeth's hands and taped the ends. "Well, then, I would try to get through to her again. If she still doesn't listen, then you should probably go ahead and tell Jackie."

"If I tell Jackie and Paige doesn't want me to, she'll hate me. Besides, what could she do? We both saw that her power has limits."

"Jackie was still able to protect us. Maybe she could figure out something to protect Paige. Just follow your gut. You'll do the right thing."

"Okay, thanks, Jennifer."

"Of course, I'm here anytime you want to talk. Not like I can go very far."

Elizabeth laughed at her dark joke, then got up from the ground to go back and check on Paige.

When Elizabeth made it back to her room, she heard the loud voice of a man. She halted outside the door and pressed her ear against the wood. Her eyes widened when she realized it was Vance. The walls and door were too thick to make out was he was saying, but she could tell he was angry. His volume was getting louder and louder.

Unwilling to stand in fear any longer, she opened the door. Just as she did, she heard Paige vocalize an alarmed scream, making Elizabeth throw the door wide. Disgust ran through her as she saw Paige, who looked like she hadn't been awake very long, holding her comforter up to her neck like it was her armor. Vance had her caged between his strong arms, with a vicious look on his face.

"What's going on?" Elizabeth said, with more courage than she felt.

Vance turned his face and gave her a terrifying grin. "None of your business. Leave us," he commanded.

"I don't think so." Elizabeth walked closer to them. Paige looked at her with such fear in her eyes that Elizabeth wanted nothing more than to rush over to her. "This is my room, and you are trespassing."

Vance only chuckled, but at least he removed his body from Paige's bed and walked over to Elizabeth. "I'm trespassing? I own you, girl."

"You don't own me. You don't own anyone," she growled.

"Such denial."

"Leave now."

"You are nothing but a...."

"Vance," Paige squeaked, interrupting him and gaining his attention. He whipped his head to face her. "I'll come find you later. I promise."

"Fine. Don't keep me waiting too long."

Vance turned back to Elizabeth and glared at her for a second before walking around her and slamming the door behind him. Elizabeth let out a breath she didn't know she was holding, feeling her heart pounding in her chest. For a minute, the two of them just stared at each other in silence.

"Are you okay?" Elizabeth finally asked.

Paige nodded, but Elizabeth didn't believe her. The fear was still apparent on her face. She knew Paige could probably sense her fear and anger.

"You aren't going to see him," Elizabeth stated.

"I don't have a choice." Paige clutched the comforter tighter.

Elizabeth refused to keep her distance any longer. She closed the gap quickly and gently placed her hands on both sides of Paige's head. "You can't. Tell me how I can help you! I'll do anything, Paige!" she pleaded, desperate.

"There's nothing to be done. It's pointless. You don't understand who he is."

"He's just a man." Elizabeth slightly squeezed the sides of Paige's head.

"A man that has us at his mercy."

"Why do you let him do this to you? Why not tell Jackie? She'd do anything to protect you, I know she would." She remembered Jackie's being absolutely distraught when Paige was hurt.

"I'm not letting him do anything." A flash of hurt crossed her eyes, "I've tried to stop him before, but he threatened to kill my brother. He can trigger any of the trackers they put in us. Give us instant death."

Frustrated, Elizabeth let go of Paige's head, instantly missing the warmth under her fingers. "He was bluffing. If he truly was going to kill your brother, then why hasn't he killed me? I'm much more of a threat than Michael."

"I'm not risking it, Elizabeth. I'm sorry if I disappoint you, but I can't let anyone get hurt because of me."

"Disappointed? I could never be disappointed in you. I just wish you'd trust me to help you."

"I do trust you. But I also want to protect you."

Elizabeth bit the insides of her cheeks. "I don't want your protection. I won't go to Jackie, and I won't tell anyone what's going on, but I'm going to help you. I can't stand back and watch him hurt you. I'll do whatever it takes." She stormed out of the room, determined to see the only person she could think of who'd go to the lengths to help her.

"Hello again, love," Priscilla purred.

"Not now," she said, not wanting to hear Priscilla talk. She just wanted to kill Vance. She wanted to enter his mind and make him hurt himself.

To her surprise, Priscilla listened, keeping silent. Elizabeth sat on the chair, then tried to dream travel to Vance's mind. Her consciousness felt around for him until she felt that sickening chill of fear he liked to spread. Reaching for him, she got ready to take over and end him, but instead she was repelled. She bounced back into her own body.

As she came back into consciousness, she felt a sharp ache in her head, like she'd pounded it against a wall. Opening her eyes, she saw Priscilla looking at her, one brow raised.

"What was that about?" Priscilla asked.

"I tried to travel to Vance to make him kill himself."

"How'd that work out?"

"Not good."

"Why are you suddenly trying to kill him? Just a bit ago you didn't seem sure on what to do, now you go straight to death. And why'd you come here to do it?"

"Paige is in trouble; Vance is going to hurt her. I need to end him. I was going to try and do it myself, but I didn't know if I could. I had a feeling it wouldn't work, from what Jackie and Paige told me before," Elizabeth admitted. "Now that I know I can't, I need help. Your help."

"Go on."

"The problem is, I don't know how to do this. I've never plotted to kill anyone. You, on the other hand, have. You want to prove yourself to me? Tell me how to do it."

"Tsk, tsk, tsk, it won't be that easy, my dear. You have to do something for me first."

"Name your price."

"Release me and come with me. I know exactly how to kill your little problem." She dipped her head and smiled, and the shadows from the light gave her a terrifying look.

"Release you? That's out of the question, and you know it."

Priscilla rolled her eyes, then unclasped her hands from behind her back. Elizabeth stepped back as fear and confusion roiled through her. Piece by piece, the rope holding Priscilla draped down her body until it was loose enough that she could stand. Elizabeth gulped, her throat suddenly feeling dry.

"Okay, so I don't necessarily need your help escaping, but I do want you to come with me. In return, I will make you a better Dream Traveller. I'll train you to become as good as me, maybe even better. And I'll take care of your problem. Your little girlfriend will be safe from Vance."

"How…"

"Did I escape the ropes? I've been slowly taking control of my guards. Remember when you got a little handsy with me?" She smirked seductively. "Well, the headphones shifted a little. I've been able to dream travel since then. Anyways, I ordered my guards to cut a piece in my ropes and to hand me a key card, which I stashed in a secret place. All I had to do was pretend I was at your mercy until you trusted me. And I so badly want you to trust me, because you are special to me, Elizabeth. You always have been."

Elizabeth was frozen, unsure of how to take this. She'd been thinking she had this woman under her thumb, and the whole time she was deceived.

"Tick tock, Elizabeth. I can leave with or without you. The choice is yours."

Elizabeth's forehead wrinkled. She couldn't tell her friends if she left; they would try to stop her. They would all think she betrayed them. But did she really have a choice? Was she willing to stay and let Paige get abused by Vance?

Elizabeth breathed in deeply through her nose. "Okay, I'll go with you."

Chapter 45

Paige was getting ready to go see Vance, after spending half the day thinking about what he had said to her.

"I'm losing my patience, Paige."

"I'm not sure what you want me to do, sir." She tried to void her face of all emotion.

"It's easy, you just have to do whatever I say."

"Well, sometimes you ask for too much," she spewed before she thought over her words. She instantly regretted saying it, feeling heat rush up her neck and cheeks.

He took a shaky breath, stalking closer to her bed. His fists clenched, showing off his muscular forearms that peeked from his rolled sleeves.

"You know what I want, Paige, and you know I always get what I want."

On her fifteenth birthday, he asked Paige to come to his office for a present, and she of course went since she had no choice. When she got there, he held a bouquet of red roses in one hand and a small gold box in the other. She accepted the flowers and was stunned when he opened the box. Inside there was a gold choker necklace, with diamonds elegantly sprinkled along the chains. He asked her to turn around so he could put it on her, and then he told her to take her leave and enjoy the rest of her birthday. That night, she tried to take it off, but couldn't find the clasp anywhere. She asked Michael for help, but he couldn't find it either.

She had to sleep with the choker on, the diamonds cruelly scratching her neck as she tossed and turned. The next day, she went to Vance's office again and asked him how to take it off. Instead of just telling her, he asked her to come around his desk to where he sat. Paige did as told, and as soon as she was in reach, he grabbed her waist and spun her around to place her on his lap. She froze, never having felt so uncomfortable around him before. She heard him shuffle for something in his desk, then he brought something cold to the back of her neck. Her neck was released from the choker, and he brought his hand around her front to place the necklace in her lap.

"You're such a good girl," he whispered in her ear.

"Why couldn't I remove the necklace?" she asked softly.

"Because only I can."

It wasn't a necklace he'd gotten her, but a collar. Another way for him to control her. Paige shivered at the memory. Now she was about to walk back to the lion's den, back to the man that had abused her for years, to protect those she loved. Just as she was slipping on some loafers, someone aggressively pushed through the door. She expected it to be Elizabeth, there to yell at her and prevent her from going to Vance. Instead, Jackie stood in her room. She was breathing fanatically, face red and forehead crinkled with concern.

"Jackie?" Paige could feel her fear.

"Elizabeth…" Jackie seemed to be having a hard time speaking while trying to catch her breath. "—she's… gone."

"Gone? What do you mean?" The worst thought came to her; Elizabeth must have confronted Vance, and he killed her.

"She left." Jackie was starting to speak more clearly.

"Oh, well, she will probably come back, right? She probably just needed some air."

"No." Jackie shook her head. "She helped Priscilla escape."

"What?"

Paige didn't understand how or why Elizabeth would do that. She found it hard to believe. The last conversation with Elizabeth ended with her saying she'd do anything to help Paige.

"We are screwed. We are so screwed." Hands shaking, forehead sweating, chin wobbling, Jackie, the woman who always had it together, was crumbling apart right before her eyes.

"How did this happen?" Paige walked up to Jackie, placing her hands on Jackie's shoulders.

"He's going to kill us," she mumbled, staring off into nothing.

Paige shook her shoulders. "Snap out of it, Jackie."

"It's over. Everything I've worked for is over."

Paige could feel Jackie's hopelessness, along with her fear and anger. She was about to have a panic attack, Paige knew it. So, she did something she'd never thought she'd have to do to Jackie. She took her emotions away.

Slowly, Jackie looked into her eyes. "There you are," Paige whispered.

"You took away my emotions," she said in a monotone voice.

"Yes, and you know I had to. You need to think logically, Jackie. Tell me everything, now."

"Right. You're right. I will. Let's get the others first."

Paige and Jackie had everyone gather in the main room, settling on the couch. Everyone was confused, especially since Elizabeth wasn't there.

"Where's Lizzy?" Jennifer asked.

"That's why I've gathered you." Jackie's emotions still lacked panic as Paige monitored her. "Elizabeth has left. And I have reason to believe she's left with Priscilla."

"She's been kidnapped?" Jennifer jumped to the conclusion.

"Maybe. We have security footage, though, and she appears to be cooperative with Priscilla."

"So, she betrayed us," Josh said matter of factly.

"She wouldn't do that," Jennifer argued.

"Are you certain of that?"

"Yes. She's loyal to a T."

"Sorry if I have a hard time believing that."

"She has put her neck on the line on multiple occasions to save people." Jennifer was trying to stay calm, but Paige could feel the rage brewing.

"Look, I'm not trying to upset you." Josh threw his hands up to signify a truce. "I'm just trying to say it's a possibility. She has been spending a lot of time with Priscilla. That woman may have been able to convince Elizabeth to join her side."

"So, you're saying Elizabeth is what, then? Gullible? Stupid?"

"Now you're just putting words in my mouth."

"Enough. This isn't productive," Michael chimed in.

"He's right," said Jackie. "We don't know exactly what happened to Elizabeth. She could have betrayed us, or she could have been controlled. It doesn't matter, we still have to go after her."

They all nodded, agreeing on something. "How do we keep this from Vance?" Paige asked.

"He already knows."

Her stomach dropped. If he knew Elizabeth escaped, and helped the enemy, he would kill her for sure.

"He already knows," Jackie said again, "and has already flown out to her most recent location. They landed in Russia, but then her tracker stopped working. It must have been removed, then broken. We are to wait for further instruction before proceeding."

"We can't wait. We have to get there before he does!" Paige was glad Elizabeth lost the tracker, that way Vance couldn't kill her remotely. Unless the removal of the tracker killed her. She shuddered at the thought.

Chapter 46

As soon as Priscilla and Elizabeth were free of the building, Priscilla grabbed Elizabeth's hand and took off, almost causing her to trip. Elizabeth dared one look over her shoulder as they ventured into the woods, feeling worried and unsure. She knew her friends would see this as betrayal, but hoped they would forgive her once she could destroy Vance. Elizabeth felt Priscilla yank on her arm, and she met her intense stare.

"Come on, love," she whispered harshly. "We won't have much time before they realize we are gone."

Picking up her pace, Elizabeth tried to match Priscilla's surprisingly fast run. The trees became denser, and twigs scraped at her face. She was glad for all the cardio Jennifer made them do, because they had been running for a while.

"Almost there!"

Elizabeth could see a clearing peeking through the trees, and as soon as they made it past the last tree, she could see a helicopter in the middle. Whoever was piloting must have seen them, because the rotor blade slowly started to rotate. Priscilla looked behind herself to Elizabeth and smiled as they continued to run. Elizabeth gave her an unsure smile in return. When they made it to the helicopter, Priscilla came to a stop, let go of Elizabeth's hand, and climbed on. Elizabeth froze, her palms feeling sweaty. This was her last chance to back out, and she wasn't sure. Priscilla's eyebrows pinched together, and she stretched out her hand to Elizabeth, eyes urging her to take it.

"You won't regret this," she shouted over the loud rotors, "I promise!"

Elizabeth took a deep breath, then hesitantly grabbed onto Priscilla's hand. Priscilla's shoulders relaxed, and she gently pulled Elizabeth closer. Elizabeth climbed into the helicopter, and it took off as soon as her feet left the ground. She feared falling from the door and grabbed onto Priscilla's shoulders instinctively.

"You're okay, my love," Priscilla chuckled.

The doors automatically began to slide closed. Elizabeth was led to one of the two seats in the back and sat to the right of Priscilla. Reaching across Elizabeth, the redhead grabbed onto the seat belt and pulled it over her to latch it securely. After making sure she was safe and patting her shoulder reassuringly, Priscilla put on her own seat belt.

Now that Elizabeth had taken a couple breaths and calmed down, she was able to take a good look at the inside of the aircraft. It was efficient and clean inside. The interior was mostly black, with hints of tan and gray for buttons and latches. In the middle was a large red cooler, and Priscilla reached forward and opened it. There wasn't much, but there were bottled waters and granola bars. The sight of water made Elizabeth swallow, realizing how thirsty she was. Priscilla handed her water first, then grabbed one herself. Quickly, Elizabeth turned the cap and guzzled down the contents. After taking in the last drop, she felt satiated and crushed the bottle.

"Good girl." Priscilla leaned towards her.

Elizabeth froze and looked at Priscilla accusingly. Overcome with thirst, she'd forgotten who she was with for a second.

"It's not poisoned, sweetheart," Priscilla assured her. "But I do need you hydrated." She leaned closer.

Elizabeth stared into her eyes, their lips almost touching. Instead of being kissed, though, she felt a sharp prick on her thigh.

"What the…" She flinched and pushed Priscilla away.

Looking down at Priscilla's hand, she saw a needle attached to a vial with all the contents leaked out, most likely into her system.

"What did you do?" Already, her vision spun.

"We can't let you see where we're going. I'm sorry, my love," Priscilla said, her tone muffled.

Fighting to stay awake, Elizabeth tried to force her eyelids open. Her attempt was futile, though. Her body slumped, and Priscilla grabbed her before she fell sideways. She gently placed Elizabeth's head on her lap, and Elizabeth could feel her hair being tucked behind her right ear.

"Don't worry, love," Priscilla whispered in her ear, "I'll take good care of you."

Elizabeth wished she would stop touching her. She wished she could just be in her own seat, but she was unable to speak. Before the drug completely took over her, she saw a shadow in the front seat move around. She couldn't see their face when they came in, since their head was covered with a helmet, but she could see the copilot taking off their helmet. They turned around and shifted down slightly so she could see them under her half-closed eyelids. She felt a sting of fear as she recognized that disgusting face.

"So glad you decided to join us." Vance spoke with an ominous tone.

His face was the last she saw before everything went dark.

Elizabeth felt like she was floating on a cloud. Her hands moved slightly, noticing softness. Around her, she heard a joyful tune being hummed, making her smile.

"Paige," she groaned, "why are you in such a good mood?" Unwilling to face reality yet, she turned her body onto her stomach and shoved her face into the softest pillow.

"Uh, oh." The humming stopped, and Elizabeth froze when it wasn't Paige's voice she heard. "I had suspected you would feel a little disoriented from the drug when you awoke."

Elizabeth flipped out of the bed. The sheets twisting around her legs causing her to clumsily fall to the floor. As she struggled to free herself, she heard Priscilla laughing, as if this was one huge joke. Elizabeth stood as soon as she could, fuming from the ears.

"Oh, I'm sorry." Priscilla tried to contain her laughter. "I shouldn't be laughing. It's been so long since I've had a good laugh, though."

"What's going on?" Elizabeth growled.

"We escaped that prison they've been keeping you at. Now we have the freedom to do whatever we want." She smiled.

In that moment, memories came rushing back: she and Priscilla ran through the halls and forest to the helicopter, then everything was a blur. Something in the back of Elizabeth's mind told her she was forgetting something important, but for the life of her, she couldn't remember.

"The reason I agreed to come with you was so you could help me get rid of Vance."

"Yes, yes. And I get to train you into becoming a better Dream Traveller."

"Wait, wait, wait. Can we step back a bit? What about the drug?"

"Yes, I had to drug you."

Elizabeth flinched. "You had to? What the hell? I thought you wanted to gain my trust!" she yelled.

"I know, I know. I didn't want to, but I had no choice."

"There's always a choice, Priscilla!"

"Not in my case."

"Ughh, whatever. Well, I guess since I'm here, let's get started. Let's take down Vance and get working on the dream travelling lessons."

Priscilla laughed. "So eager, I do love that about you. However, first you need to eat. Then I will give you a tour of the place."

Elizabeth frowned; she didn't want to make nice with Priscilla. This wasn't her new home, and she didn't plan on staying here long. She also had to find a way to contact her team, to let them know she didn't abandon them. While deep in thought, Elizabeth didn't notice Priscilla coming over with a plate of hot food. Pancakes, sausage, and eggs steamed on the plate, and delicious smells filled the air.

"You've been out for quite a while, and we have a lot to do today, so make sure you eat as much as you can," Priscilla said as she placed the food on a side table. "I'll let you get settled in and fed, then I'll be back in a half hour. Sound good?"

Elizabeth nodded her head, happy that she would at least have some time to let everything sink in. Her stomach growled, and she began to shovel the food into her mouth. It was delicious, with just the right amount of sweetness and saltiness. She ended up eating every piece of food on her plate, then set it back down on the table.

Pushing the covers off, she noticed she still wore the same clothes she left in, then began to take in the room. The decor kind of reminded her of a Viking and medieval mix. Animal horns hung on the stone walls, along with a couple scenic art pieces. The ground was also stone and had tasteful rugs thrown about. There was one large bed, with a velvet canopy over it, and side tables on both sides. Across the room was a dresser and a body length mirror that matched the side tables.

She went to snoop through all the drawers to see if there were any weapons she could use, but found none. With just fifteen minutes left before Priscilla came back, she decided to find a bathroom and clean herself up. She walked into a small room attached to the room she awoke in and turned on the lights. Unsurprisingly, it was exactly what she was looking for. There wasn't a shower, but there was a large tub with claw feet. There was also a toilet and a mirror, along with the basic accessories. Finding some soap under the sink, she began to fill the tub with hot water, and then poured soap in when the water was high enough.

Peeling her dirty clothes from her body, Elizabeth dipped her toes in the water. Deciding the temperature was perfect, she dunked the rest of her body in, loving how the smell of lavender and peppermint invaded her nostrils and the mint tingled her skin. She wasn't just there to relax, though; she thought now would be the perfect time to try and travel to her team, if it were possible. Not knowing if she could travel to someone specific from a long distance, she still felt she had to try. So she closed her eyes and fell into a deep relaxed state. She thought of Paige and demanded her consciousness to travel to her. She felt herself leave her body and was successfully floating away, but then hit a wall, one that made it impossible to travel.

"Odd," she thought to herself.

She wasn't deterred, though, so she kept trying and trying until her head hurt. She groaned and placed her hands over her eyes.

"It's blocked."

She shrieked at the sound of Priscilla's voice, then covered herself under the water.

"Dude! Knock!"

"I did, actually, you just didn't respond. I wanted to make sure you didn't fall asleep in the water. I knew exactly what you were doing the moment I saw you."

"Okay, can you leave? Or at least turn around?" Elizabeth yelled.

"Yes, of course." Priscilla quickly walked out the door.

Elizabeth climbed out of the water, dried herself off, wrapped the towel around her chest, then walked out to the bedroom. Priscilla stood with a pile of black clothing in her arms. Priscilla looked at her as if she hadn't just seen her naked.

"Okay, finish getting ready and meet me outside the door. I've brought you some clothes, which I'll leave on the bed."

Elizabeth watched her as she left the clothes and walked out the door. Eager to get something on, she wasted no time in looking at what Priscilla brought her. It was a simple black tank top, a black zip-up hoodie, some black leggings, and undergarments. She tried not to think about how she knew her sizes and style. As soon as she had clothes on, she walked to the door and carefully opened it. As promised, Priscilla was standing right outside her door.

"Ready?"

"I guess."

Unlike Elizabeth, Priscilla was wearing a dark red jumpsuit and thigh-high black boots. Her hair was worn loosely, and her lips were painted to match her outfit. Priscilla turned down the hall, her steps silent, and Elizabeth followed. They passed many closed doors; she wondered what was behind them, but Priscilla walked too quickly.

While they were walking, Elizabeth remembered not being able to dream travel to her friends. "What did you mean when you said I was blocked?"

"Just that you can't travel unless I give you permission. At least, until Master says you can. Wouldn't want you telling people what's going on here, or finding out secrets you aren't permitted to know, now, would we?"

They came upon one room with an open door, stopping in front of it.

"This is my room," Priscilla said.

Elizabeth curiously peeked her head in. It had a similar setup to her room, but there was more stuff in it. Priscilla had perfumes and jewelry scattered along the dresser, a couch, and a plush purple rug covering the floor.

"Just remember this in case you ever need anything in the night. I'll always be here for you."

Elizabeth could tell she meant it. Not letting Elizabeth stare inside for too long, Priscilla kept walking.

"The closed doors are off limits, by the way. They are of course locked, but knowing how resourceful you are, you could probably get in," Priscilla complimented.

"What's inside them?"

"Bedrooms," she said shortly.

Elizabeth guessed she probably didn't want to say more, but she did wonder who lived inside the rooms. It wasn't like there were people roaming the hallways. Maybe she would see them later.

Finally, the end of the hallway came, and they reached a large, open space. It was octagonally shaped, and there were railings placed around the middle. Elizabeth walked over to the railing and looked down the middle. She gasped as she saw how far down it went.

"How many floors are there?"

"Just ten. We are currently on the ninth floor."

"And what are on the other floors?"

"We will be exploring most of the floors today, but I'll give you a little overview," she said, joining Elizabeth by the railing. "First off, the tenth floor is off limits. That is where the master of this place stays. If I were you, I'd avoid him as much as possible. The next four floors are filled with bedrooms. There's nothing interesting on those floors, and all those rooms are probably locked. Then we get to the fifth floor, where you will find most of your amenities, such as a cafeteria, training rooms, and entertainment. The next floor is where we have most of our technology and meeting halls. The next three floors are below ground. Floor three contains vehicles and equipment necessary for fighting or carrying out other missions. Then the last two are where we hold prisoners and interrogations."

"Wow," Elizabeth said softly. It was a lot for her to wrap her head around as she tried to memorize each floor. The most intriguing floor for her was the tenth floor. "Will I get to meet your master?"

"Hopefully not."

She would have to sneak up there when she was alone at some point, to snoop and figure out who this master was.

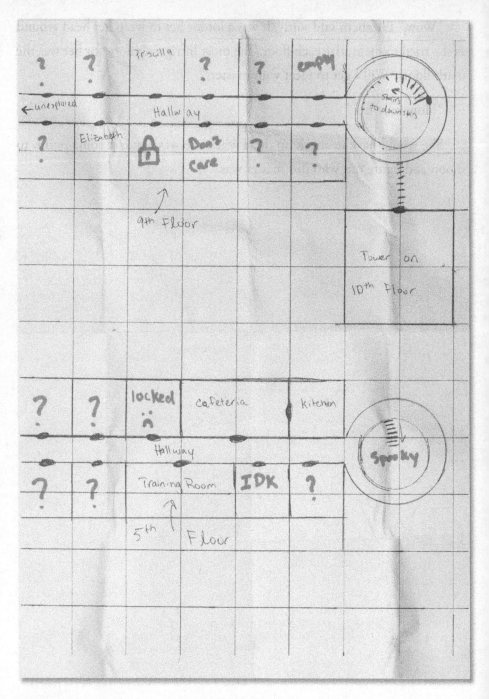

Map drawn by Elizabeth Voltz.
The Castle.

Chapter 47

Elizabeth followed Priscilla as they descended three flights of stairs. Priscilla seemed to be conscious of Elizabeth's curiosity and didn't rush her as she looked around to take in her surroundings. Just like her room, the walls were made of stone decorated with medieval-style paintings and intricate tapestries. The halls were lit by oil lanterns hanging from the walls; she wondered who was tasked with lighting and extinguishing them. The stone staircase was covered in a deep reddish carpet, and there were very few windows, but they finally came upon one, and Elizabeth wasted no time in looking to see where they were.

Seeing only blizzarding snow, Elizabeth couldn't distinguish any landscape. She frowned with disappointment. Priscilla seemed to understand as she put a hand on Elizabeth's shoulder.

"Maybe I can take you on a snowmobile ride sometime in the future. Show you around the land. Unfortunately, my master doesn't trust you yet."

"Your master?" She continued looking longingly out the window.

"Yes."

"Why do you call him that? Who is he?"

"I call him that because that's what he is. He has been my master for as long as I can remember. He tells me what to do, and I do it. In return, he provides for me. As for who he is, I can't tell you yet. You will find out in time."

"I think it's kind of odd that you have a master. Normal people don't call others 'master.' Does he pay you?"

"No, but he feeds, clothes, and shelters me."

Elizabeth shook her head, then stared Priscilla in the eyes. "That's not okay, Priscilla. You make it sound like you're a slave."

"Well… he did buy me when I was a child."

Elizabeth's eyes widened in horror. She was really beginning to regret escaping with Priscilla. What kind of person buys a child? What if her master tried to keep her? Make her his slave?

"You got me out of one prison into another, Priscilla! I'm now under the thumb of someone who buys children! What have I gotten myself into?!"

Elizabeth internally scolded herself for her stupidity.

"Don't worry, love," Priscilla tried to reassure her. "I will protect you."

"Is that why you hurt those people? Is that why you hurt Daisy?"

"He ordered me to. I must always do what my master tells me to do. Except when it comes to you. He promised me he wouldn't hurt you."

Elizabeth gulped. She remembered seeing Priscilla's memory of herself chained up in a room. What horrid things had she gone through to make her so complacent about committing such terrible acts? She was sure she just saw the tip of the iceberg.

"Well, sorry if I don't take your master's word for it."

"Master may seem cruel at times, but he's never lied to me."

"Back in the cave, you mentioned something about Daisy's father. What did he do? What did he have to do with your master?"

"Master doesn't tell me the specifics, but my guess is they were involved in some sort of business together. Mr. Chatawick did something to betray him."

"Business? Like human trafficking?"

"I'm not sure. Master is involved with many things. He's a busy man."

Staying quiet, Elizabeth didn't know how to respond. Priscilla seemed too brainwashed to reason with. She didn't know how she'd be able to get rid of Vance in her current situation, though. What was in it for her master to get rid of him?

"Let's continue. I want to show you the training rooms." Priscilla interrupted her thoughts.

Dropping her hand from Elizabeth's shoulder, Priscilla led Elizabeth down the stairs until they got to the fifth floor. She walked off to the right, then around the railing to the hall. Elizabeth noticed, just like on the rest of the floors, there was only one hallway to the left of the staircase. Once they came to double doors that almost reached the ceiling, Priscilla twisted both the handles and swung the doors open.

"This is the cafeteria," she said as Elizabeth followed her in. "It's one of the few rooms that aren't locked."

"Thanks for not starving me," Elizabeth replied sarcastically.

Giving her a coy smile, Priscilla walked over to a metal door. Elizabeth froze, recognizing the door from when she was inside Priscilla's head. After noticing that she was no longer being followed, Priscilla turned to Elizabeth, then furrowed her brows with concern.

"Don't worry, my love, it's just the kitchen."

Elizabeth relaxed, then continued on her way. Having slightly more trouble opening the metal door, Priscilla pushed it till it gave. Inside was a full kitchen with large refrigerators on the left wall.

"We don't have chefs here, unlike your cage back in the United States, so you'll be in charge of making most of your food. If I'm making food, though, I'd be happy to make some for you too." She glanced at Elizabeth, a maternal look in her eyes. "I assume that you'll be hungry sometimes when I'm not around, so you should feel comfortable to make anything you want."

"Great. From one cage with personal chefs, to another without."

"There's no perfect world for people like you and me. At least we have each other now, though. No one will get you like I do."

"Oh, joy."

Priscilla grinned, ignoring Elizabeth's sarcasm. "Next, the training room."

Elizabeth followed her for the entire tour. She barely spoke, only doing so if necessary. She could tell that Priscilla was trying to make conversation with her, but how could she talk to her when she'd done so much. How could one talk to someone like that? She allowed, encouraged, the rape of a teenager. Being near her was revolting; even looking at her face made Elizabeth sick. She wondered what other heinous acts Priscilla had participated in. She was sure about one thing, though: as soon as Priscilla helped her kill Vance, she'd escape her. Although Priscilla would probably be able to find her. Somehow, Priscilla had been getting into her head since she first travelled. She was certain there would be no place she could hide where Priscilla couldn't find her.

Priscilla finished the tour by showing Elizabeth their garage filled with different types of vehicles. Unfortunately, every room that had something useful for her escape required an eye scan, so Elizabeth would have to find someone she could travel to and control. She would need to grab weapons and supplies, and she would need to think about which vehicle would best suit her escape. She could steal a snowmobile, but she honestly had no clue how to drive one and she wasn't sure how far or fast it could go. Taking a helicopter proposed the same issues. There was a Jeep, which would probably be her best option, but then she had other unknowns; she had no clue where to go. All she knew about their location was that they weren't in the United States, because of Priscilla's comment in the kitchen, and that they were on a snowy mountain. They could be in Italy, China, or Japan; the list was too long for her to be sure.

"That concludes the tour!" Priscilla exclaimed.

"What about the dungeon?"

"Oh, no, you don't want to see that."

"Why? Do you have prisoners down there?"

"I can't tell you. Besides, it wouldn't matter. I wouldn't take you down there either way." She mumbled the last part.

Elizabeth sighed. "All right. So, what now?"

"Now we are going to work on your dream travelling."

Elizabeth followed Priscilla, excitement running through her. As much as she hated being near Priscilla, she was excited to start increasing her travelling skills. As a Dream Traveller, everything she learned had been by mistake and experimentation. Having the chance to learn from another traveller was a priceless opportunity.

Once they made it to Priscilla's room, Priscilla opened the door and had Elizabeth sit next to her on the soft, gray couch.

"Today, we are going to work on travelling together."

"Can we do that?"

"I actually don't know. You are the only traveller besides myself that I know of. I assume, though, that since I can talk to you while you're in my head and vice versa, we can travel together too. We will have to cooperate with each other, though. So, you're going to have to listen to me."

Priscilla smirked, knowing Elizabeth wasn't the best at listening to instructions.

"I will listen." She was desperate to learn.

"Good girl," she praised. "Okay, close your eyes and let me in."

"Wait, why are we going in my head? Can't we go to yours?"

"Elizabeth, you said you'd listen. You have to trust me."

Elizabeth laughed. "Trust you? I'm not stupid."

Priscilla dropped her chin, shadows falling under her eyes, and her green eyes squinted at her. A chill ran down Elizabeth's spine.

"I don't have a choice, do I?"

Priscilla shook her head slowly, and the next thing Elizabeth knew, she could hear Priscilla's voice in her head.

"I would prefer you to be willing, but I don't need your consent."

Elizabeth couldn't move. She couldn't speak. She started to panic; her head ached.

"Relax, dear, your passing out won't stop the session." Priscilla forced Elizabeth to take deep breaths. "It will be better for you if you go along with it. I promise I won't hurt you, and I promise I won't go digging in your head. I know everything about you anyways, so there would be no point. I have no ill intentions toward you. I only want to help."

Elizabeth's head stopped aching, but she was still afraid. She had never lost control of her body before. Now she knew what a horrifying experience it was.

"Have you ever been inside your head?"

"Inside my head?" she thought.

"That would be a no. Come inside."

Darkness consumed her for a second, and then she was inside her own head. She blinked a couple times, feeling disoriented.

"It's strange... being in your own head," she heard Priscilla say behind her.

Elizabeth tried to turn. Her body felt like it was in wet concrete, making it difficult to control herself, but eventually she moved. Priscilla stood behind her in solid form, looking confident. "It feels like I'm in a dream."

"That's because you're in your body and your head at the same time. It's disorienting at first, but you get used to it. For now, just take my hand and I'll guide you."

"Why are we here?" Elizabeth could hear her own voice echoing off the walls.

"If you can master your own mind, you can do anything. You can get out of any trap, control anyone, control multiple people. You can even make it so you don't travel at all. You wouldn't need to wear those headphones to sleep."

"Can I stop people from getting in my head?"

"Yes."

"Even you?"

"Even me. You'll need to practice often if you want to be able to do any of that, though. I would escape into your own head every day. That's what I did when I was learning."

"How did you learn?"

"Master had a journal from his previous Dream Traveller. He gave it to me so I could learn how to control my powers."

"There are more than just us?"

"Were. We are the only two at this point in time. I know, because I've searched."

Curious, Elizabeth wondered if Priscilla was lying. It would be in her best interest to hide other Dream Travellers from Elizabeth, after all, to keep her for herself and prevent her from learning with anyone else.

"I'm not lying, Elizabeth. Don't forget, I'm in your head, so I can hear your thoughts."

Rolling her eyes, Elizabeth said, "Do you know why we are here? How do we have our powers?"

"I don't know the answer to either of those questions."

"What happened to the dream traveller whose journal you have?"

"He's dead. He lived a long time, though, all because he was able to master his own mind."

Elizabeth contemplated all the things Priscilla just shared with her. There had to be a reason why Dream Travellers existed. There had to be a reason why she was a Dream Traveller.

"Why do we only travel to people going through something... traumatic?"

Priscilla tilted her head and looked at her quizzically. "You go to the victims?"

"Yes?"

"When I travel, I'm drawn to the perpetrator. I see the victims getting hurt."

"You don't stop them?"

"No."

"Of course not. For a second, I forgot that I'm talking to a psychopath."

Priscilla flashed her green eyes to the side, as if Elizabeth might have hurt her feelings.

"That's enough for today." Priscilla disappeared, and the next second Elizabeth opened her eyes to see Priscilla standing in reality.

Elizabeth scrunched her eyes and shook her head, trying to get used to coming back from inside her head.

"You will get used to jumping back and forth. For the next few days, I will help you go to your dream world and back to reality. Then I will expect you to be able to do it yourself, but I'll still accompany you. Wouldn't want you getting lost, now."

"Can we…"

"It's late," Priscilla interrupted. "I will see you in the morning." Without another word or glance, Priscilla walked out the door.

Chapter 48

Once Priscilla left her room, Elizabeth lay flat on the bed. There had to be information somewhere about why Dream Travellers existed. If there was a Dream Traveller that lived here before Priscilla, and one that had been on Jackie's team, then there had to have been more.

At that moment, she missed her friends. She missed Jennifer and Paige.

Jennifer would have jumped up and said, "Well, let's go find it'. Paige, on the other hand, would have sat there and offered her support, then gone behind her back to find information and tell her later. She wondered what they thought of her right now. If she was ever able to make it back to them, she would explain everything. For now, though, they probably thought she had officially lost her mind.

She groaned and rolled to her side. The bed creaked with her movements. Priscilla had said it was late, but without a clock and windows in her room, she had no way of knowing how late. She wasn't close to being tired, either. Lying in bed waiting for Priscilla to come back wasn't an option. Inching her way off the bed, she made her way to the door and peeked into the hallway. It was quiet; only the soft glow from the lanterns could be seen. She stepped out and walked on the balls of her feet.

When passing Priscilla's door, Elizabeth expected her to come out and give her that obnoxious hospitality she'd been doling out all day. Her shoulders relaxed when Priscilla didn't appear, and quickly tiptoed to the stairs. She gave one more glance over her shoulder to see if Priscilla was coming, then descended down the stairs once assured she would be alone. Finally, Elizabeth could see the floors she so desperately wanted to explore.

Since Priscilla told her not to go into the dungeon, she of course had to see it. Running down the cement stairs, she found herself in front of a metal door, different from the rest of the architecture. There was a simple metal latch, which surprisingly wasn't locked. They probably wanted easy access to torture their victims, she thought. The door creaked loudly as she pushed it open, and she cursed under her breath. She let out a sigh when it seemed nobody was coming.

There weren't oil lanterns lighting this hall, but instead overhead lights, similar to her underground prison in the DUST facility. It smelled of sulfur and bleach, so intensely that it hurt her nostrils. She came to one room with a door left ajar and peeked inside. Uninterestingly, it held just a stool and a bucket, with flickering lights overhead. She continued walking until she found a door that felt familiar somehow. Giving it a go, she pushed the metal door open.

Elizabeth's heart dropped. She tasted bile on her tongue. The room. The room she saw inside Priscilla's head. Chains hung from the ceiling; whips and knives were strapped to the walls. This wasn't just a place for prisoners to be tortured, but where the master of the castle abused his slaves. It was where he hurt Priscilla.

Elizabeth regretted not listening to Priscilla. She slammed the door shut and ran out of the dungeon as quickly as possible. She choked on her sobs on her way up the stairs, almost falling as she stumbled clumsily. She was scared. Would the master hurt her like that? Would he try to turn her into Priscilla? Brainwash her until she was willing to do his every command?

Elizabeth halted at the top of the steps, forcing herself to calm her breathing and regain her composure. This might be her only chance to sneak around without supervision. Even though she wanted to return to her room and hide, but she had to take advantage of this opportunity. It was time to figure out more about this man. Thankfully, Priscilla had pointed out exactly where he may have kept his secrets. The tenth floor.

After climbing flight after flight of stone steps, Elizabeth came to an elegantly carved door. Whimsical glyphs were engraved into the wood, seeming to hold no pattern. To make sure nobody was in there, she opened the door for a peek. When she heard no noise, she stepped all the way in.

It looked like a king lived there. There was a four-poster bed with thick evergreen-colored sheets, a stone fireplace with matching green chairs by it, ceiling-high shelves with ancient looking books, and mannequins with medieval-like armor.

"Who are you?" she asked herself.

She looked around in awe, never having seen such elegance in her life.

"I guess being disgustingly evil pays well," she muttered.

Discovering a wooden desk with drawers in the corner of the room, she decided that was a good place to start looking. The wood was carved with the same symbols as the door, but she paid no attention to the details. It wouldn't be long before Priscilla or someone else realized she was missing, so she'd better start looking now. Elizabeth rummaged through the drawers, finding stacks of loose paper with names and numbers written on them, but no other clues as to whose room she had found. She made sure to shut the drawers, so that it looked like no one had been there.

There was a trunk at the end of the bed, and she decided that would be the next place to look. Unfortunately, it had a padlock.

"Of course," she groaned. "Now, where would he be hiding the key...?"

"This key?" she heard a familiar deep voice ask.

Without turning around, she froze. She could hear her own heartbeat as her veins seemed to ice over. She heard his feet walk closer to her, until she could feel his heat radiating on her back.

"Hello, Elizabeth," he said smoothly. "What is it that you were hoping to find in this room?"

"Vance," she managed to choke out.

Then, slowly, she turned to face him. Sweat formed on her upper lip. She had never been so scared in her life. The man responsible for Priscilla's actions, the one who had been puppeteering her, had been under their noses the whole time.

Without a word, he brought his hand under her chin and lifted her head, so she looked into his eyes.

"It's a real shame that you've stumbled upon my space. I wasn't ready for you to find out. Now you've put me in a difficult situation."

Elizabeth gulped. Sweat rolled down her temples. She was now at the mercy of the one man she wanted to kill. The reason she had left with Priscilla in the first place. She was tricked. Priscilla delivered her right into her enemy's arms. She was certain he was about to kill her. Who would protect Paige then?

Before anything else could be said, she heard the door slam open.

"Master! I'm so sorry! I left her mind for just one second! Please don't—"

"Enough!" Vance cut off Priscilla's hysterical cries and let go of Elizabeth's face. He stepped back and stood so he could see both women. "Come, Priscilla."

Instantly, she fell to her knees and crawled over to him. She wore a red robe over long black satin pajamas. Once at his knees, she placed her head on the floor, like she was doing child's pose. Vance stepped away from her for a minute, and grabbed a cane hanging on the wall by the fireplace. He stroked it like it was a pet, and calmly looked Priscilla over. Then, without warning, he struck. Over and over again. Elizabeth heard the swish and slam against human skin. Priscilla shuddered, not breaking from.

Elizabeth was stunned for a moment, but once she heard Priscilla whimper, she jumped into action. She lunged for Vance and pushed him away from the cowering woman. Never in her life had she seen such anger. His face turned red, and his brows furrowed so deeply they almost covered his eyes. He wound the cane back and whipped it across her face. She screamed, not from the pain, for her adrenaline was too high to feel any, but from the impact. It was as if her brain was wobbling inside her skull. She felt completely disoriented.

"You promised you wouldn't hurt her!" she heard Priscilla yell.

"That was before you let your little pet explore unattended."

She heard Priscilla growl in frustration, then there was silence. There was a loud bang, as if someone fell to their knees. Worried Vance was hurting Priscilla again, she looked up. To her surprise, it was actually Vance on his knees.

Priscilla looked at her with a worried expression on her face, the first genuine look Elizabeth had gotten from her.

"I can't hold him for long," Priscilla yelled. "Run! Go find a vehicle. The red jeep has enough fuel to get you to the closest town. Go now!"

Elizabeth didn't want to leave, though. She wanted to do what she came here for: kill Vance. Finding a metal vase on his dresser, she grabbed it and charged for him, ready to bash him in the head.

"No!" Priscilla screamed.

Then Elizabeth lost control of her body. Forced to stop, her hand let go of the vase, the metal crashing against the stone floor.

Taking control of Elizabeth must have faltered Priscilla's ability to control Vance, because Elizabeth saw him try to stand, and then he lunged for her. As he tackled her to the ground, her head hit the floor, causing her already injured skull more damage.

"Ugh!"

Vance once again stopped moving, and Elizabeth could move her limbs again.

"Elizabeth, run! I won't let him hurt you, but you need to run!"

Elizabeth scrambled to get to her feet. Her head hurt so badly she felt drunk. She couldn't even remember running once she made it to the stairs, but she kept going. Then she heard blood curdling screams. Priscilla's screams. She couldn't leave her here. At that moment, she didn't care about the evil Priscilla had done. She only thought of how she was a victim of abuse to a powerful man. Backtracking, she made her way back up to Vance's room.

Priscilla lay motionless on the floor, her beautiful face covered in blood.

"Stop!" Elizabeth yelled before Vance could strike again. This time, he wasn't holding a cane, but a long chain rope.

She looked for a weapon and found a sword standing next to one of the fancy mannequins. She grabbed it without thinking and held it out in front of her, doing one of the stances Jennifer had taught her. It did no good, though. He whipped his chain at her and effortlessly smacked her hand, making her drop the sword. That time, she felt the pain, and she screamed. She was sure her hand and wrist were broken.

"You should have run like Priscilla told you to. Although I would have found you anyway." He stalked towards her. "I'll be glad to get rid of you, though. I only need one Dream Traveller to succeed. Once Priscilla heals, I'll make her forget all about you, and she'll be back to being my little whore."

Before she could react, Vance grabbed Elizabeth's hair and dragged her to his feet. She clawed at his hands, but failed at dislodging him. Then, he wrapped the chain around her throat and squeezed so hard her airways were blocked. She tried to pull the chain away, but he was much stronger than she. She felt the chain digging into her neck, so tight she feared it would draw blood. The room started to become darker, and her grip on the chain loosened. She was dying; she knew it.

The next time she blinked, though, she found herself on all fours, coughing as her body tried to push oxygen back into her system. She looked up and saw Priscilla staring past her with fire in her eyes. Elizabeth turned around and saw Vance, once again on his knees, with his hands on his head.

Looking back, confused, Elizabeth found Priscilla's eyes now on her.

"Elizabeth! If you're adamant about not saving yourself, then I need help knocking him out!"

She tried to speak, to ask how, but her throat felt like it split open when she tried.

"Enter his mind with me!"

Closing her eyes, Elizabeth easily entered Vance's mind, like there was a door held open for her. Inside, she saw absolute chaos. Priscilla sat on the ground; her hands spread out on the ground. The ground quaked, and Elizabeth felt like she was being pulled into multiple directions. Static blared through her eardrums.

"He's fighting me! I need you to help me!" Priscilla shouted.

"How?"

"Put your hands on top of mine! I'm trying to make him unconscious."

"Then what?"

"I don't know."

Hurrying to Priscilla, Elizabeth knelt and put her hands where instructed.

"What now?"

"Just make his body sleep! Hurry!"

Elizabeth did what she normally did when commanding people's bodies: collect all her emotions and use them to fuel her powers. She already felt a lot from the beating Vance gave her and the sight of Priscilla's battered body, but she could conjure up more. She thought of how he beat Jackie, how he groomed and abused Paige, how he bought Priscilla as a slave, that he'd threatened and chipped her and her friends, and how he treated them as nothing but pets.

She felt anger unlike anything before. Her skin prickled, like electricity ran through her, and her body felt lighter. She demanded that he sleep, but she wanted him dead. Looking into Priscilla's eyes, she saw fear.

"Elizabeth? What are you doing?"

"Making him sleep."

Grounding herself, she commanded his body to sleep. The air around her forcefully expanded, sending Priscilla flying. Like an explosion going off, Elizabeth as the bomb, the walls around Vance's mind blew apart. Only darkness was left behind.

He had no thoughts. No feelings. Nothing.

Then Elizabeth felt herself being ripped from Vance's mind, her exhaustion making it easy for Priscilla to control her. Out of the corner of her eye, she saw Vance staring straight ahead, with no expression on his face. Then he fell forward.

Gripping the sides of Elizabeth's face, Priscilla stared at her, eyes wide and forehead crinkled. Blood dripped down Priscilla's cheek, and Elizabeth could feel the warm, sticky liquid covering her skin where Priscilla touched her.

"What did you do?" Priscilla asked.

"Put him to sleep, like you asked," Elizabeth grumbled.

Her vision waned. She wanted to sleep, too.

"Stay with me, Elizabeth!"

"I'm trying…"

Next thing Elizabeth knew, she was being pulled into her own head. It disoriented her at first, but it took less time to get used to dream travelling to herself. Priscilla stood across from her.

"I'm so sorry." Priscilla's dream form ran to her. "He promised he wouldn't hurt you! I'm trying to keep you awake for the time being, by keeping you in your head to preserve energy."

"We can talk about that later. We need to get out of here, though."

"Yeah, we can leave once I'm healed. We can hide from Vance. We can find a place, just you and I…"

"No. We need to go back to my team. We need to tell them everything."

"But I thought we were going to train together. You promised."

"Yeah, so did you. Looks like we both have made promises we can't keep. We can still train together back at the headquarters."

"No. They'll never let me help you. They'll lock me away."

"Priscilla, please. I came back to save you. I could have just left. Please. Trust me. We will figure it out. The sooner we get help, the sooner we can both get better. Let me travel to them."

Priscilla stared at her, contemplating. "Fine."

"Thank you. Where are we?"

"Russia."

Chapter 49

"I'm going to dream travel now," Elizabeth told Priscilla, in case Priscilla was still blocking her. "Fine, but no falling asleep. We need to stay as awake as long as possible. We don't know the extent of damage done to you."

As Priscilla spoke, Elizabeth felt the throbbing in her left cheek where Vance struck her with the cane. Her throat ached, and when she reached up to touch it, she winced at the sting.

"Try not to think about it too much." Priscilla interrupted Elizabeth's self-exam, pulling her back into her mind. "Don't want you to panic."

"Well, now I'm kind of panicking…"

"Let's just go."

"I don't know if I can. I was able to travel to Daisy whenever I wanted, but I don't know if I can do that with just anyone."

"I'll create the connection. You just have to travel."

"You can create the connection?"

"Yeah, it's easy. I'll show you later when we have time."

"Okay. I'll travel to Jackie."

Elizabeth left her head. Then she felt the pull of Priscilla's mind guiding her. Next thing she knew, she found herself in Jackie's office. Elizabeth felt her hands tugging at the roots of her hair. She felt all of Jackie's emotions, stress, anger, and worry.

It didn't take long for Jackie to realize someone was in her head. Letting go of her hair, sitting up straight, she thought, "Elizabeth? Is that you?"

"Yeah, I'm here with Priscilla."

By Bethany Drier   Page 337

"Are you okay? Where are you?"

"Jackie, I need help. Priscilla and I are hurt bad. I'm not sure how long we'll be able to stay conscious."

"What happened?"

Elizabeth could feel Jackie's suspicion.

"Vance."

"Vance?"

"Yes. Vance hurt us. He tried to kill me."

"Start from the beginning. Why did you leave?"

"We don't have time for this" Priscilla spoke up. "We need help now. Our coordinates are 61.00658 degrees north, and 69.00593 degrees east. We can explain while you're on the way."

Already starting to feel weak, Elizabeth wasn't sure how long she'd be able to hold on. Her body called her back to it.

Turning on her computer, Jackie looked up the coordinates on the map.

Overcome with worry, she asked, "How long do you think you have? Do you have time to wait for me to come get you personally? Or do I need to have agents stationed closer to you extract you? You are really far from Kentucky."

"Send your agents. Elizabeth won't last much longer before she passes out. I can feel her body weakening."

"Okay, okay, I'll do that right now."

Jackie picked up her cell phone and called William, telling him about their situation, who to call, and where Elizabeth and Priscilla were located. Elizabeth could feel herself becoming weaker. She knew she didn't have much longer before her body gave out. Then she would be at the mercy of whoever Jackie sent over to them.

"Okay, ladies. William will be sending out DUST agents that are placed in Russia, but they won't be there for a couple hours. I wish I could do more for you, but that's the best we can do. A doctor will also be with them."

Jackie's tone was casual, but her feelings and thoughts were anything but.

"Okay, thank you, Jackie," said Elizabeth.

"Now, tell me why you left, Elizabeth. Why did you escape with Priscilla?"

Elizabeth knew she couldn't tell Jackie the exact reason why she left, but she hoped her explanation would be enough.

"I decided Vance had gone too far with punishing you, parading us around his friends, keeping us captive, threatening our lives… I had enough. I wanted him dead, and I figured Priscilla would be willing to help me. I don't know why; I just had a feeling she would. The rest of you are just… too good. You wouldn't have killed him. I wanted him dead. I didn't kill him though. Death would be too good for him."

"I wish you would have come to me…"

"And what would you have done? He beat you, and you did nothing. You just let him."

"I did what I thought was best."

"I know, that's why I didn't go to you. Anyways, we took a helicopter ride, and Priscilla drugged me so I would be asleep the entire time. I woke in this huge castle. Then I went exploring up to the tenth floor, where Priscilla said her master lived. Jackie, her master is Vance. Vance bought her when she was a child. He was the person behind the terrorist attacks. He's been the evil under our noses."

Shock and disbelief overwhelmed Jackie's feelings. "I knew he was bad, evil, but I never would have suspected this…"

"There's stuff in his room that might provide more information. There's a chest that requires a key, and the key's on his body."

"His body?"

"Priscilla and I put him to sleep. I'm not sure how long we have before he wakes."

Jackie's thoughts were filled with concern. She didn't know what would happen if Vance woke before their agents got there. And she didn't know what to do once they got him back to DUST. Would there be enough evidence to back Elizabeth's claim? If not, he would kill them all.

"Okay… I'll make sure the agents know to bring everything from his room. Is there anything else I should know?"

"I'll make sure Vance's people know we are having guests. He had everyone leave for the safe house, since Elizabeth was coming," said Priscilla. "That way they won't attack when they arrive. They'll believe me."

"I'm feeling worse, Jackie. I don't think I can hang on much longer," Elizabeth warned.

"Okay. We will deal with everything when you get here. Just try to stay alive."

"If I don't make it, I'm sorry. Tell Jennifer and Paige I'm sorry."

"You'll make it. You will."

Jackie seemed hopeful, which made Elizabeth feel better. She still had to say it, though, just in case.

Before she could say another word, she felt herself slip from Jackie and back to her body. As she opened her eyes, her throat felt swollen enough to make it hard to breathe. Her head throbbed even worse, like her brain wanted to jump from her skull. Priscilla dragged her body close to Elizabeth and grabbed her hand.

"Stay awake for as long as you can, Elizabeth."

Nodding her head, Elizabeth did her best.

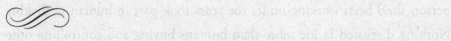

"How is she?" Jackie asked the agent that contacted her after DUST had retrieved Elizabeth, Priscilla, and Vance.

"Stable, ma'am. The doctor is working on her. She was still breathing, but barely. We have to give her medicine to bring down the swelling in her throat and put a breathing tube down her nasal passage, but she will be okay. The other woman, the redhead, we can't see anything too wrong with her, she's just bruised up. We gave her some pain meds. Vance is unconscious, but we can't find anything physically wrong with him."

"Yes, I think Elizabeth said he had a stroke," Jackie lied. She wasn't sure how the agency would react if they knew Elizabeth went away to kill Vance, so she decided to keep that to herself.

"Okay. Do you want us to take them straight to the base?"

"Yes."

"Okay, Jackie. We will see you in twelve hours. I'll let you know if anything goes wrong."

"Thank you."

Leaning back in her chair, Jackie tried not to let her nerves get the best of her. So many things could go wrong. The board members could find out about Elizabeth's secret quest to kill Vance. They could ask to have her imprisoned for her escape. Jackie would have to come up with a plan, but first she would need to see if Elizabeth told the truth. She thought she probably had, but how would she prove it? Hopefully information was included in the things the DUST soldiers picked up.

Jackie couldn't believe the connection between Vance and Priscilla. She knew Vance was a terrible person, but nothing could have prepared her for the news of his buying a child, operating as a double agent for the Society. The person she'd been working under for years took part in human trafficking. Nothing disgusted Jackie more than humans buying and controlling other humans. After all, she knew what it felt like to be controlled.

Also, Elizabeth's hiding her plans for Vance made Jackie feel helpless. She wanted to be someone her team could trust; someone they went to when they had issues. Instead, Elizabeth took matters into her own hands. She left without a word, consequences be damned. Vance could have killed Elizabeth. He even could have killed Jennifer just to punish her. Maybe he would have killed Jackie for letting her escape. Her chest tightened at the thought.

Any trust Jackie and Elizabeth built over the past few months diminished the longer she considered things. She thought she finally got through to Elizabeth, showing she had her best interest at heart. Now, Jackie didn't know what to feel. Fear? Anger? Betrayal? Overwhelmed, she just hoped she would still have hair left, after pulling at it since Elizabeth disappeared.

Dream Traveller

Chapter 50

Looking down, Elizabeth saw her hands chained to the bed.

"What in the world?" She spoke softly, since it felt strange to talk.

"Just a precaution," she heard Jackie's voice say.

She looked up to see Jennifer and Jackie, standing in front of the bed. Jennifer's expression was unreadable, but Jackie had that annoying judgment smeared on her face. Paige stood to the left, her head bowed, eyes on the ground, forehead wrinkled, and eyebrows raised.

"A precaution for what?" Elizabeth asked.

"You helped a prisoner escape, Elizabeth," Jennifer responded. "We aren't sure what to think."

"Right."

There was silence for a moment, Elizabeth looking back and forth between Jennifer and Jackie.

"So, am I a prisoner now?"

"We couldn't be sure what happened, Liz. We don't know if your mind was or is being controlled by Priscilla, if she threatened you, or if she manipulated you. We didn't want to risk you waking up and putting us, or yourself, in danger."

"Okay, but now that I'm up, can you unlock me?"

"I have to make it look like we are taking all the right precautions, for the cameras," Jackie said telepathically to Elizabeth. "Whatever you do, don't say anything about killing Vance."

"Why'd you leave? Why'd you help Priscilla escape?" Paige asked.

"Priscilla told me she would lead me to her master, but only me. I thought I was doing something good for the team. And I didn't help her escape. She had that figured out on her own."

Jackie nodded, indicating she accepted this explanation.

"So you just left? You left your team behind? You could have at least warned us!" Jennifer yelled.

"I had no time. She said the helicopter was there, she was leaving with or without me. It was my one chance. And you would have tried to stop me."

Paige tilted her head, crossed her arms, and lifted a brow. Jennifer, watching Paige's reaction, seemed to doubt Elizabeth too.

"Did she seduce you or something? You can tell us the truth," Jennifer encouraged.

"No!" Elizabeth became defensive, "I'm telling you everything that's relevant. The main reason why I went is because I thought I could take down the person who was actually behind the terrorist attacks."

"And did you find them?"

"No."

Jennifer looked to Paige, who was shaking her head.

Shifting in the bed, Elizabeth remembered: she left with the woman that hurt Paige. How did she not think of how that would affect her until just now? A rush of guilt filled Elizabeth as Paige studied her.

"Are you and Priscilla…" Paige began. "Are you… I mean do you… have feelings for each other?"

There was disappointment on Paige's face, and it hurt Elizabeth's heart to see her look so sad. "No, I promise."

"Then why were you holding hands?"

"I wasn't holding her hand. I was passed out."

"But she must care for you."

"She might."

Elizabeth tried to reach out for Paige's hand. The chains got in her way, however, and she groaned in frustration. "Get these chains off me! I'm telling the truth!"

Jackie walked over to Elizabeth's bed and pulled a key from her pocket. She leaned over to unlock her hands, then left.

Once the door was closed, Jennifer walked over to her and grabbed her hand. "We used to tell each other everything. We were a team. What changed?"

"Nothing changed. We're still a team. I did this for us. I did this for the team."

"Then tell me the whole truth. I know when you're lying."

Elizabeth stared into her sister's concerned brown eyes. She knew it hurt her to not know this secret, but it wasn't hers to tell. "I told you the truth."

Jennifer shook her head, pulled her hand from Elizabeth's, then left without another word.

Elizabeth sighed. Tears began to burn her eyes.

"Did you leave because of me?" Paige whispered.

Elizabeth turned to her and saw tears flowing down her cheeks. Elizabeth quickly sat up, ignoring the pain shooting through her skull, and reached for Paige. She grabbed her hand and pulled her towards herself.

"No, why would you think that?" Elizabeth lied. Again.

"I'm an empath. Or have you forgotten? I can tell when someone's nervous. Is it because of Vance? Because I wouldn't do anything to stop him? Were you mad at me?"

Elizabeth placed her hands on both of Paige's cheeks, using her thumbs to wipe away her tears. "No, Paige. I wasn't mad at you. I did this because I felt like I had to."

"But if I would have just let you help, then you never would have left. You never would have put yourself in danger."

"Paige, we were all in danger as long as that man was still walking around. You just gave me that bit of incentive I needed to take him down."

Paige pushed Elizabeth's hands away and stepped back. "Then why did you go alone? You could have had Jennifer go with you! You could have done anything else than what you did. You could have been killed, and I would have blamed myself. Did you think of that?"

Elizabeth got off the bed, then walked towards her, but Paige backed away. Elizabeth took another step to Paige, but stopped again when she saw her eyes widen.

"Paige? Why do you look scared? You know I'd never hurt you."

"I… the way you're walking towards me…"

Chills ran through her body as her stomach dropped. Elizabeth realized she'd triggered Paige. In some way, her approach had made Paige think of Vance. Leaving with Priscilla must have made Paige lose her trust and sense of safety with Elizabeth.

"Paige, I'm sorry. I should have told you. I know I messed up," Elizabeth apologized.

"I don't believe you. If you were really sorry, you never would have left."

"Paige, please…"

"No! Go be with Priscilla. She's probably more interesting than me anyways," she sobbed, before sprinting out of the room.

Elizabeth wanted to run after her, but she knew Paige needed some space. Also, she felt exhausted, and everything neck-up hurt.

This wasn't the reunion she'd hoped for.

Hours had passed since anyone had checked on Elizabeth, making her feel isolated.

It had been years since Elizabeth felt completely alone. Now, in the middle of the night, even sleep had left her side. All she could do was lie in her bed, thinking of all the ways she messed up. Guilt gnawed away at her. She hurt her friends, her team, her sister, and herself. She never should have left with Priscilla. She wished she had told Priscilla no and alerted Jackie as soon as she heard her plans.

Hours of dwelling on her problems had given her a stomachache and a headache. Elizabeth tried to travel to Priscilla, but there must have been something blocking her, because she couldn't be found. She didn't even know if Priscilla was okay, and didn't think she should ask, since it seemed to be a sore subject. It annoyed her that she cared about the psychotic woman, but she couldn't help it.

Elizabeth felt at war with herself. She didn't know if she should hate Priscilla or have sympathy. Whatever abuse she'd endured was probably what made her so terrible, not that it was an excuse. But if Priscilla had lived a normal life, had been raised by a loving family, maybe she would have grown up to be a good person.

Lost in her thoughts, Elizabeth didn't notice the room darkening. It wasn't until she heard a whisper that she looked up.

"Elizabeth…" an unidentified being whispered.

The whisper scared her so much that it felt like her skeleton jumped from her body. Looking around, she saw no one, but noticed a mist spreading around the room.

"Is someone there?" she called out.

"Elizabeth…"

"What do you want? Who's there?"

"I have something to show you…"

Gulping, Elizabeth slid the covers from her body and got ready to run to the door. She didn't care if they had something to show her, whatever was calling to her gave her a bad feeling.

Before reaching the door, Elizabeth was thrown backwards. Expecting to hit the wall, she closed her eyes, but seconds passed, and she felt no pain. Breathing heavily, she heard a faint noise become increasingly louder, until she recognized the sound of a woman screaming.

She opened her eyes and found herself standing in front of a young woman strapped to a bed, surrounded by people dressed in lab coats. The woman thrashed, screaming like a wounded animal. Nobody touched her, and she didn't appear to have any marks on her scantily clothed body. Elizabeth didn't like the way everyone observed her, though. Like an object to be viewed. They looked like doctors, but they weren't doing anything to help her with whatever pain she was going through.

"Status?" said an older man to the younger people.

"We injected her with a concoction of valerian root, lion's mane, and LSD. This is one of our weaker Dream Travellers, so we thought certain drugs might enhance her abilities. It has been three days since injection, and she has not awakened. We had him," —the young female doctor pointed at Elizabeth— "enter the subject's mind, and he discovered she's stuck in someone else's head. The person she found seems to have a taste for torturing and murdering college women. She has been experiencing the murderer's memories. Eli has been trying to get her out, but it seems she's forgotten her identity."

"Interesting. Keep trying, Eli." The older man looked at Elizabeth. "I want to know how this experience affects her once she's back. As for the rest of you, obviously the mixture of whatever you gave the subject has been a failure. Find another defective traveller for the next vial you come up with, then report back to me. Try to put more thought into it next time. It's not like we have an endless supply of subjects."

"Yes sir," the group muttered.

Right then, the woman tied down started to maniacally laugh.

"And someone gag her or something. I don't want to disturb everyone with her obnoxious wailing."

The man left the room, and Elizabeth, or Eli, the man she inhabited, followed.

"Sir?" he called out.

"Yes, Eli?"

"May I ask what our intentions are with these drug administrations?"

"Very few Dream Travellers are as talented as you, Eli. You are a rarity. Mr. Thorndale is looking for a drug to enhance… lesser subjects. If you can get that woman out of whatever situation she's stuck in, we can try another sample on her."

"Okay, sir."

"If that's all, I have to get going. There's lots of work to do."

"Yes, sir."

Then, Elizabeth was pushed back into her own body. The mist had gone, and the lights were back to normal. She still felt Eli's presence, though.

"Come find me, Elizabeth…" he said, before fading from her mind.

Elizabeth's fingers clenched the blankets. She had never left her bed as she previously thought, which meant Eli, another supposed Dream Traveller, entered her mind and made her see things that weren't there.

If what he showed her truly existed, then that meant there were way more Dream Travellers out there. Why would there be a lab containing a bunch of them? Who was Mr. Thorndale? And why did Eli feel the need to contact her?

She didn't know what to think of this Eli character, or even if what he showed her actually existed. One thing she did know, however: she would find out.

###

Dream Traveller

About The Author

Bethany Drier is a software developer by day, and an author by night. She is an avid dreamer, and understands their power.

Bethany advocates against human trafficking, and violence against women and children, giving her the inspiration to write Dream Traveller to increase awareness for victim empowerment worldwide.

Dream Traveller Playlist

Panic Room . . . . Au/Ra

Protection . . . . Massive Attack & Tracy Thorn

You know What I Mean . . . . Cults

Bed Case . . . . Tancred

Where Is My Mind . . . . Pixies

Battle Of The Larynx . . . . Melanie Martinez

Only In My Dreams . . . . The Marias

Lipstick on the Glass . . . . Wolf Alice

Rescue . . . . Lauren Daigle

No Rest For The Wicked . . . . Lykke Li

Cold Cold Cold . . . . Cage the Elephant

Monster . . . . dodie

Man's World . . . . MARINA

Save Me . . . . Aimee Mann

Player Of Games . . . . Grimes

Dream Traveller Will Continue

Dream Traveller
ORIGINS

Sign up for the Dream Traveller newsletter and

connect with Bethany Drier at:

www.dreamtravellerbook.com

Autographed copies available from:

www.whereverbooks.com

CPSIA information can be obtained
at www.ICGtesting.com
Printed in the USA
LVHW032012020623
748745LV00041B/1059/J